TO GUARD AGAINST THE DARK

TO GUARD AGAINST THE DARK

Reunification #3

Julie E. Czerneda

WITHDRAWN

DAW BOOKS, INC.
DONALD A. WOLLHEIM, FOUNDER
375 Hudson Street, New York, NY 10014

ELIZABETH R. WOLLHEIM
SHEILA E. GILBERT
PUBLISHERS
www.dawbooks.com

DAW TRADEMARK REGISTERED
U.S. PAT. AND TM. OFF. AND FOREIGN COUNTRIES
—MARCA REGISTRADA
HECHO EN U.S.A.

PRINTED IN THE U.S.A.

To Trudy Rising, My First Publisher and Dear Friend

In the dedication for *Gulf*, I told you how the idea for the Clan came from my studies under Dr. Jan Smith. In *Gate*, you met Lili Pasternak, who reinforced my passion for biology and introduced me to writing nonfiction.

It's my pleasure, now, to introduce to you, the remarkable Trudy Rising. If you've used a textbook in Canada for science or math or other specialized topic that was exceptionally well-done? Most likely you'll find Trudy's name inside. Whatever's acknowledged will be the tip of the iceberg of her contribution, for she takes her work to heart in the best way.

I'll back up a bit. My introduction to Trudy happened thus. I was in my third month of being a full-time mom when our friend Mike Lamarre, a science teacher, called. He'd given my name and number to a textbook sales rep, saying he knew someone with a biology background who—wrote.

I add the em dash because what I wrote was my science fiction, for fun and for no one else. Yes, the stacks of paper in our house were hard to hide, but only one friend, Linda Heier, knew *what* I wrote and she wouldn't tell on me. (Roger, on the other hand, was gleefully supportive of my then-hobby and did boast I was writing books.) Oh, dear.

The call came, from an editor named Jonathan Bocknek (from John Wiley & Sons). He explained they were mid-project and needed someone who could express complex biology in an accessible manner. Would I give it a try? After my shock (I honestly didn't think textbooks were written by anyone other than aged/dead academics), I agreed to his test: to write a one-page description of the human circulatory system.

Okay. I treated it as though explaining the nuts and bolts to my father-in-love, using a tube of toothpaste as an analogy, as I recall. I had a blast writing it, but didn't think it particularly special. Just biology.

Jonathan called to request an urgent face-to-face meeting, with Trudy Rising, in the Wiley office.

It is here I confess I was terrified. I brought Roger to the meeting. Because, you know, PUBLISHERS.

I'd seen the movies.

Trudy was a well-dressed, tiny person. Why all the truly powerful women in my career are shorter than I am, yet seem SO MUCH TALLER remains, to this day, a puzzle. She was a bit surprised I'd brought Roger, but didn't do more than blink. I was glad, because Trudy went on, with what I soon learned was her usual dynamic efficiency—something like a fighter jet at Mach 2—to invite me not only to rewrite a couple of chapters, but start a career.

They'd really liked the toothpaste.

My first nonfiction came out in 1985, and Trudy Rising wasn't just my publisher/editor, she let me *in*. From her, I learned every step of the process, from concept to print, from curriculum development to sales. We shared the same drive for perfection, though I've never come close to Trudy's ability to warp the hours of a day. (She and Sheila? Peas in a pod on that score.)

At a time when working at home was a rarity, I'd a rewarding job to stretch every brain cell and use everything I could learn. Fabulous!

Trudy Rising, with Grace Deutsch and Mary-Kay Winter, went on to form the acclaimed publishing house: Trifolium Books. If the name's familiar? Trifolium published my *No Limits: Developing Scientific Literacy Using Science Fiction,* as well as the *Tales from the Wonder Zone* anthology series. Technically, they published my first work of SF, a story in that series, but I wouldn't accept payment for it, being the editor.

In a sense, Trudy ended my nonfiction career, too. She added her voice to Roger's, firmly pushing me to send out my stories, and no one was happier when I succeeded. I must add it's the fault of Jonathan, my first editor, too. He's the one who sent me to my first convention, Ad Astra.

Trudy, we are the sum of our experiences and passions. What we create comes from that well, and I've been fortunate indeed to have had such teachers, role models, and friends in my life. And yes, Trudy, to this day I'm careful about page count.

Oh, and another confession: you were the model for Sector Chief Lydis Bowman, one of my favorite characters.

You taught me well. You turned me into a professional author and editor. I will always be grateful for that, and your friendship.

Thank you.

Previously, in the Clan Chronicles

Jason Morgan had a starship.

The decommissioned patroller, then ore freighter, had been stripped and lifeless when Morgan first stepped inside her air lock. Her name then had been an ignominious fifteen-character code and her fate? To float in orbit, waiting her turn at a scrap-station.

Instead, Morgan had her refitted, giving her a new name and purpose. The *Silver Fox*—with Morgan as captain and crew—plied the star lanes with cargos needing swift passage, soon gaining a reputation for reliability and discretion.

And luck, for Morgan was that rarity, a Human telepath of significant ability, possessing an unusual gift: to *taste* change. Nothing specific, but warning enough to help him avoid trouble. Mostly. There'd been a brush or two with authority; the occasional close call with pirates. He cared for his ship, played it fair but smart, and relished the peace and privacy of the *Fox*. Other than a few friendships, longest and most importantly with the Carasian Huido Maarmatoo'kk, Morgan kept to himself. Other than the odd side job for a certain Trade Pact Enforcer, Lydis Bowman, who'd an interest in the mysterious Clan, Morgan considered himself free of any ties and glad of it.

Until the morning on Auord, when he met Sira.

Sira, who'd believed herself Human and known only that she had to flee that planet. Who'd had nothing, not even a name.

He'd known who she was and what. Of the humanoid Clan, aliens living, scattered, on Human worlds. All Clan had an innate ability to move their thoughts—and bodies—through what they called the M'hir, an ability they used to manipulate Humans vulnerable to mental suggestion and to keep their true nature secret.

Of interest to Bowman. Of—some—interest to Morgan, it being the Clan's nature to use or dispense with Humans like him, who weren't vulnerable but possessed some power.

Sira wasn't a threat, far from it. He let her board the *Fox,* having been ordered by Bowman to deliver her. A job, nothing more. Soon, though, Morgan knew it would be a terrible betrayal. Sira wasn't a pawn, to be dispensed with or used. She was—

—crew, in the beginning. Young, he'd thought. Curious and determined, yet with something about her.

Then they shared a dream.

It began there, the connection forged between them. Grew until they could feel one another's pulse, as though their bodies tried to come close before their minds. Stunned, Morgan pushed away her advances and did what he could to teach Sira the difference between attraction and love, between a juvenile crush and true, lasting feelings.

He did more than he knew, for Sira was fighting a compulsion that had nothing to do with any Human drive: the urge to Choose. She was the most powerful of her kind yet born, a female ready to Join for life and Commence, when her body would at last become reproductively mature. To the dismay of her kind, no unChosen matched her strength in the M'hir; those who tried, died. Deliberate breeding for power like Sira's had brought the Clan to the brink of extinction; within a generation no Joinings would be possible.

The more Sira, ignorant of all this, came to truly care for him, the harder it was for her to protect him from that terrible instinct. She only knew the longer they were together, the more dangerous it was for him. She decided to leave the *Fox.*

It was then Morgan realized how empty his life would be if she did.

Together, they restored her mind and memories. Within the M'hir, Morgan learned Sira's true nature: a being of astonishing power, burning like a sun to dispel the Dark. In the solid world, older and wiser in some ways, charmingly naïve in others, but above all, fixed in purpose: to prevent harm and save her people.

And to stay with him, always. As Morgan wanted nothing more than to be with her, for they'd completed each other even before they Joined in the way of the Clan, and once they'd resolved the threats against her, their future was together. Chosen. Lifemates. Crewmates.

He should have *tasted* change along with the joy. Should have distrusted being so damn happy. Should have KNOWN.

They'd no future at all.

The attack had come without warning. The Clan had made enemies—too many—and when Sira brought the Clan into the open, into the Trade Pact, those enemies had struck.

Assemblers had led the assault, killing most of the Clan in one dreadful sweep. Morgan willingly burned out the engines of the *Silver Fox*, to help Sira save the survivors, only to see his ship destroyed.

It should have been a sign. They'd no future; no home, but Sira didn't give up. She found a way, as she'd done before. Created hope from nothing. They'd taken flight through the M'hir, sought the birthplace of the Clan, sought the truth—

If they hadn't found it, would he be alone now?

The truth. That the Clan hadn't evolved, but been made through meddling and experimentation. That they'd been made for a single purpose: so that the Hoveny Concentrix, what remained of that galactic empire, could again connect their technology to the null-grid and draw from its limitless power, a power accessible only by beings who could enter the Dark of the M'hir.

Which wasn't, it turned out, the truth at all.

The original Hoveny hadn't discovered a new power source. They'd *breached* what separated two very different universes: Between. The M'hir. The Dark.

Call it what you would. It kept his reality safe from hers.

For Sira had never belonged in the Trade Pact. The Clan didn't. They were noncorporeal beings, Singers, living in their universe. A universe protected by entities who'd taken offense at the Hoveny sucking its life to use in their machines.

Who'd *taken* the Hoveny Concentrix, and destroyed it. To prevent it happening again, to save all she could, Sira returned the Clan where they belonged.

Then spent her life to send him back to the Trade Pact.

The truth?

Their love—their life together—had been a dream.

Nothing more.

Prelude

SEEKING THAT WHICH STOLE from AllThereIs, the Great Ones felt neither strain nor effort as they *reached* along the bridge, crossing Between into NothingReal, the space occupied by beings of flesh.

Until they *reached* through the portion where Between had begun to *rot*.

They faltered, impeded. Experienced *dislocation*. The universes had an order. They were part of that. Disrupting it had consequence—

But their task was unfinished. They *reached* with *FORCE*.

Uncounted Great Ones winked from existence, leaving gravity holes to warp AllThereIs, swallowing light.

Others were created, cataclysms of wild, vibrant energy to fill and alter what had been.

The Dance changed. The change took place before the Singers could perceive it. If they could. To them, AllThereIs was the fabric of the universe and eternal.

But the Watchers saw. They learned a new and terrifying truth about the order of universes.

All things begin.

And all have an end.

* ✸ *

At the same instant, in the universe where the life cycle of stars and their planets were predictable and of note mainly to astrogaters:

On Cersi, an Oud had died, having crawled to its final rest. Unlike other Oud, this one had stuffed its ventral pouches with objects that were not Oud, but when iglies swarmed to consume the corpse, as was their role, there was nothing left inside.

On Deneb, a Human inner system, in the fortified hillside estate of the new leader of the Gray Syndicate, a gem-encrusted raygun disappeared from where it had been tossed in a drawer, its new owner frustrated the thing didn't work.

In the well-protected vaults of the First, the aging collective of species who'd begun the search for the Hoveny and remained transfixed by its mysterious sudden collapse, cases filled with artifacts emptied. Those thefts went unreported; the fortunes of the First were scant enough in this era of peace within the Human-inspired Trade Pact.

Little did they realize the theft was happening on every world gifted by the Hoveny Concentrix with its technology, for everything once able to rob AllThereIs of its living energy had been, finally, removed from existence.

A handful of archaeological sites emptied; most remained unaffected. Still, panic could have spread, for such happenings had no precedent—

—but they were over as soon as they'd begun. In the aftermath, few wanted to admit what they'd lost, fewer still what they hadn't. Curators on several worlds retired their costly "Hoveny" displays and looked for new jobs.

What had happened? Speculation was rampant, whether secret or in public. The Hoveny built with materials no one in the First or the Trade Pact yet understood, but if they'd a finite lifespan, where were the products of that decay? If, as Turrned missionaries preached, the former Hoveny Concentrix was cursed, why this consequence? And why now?

* ✱ *

Unknown to the rest, heedless to the order of universes and consequence, was another opinion entirely.

/~!~/anticipation/~!~/

Trade Pact Space

Chapter 1

STARS.
    Fingers interlaced, her hair stroking his cheek, they'd walked the nights of ninety-nine worlds. Floated in space to watch planets spin. Lain naked on mossy ground, lost in one another, under so many stars—

Those had been real. These couldn't be. The ceiling lay beneath a covering of formed concrete, plas, and a significant amount of natural stone, a roof he'd built to keep out more than the night sky. Could be a dune curling overtop as well, it being sandstorm season.

Yet, still, stars twinkled overhead, wheeling in formation as if he watched them through time.

A dream. That was it. He shut his eyes, fingers straying to the cool metal band around his wrist. Touch seemed odd, for a dream.

He opened his eyes. Looked up. Surely only in a dream could a segment of that starry scape flex . . .

Bend . . .

Lean down, closer and closer, those stars about to crush him—

/need/~location?~/urgency/

For the— "No more!" he shouted, furious. "Get out of here!"

A heavy arm—something arm-ish—plopped across his chest

and slid away. Jason Morgan squirmed in the opposite direction. "On! On full!"

The portlights obeyed, blazing into every corner of the room. He was alone.

* **✹** *

"I heard you the first time." Huido Maarmatoo'kk emphasized the "first." "A Rugheran was on your ceiling. The starry kind, like the ones you saw on Cersi, not the dark greasy kind here. Your shout woke me from a most pleasant dream, you know." A sigh like rain on plas.

His hands wanted to tremble. Morgan wrapped them around his warm cup, guiding it to his lips with care. The kitchen felt strange. Too bright. He hadn't, he thought abruptly, sat at this table for—he hadn't, since, that was it. Hadn't left his quarters.

Hadn't bothered to move, in case it hurt. Fine plan, that was. All of him hurt.

Most of him stank.

Not that it mattered.

"Yesterday, you saw a Rugheran in the accommodation. You shouted then, too. And threw a jar of something at it, making a mess, at which point it disappeared. Can't say I blame it."

Morgan glowered through the steam at his companion. Gleaming black eyeballs, each on their stalk, lined the opening between the gently pulsing disks that served as a head. Unblinking eyeballs. He should know better by now than try to stare down a Carasian. "It's not my imagination. They travel through—" the M'hir, he almost said, and flinched. "They don't use doors. You know that. They're here and they're real."

Unlike what else he saw when alone: the curve of a smile, the luxurious flood of red-gold hair, somber gray eyes flashing with sudden heat—

Sira.

Always, always, no matter how he tried to stop there, stay, the ending followed. The furious boil of waves on an unreal beach—

Her fingers, letting go—

That hollow, inside, where she'd been.

He'd curl into a ball and shiver until he fell asleep or passed out, always cold. So very cold—

A soft *chink* as clawtips met under his nose. Morgan refocused. "What?" He tried not to snap, wearily grateful Huido bore with his tempers and accepted his silence. He wasn't ready to talk.

They hadn't spoken in what might be days, come to think of it.

Something was different. He blinked. His friend's massive carapace was peppered with gleaming metal fragments, between the usual hooks for weaponry, the fragments from a groundcar that had exploded too close. Huido'd removed the largest to keep as souvenirs—but that wasn't it.

The black shell was a maze of fresh scrapes and gouges, some deep. "What happened to—" Morgan's voice broke. Gods. "What did I do?" a whisper.

"You weren't yourself," Huido informed him. The big alien eased back, wiggling the glistening pink stub of what had been his largest claw. "Nor am I. After molt, I will be magnificent once again! We need more beer." In a confiding tone, "Beer speeds things up."

He'd hit bottom, that's when they'd last spoken. When he'd— Morgan's face went stark with grief. "I cursed you. Ordered you to leave."

"Bah. Why would I listen? Your *grist* wasn't right." The intact claw, capable of severing his torso in half, tugged gently at his hair. "Better. Still stinks."

"I attacked you." Morgan remembered it all now, too well. He'd been wild, raving. Huido had squeezed himself into the door opening to seal him in his quarters. Morgan had struck out with whatever was in the room—until he'd collapsed, sobbing, at Huido's feet.

Eyestalks bent to survey the marks. "You tried," the Carasian corrected smugly, then chuckled. "I'm glad you didn't hurt yourself."

Morgan reached up. After a second, the centermost cluster of eyes parted, and deadly needlelike jaws protruded, tips closing on his hand with tender precision. "Huido—"

The jaws retracted and Morgan found himself reflected in a dozen shiny black eyes. "The past." The lower claw snapped. "The present! Why are the Rugherans here?"

The Human dropped his gaze, staring into the sombay. "They're looking for—" His sigh rippled the liquid. "For her."

"To the Eleventh Sandy Armpit of Urga Large with them!" Huido roared, shaking dishware and hurting Morgan's head. "Tell them I said so!" After a short pause, he went on in his normal voice. "You can talk to them, can't you?"

"I don't want to." It sounded sullen even to him, but Morgan couldn't help that, any more than he couldn't help but *hear* the Rugherans: their matrix-like speech, emotion blended with single words or the simplest of phrases, flooded his mind despite his tightest shields. Cruel, to come to him here—

—where he came for peace.

It hadn't always been so. The first time Morgan set foot on Ettler's Planet, he'd been dumped there. His own fault, having yet to gain the most rudimentary knowledge of what offended non-Humans. The Trants could have removed his limbs for suggesting—well, being dumped had been the best option, suffice it to say, and one reason he'd gone on to learn everything he could about the manners of others.

That sorry day, he'd prided himself on a close escape. Instead, he'd been left in the worst place for a telepath, even one of his latent ability, for this world's Human population contained more than its share of the minimally Talented: those whose thoughts leaked constantly, without self-awareness or restraint. Morgan's natural shields protected his mind from others.

He didn't know how to keep their minds out of his.

Half-maddened by the bedlam, somehow Morgan had taken an aircar and flown out into the desert, unable to stop until he reached *quiet.*

There—here—he'd stayed to recover. Only Huido had been welcome, the painful maelstrom of Carasian thought patterns at a level easy to avoid.

Later, healed, and having traded with Omacrons, non-Human telepaths, for their mind-shielding technique, Morgan was able to protect himself. In space, in the *Fox*, he hadn't needed shields at all.

With Sira, he'd wanted none. Her thoughts had been his—her mindvoice the last he'd *heard*. The last he ever wanted to *hear*. He'd never open his mind to another's again.

Till the Rugherans, who had no right—

The Human set down his cup. It tipped, spilling dark liquid. Unfair. Huido kept the kitchen spotless. "I'll get that." He rose and was forced to grip the table to steady himself. It took longer than he remembered, walking to the counter, and he had to concentrate: pick up the wipe, return, clean the mess.

Eyestalks twisted, following his slow progress. "You need a molt, too."

"Wish I could." Something about molting— "Order as much beer as you want."

A chuckle. "Fear not, my brother, I've taken care of it—and a case of Brillian brandy, for variety." A less happy, "If not the storms." The Carasian loathed sand, claiming grains worked into the seams of his shell. He cheered. "While we wait, I could take care of your unwanted visitors." With a disturbingly coy tilt of his carapace, Huido indicated the weapons, most illegal even here in the Fringe, housed on the pot rack.

Morgan shook his head. "Let them poke around till they're satisfied." No need to point out the unlikelihood of any weapon affecting beings of the M'hir.

As for the Rugherans' reaction . . . should more than a jar be tossed at them?

He'd prefer not to—

The kitchen tilted. The Human lurched into his chair, sending the rest of his sombay, and cup, to the floor. He cursed under his breath. A newly hatched Skenkran was stronger. "What's wrong with me?" under his breath.

Shiny black eyes converged on him, then aimed idly—and simultaneously—anywhere else: the weapon-containing pot rack, the ceiling, the floor, the walls.

Done it to himself, that meant.

Morgan let out a slow breath, tasting the stink on it, the truth.

He'd ignored his body's needs. Refused food. Drank himself to sleep. Refused to move. He'd a vague memory of feeling the pinch of shots. Stims, likely.

For how long?

Judging by the tremor in his hands, it could have been weeks.

Neglect? Cowardice. He winced. Hadn't he told Sira: *Let go and live?*

Hadn't she asked the same promise of him?

Shouldn't have taught her to be a trader, he told himself, meaning not a word.

Morgan summoned his remaining strength and stood. "Tomorrow," he announced.

One eyestalk swiveled back to him.

"Tonight, then." Three more joined the first. Doubt, that was. "Some supper—just not—make anything," he capitulated. "I'll eat it." No guarantees it would stay down.

The full force of the Carasian's gaze returned. "At the table?"

"Don't rush me." The Human pretended to squint at the lights. "Too bright. And the Rugheran ruined my sleep."

But his lips cracked, stretched by the ghost of a smile. The first—since.

Interlude

Plexis

PLEXIS SUPERMARKET sped through the fringes of Trade Pact space, its myriad stores and services offering far-flung customers whatever they could desire—and afford. The only resemblance the former asteroid refinery bore to its previous incarnation was a thick, scarred outer hull, festooned with starship docking ports.

That the largest scar had been made when a pirate ship had torn itself free of lawful connections, spilling atmosphere and hard-working staff into vacuum, merely meant Sakissishee—Scat—ships were requested to park at the aft end of the station, where the bulkhead was reinforced and security had extra bite.

Not that other options hadn't been considered. The Trade Pact frowning on Sapient-specific bans, Plexis had designated the Scat preferred food item as a noxious pest—that hadn't lasted either, since it was and no one cared. In the end, practicality ruled. Why? If Plexis banned every alien race who misbehaved, it'd be out of business in a standard day. No, better to absorb the bumps that came with being an open market.

Though it meant repairing the damage done to a famous restaurant for a second time.

* ✳ *

Leaving the repair crew to their own devices—after all, they were probably the ones who'd been here the last time, Humans being impossible to tell apart, and likely knew better than he what needed to be done—the Carasian hurried down the just-opened corridor behind the *Claws & Jaws'* kitchen.

At last.

An elbow scraped a line in the fresh paint along one wall. He paused to eye it worriedly. Should he fix it? Could he?

Later. He continued to the door, rocking a little on his spongy feet. If his handling claw trembled as it neared the shiny new keypad?

No shame there. He'd good reason. So many that he'd lost sleep these past weeks. Behind this door? Everything he'd ever wanted.

He'd only to key in the code.

His very own code, Tayno Boormataa'kk thought with delight, the silly Humans doing the renovations unable to tell one mighty Carasian male from another.

And it was his restaurant now, wasn't it? Huido had left him in charge. Of all it contained.

Which included a pool. A pool filled with wives.

The keypad flashed a familiar orange. Refused.

No. It wasn't possible. He'd been clumsy. Hasty.

Lonely, neglected wives, Huido having deserted them to aid his Human friend, not that Tayno found fault or would ever suggest or think to himself in any way whatsoever that the formidable Jason Morgan, with his uncanny ability to tell them apart, wasn't worthy.

Opportunity being rare, it mustn't, Tayno thought cheerfully, be missed.

With exaggerated care, he reentered the code. He rose to his full height, greater claws outstretched, but tactfully closed, eyestalks alert. All the practice before mirrors, the polish, had led to this splendid pose. He'd impress his new wives. They would accept him—

The code pad blinked. The door to his dreams opened.

Vacuum sucked him forward.

Tayno's dismayed cry was lost as klaxons sounded the alarm. Just as he was about to be pulled through the doorway into the chasm beyond, his claws, still out in rigid display, caught the doorframe to either side and stopped his forward motion.

A disadvantage to the pose he hadn't considered—

The door swooshed shut. Tayno staggered back, eyestalks spinning.

The alarm ceased.

"Tsk. We haven't fixed that yet, Hom Huido," the Human informed him, reaching past to slap a yellow sticker over the keypad. One of the workers from the kitchen. Or the construction foreman. Male. Maybe.

"There was a room—" the Carasian pleaded.

"There was a docking port," the Human corrected, "with an autonomous lifepod." His shoulders lifted and fell. "Must have evacuated during the, ah, incident."

The attack by those small nasty things. Tayno sank down, claws sagging to the floor, his misery boundless. The wives were gone.

The Human waved a noteplas at the nearest of Tayno's eyes.

"What is it?" he asked listlessly. Why wouldn't the creature leave him alone? Nothing mattered. Not anymore.

"We've orders to restore everything. Means you get a new lifepod in there." He closed the skin over one eye for no reason. "Plexis is paying."

Restore meant make things the same as before—they'd said that repeatedly to him during the work on the kitchen. He'd have a pool?

Tayno surged erect, sending the Human back a few paces. With a pool, he could attract his own wives!

An outcome, he reflected in a burst of rare common sense, surely safer than his original plan, should Huido return for his own.

"Do that!" Tayno ordered. "Build it again, but make mine much bigger—no—wait." Huido's pool had successfully attracted wives; he wouldn't take chances. "It must be exactly the same."

"It would have to be," the Human pointed out. "Plexis has the specs."

"Wait. You must finish the restaurant first. What is your name? Can you make sure?"

"Mathis Dewley. I'll do what I can for you, Hom. It'd be a pleasure." With that startling facial grimace Huido insisted was friendly.

Why, he'd found a Human friend of his own! Tayno managed not to rock with delight. "Hom Dewley," he repeated with care. He'd write that down. "The restaurant must open as soon as possible. And must be successful. I must be very successful!"

Carasian females being selective about their retirement prospects.

"I'll inform the crew."

Before his wonderful, helpful new Human friend could escape, Tayno blocked the way with a quick claw. "One more thing—

"I'll need a cook."

* ✳ *

Noteplas tossed into the first dispenser, Mathis Dewley walked through the kitchen. He pushed through the group of Neblokan, costing them their combined grip on an awkward section of new countertop. It dropped, cracking in two.

The seniormost spit after him. The green blob struck the back door as it closed, sticking in a mass of odorous bubbles. Thwarted, the seniormost spun to turn its ire—and spit—on subordinates only to discover they'd beat a sensible retreat into the restaurant.

Dewley went down the short corridor, stepping without hesitation into a machine world.

The tunnel access, like others threaded throughout Plexis, connected every permanent rent-paid-in-full establishment with automated services, from servo-freight to disposal. "Better be on time," Dewley muttered darkly. "Better be as promised." He moved between waste canisters, busy chewing their contents, eyed a flying messenger, then chose a slow-moving servo-controlled cart. Taking hold of a handle, he let the cart lead him through similar traffic, reserving his full attention for the tracker cradled in his left palm.

At its flash, he laughed and jumped on top of the cart, crushing bags of spun Detin sugar as he turned to take position.

A flock of messengers diverted to zoom low over the cart.

Once they'd passed, Mathis Dewley was gone.

And each flying machine had a passenger.

Chapter 2

SUPPER STAYED DOWN, if he counted the single mouthful he'd managed to swallow. Morgan set the bowl on the floor and gave it a push, lying back to stare at the ceiling. This was ridiculous. He'd consumed anything and everything to survive, a fair share of that disgusting, not to mention subsisted for entire voyages on e-rations.

Now he choked on a dish made for him by the founder of the *Claws & Jaws: Complete Interspecies Cuisine,* creator of the Poculan Truffle Frenzy?

A dish, moreover, he'd promised to eat.

Morgan groaned and rolled over, flinging out an arm, fingertips fumbling for the bowl. *Things* scurried away. He'd come to an accommodation with the vermin; after all, they were no more native than he. Starships—his, too—spread such hitchhikers throughout the Trade Pact. They left him alone; they were welcome to clean the scraps.

Finding the bowl, he pulled it close. Huido, being who he was, would have laced this—goop—with what Morgan's neglected body needed most.

All he had to do was negotiate the next spoonful past his teeth.

To distract his stomach, Morgan watched for another Rugheran. Or the same one, he corrected. They didn't come from any sane mold. He'd met a glistening black blob with five fibrous arms somehow squeezed into the *Fox*'s corridor, seen others—called *rumn* by Om'ray—who were aquatic and sleek, with elegant starlike phosphorescence disguising their true shape. At home? Rugherans coated their planet as a heaving, glittering mass—whether uncountable numbers or fused into one organism seemed a moot point. A planet in a system not so far from this one, as it happened; not a place for a return visit.

For they, and their world, existed within the M'hir as well.

Making Rugherans as dangerous as they were strange. They'd almost killed Sira in their fervor to have her reconnect an aspect of their planet, White, through the M'hir to Drapskii, home of the Drapsk. Whatever debt Ren Symon owed, he'd paid when he exhausted his Power, dying so Morgan could reach White in time to save Sira.

Not even Huido knew Morgan had done so by *pushing* his starship through the M'hir, circumventing normal space.

Given the consequences of that being discovered? It was a secret he'd take to his grave, thank you.

Until Morgan, only Clan had the Talent to *push* themselves through the M'hir; 'porting, they'd called it, using their Power and will to arrive at a remembered place. It was how they'd lived in secret among Human societies as long as they had. How they'd arrived in the Trade Pact in the first place. How they'd left it.

How she'd left him.

Morgan's throat tightened. He made himself relax and forced the morsel down.

In their last moments together, Sira had tried to explain. The M'hir was really "Between," that seething void a boundary between this and a far different dimension. "AllThereIs," she'd called it. The beings who'd lived in the Trade Pact as Clan, alien but easily mistaken for Human, hadn't belonged in those flesh bodies. They'd been stolen from their rightful home and forgotten it.

AllThereIs did not forget them, and that was the mind-wrenching part; for there, the Clan were Singers, noncorporeal beings. Infinitesimal and infinite. Carefree and joyous, yet their combined song, she'd told him, defined their existence. Those who'd been Stolen were returned to that existence, reunited with all those they loved, if they lost their way in the M'hir, or when their bodies died, freeing them to go home.

AllThereIs did not forget, nor forgive. There were "entities" within it, Sira'd warned, who reacted to threat. When the Hoveny breached their home with devices designed to feed from its energy, those entities responded. Their defense had ended the vast Hoveny Concentrix.

How, no one had known.

Until the next time. Morgan shuddered, remembering the destruction of Brightfall, the Hoveny Homeworld. Prodded by a new intrusion, those same entities had *reached* into normal space to pluck out whatever they deemed a danger. Hoveny devices. Buildings.

A moon.

Unthinkable power, pacified only when Sira closed the breach. To do so, she showed the final remnants of the Clan the truth and sent them home, but the threat ended only when she, the last of her kind, severed her Joining to a Human, and died to send him home, too.

Yet hadn't died, except to him. Morgan didn't understand— could any Human mind?—where Sira and the Clan were, or what they were, now. He supposed he didn't have to: they hadn't belonged in his universe.

And he didn't belong in theirs.

His fingers found the cold of the bracelet she'd pushed on his arm.

Where did Rugherans belong?

There was a question to ruin any chance of eating.

* ✳ *

Ettler's Planet, the central continent, a patch of nowhere hidden in a sandstorm stretched to the horizon and promised to last another four days—

The last thing he'd expected to wake him was the door alarm.

Morgan relaxed at the ensuing noisy clatter, like a maddened servo shedding parts, of Huido in rapid motion. A delivery. Odd that. *Mal's Anything-Anywhere* pilots were locals; they'd know better than cross the Singing Sands when they howled like this—

SnapGRRRR

Not good. Only one thing in this building made that sound: Huido's favorite disruptor prepping a load. Stealthy it wasn't: the thing was the size of a Human leg and that ominous glow?

If this wasn't a delivery—if there was trouble, he should be out there—

And do what? Lean on the wall?

Railing inwardly at his own weakness, Morgan propped himself on an elbow to peer through the gloom.

Silence. Silence was good, he assured himself. He'd been imagining things for days now. Longer. He'd imagined the *snap,* that was all. Probably the door alarm, too. Huido was merely puttering—loudly—in the kitchen. Cleaning weapons, that was it.

Morgan flopped down, kicking irritably at the mess of disks, clothing, and who knew what had accumulated on the mattress until he had a comfortable space. He closed his eyes, relishing the silence.

Light reddened his eyelids. "Off," he ordered the portlights, throwing an arm over his face in case Huido didn't take the hint.

"On. You aren't much to look at," a woman's voice informed him, "but I'd rather not trip."

He sat up, the room spinning, and blurted, "You're dead."

"Not yet." The expression on Lydis Bowman's face wasn't pity; her eyes held too clear an understanding for that. "Hello, Jason. We can talk. Or I can leave."

Sand dribbled from every crease and seam of her clothing. She'd pulled free her hood and mask. Beneath, she looked much as she had when he'd last seen her, in the cabin of the *Silver Fox.* Determined. Grim. Better fed and the burn along her blunt jaw had faded to a pale scar. The angry puckering from her chin to her collar was new. Battle wounds.

But what captured Morgan's notice was her raised hand, with a piece of torn plas between two fingers.

The note he'd left behind, that impossible day.

Strange to feel a weight shift, somewhere inside. Not peace, never that, not again, but something akin to relief.

Someone else knew.

It had been real.

"Talk," he chose, annoyed how rusty his voice sounded. He rolled off the mattress. Sniffed and made a face. "Give me a moment."

Her nod shook more sand onto the floor. Huido gave the tiniest clank of distress, but otherwise remained in the doorway.

With, Morgan observed, his disruptor. Not wrong, that caution.

Bowman was a friend, but what came with her?

Trouble.

Aside: The Papiekians

THE YOUNGLINGS weren't sleeping well.

That, all agreed, was the first sign. While younglings could react in unison to many things, from overexcitement to a virus, this, all agreed, was not the same.

Since every youngling of the world stirred in their night, crying out.

And every youngling wept.

The second sign was the disturbing end of Alla'do Go.

A humble, particular being of little ambition and less talent, Go believed, as did his kinspread, he'd be the next invited to ascend the Tower of Blissful Dark, to become a caretaker-devout.

Instead, he climbed the tower and threw several priceless examples of Teeng-era pottery from the top, then followed them to the rocks below.

Which would hardly seem as significant as weeping younglings, save for what Alla'do cried out as he fell, words *felt* with painful clarity by the sages inside the Tower, and auto-recorded by the monitoring system outside.

"The Dark *BLEEDS*—"

The information was collated and sent to the Consortium.

Chapter 3

IT TOOK MORE than a moment. In the fresher, Morgan shed hair as well as grime, honestly startled by the feel of bones jutting under his skin. He'd hit lean times before. Not like this; the gaunt face in the mirrored tile was a stranger's, with sunken listless blue eyes above a tangled beard.

His "don't forget what I am" beard; a statement he'd made when he'd been the only one of his kind.

The Human used handfuls of depilatory cream to sweep the growth from his jaw, cheeks, and neck. The result was—he turned away.

Clean was good. He felt steadier as well, his head clearing by the second, and he was grateful for Huido's concoction. Especially given who'd arrived.

Morgan stepped back into his quarters only to stop in his tracks, appalled. The mattress was a cluttered island in an ocean of debris, an ocean swarming with vermin. Most scurried into their nests, but some paused and sat up, regarding him with their little red eyes, and who knew what else crawled in the mess? Swathes had been plowed to connect the doors; by their width, Huido's doing.

No spacer lived like this.

Averting his eyes from the mess, Morgan pulled on the first

clean clothes he came across—a sleeveless shirt and pants, neither of which fit as they should—and padded barefoot to the kitchen.

* ✱ *

Bowman sat at one end of the table, a bag at her feet, looking like a vistape salesbeing—no, the rugged clothing and toolbelt hinted at an itinerant plumber. This time. With her, you never trusted appearance, nor that she was alone. Good odds her battle cruiser, the mighty *Conciliator*, orbited overhead.

She went oddly still when she saw him.

"That bad?" Morgan asked lightly.

"I've seen prettier corpses," she concurred. "Sit before you fall."

He took her advice. Huido lowered to a polite crouch at the side, eyes divided between the two Humans.

"Brought beer." Their visitor pulled a small keg from her bag, thumping it on the table. Morgan didn't recognize the label.

Huido did, by the way his eyes converged. "I'll get glasses," the Carasian boomed happily.

Morgan met Bowman's level gaze. "Thanks."

No need to ask how she'd found his refuge. That incident when his bighearted friend had rushed here to save Sira's cousin Barac from the clutches of an out-of-control Chooser? Ruti and Barac had Joined successfully, to their mutual joy—

—were still together and happy, he reminded himself, in some impossible way—

—the point being, Huido had flown here in one of the *Conciliator*'s aircars, piloted by none other than Bowman's ever-loyal constable, Russell Terk.

Who'd, as a matter of course, planted an assortment of sneaky devices before he left.

Given they were, usually, allies, Morgan hadn't had the heart to remove them all. It did raise a question. "I'd expected you sooner," he continued as Huido dealt with the keg's contents. Much sooner. With a demand for a full briefing: on where he'd been, the Clan, the Assemblers—why he'd returned alone.

"I'd this," the scrap of plas twirled slowly between Bowman's fingers. "Very helpful."

Morgan's eyes locked on the scrap. "Was it?" He half shrugged. "At the time, I—" He'd used no names. Hadn't dared without knowing who'd find the note, if it was found at all, buried beneath Norval. Written: *It's over. They're going home. Tell the big guy I'm happy. She and I will be together, always.*

They'd tried, gods knew. What hope did they have when not one but two universes worked against them?

He'd have died with her in either, but Sira hadn't wanted that. *Let me go, knowing you'll live,* she'd asked, her eyes full of love. *Promise. As you love me.*

"Morgan?"

He came back to himself. "It doesn't matter," he finished more harshly than he'd intended. "Ask your questions."

Bowman studied his face, her own inscrutable. "I've one," she said at last, tucking the scrap into a plas notebook, new and shiny. "From this—and the fact you're wearing Barac's band on your wrist—am I to gather the Clan are no longer my concern?"

He touched the bracelet. Concern? They'd been her life's work. Bowman—and her most trusted aides—had Drapsk-made implants punched into their skulls for protection from the Clan. As an enforcer, she'd done her utmost to keep them from harming anyone else. Morgan had been one of her informants.

What he hadn't known then? As a direct descendant of Marcus Bowman, the first Human to encounter the Clan, Lydis had known what the Clan's ancestors had erased from their minds: their origin on Cersi and how they'd come to live among Humans. Like Bowmans before her, she protected the secret of their existence and tried to protect them from themselves.

It wasn't until Sira had come along, revealing her species had bred itself toward extinction, that Bowman had become an active participant in the Clan's future. She'd helped them move into the open and join the Trade Pact. Find new hope.

"The Clan are no longer anyone's concern," Morgan told her. Bowman, of all people, would want the unvarnished truth. "They're gone."

Huido made a sound of distress.

"Define 'gone.'" Bowman sat back, steepling her fingers. Not moving without the rest of it, that meant.

Fair enough. "They found their way home."

"Sira wouldn't leave—" With sharp conviction, Bowman having been witness to their love and their bond. A pause, then heavily, drawing her own conclusion, "I'm sorry, Jason. When you arrived alone, I feared she was dead. I'd hoped to be wrong."

"In the end, Sira didn't have a choice." Choice. The word resonated through him, with all it had meant to them both, and, for an instant, it seemed there was no air to breathe.

The next, it came to him Bowman deserved more: to know she and her family hadn't failed. "Sira and the Clan are happy. Home and together. All of them. Including those who died here and—" Cersi and Aryl Sarc were topics for another time, if ever, "—anywhere. Don't ask me to explain." He glanced at the Carasian. "Your wives were right. The Clan didn't belong here. Sira didn't." His voice threatened to fail; Morgan made himself go on. "And they can't come back."

Keeping this universe safe from theirs.

"The Clan are gone," he finished.

"I see." A glass brimming with amber liquid and foam appeared in front of Bowman, the Carasian having exquisite timing. Bowman raised it toward Morgan, and for an instant he thought her eyes glistened.

Before he could be sure, Bowman poured half the contents down her throat, then put the glass aside with a brusque, "That complicates things."

Morgan blinked. "I don't understand."

"Here's me, hoping you would." Her lips twisted. "Guess I made the trip for nothing." She stood. "Take care of yourselves."

"Not so fast!" Thrusting Morgan's glass into his hand, the Carasian placed himself in Bowman's path. He wiggled his stub in her face. "Look what she did to me! Tell me she's dead."

Morgan frowned. "Who?" The Carasian had stood guard while he and Sira led the surviving Clan away from the Assemblers. Been injured. He shuddered inwardly. How had he not asked what happened? About Huido's own concerns: his wives, his restaurant. About anything?

He hadn't cared, was the bitter truth, busy wallowing in his grief. No more. Morgan straightened in his seat, unaware his eyes flashed with their old fire. "What happened on Norval after we left?"

Huido expanded in size. "I was attacked from behind! If not for Terk, I would be dead!"

"Ambridge Gayle," Bowman explained.

There were reasons Morgan had avoided going finsdown on Deneb; top of the list, the criminal syndicates who ran the system. "Leader of the Grays."

"Not anymore."

"Excellent!" Huido boomed, immediately in a better mood. He poured beer from a handling claw into his hidden mouth with a triumphant slurp. "May oort dispense with her bones."

"Your plan worked." Almost got them all killed, granted, but to be the bait, then turn the trap on her pursuer? Classic Bowman. The assassin, however, hadn't been her target. She'd been after the mysterious smuggler king; the one who'd put Assemblers where they could do the most harm to the Clan. "Did she give up the Facilitator?"

"Still waiting on that." At Huido's deep agitated rumble, Bowman gave a tight smile. "I appreciate your feelings, but it's hard to get answers once they're dead." She made a little gesture with her hand at the Carasian. Out of my way, that was.

Huido didn't budge. "What about the nasty things? What was done about them?"

Bowman looked to Morgan. "Let me guess," he said flatly. "Nothing."

"Not quite." She eyed Huido. He eyed her back, dozens of times over. "Stubborn, aren't you." It wasn't admiration. Sitting back down, she pointed to her glass. "A firmly worded memo went from our new Board Member to the Assembler homeworld condemning the attacks."

" 'Memo?' " The Carasian shook himself, as if to remove the word, then stalked over to the keg muttering, "I'll write them a memo. And deliver it."

"Wouldn't have that much if our late Board Member hadn't conspired with them to commit species-cide." Bowman caught Morgan's eye. "Accident in transit. Shame. Cartnell had more to tell us."

Her stubby forefinger circled in air. "As for any crime? Scale, my friends. The number of Clan reported dead? Less than a cruiser's complement. Add to that, the incidents were on Humanocentric worlds. We're one species among thousands, each with problems they've a right to consider first." She snorted. "Doesn't help the Assemblers—and the Clan—pretended to be Human. Most of the Board can't tell us apart, including the ones who like us. No offense," with a nod at Huido.

Not a surprise, but it left a foul taste. The Clan's rebirth didn't change the fact that the Assemblers had murdered them in their hundreds. Deaths of terror and pain.

Deaths Sira had *felt*.

For that alone, he thought grimly, the Assemblers should pay. But Bowman hadn't come about the past. "Your hands are tied anyway," he concluded aloud. "Assemblers aren't in the Trade Pact."

Her eyes went cold, but she didn't argue. "They push another species who is, I get to push back. Till then?" Her hand tipped, palm down.

"I pay my taxes. There's other Human authority," Huido rumbled. "What about them?"

"Port Jellies claimed lack of jurisdiction, the Clan being non-Human—or requested formal complaints from next-of-kin. When I pointed out the next-of-kin were dead as well, I was invited to lift offworld and look after aliens."

Morgan raised an eyebrow.

Her answering shrug was eloquent. Strictly speaking, Trade Pact Enforcers had no jurisdiction dirtside, but this was Bowman. Heads would have, figuratively, rolled.

"The Assemblers attacked the Clan with a species-specific toxin. You'd think that would matter to someone."

"Oh, it matters." With a nod, Bowman accepted a second beer. She drank deep before continuing. "What to do about it is the problem. We couldn't get rid of Assemblers if we tried. The individual bits slip by Port Authority as easily as vermin. Unified?

They've no traceable affiliations, no travel records, no idents. The perfect infiltrators. But—tell me something, Morgan." That finger stabbed the air at him. "You've been in the Fringe; seen enough. Does it track Assemblers came up with this grand scheme to eradicate the Clan on their own?"

She'd a positive gift for turning things inside out. He wrenched his brain to follow the question. The Assemblers he'd traded with argued with their own parts. He'd watched a couple fragment trying to get through a door simultaneously. "Rumor was," Morgan mused, "they couldn't work together."

"Like putting a Scat and Whirtle at the same table," Huido contributed, the former species an obligate predator constrained to live food, the latter unfortunately of the hapless, tasty variety. "Or two pox in a hole. Or—"

Bowman coughed before the Carasian could expand on the mutually incompatible, as much a problem in the restaurant business as in gatherings of the Trade Pact Board. "Just so. It's smelled like a setup to me from the start. My guess? The little monsters were aimed at the Clan by someone, multiple or solo." A finger tapped. "Same someone," another tap, "developed and gave them the toxin. Could do it again's the rub." A sober pause, during which her clear gaze found them both. "Can't prove a thing. Assemblers fragment before giving up a secret. My usual sources are dry on the topic; my latest isn't willing to talk about it. Rot them all," she stated, her tone sending a shiver down Morgan's spine. She leaned back, as abruptly composed. "So I'm coming at the business from another angle."

"The Facilitator."

"Who helped the Assemblers reach their targets." Bowman nodded. "I've a lead. Could use help following it."

Huido's claw snapped in protest before the Human could respond. "You see how he is."

"I do." She gave Morgan a speculative look. "But I know what he is."

His bones hurt. His stomach wanted to reject supper, let alone the beer. The lights were too bright.

And Lydis Bowman? Never told the whole truth.

"What I am is curious," Morgan countered. "Why today, in a sandstorm?"

Gods, that earned him an honest, if predatory, grin. "That's the thanks I get for keeping your hideout off scans."

Everything was convoluted with her. He wasn't sure if his head hurt or was waking up. "The storm's convenient," he dismissed. "You came today, and it's not because of your 'lead' on the Facilitator. It's something else. Something you believed involved the Clan till I told you they were gone. Tell me. Or we're done here." And he could go back to bed—

Instead of a direct answer, Bowman pursed her lips, then held up her glass. "You still do that trick? The one where you make things go poof?"

When had she—how—Morgan shook his head, well aware of the futility of such questions. "You mean this?" He concentrated on the glass . . .

. . . *pushing* it into the M'hir.

He'd have been gratified to see Bowman's start when the glass vanished, but the effort drained what little he had left, and this wasn't—in any sense—about tricks. "Why?"

"There've been thefts. Locked room stuff—situations where an ability like that might have explained things."

Huido rose, offended. Morgan eased him back with a gesture. He had to see, or touch, an object to give it a *push*.

And it wasn't an accusation, not yet. Besides, Terk was the one with a low opinion of his honesty. Bowman?

Knew him a little too well. "I've been here," Morgan reminded her.

"These thefts occurred shortly before you showed up," she confirmed comfortably. Her head tilted. "They landed on my desk because the Trade Pact takes a very dim view of coordinated crime across member systems. You see, the robberies weren't simply close in time. They were simultaneous. That takes remarkable planning."

No. It took unthinkable power.

His heart labored in his chest. It couldn't be. "What was stolen?" But he knew. He knew. The M'hir touched everywhere.

Why had he thought AllThereIs wouldn't?

Her gaze sharpened. "What is it, Morgan?"

"What was stolen?" He found himself leaning over the table at her, braced on shaking arms.

Bowman didn't pull away. "Hoveny artifacts. Priceless, I'm told. Taken from several museums."

Taken from the Trade Pact.

Taken from this space.

"They'll all be gone," he whispered, sagging back down. He missed the chair. Huido caught him in a grip like a metal vise. "From collections. Secret hordes. Packing crates. From anywhere. Everywhere."

By rights, the darkness that was the M'hir should be awash in a civilization's sad debris; the Hoveny's doomed technology, the billions of their dead, bumping into harmless oddments like a beer glass and sheets—

—but hadn't Sira told him? The entities from AllThereIs didn't take, they destroyed.

"How can you know that? What's this about? Make sense!"

"There's life in the M'hir. You've seen it." Trust the Drapsk to put it on a viewer. "This is more. This is instinct." He found himself in the chair and tried to focus. "Self-defense. The Hoveny disturbed—couldn't have known—we're safe now. It's over." Morgan thought he spoke clearly, but there was something wrong with Bowman. The look on her face—he'd never seen anything like it, not once in all the years. He tried to smile. "It'll be all right. AllThereIs won't pay attention to us anymore. It's why the Clan had to go, you see. It's why Sira left me. To guard against the dark—"

The table rose up and hit him in the face.

Interlude

An Undisclosed Location

" 'A COOK?' " Ivory-tipped fingers drummed thoughtfully, then were lifted for their fresh manicure with diamond insets to be admired. "The fool doesn't know he needs a Trade Pact Certified Multi-Species Master Chef. I'll arrange it. I believe that's the final item. Questions?"

There were, at that instant, three beings in the spacious apartment; unified, the Assembler counted for less than the sum of its parts. The two summoned to this meeting, the Assembler and an elderly *sept* from Omacron, stayed well back from the wash of natural light pouring in from outside—

There being no window at present, and their host reputed to use the opening, and the sixty-story drop on the other side of it, as a convenient expression of her dissatisfaction—

Not that their host showed any such at the moment, but Brill were volatile—this one more than most—and these two hadn't survived her company by taking risks.

Unless needful. Gryba's hand raised, the Omacron's long fingers trembling as though caught in a breeze. "This humble one inquires why we would aid one of the shelled ones."

"You waste time." Mathis Dewley's left foot twitched. The right stepped on it. "You always do. WASTE TIME!"

Distressed by the vehemence—and spittle—sept curled back over the upper of its two supple waists.

"See? You're doing it again!"

"Dewley, mind your betters." The Brill rose to her feet, folds of smooth blubber revealed by the issa-silk of her raiment. Larger than most, this one, too. Choiola was her name, highest in the ranking of her kind among aliens, Board Member for the Brill in the Trade Pact.

Less high among her own kind, it patently beneath a founder of the First to consort with an array of unproven new species for the sake of, of all things, peace and commerce. The only unifying interest of the First had been to learn why the Hoveny Concentrix had failed so that they didn't.

That, and the entertaining dance around mutual extermination. Theirs hadn't been, she thought wistfully, a peaceful civilization at all.

Now? The First had been overrun by swarms of humanity, starting with the Commonwealth. Worse, than that. Diminished to history, its once-weak members falling over themselves to embrace the upstart Trade Pact, seeking safety within its cooperation, its inclusiveness. As if every species were equal.

As if none deserved to rule the rest.

Not for long. The new First would be stronger, better. They'd leave behind the weak and useless, and the Brill would lead the way!

Until then, each served, Choiola reminded herself, stopping where she could stare down at the fragile Omacron. Hard to credit Gryba's ancestors were founders, too. Perhaps an unfortunate genetic drift had reduced them.

The creature uncurled, flashing wide the lids of sept's oblong eyes to expose their outer ring of black. Words, unwelcome, unwanted, slammed into her mind: *We ruled twenty systems more than the Brill. We will again!*

She envisioned the "humble" Omacron being skinned alive and made, yes, into a carpet.

Choiola smiled as Gryba flinched and lowered sept's lids. Teach sept to eavesdrop—for now. "Your inquiry is reasonable. We suspect Huido's establishment on Plexis—this *Claws & Jaws*— is used by the Consortium."

A hand dropped loose to run under a chair, but the rest of Dewley was made of sterner stuff—or noticed he was now between the Brill and the open sky, and nothing tempted a Brill more than a moving target. "The equipment was installed, Fem Choiola. Just as you wanted. Just where you said. I swear it."

"I should hope so. We shall do all we can to ensure this restaurant opens and succeeds. With patience comes opportunity." The Brill struck her chest with a fist. "We will snare those who've eluded us, and it will be your turn, Gryba, then." She watched as the Omacron's skin suffused a telling green and yellow, a display of no utility among aliens, bizarre in this dwelling of metal and glass, but nature wouldn't be denied.

Unlike most Brill, she'd made a point of studying the species who were, for now at least, their allies. Such a display had but one meaning. The prospect of using sept's mental powers against other sapients—especially against any of those who'd so successfully curtailed their previous attempts to destabilize the Trade Pact and restore the First to glory—aroused the disgusting creature.

"No need to thank me," Choiola assured sept.

Gryba had better be far from her living space before doing whatever sept must to relieve septself, or she'd have one less ally.

∗ ✳ ∗

Aboard the *Ikkraud*

Allies.

Eyes half-lidded, Wys di Caraat let her gaze follow the pacing Scat. Efficient things, Scats, with much to commend them. She'd no complaint so far. There was, however, always the worry someone would outbid her for their services. Scats being pirates by trade and inclination, trust wasn't in their nature.

One of the few things they had in common. This Scat wasn't the ship's captain, but an ambitious second, bright enough to grasp the potential gains afforded by insinuating itself close to the Clan when most of its kind openly loathed "mindcrawlers."

Enlightened self-interest, that loathing. The Clanswoman indulged herself in a sigh; she did prefer her allies mind-wiped and controlled, but finding susceptible individuals without attracting unwanted attention wasn't easy. These days, it was nearly impossible.

She remembered when anything was, when the House of Caraat had been recognized for its potency among Clan and she'd controlled their rich holdings on Camos, itself the seat of the Clan Council. Not that di Caraats sought political power.

Why should they? It came to them, for among Clan, those of greater strength ruled, and her son, Yihtor, possessed Power unmatched save by one: Sira di Sarc.

Had her son Joined to Sira, as he should, they'd have witnessed the birth of a dynasty. Wys would have raised their offspring to be a true di Caraat and begun the rise of her House to rule all other Clan.

Except Sira refused his Candidacy, and the Council ruled in her favor.

Not to be denied, Wys had led those loyal to her and her son into a new life, free of rules, only to watch in horror as Sira Commenced for a Human's bastard Power—allowed an alien to contaminate the M'hir—*fought* her son, and defeated him.

These days were different, yes. Wys allowed herself a tight little smile. The mighty Sira was dead, taking Jason Morgan with her, while she had those utterly loyal to her and to her House.

And to their shared future.

In the meantime, this Scat would have to do.

"Stop pacing," she told it, tiring of the prick-prick of its clawed toes in her carpet. "Word will come."

"Or not. Our intermediary was-ss unreliable." Crests rose behind each of its slit-pupiled eyes. A black whiplike tongue daintily recovered a feather lodged between two fangs, the intermediary having paid for its failure. "We could have obtained the final item of the shipment directly."

"A Scat ship on Camos?" A known pirate, landing on a wealthy inner system world? Lucky if they were only searched to the bulkheads. She didn't hide her scorn. "This is why you're not the captain."

Though Camos itself . . . For an instant, Wys contemplated its unseeable wealth, the ease of passages burned through the M'hir to every other Clan holding, encompassing hundreds of Human worlds.

None to Acranam, the world she and her son had claimed for their own.

Acranam. Whose Clan sided with Sira di Sarc and her *Chosen*, the foul Human telepath Jason Morgan—the pair responsible for the capture and destruction of her son! Acranam. Who'd pleaded to be part of the Clan again, under Council's thumbs, even to be part of the Trade Pact.

Spat her out, hadn't they? With her Chosen and all those still loyal to the di Caraats. Forced them to live like this, hidden in space, running between worlds.

Another cruel smile flickered along her lips. Who'd the better of that bargain, now?

For Acranam had burned. She'd laughed as the Watchers wailed in the M'hir, for their howls were her triumph. Kept careful track, to be sure every Chosen, Chooser, unChosen, and child who'd opposed her was dead. The last had disappeared from Stonerim III, leaving nothing but ghosts.

Believe in destiny? She was destiny. All the Clan who continued to exist were hers, and she'd given them a new name, one to remind them forever of their first, great leap forward together. Taken that of the cruise ship and crew they'd destroyed in order to escape Council and be free.

Destarians.

"Word will come," Wys repeated. In days, perhaps. More likely weeks.

Then, she would begin her dynasty.

Chapter 4

Three Standard Weeks Later

AUORD'S SHIPCITY played itself on flickering screens that covered the walls of the small room, the towering starships and gantries like toys sparkling with portlights, planetary freighters hovering overhead. While there was, by agreement, no official surveillance of the ships finsdown at port—many being homes as well as transport—nothing went unnoticed. Every entrance was monitored, along with the changing perspectives fed from vids attached to Auord's fleet of docking tugs, here.

"Peaceful night. May it stay so." With that, Thel Masim stretched and rose from her easi-rest in front of the large center screen, the paired luck beads in her gray hair tinkling. "You ready?"

The Human paused his sweeper. "You hired me to clean." His voice, like his face, gave nothing away, shared nothing, but she'd never seen self-doubt in those remarkable blue eyes before.

Jason Morgan. She'd never thought to see him arrive at the shipcity in third-hand spacer gear, without a credit to his name. Damaged goods.

Lost his ship, *The Silver Fox.* Destroyed on Stonerim III, she'd heard. As for Sira Morgan, his lifemate and crewmate?

Some questions, Thel knew, weren't to be asked.

"I hired you to help out," she said. "Tonight, you cover the boards while I get a decent supper. Shouldn't be more than the scheduled tugs. Best not be a problem." This with a snap. "You aren't the only one wanting work." It was the ugly truth. Dozen a cred on Auord, down on their luck spacers like him, and everyone had tech skills. No wonder recruiters did well.

His shoulders hunched. Morgan parked the sweeper. "You're the boss."

"That I am. Don't break the place." She locked the door behind her.

* ✳ *

Morgan straightened from his slouch the moment he was alone, lips quirked in a half smile. What Thel Masim was? A friend, the best kind. Among spacers, her prickly kindness was as legendary as her memory, not to mention her lack of tolerance for those trying to cheat the system or one another.

He felt a twinge of guilt as he unlocked the door, then slipped into the still-warm easi-rest. Easy to fall into old habits: find a hole to sleep in, keep away from authority, cautiously approach an old friend. She'd taken one look at him and given him work. He'd not only expected Thel's trust.

He'd counted on it.

Over Huido's extremely loud protest, Morgan had brought nothing but the bracelet, these clothes, and traded his good boots for a pair with worn soles. Plus his twin sets of little force blades, snicked in their holders at left wrist and ankle, but physical struggle wasn't the plan. He was here to watch Auord's shipcity by night.

This night, in particular.

Seated, he let his gaze flick from screen to screen, leaving the centermost set to the main thoroughfare from the portcity's warehouse district. There were other traffic flow stations like this one, but they were automated through the quiet evening hours, their images shunted to Thel's. From here, Morgan had access to the sprawl of starships between the rugged sea cliffs, the landing field, and the start of permanent buildings.

Shipcities were dynamic communities, their proportions changing with the ebb and flow of trade as local seasons changed availabilities. They changed with whispers, too.

The attacks confined to Human worlds hadn't been a rumor. Small, family-run freighters, with their minimal margins, couldn't afford trouble. Non-Human systems had seen an upswing in business since. Enough to boost prosperity.

Even on Auord.

Uniformed beings oversaw the entrances at every hour, monitoring the comings and goings between ship and portcities for any hint of fee evasion. Smugglers, if they were smart, paid like the rest. The uniforms were the green of Auord's Port Authority, there not being a current emergency requiring Trade Pact Enforcers, with their distinctive red and black—or gray of battle armor.

No emergency the planetside Jellies wanted to share, anyway. After Bowman's comments, Morgan guessed enforcers were less welcome than usual. Which didn't say much.

His attention caught, he flipped the feed from an upper screen to the center, leaning forward with a frown.

A starship sat where it had landed at the near edge of the field, ready to lift without being carried into position by one of Auord's docking tugs; a privilege granted, or rather afforded, by very few indeed. Put that location together with the ship's curved design and unusual size?

"Drapsk."

The ship would be crewed by hundreds of impossible-to-tell-apart beings, all of the same highly motivated tribe. Polite to a fault, but Morgan had seen more than one rowdy bar cleared by the entrance of a single little Drapsk, the most inebriated patrons aware the rest wouldn't be far behind.

Morgan's fingers strayed to the metal bracelet on his right wrist. Turned it absently.

Drapsk could be—and had been—wonderful allies and friends. As easily, they could—and did—thwart the best-laid plans of any rational non-Drapsk for their own mysterious reasons. Random elements, that's what they were. They shouldn't be here. Auord wasn't on any of their routes—the pickings were too lean for such consummate traders.

Just his luck. He'd hoped to avoid meeting any Drapsk before he was ready. If he ever was. The beings knew of the M'hir, what they called the Scented Way; more importantly, they adored Sira as their Mystic One.

Maybe they were here for the bertel nut harvest.

He called up the ship's public manifest. The *Heerala* had come here via Plexis. No earlier stops listed, but there needn't be. Plexis was a port others trusted to be strict with contamination protocols, its atmosphere and resources such as water limited in a way no planet experienced.

No postings for trade, either desired or offered.

Again, there needn't be. The Drapsk weren't like free traders, dependent on local supply and demand. The *Heerala* could be here on business of her own, arranged offworld.

Drapsk didn't miss an opportunity. That lack of posting?

Morgan jabbed the vid feed control harder than necessary, resuming his search. Mysterious Drapsk were the worrisome kind—

"Anything?"

"Not yet." He didn't turn around. "Lock the door."

"Done." Constable Russell Terk grabbed a stool and pulled it close. The legs creaked under his weight; shorter than Morgan, the enforcer was half again as wide, most being muscle.

Morgan glanced sideways and grinned.

Gone was the uniform that strained to cover the other Human's oversized shoulders. Instead, a jacket of some brown scaled hide gave up the attempt, stretched open over an unpleasant swath of shirt printed with gaudy flowers—no, upon close inspection, those were little crustaceans holding claws. A belt with a clasp shaped like a bunch of bertels held up pants that stopped at his ropy calves. The pants sported a ridiculous number of pockets, bulging, no doubt, with the latest enforcer tech.

To finish, Terk's thick hairy toes, nails painted a vile orange, protruded from sandals.

Catching Morgan's look, he growled, "I'm blending."

"I can see that." The garish, memorable outfit, coupled with that face of harsh angles and perpetually grim expression? Any Auordian, from Port Authority to child, would peg him as a recruiter, out to prey on the shipcity's dregs.

Slavers, was the truth of it. Recruiters worked the bars—or hunted in alleys. Whether they drugged a drink or simply stunned a candidate, the result was the same: a one-way trip, sold to any Fringe world desperate for skilled labor.

Abandoned in Auord's All Sapients' District, away from the Clan for the first time in her life and vulnerable, Sira had been swept up by recruiters. It happened moments after she'd accosted Morgan, asking for his help to leave the planet. He'd believed her one of his own, out of work, and sent her on her way with a few credits for food and a bath, and Thel's name.

A memory still able to make him wince, though Sira had escaped and made her way to the *Silver Fox*. And him.

"I've the talent," Terk claimed modestly. "You, on the other hand, look like a dried-out crasnig dropping. You should eat more." He leaned forward, risking the stool. "So where do we start looking?"

Not: where have you been, what happened to you, where's Sira and her people, how could you have left us mid-battle—questions he'd expected. Had even planned to answer, owing Terk that much and more.

Either Bowman had briefed her constable, or Terk was being kind.

Briefing, Morgan decided and relaxed slightly. "I've sent a tug to make a pass. It'll be in position shortly."

Meanwhile, little was happening in Auord's sleeping shipcity, the varied feeds a monotony of vacant shipways, cables, and locked ports. The hour was late for business, the portcity frowning on anything that kept spacers out of its entertainment sector, and much too early for those spacers to stumble back to their ships.

Inside some of those ships, traders with families would be putting their children to sleep, while those scheduled to lift in the morning would run final checks on their cargoes and dig into vistapes for anything pertinent ahead of their next stop. He'd wanted no more than that life until Sira and beyond any imagining? She—the most powerful member of the Clan and leader of her kind—had wanted it, too. What might have been—

Morgan pulled his thoughts out of that too easy spiral. It led to darkness, and he wasn't the only one grieving. Terk's long-time partner, the Tolian Ptr-wit-Whix, had perished in the Assembler attack beneath Norval.

"Huido told me about 'Whix," he said. "I'm sorry. He'll be missed."

Predictably, that sympathy received a scowl. "At least the featherhead took his share of Splits with him. M'new partner's waiting on the *Conciliator*."

Fair enough. "You should have introduced us." He'd made his own way to Auord, but the *Conciliator* had shaved that time in half by taking him from Ettler's to Radulov first. Not that Morgan socialized on the cruiser—Bowman having invited him, politely, to stick to quarters and keep his nose in the newsvids to catch up—but he'd bunked with Terk. "Let me guess. That Neneman wrestler, Chert the Masher Nyquist?" Good choice, if Bowman wanted a matched set.

"No."

A touch too firm, that denial. "Then—" pronouns being tricky beasts, Morgan settled for: "—who?"

"You'll find out soon enough," in a defensive mumble.

Curious. "Terk—"

"Her name is Two-Lily Finelle. Satisfied?"

A Lemmick. Morgan pressed his lips together. Nonetheless, a tiny *huph* escaped.

Terk glared at him. "Twenty years of field experience. Combat rating off the charts. Would have promoted outsystem before now, but not everyone appreciates Finelle's qualities."

Being a Lemmick. The only species in the Trade Pact with a natural body odor so debilitating to the majority of the rest, including Humans, that their Board Member had to don a personashield for meetings. Otherwise, no one else would attend.

He had to know. "What did you do?"

The enforcer clenched fists half the size of Morgan's head. "The Neneman was the commander's first pick. He claimed I insulted him. No sense of humor."

Understanding dawned. Morgan hid a smile. Terk mourned 'Whix in his own peculiar way. The problem was, Bowman needed a functional team.

"Just how many potential partners did you insult?" There wouldn't be many qualified, not with clearance to work on her personal staff.

Terk growled in his throat. "Three. Then came Finelle. You can't," with real despair, "insult a Lemmick. They expect it. She congratulated me on my originality."

Morgan burst out laughing, faintly surprised he still could.

The other tried to glower, then gave up, sighing with all the air in his cavernous chest. "The commander ordered me to give Finelle a fair trial—in the field, no less. Anyone we're after will smell us a block away. I expect to be killed in action. Gravely wounded. Maimed! No, killed." Considering this dire future, Terk shifted; the stool protested with a creak. "Should get a medal anyway," he concluded gloomily. "Can we get back to business?"

"You take those," Morgan said waving to the screens on the right wall, nearest the enforcer. "Sure it's tonight?"

"Bowman made sure," with grim satisfaction. "One of Gayle's associates on this dirtball planet squealed the buyer accepted delivery of less than the complete shipment. So happens the ship with the final two crates got caught in an unscheduled mole fly inspection. Delayed till today." Terk's broad shoulders rose and fell. "Ask me, this is a wilder shot than usual, even for Bowman. The shipment's routine contraband. The Facilitator won't show. Why should he?"

"You might be right," Morgan replied, carefully noncommittal. If Bowman hadn't told Terk this wasn't about the Facilitator—though that ghostly player could well be involved—she'd her reasons, reasons having nothing to do with trust and everything to do with how dangerous the truth was.

Making Bowman's confidence a particularly disconcerting gift.

He'd needed a purpose; she'd offered him one: to find who'd been behind the Assemblers. This shipment—whatever it contained—was proof the aliens hadn't acted alone. As their bombs exploded, the vast wealth of the Clan had evaporated, sucked from every account and holding by the syndicates. Others had come later, with the skills to thwart official seals. They'd brought grav carts and the tools to open vaults, and might have raided empty Clan homes without being noticed at all.

But Bowman had been reinstated. Back in charge, she'd had every item in those homes tagged with the latest, undetectable enforcer tracer tech, then waited. Didn't matter that what was taken hadn't appeared worth the risk. Oddments of furniture and a few keepsakes. Clothing and some chests full of the Clan version of documents. What did? The tracers reported each item's journey through a variety of ports, via hands and other appendages, moving in a bizarre number of directions until, ultimately, converging on Auord.

Where the signals had stopped. Someone had found the tracers and disabled them; "undetectable," in Morgan's experience, more a matter of "for how long." Bowman wanted idents on the ship receiving the cargo and any beings involved. Discreetly.

"Damn straight I'm right," Terk stated. "The shipment's nothing but junk." He fished in his pockets. "Found this in one of the crates."

The crates they were to observe, from this carefully distant, discreet viewpoint, without risking contact.

"This would be why you've a Lemmick," Morgan commented dryly. Such rash impulses had been 'Whix's job to contain, whenever possible. No wonder Bowman was desperate to find Terk a partner.

"No one saw me. The stuff was in the freightyard. So happens—" an unrepentant grin, "—I was, too." With a grunt of triumph Terk pulled out his find. "See? Junk." He tossed something small and white to Morgan, who caught it with one hand.

"You shouldn't—" The words died in his throat as Morgan

found himself holding a waferlike crystal, oval, cloudy, and terribly familiar. "This isn't junk," he said after a moment. He lifted his hand, the crystal catching glints from the screens. "I've seen one of these before."

It had housed Aryl di Sarc's consciousness until she could enter her great-granddaughter's—Sira's—unborn. The baby had been mindless—a Vessel, as the Clan called it—waiting to host a personality.

Host? Trap was the better word for it, for Vessels were how those from AllThereIs were brought into this universe, Stolen, forgetting who and what they were.

Terk looked unconvinced. "Looks like a chunk of window plas to me. What is it?"

"I don't know what they're called, but there was a box of these at Norval." Specifically, in the lab where Sira's mother, Mirim, had worked with her group of M'hir Denouncers to restore the M'hiray's past. Sira had shared her memory of being shown the box. Its contents had been found by the group among other relics of Cersi.

How and why the crystals had arrived on Stonerim III, no one was left to explain. Marcus Bowman had given the M'hiray crates of Hoveny artifacts; maybe one had held a different type of treasure, but his records were gone too, prudently destroyed by Bowman's grandmother. A family tradition, to act against expectation.

"Can't be from there," Terk protested. "Bowman sealed everything Clan."

"Seals can be broken."

"I suppose you'd know how."

Morgan didn't rise to the bait, busy studying the crystal. On Cersi, the Vyna had put their dying Adepts inside such orbs, storing them as their Glorious Dead to live again and again in a sequence of new Vessels. Was he holding such a—a Presence in his hand? Someone who'd last been alive before the Clan entered the Trade Pact?

If so, they didn't belong here.

His fingers were averse to closing over the thing, but he forced them into a tight fist. Bowman would be the first to realize her plan was no longer the priority, in any sense.

Saving the Trade Pact from another, potentially disastrous, incursion by the entities of AllThereIs was.

"We have to get the rest."

Then he'd deal with what to do with them.

Interlude

A WATCHER *STIRRED* IN ALLTHEREIS, tempted to slip Between, into what the Clan had named the M'hir, to find what disturbed it.

For that's what Watchers did. What they were. While Singers flew and created and loved and, yes, lifted their voices, their Song weaving into the dance of the Great Ones, those who Watched paid *attention* to what was beyond.

What lived there.

What might become threat.

The Great Ones knew about the Watchers, or didn't; what consciousness they possessed was on another scale than that of Singers. Singers knew, though. After all, Watchers were Singers, too. Most lingered but briefly at the edges of AllThereIs, briefly as measured against the vast movements of the Great Ones, waiting for what only they knew. When done, they returned to add their voices, notes fresh and triumphant, or deep and grim, to the rest.

Some, a very few, couldn't let go; they became strange to their fellows and mute. They knew their duty, nonetheless.

The Watcher who'd stirred settled once more, the temptation passing. It had purpose, here, for it Watched what was new. Not threat.

Not yet.

The buds of Between shone with inner light, within each a Singer who'd been Stolen and was now coming home. Each bud grew, walls thinning, as its inhabitant let the minuscule span of their lives in NothingReal fade to memory, supplanted by the joy of remembering what they'd been. What they were.

Loved ones sang encouragement and stayed close, eager to welcome them home. A swift, easy journey for most; it would be longer for those in buds hanging loose, their walls shriveled, for those within lingered, caught in a dream of their own making. They would be free in their own time. Or not.

The Watcher's attention was for a bud unlike all there were or had ever been.

This bud was armored in *darkness* that *boiled* and *hissed* and stung those who flew too close. Many did nonetheless, their songs filling with despair.

For in the violent flashes of light that illuminated it, someone could be seen inside. Someone loved by all who'd been Stolen, by all who'd heard, which meant, here, by all.

Someone trapped.

Disturbance.

Here, the Watcher knew, not Between. Aware, now, she *reached* outward, seeking. Another of her kind approached. For a Watcher to change position in AllThereIs took *purpose* and *direction,* for without song, they did not fly. Such a change imposed on the Dance, affecting all.

Especially when a Watcher moved this quickly.

With—*ALARM!*—dragging Singers in his wake.

The Singers around the buds scattered, some flying into the living vastness of AllThereIs, others wheeling about to join those *caught* by the oncoming Watcher.

ALARM!

No, the Singers *bound* themselves. Willingly. More and more Singers joined; the Watcher's *purpose* and *direction* become theirs.

Together, they sang.

The thing about space travel? It's noisy, but you get used to it. The comforting din of rumble, whoosh, and whine lulls you to sleep. Then there's an assortment of pops, clanks, or dire hissing that will have you on your feet before you're awake, scrambling to the engine room. Or to the nearest spacesuit, vacuum being what it is, or rather isn't.

Footsteps? Those were new.

With no place in my reality. Mine, you see, alone. My choice and that part was clear to me, if little else was.

How could there be footsteps?

I went to the cabin door and hesitated, fingertips brushing the cold metal. I leaned my forehead against it, closed my eyes.

The footsteps weren't his.

These were heavier. Aimless, as his had never been. They wandered, as if lost, then stopped as though on the other side of the door.

A door suddenly much too thin for my liking. I'd known creatures who looked like feet. I rolled my forehead from side to side in furious denial. Couldn't be Assemblers. They scurried on fleshy cilia.

Most importantly, I was alone. Would always be alone.

Yet wasn't, for someone stood on the other side. A stranger. Waiting.

For what?

I jerked back, eyes wide. Waiting for me to open the door. To let a stranger into *my* reality?

"NO!" It wasn't a word and wasn't a shout. It was the outpouring of my pain and grief and determination to stay as I was, where I was—

To never forget him. Never!

The footsteps resumed, grew fainter, were gone.

A wave of *PAIN* and *GRIEF* surged through AllThereIs, *shattering* the Watchers into fragments. Singers tumbled, their song a wail of fear.

A Great One *paused . . .*

—everything did, as if AllThereIs could hold a collective breath—

. . . then *continued.*

The Singers returned, their song of *resolve*, even as the Watchers *rebuilt* themselves and a third joined them.

<<*AGAIN.*>>

I stepped from the fresher, tossing still damp hair back over my shoulders, and pulled on my coveralls and boots. For the next few moments, for days uncounted, I would feast my eyes on his paintings, dwell in the memory of this leaf or that flower, recall the aroma of a planet's night. When I could take no more, I would undress and climb naked between sheets that never warmed, and fall asleep, or what passed for sleep, here.

To wake again and walk to the fresher.

The ritual was mine, one I kept having left the rest behind, no longer in need of food or drink or activity. Sometimes I would let a finger's tip touch the com button. Others I couldn't bear it.

I'd just closed the top fastener when I heard footsteps.

Again.

They sounded different.

I went to the door and pressed my ear to the metal to listen more carefully. The heavy footfalls were back. The same.

They weren't alone. Another set marched with them down the corridor. No, not marched. Purpose to these steps and direction, yet their rhythm was as if they walked to music.

"No music here," I said or I thought as I turned away.

The footsteps slowed and stopped, distracting me from a curl of vine. Stopped outside my cabin door. Two strangers now.

Two wanting in.

Annoying.

I couldn't rouse myself to shout this time, so tried reason. "There's no room." The cabin had been barely large enough for two.

Without him, it was so much smaller.

They hadn't left. I could tell. "You can't come in unless I know you," I told them, feeling clever.

<<*Heart-kin . . .*>>

I whirled, throwing the bedsheet at the door. "Strangers!"

<<*Sister . . .*>>

I stood where I meant to stay, panting though I'd no need to breathe, in our cabin. Unfair, to *breach* my walls.

My mood darkened. Unwise. "Keep away."

<<*You don't understand . . .*>>

They deemed me oblivious; I was not. Outside this cabin was AllThereIs, filled with Singers—my joyous, happy kind—part of the Dance of the Great Ones. I'd heard their Song, its strands woven by everything they were and experienced: love, imagination, and laughter, remembrance, curiosity, and joy, fascination, mystery, and wonder. They created. Lived.

I was glad for them.

They believed me trapped, unable to reach them.

I wasn't. This bubble of reality was my strand, my creation, and if that made me a dissonance in their Song, a tiny misstep in the Dance?

Let them end me.

I turned my back on the door and went to sit cross-legged on the bed, counting the petals of a flower I remembered from Acranam.

I should have remembered what my sister could do.

A form *appeared,* hovering in the air above the bed. A torso so insubstantial I could see petals through it. No legs. Hands without arms. The barest shape of a face followed, framed by the sweep of long black hair. A face my memory granted expressive green eyes and a generous mouth. Had hers lost them?

Worse, I feared. Like the other Singers, she let what she'd been in NothingReal slip away and be, if not forgotten, then less.

Could any of them understand that was why I remained in here? That I valued Jason Morgan—each moment of our life together—over anything AllThereIs had to offer?

Slowly, as if drawing forth that other life took effort, her skin became opaque, then smooth and pale, a hint of pink over high cheekbones. A nose followed, arched brows, and there they were, at last.

Those eyes and that mouth, both filled with regret.

"Rael." I acknowledged sadly, shaking my head.

My younger sister had been betrayed and murdered on Deneb, along with her Chosen Janac di Paniccia, becoming a ghost in the M'hir to howl her warning to the rest of us. A terrible end—but there was more. What was really Rael, her mind, her personality, her passions, had been guided home by the Watchers. Free in AllThereIs to Sing in unending joy with Janac and our sister Pella and all those she loved.

Except me. I should have realized Rael would be the one to reject my defenses. Well, I'd resisted her plans and those of others on a regular basis before; I trusted she remembered that.

I had my doubts. She'd forgotten her arms and legs—which was, I had to admit, becoming rather disconcerting as the rest of Rael continued to solidify in front of me.

"You don't belong here," I told her.

"Where are we?" My sister's projections weren't like a holo or vid; she was, in part, physically present, enough to look around. I saw her recognize her surroundings. "Morgan isn't here."

As if surprised.

"Of course, he isn't," I replied. "He's in Trade Pact space." I should know. I'd died in the M'hir—my body had—'porting him there, along with Aryl and Enris, Barac and Ruti, being the truest of heart-kin and determined Morgan should have a future.

I frowned. "You thought I was stuck in a lie."

Pink became rose, flooding over those cheekbones; Rael had never been able to hide her emotions. "If I'd lost what you have, Sira, I couldn't have done otherwise."

"I choose the truth," I said simply. Nothing between Morgan and me had been false. I wouldn't start now.

"I'm glad of that, though I wish you'd choose more. Choose us." Rael tilted her head, hair flowing over a shoulder to cover a nonexistent breast. "Share your love, Sira, in the Song instead of locking it in this place. Will you, ever?"

She'd remembered me, now. Enough, at least. "No," I said as gently as I could. "I've no need of AllThereIs. You've no need of me. Leave me as I am, Rael. Sing that to them."

Tears glistened in her eyes but didn't fall. "I would, heart-kin. For you, I would, but that's why I'm here. We do need you."

I laughed, the sound harsh and bitter, burning in my throat like bile. She flinched, but didn't vanish, and I stopped. "I've done everything. Lost everything. This," I waved my hand at my spacer coveralls, "is all that's left. What more could you possibly ask of me now?"

Footsteps resumed in the corridor. The heavier ones. Pacing, though impatience wasn't something I associated with Singers, granted a universe to explore.

Rael's long-fingered hand moved with its former grace, sketching the Clan gesture of appeasement to one more powerful.

Unpleasant, that reminder of what we'd become among Humans. "I need you to leave, Sister."

But her apology hadn't been offered to me.

The footsteps stopped at the door, Rael lifted her hand once more, and a second figure began to *appear*. In my cabin.

Before I could be outraged, before I could summon that oh-so-useful *PAIN* and *GRIEF*—

—the figure was whole.

My next breath came out as fog, as if I'd stepped into an ice-cold cargo hold, and part of me wondered why I breathed at all.

"Sira."

Yihtor di Caraat.

Chapter 5

"THERE IT IS." Seizing the manual control, Morgan slowed the tug's progress past a lean, ominous shape. "The *Worraud.*"

The starship's main port was shut, its pitted hull revealed only in the flashes of the tug's caution lights. Two figures loitered by the ship's ramp, claw-tipped fingers hooked around weapons any other Port Authority would confiscate. But those crested heads dominated by elongated snouts, swinging with predatory grace to aim at the tug?

Auord's Port Jellies weren't about to challenge a Scat ship, so long as its piracy took place offworld and to Auord's profit.

Some things, Morgan thought, didn't change.

Everything else could. Had. He swallowed to ease the tightening of his throat.

Terk leaned forward, elbows on his thighs. "They haven't taken the shipment yet—not with guards standing around—I can get down there first and intercept." His big head turned. "Not saying I don't like the play, Morgan, but orders were to keep our distance."

"Bowman will approve this. Trust me."

"I don't." A sudden predatory grin. "But, as I said, I like the play." He started to get up.

"Wait." Before the Scats could grow suspicious, Morgan eased the tug along its path. Its rear vid feed showed more figures to the side, indistinct in the shadows. "They're ready for trouble."

The other growled something improbable with Scat anatomy and leaned forward again. "Figures. And you can't tell me why these things matter so much."

"You wouldn't believe me," Morgan admitted.

"Clan," Terk retorted, as if that said it all.

Didn't it? Even not knowing if the crystals housed any Stolen— or if the entities of AllThereIs could detect them in that state—

Or if they'd *reach* into this space after them, as they had after the Hoveny, and this time take an entire world—

"I'll go." He'd 'port the crate into the M'hir. Let the entities find it there; at least it'd be out of the hands of any meddlers in the Trade Pact. The thought of anyone releasing one of the Clan—making Sira's sacrifice for nothing— "I just need to get close—" If the guards caught him, Morgan thought bleakly, so be it.

"Ease your jets," Terk objected. He waved at the screens. "These are the only eyes we've got down there—and you'd best be sitting here when Thel gets back. 'Nother option?"

"If we can't steal the crate, we destroy it." Morgan lowered his voice. "Are you equipped?"

"I think I'm insulted." Terk put two fingers under the collar of his jacket and produced a thin black strip. "You know I travel prepared." He flourished the strip. "Targeted digester—like the one that ate that rust bucket of yours. Eats anything. Crate'll be empty before they know it. Trick will be the guards and the not-getting-dead part." A dour grin. "Don't want a medal that much."

"The ship won't waste time once the shipment's loaded. They'll call for a tug—wait—" Morgan checked the listings on Thel's sheet. "They've requested pickup in an hour. I'll assign one and disable—" his nimble fingers flew over the control panel, "—its rear access proximity sensors. That'll get you close without alerting the Scats, but—"

"Close'll do." The enforcer pulled what looked like a standard-issue stunner from another pocket. After popping off the muzzle's tip, he rolled the lethal strip into a tube and slipped that into the opening, then aimed the "stunner" at Morgan. "Gotcha."

Morgan eased the muzzle aside with a finger. "If you miss," he warned, "I'll send the tug into the ship. Foul her fins and ground her."

Terk gave him an unreadable look, then swore. "You'd do it, too. Cost your job, you realize."

Knowing as well as Morgan it could cost a great deal more. The Scat ship would be armed, no question. If such a collision set off those armaments, it would blow a hole in the shipcity, starting a chain reaction of explosions in its unfortunate neighbors. Murdering innocents as well as Terk.

Better that, Morgan thought, than the entire world. Than—horrors—multiple worlds. If the entities had, as it seemed, no limits?

He couldn't afford to have them either.

"Then don't miss," he told Terk.

* ✳ *

The enforcer left for the line of docking tugs well before the sound of the lock opening announced the return of Thel Masim. She'd a bundle in her hands, a bundle she handed Morgan as she took her station, eyes scanning the screens.

He was surprised to find it not only warm but emitting a delicious aroma. "Thanks."

"No need. You're so scrawny I was too guilty to enjoy my supper." Thel settled back. "Scats get up to anything while I was gone?"

Of course, she'd be aware who was finsdown. Morgan's lips twitched. "Not that I saw," he replied easily, taking her casual tone—and the bundle—as an invitation to take his own break. Going to the stool, now back in its corner, he opened the wrap, finding a crusty roll stuffed with still-steaming *hortsal,* the local and spicy version of white fish in butter sauce. "From *Gordon's Legion?*"

"Where else?" She'd a knack with the feeds, streaming view

after view on her main one until Morgan blinked and focused on navigating the dripping delight to his mouth. "Ah."

He lifted his eyes and froze. The main screen displayed the feed from a docking tug: the rear feed, to be exact, somehow reestablished in time for a too-clear view of a chest covered in small crustaceans. Terk, climbing aboard.

Without looking away, Thel pointed beside her. "C'mere."

Morgan rewrapped his supper and tucked it in the cleaner of his pockets, then brought himself and the stool. "You were watching," he concluded.

The corner of her mouth deepened. "I'm always watching. You should know that."

"Maybe I thought this time you'd trust me."

"If I didn't," she informed him cheerfully, "it'd be Port Authority in here to haul you off. And you wouldn't have that nice supper. Eat it while it's hot, lad."

Slightly dazed, Morgan took out the fish sandwich.

"Can't say I've the whole thing straight," Thel told him while he chewed. "But if your pretty bud's going to make those Scats sorry they picked my shipcity for their piracy, I'll be glad of it. But no using my tug as a weapon." Pointedly, she took the tug control in one hand, switching it to manual, then started it in motion.

"It's too—"

"—soon?" she finished for him. "No point being late, is there?" A moment passed, then, "What I don't get? The act. We go back, Jason, you and me. I'd have thought too far for that rowlas' dung."

"You're right." About to lie, to blame Bowman's demand for secrecy, Morgan changed his mind. "I thought if you believed I was now dregs, like your other waifs, you wouldn't ask any questions. About where I'd been. About . . . things I can't answer."

"Had your head on backward, you mean. Forgot, did you?" She made a rude noise. "I don't care what's blown out the air lock. Never have. No more of it, hear me?"

"Understood." That this old friend would take him back at face value, accept his word, warmed someplace inside that had grown very cold indeed.

"Hope Terk enjoys the ride." Thel had a wicked chuckle. "I remember sneaking you on the *Fox* same way a time or three. Seems to me you complained of bruises."

"Terk's tough." Morgan took a bite of his fish.

* ✳ *

You didn't order up a docking tug before you'd finished loading and secured your cargo; shipcities everywhere leveed stiff penalties if one of their tugs was kept waiting in an aisle. If traffic control made a mistake in your favor? Well, no one minded that.

Morgan watched, riveted, as Thel sent the docking tug around the final turn to the Scat starship, feeds catching an incoming freight-servo in the opposing lane. "Now that's good timing," she declared, speeding the tug a notch to claim right-of-way through the intersection. The train was forced to pause as the much larger—and slower—tug passed, then started up again, its five cars powering in turn.

Thel closed in the vid, but their loads were too well-wrapped to make out more than the shape of crates. "You know which one?"

"Terk does." The enforcer should have a clear shot—Morgan cursed under his breath. "We've a problem."

"I see it." Widened out, the feed revealed the flesh-and-blood driver operating the servo. All Morgan could discern in the slashes of light and dark provided by the tug's warnoffs was a humanoid. Auordian, best guess. Burly and doubtless well-armed.

And in perfect position to see the access panel of the tug open on Terk and his stunner.

Morgan lifted the com. "Hold."

"More company," Thel announced as a groundcar, low and sleek, came up from behind, accelerating past both freight and tug. "Busy night. What do you want to do?"

Get down there himself. That being impossible, Morgan thought quickly. "Push them, Thel. Put the tug right in their snouts and tell them you're on time."

"And why aren't they ready. My pleasure." As she maneuvered

the tug closer, Thel opened a channel to the Scat ship. She began at full volume, "Get that junk out of my way! I'm here to pick up your ship . . . Don't give me that, I make the damn schedule, you miserable excuse for—"

Morgan didn't bother listening to the ensuing spit and hiss of infuriated Scat, busy watching the groundcar stop at the ramp leading into the Scat ship. Three figures got out, standing in the spill of light from the now-open port above. They weren't spacers, by their portcity garb. The groundcar sped away.

Passengers as well as cargo? Unusual for Scats. They'd well-known difficulties dealing with species that refused to eat live food.

"Could be on the menu," Thel commented, nodding at the screen, then resumed swearing enthusiastically at the captain. The ship loomed larger and larger in the screens. By now, the passengers and the Scat guards were looking toward the tug. Three more Scats appeared from the shadows, one waving the freight-servo to hurry. Two darted up the ramp, opening the cargo port. The passengers were hustled to one side of the ramp, out of the way. One was protesting.

"What's going on?" Terk, in an aggrieved whisper.

"Hold till I give the word," Morgan told him. In the organized chaos, the driver climbed out to argue something with a Scat—presumably payment. Hands went to weapons. Mouths opened in shouts. The tug continued to close in, its flashing lights disorienting— "Now!"

Terk eased out of the tug, dropping to the ground as he angled for the best shot—

Only to be blocked as a piece of night descended to hover across the ramp. The massive aircar's roofing shield peeled back to allow dozens of little white Drapsk to spill over the rails. Armed Drapsk.

Heading for the cargo.

"Don't engage!" Morgan shouted into the comm.

"You think?" The enforcer scrambled back into the tug.

Thel slowed and stopped it, turning off the Scat captain—who'd know shortly he'd a bigger problem than traffic control—mid-hiss.

Together, she and Morgan watched in silence as the Scats on the ramp abandoned their cargo and passengers, running into the ship and closing the port behind them. Their erstwhile passengers—and the driver—disappeared into the night.

The Drapsk focused on the cargo, quickly and efficiently hooking anti-grav units to each of the five cars, then tethering those to their aircar. Done, they swarmed back on board and lifted away.

"Well, now," Thel observed. "Don't see that every day."

Interlude

"SIRA."

    I knew the voice—recognized the face. How could I not? Yihtor, the lawless, powerful Clansman who'd set out to build a new Clan empire on Acranam. Yihtor, who'd murdered his own kind and worse. Who'd tortured Morgan and tried to force Choice upon me.

Only to fail. I'd last seen him after the Clan Council had reduced him to a mindless, drooling nothing, their foul plan to use Retian technology to breed the two of us and ensure the Power—my Power—would pass into a future generation.

The Clan Council no longer existed.

Drooling husk or glorious Singer, Yihtor had no right to exist here in my reality. I focused on a vine painted with tender accuracy. "Get out."

"We need you."

As if I'd find that more palatable from him? "Go before I destroy you." And I could. There were rules here.

All of them mine.

"Look at Rael. Look at me."

"Go now—" Even as I spoke, I involuntarily shifted my gaze to my sister.

Something was wrong with her projection. Lines grew at the

TO GUARD AGAINST THE DARK

corners of her eyes, eyes that lost their brilliance. Her lips thinned and cracked. Bled.

I gasped as her lustrous, living hair, that hallmark of a Chosen Clan—or rather Hoveny, for that was what we'd been as flesh—vanished, replaced by a coarse stubble no longer than the last joint of my smallest finger.

And where she'd forgotten arms and legs—where her torso had been mercifully indistinct—all became solid and clear, and I wanted to weep.

Punctures tracked her arms and legs. Holes, regular, of specific size, gaped in her throat, chest, and abdomen, opening on the slick shine of mesentery and organs.

"Now me."

Gladly, I looked away from Rael, but what I saw next was worse. Yihtor had been handsome by any humanoid standard, exceptional even for Clan.

His thick blond hair had been shaved to the scalp. His eyes—his eyelids were shut, top and bottom marred by rows of tiny punctures. The same punctures lined his lips, kept tight together. His body was marred by holes, larger than Rael's, but his arms were clear. His legs—

The kneecaps were missing, the bone below exposed, slivered tendon jutting outward.

Though I no longer ate, I twisted to retch over the side of the bed.

"Our Vessels haven't died," Yihtor said, his voice hollow. A voice that couldn't come through those lips. "Their flesh still binds us."

Lips and eyelids sewn shut. Holes where tubes would be inserted. Needle marks. The knees—I didn't want to know.

"Sister, we need you."

Reluctantly, I sat up on the bed, arms tight around my legs. Rael had blurred her projections once more, but the reality couldn't be unseen. "You're in stasis." I'd been drugged and put into a stasis box once, but there hadn't been this mutilation.

Then again, Symon had wanted me to arrive in perfect condition.

Rael nodded. "They were too quick for me. I tried—" with abrupt passion, "—to die first."

I glanced at Yihtor and away again. My sister's face was easier to bear. "Why force yourself on me?" Stasis units were safe, reliable tech—and in Trade Pact space, another reality altogether. "There's nothing I can do." I didn't bother saying what both would know: they'd only to wait. The units would ultimately fail—power cells didn't last forever—or those bodies would be awakened and die from whatever was being done to them.

"We don't need help—" Rael started to say.

"NothingReal does," Yihtor interrupted. "Your precious Trade Pact and its aliens—and your Human—are at risk because you didn't finish what the Great Ones asked of you."

"I wasn't 'asked,'" I corrected, very quietly. I found I could look at his face after all, taking a distinct pleasure in its scars. His body, mine? Should never have existed. Our ancestors had been made by the Tikitik: an experimental blend of Hoveny—whose unborn could *lure* Singers inside—and Oud, who'd innate Power Between. Why? To produce us, living keys able to *breach* what protected AllThereIs from NothingReal.

To produce me, a Founder who, like a fool, reconnected Hoveny technology to the null-grid.

The first such *breach* had destroyed an empire; the second, mine, had almost ended billions of innocent lives. I'd made sure there wouldn't be another.

"I brought the Clan home. It's done. Go." I dropped my forehead to my knees. "And don't come back."

"Done? Then where are my heart-kin?!" More wail than words. "Where are the ones who were my House, my family?! You left them behind in NothingReal!"

No. It couldn't be. "Ask the Watchers," I told them, not raising my head. "They counted the dead, not I."

All at once, I felt a voice, no voices, deep inside. Hollow, echoing, *HARSH*. <<*We did. That's why we've come.*>>

Voices that were *here*.

My sister and Yihtor.

Watchers themselves. Or, I thought with some self-pity, they'd brought Watchers trailing into my cabin like lint in nonexistent pockets.

Watchers were trouble. They were Singers consumed by the desire to protect AllThereIs, maintaining an awareness of Between, the M'hir, and alert to any connection through that to NothingReal.

They weren't always sane, in my experience. Too much time in that seething Dark when they should be singing.

I lifted my head. "If there are Clan alive in the Trade Pact—"

<<YES!>>

Unfair. Even here, it hurt when they shouted at me. I glared at Yihtor, finishing with, "—There's nothing I can do about it. Being dead." In case they'd forgotten that, too. I shrugged. "Besides, without knowledge of the null-grid, or any device to use it, what harm can they do?"

<<HARM!!!!!>>

"The Watchers have seen," Rael answered, her eyes flashing their old fire. "The rise of the M'hiray affected more than the Balance on Cersi. We harmed Between."

Deluded, I thought with some pity. The link to their damaged bodies—

<<Between SUFFERS!>>

As if he'd heard the voice, or been it, Yihtor's blind head nodded. "From the start, 'porting has sliced through Between like a knife through skin. Some wounds heal, but passages cut too deep. They've begun to rot."

"We've weakened Between, Sira," my sister continued. "Continue to weaken it."

The roiling deadly Dark of the M'hir—Between—was beyond vast, beyond understanding, but it had been *ours*. I'd been proud of my abilities there. Resented the Drapsk showing me the Clan weren't the only life to be part of it. Been outright offended to discover worlds having their version of sex there.

That I—and others like me—had been causing it to rot? I liked this view least of all, not that my opinion mattered.

Nonetheless, I offered it. "Then be grateful any Clan in the Trade Pact are the last." I didn't look at Yihtor. "It doesn't matter

if Acranam's exiles escaped. They're too old to breed again."
Clan genealogy had been my obsession; this group had earned
my special, unflattering attention. "No more Vessels. Once the
exiles die, no one left to 'port. The problem ends."

"My mother has other plans."

Wys di Caraat. Of course, she did. I wanted to spit, but my
mouth no longer held moisture. I settled for a shrug. "Let her try.
The end will still come."

<<*TOO LATE!*>>

I grimaced at Rael. "Immortals. Eternity. Why the rush?"

"The Great Ones remain uneasy. They *hear* silences in the
Song."

<<*The Stolen have no voice.*>>

"So they listen harder. Grow more unsettled. Sira, we can't let
them *reach* out again. Above all, not to the Trade Pact. It's the
part of Between we've damaged the most. It's become unpredict-
able. Riddled with rot. If the Great Ones enter it, force themselves through—"

<<*ALL WILL END.*>>

It wasn't as if any force or persuasion existed to stop what were
the equivalent of stars and planets in that other reality. While a
topic I'd have enjoyed discussing with my Human over sombay—

It being safer to think of that—

Safer than remembering a world scoured and ruined, a moon
plucked from its sky, a civilization ended—

Than to think it could happen to the thousands of worlds com-
prising the Trade Pact—

—to Morgan.

FURY! FEAR! I lost myself as they fed one another, those all-
consuming emotions, clashing to rise in giant waves of turmoil
and despair.

What little of me remained in control knew the danger: in this
place, where a Singer's Song became part of the Dance?

If they *heard* mine, the Great Ones wouldn't be "uneasy."

They'd respond.

I fought for control. The projections of Rael and Yihtor
flickered—a warning this was a battle I could lose.

No. I refused the possibility. Stopped fighting. Instead, I thought of Morgan. Of nothing but Morgan.

How, if he were with me, I'd feel his belief in me; of how I'd draw upon his bottomless well of strength and resolve.

He wasn't here, and I'd no help. Still, memory *resonated.* As you love me, we'd said to one another. I remembered. And there it was.

That love.

Rael and Yihtor became solid. Both were tense and broadcast *fear* of their own, but it was over, and I gestured apology.

"What," I asked then, fragile myself in the aftermath, "do you need me to do?"

Chapter 6

"I'LL SAY THIS FOR YOU, lads." Thel Masim sat back. "You do liven up the place."

Terk's craggy features collided in a ferocious scowl. Before the enforcer could say anything Thel'd make them regret, Morgan passed him the last of his fish sandwich. "The *Heerala* hasn't lifted," he pointed out. Whatever the Drapsk were up to, it was more complicated than robbing the Scats.

Who hadn't reported any theft. Who'd, in fact, requested a docking tug—please—and would traffic control—we insist—accept a bonus for their prompt service? Thel had assured them, with choice adjectives, it'd be Auord's pleasure to see the last of their ship.

Terk had been stuck inside that tug for the duration of its task: picking up the starship and, with excruciating slowness, trundling down the long aisle with its burden to the landing field, setting the starship in place, then returning home to its spot in line. Suffice it to say the experience hadn't improved his mood.

Accepting Morgan's peace offering, the enforcer took a huge bite, eyes promising this wasn't over.

Which, of course, it wasn't. "Thel, play it for Terk."

She nodded and flipped a control. The main screen showed the Drapsk aircar descending in slow motion, flashes from the tug's warnoffs absorbed by its black hull, instead of reflected. Terk grunted in acknowledgment of what that meant: not an average vehicle, not with that stealth tech.

"Now watch the ramp," Morgan told him.

The driver dropped to the ground and ran away.

At first, the passengers seemed too stunned to move, their reactions comical, mouths flapping, arms waving—

Then one *fragmented,* components scurrying over the sides of the ramp and away—

—as the other two vanished from sight, without taking a single step.

Terk stared. Swallowed, hard. "Got to be a mistake. Problem with the vid."

"My equipment's prime—"

"No mistake," Morgan said heavily. The Assembler? Given the source of the cargo, he'd have been surprised not to find one or more involved. As for the others?

"Don't take this wrong, Morgan, but I thought the Clan were extinct," Terk grumbled, as though this shift in his universe was a personal affront. "Thought the Assemblers made them extinct. We were sure."

"We were wrong." Morgan rose to his feet. "Thel—"

She sniffed. "Go on, then. Shipcity's full of those who want work. Daresay most'll do a better job."

He had to smile. "Thank you."

An impatient wave dismissed him, her small eyes back on the screens.

Terk climbed to his feet, rubbing his backside. "What now?"

"The Drapsk have what we want."

The enforcer grimaced. "I was afraid you'd say that." But he headed for the door.

Morgan was about to follow him through when Thel said very quietly, "Jason."

He turned. "What is it?"

"You and your pretty bud are all hot about this batch of cargo." She tipped her head back over her seat, luck beads dangling, to regard him upside-down. "For what it's worth, Scats didn't lift empty. Took deliveries yesterday and the day before that. Food-stuffs. The usual dregs." She made a face. "Shouldn't be doing enforcer work, mind, but I don't like pirates."

Morgan strode forward and planted a kiss on her forehead before she could evade it. "Keep safe, Thel," he told her. "What you've heard—"

"Out of the air lock," she scolded, sitting up and rubbing her forehead. "Get. Lock the door on your way."

But he could hear the pleased smile in her voice.

✴ ✳ ✲

Constable Russell Terk could express his deepest, direst doubt as to the wisdom of an idea without saying a word. He did so now, looming like a cloud as he walked beside Morgan, his breath coming out in machinelike rasps. The effect was, admittedly, diminished by the cheerful slap of his sandals on the cobblestones of the portcity.

Morgan felt Terk's doubt as a tangible weight. Doubt of him—perhaps. Or of where they were going, for he'd been the one to arrange a face-to-no-face with the Drapsk. That it would take place in arguably the lowest of the dives that preyed on spacers? Couldn't be it. The enforcer relished any place where fights promised smashed furniture and beer.

No, he decided. Terk had sent a squeal to Bowman, and she'd replied.

Now the enforcer fretted about the Clan.

Well he might. A Master Trader had to remember faces and Morgan had recognized both, however distorted by panic they'd been. He'd last seen them on Acranam, in the grand hall of Yihtor di Caraat, along with over a hundred of the faithful.

Gathered to watch their leader attempt to force Choice on Sira di Sarc.

The attempt had failed, in part because Morgan had arrived in time with Rael and Barac, but mostly because Yihtor hadn't come close to being a match for Sira's Power.

Morgan knew who the Clan were. As for how they'd escaped the Assembler attack? From what he'd seen—possibly by aiding it.

Implying these two were among the Clan who'd followed the di Caraats willingly. Lawless. Dangerous.

He'd kill them and send them where they belonged without a qualm, but if there were two—

"Can't just be two," Terk said abruptly.

Morgan snorted. "Sure you're not a telepath?"

"Bad enough you are," the other retorted. "So if there's more, where've they been hiding?"

"These were taking a Scat ship. Maybe they've an arrangement." Though it was difficult to imagine a species who loathed "mindcrawlers" more than the reptilian bipeds. Still. "There's history. Roraqk worked with Yihtor."

To kidnap Sira. He'd perished for that, as well as for those he'd killed on Plexis. A death Morgan did not regret.

Terk nodded. " 'Nuff creds buys allies. Not that you'd trust the sort you can buy. Sira, now—" with a sideways glance, "—she did all right with Scats. Rek, wasn't it? Might be worth making contact."

While Sira's bold ploy to pit one captor against another had gained Rek a ship of her own and earned the Scat's respect, from what he knew of the species? "Rek has no reason to trust me or anyone else." He fell silent as they passed a line of spacers waiting to enter a garishly painted door. Once clear, he continued, "Bowman's got the ident for the Scat ship. Whatever else they've loaded, or if there are more Clan on board, that's her call. We've our own job. The Drapsk have our box."

"Dear Drapsk. Please give us what you stole from pirates. Yeah," Terk spat into the gutter. "That's going to work."

"You could go back to your ship."

The other feigned shock. "And let you go to the—where're we going again?"

"*The Raunchy Retian.*"

"Great. A toad bar." Terk rolled his eyes. "That settles it. Can't let you go alone."

They turned the corner and entered the entertainment district. Buildings leaned overhead, top floors wider than lower ones. There'd been a shower earlier in the night, sufficient to fill the gutters on every roof, but the resulting musical tinkle as drops hit the chimes suspended below hadn't a chance against the bass thumping from the bars to either side.

Their destination wasn't one of them.

Morgan led the way down an alley; the All Sapients' District of Auord's portcity was riddled with them, all, as far as he'd been able to tell, used for waste disposal. Piles of refuse crisscrossed their path. He smiled to himself when Terk swore and danced, his sandal having landed in some of it.

What lighting there was came from dim fixtures over widely spaced—and closed—doors, leaving pools of darkness between. Morgan twitched his wrist to drop a knife into his palm. Terk had something larger in his hand. They should be taken for recruiters, too dangerous to be targets.

But the desperate lived here. Morgan could hear them, moving among the bags and cans. If he lowered his mental shields, he could *scan* for any threatening intention, but that came with its own risk. There were species sensitive to the merest *touch*.

He might *taste* change before an attack.

Might not, just as easily. Useful as the Talent was, he didn't trust his life to it. Instead, Morgan kept his head up and gaze ahead, aware Terk did the same. Beings of purpose, that broadcast, uninterested in whomever—whatever—lurked in the shadows.

That, combined with Terk's distinctly intimidating self, got them to the stairs leading up to the bar without incident.

The Raunchy Retian did have a sign on the leftmost of its paired doors, of a sort. The name "Retian" had been scratched thin, with "Toad" scrawled overtop, but none of that species would care, being disinclined to venture from their mudball of a world and even less to participate in the sort of activities that had Terk eagerly reaching for the door handle.

The Humans paused inside to adjust their eyes. Far from dim, the interior of the bar blazed with an unfortunate number of portlights, making it easy to see clusters of wizened grapes were the main decor element. Retian eggs or close enough. Again, not a concern to their parents, who produced such offspring in massive streetside orgies once a year, leaving them to squirm their way into the swamps and grow. That Ret 7 had yet to suffer a population explosion spoke volumes about the challenges that growth posed.

It worked for them.

As the lights worked now. "No Drapsk yet," Morgan shouted over the flutes.

Flutes in a spacer dive. Mind you, they were Ordnex flutes, resembling engine parts and requiring multi-jointed arms and fingers—which Ordnex had—to play. The sound produced was, Morgan had to admit, loud and rhythmic.

If you liked feeling trapped inside a water pump. A very large water pump. A pump having, he listened a moment then nodded, a vane about to fail.

To his ears, but *The Raunchy Retian* didn't cater to humanoids. The only Human Morgan could see from this vantage, ten stairs up, midway between ceiling and floor, was Terk. The enforcer plunged joyfully through the multi-species' crowd, using his shoulders to make a path to the bar—charmingly willing to offend any and all beings in the name of a good time.

Which they weren't here to have, but as a cover for a clandestine meeting? Terk did have the locals fooled. Shaking his head, Morgan stepped down, then followed the walls around, slipping quietly between tables and booths. By the time he reached the bar, Terk had claimed an inordinate share of it, big elbows spread wide. "Waited for you," he greeted, making room before raising a mug of beer to his lips.

Morgan leaned on the bar—some type of plas, pressed and colored to resemble, vaguely, wood—and kept his eyes on the entrance, the door in plain view over the various heads and body parts. No need to guess why the Drapsk had chosen this spot in the All Sapients' District: it might not be clean or quiet, but the air was clear, free of the usual ysa-smoke and other overly shared contaminants.

Perfect for a species reliant on airborne chemical signals.

"What can I get you, Gentle Hom?" Deep that voice, with an underlying rumble.

Morgan turned to face the bartender, unsurprised to find a Brill. Male. Almost dainty, for his kind, being hardly bigger than Terk; a yellow apron printed with more purple egg clusters strained to cover his leathery bulk.

"This enough for a beer?" the Human asked, dropping a few coins of local currency on the bar.

The Brill swept them up with a click of ivory-tipped fingers. "Anywhere else, it gets you the door," with a booming chuckle. "Lucky for you, tonight I have the soft spot for spacers." Filling a mug to overflowing at the tap, the bartender held it just out of Morgan's reach. "One," he warned, then put it down in front of him.

"My thanks." The Human inclined his head, a gesture their species shared. "I beg the honor of your true name, good Brill, that I may record your kindness for my many progeny." Terk's eyebrow twitched upward.

"Grasis' Glory!" the bartender boomed, appearing sincerely touched. "To find such manners in a Human!"

"I've manners, too, you know." Terk raised his mug. "Cheers!"

"Ignorant pisspot, you are." The Brill regarded Morgan, then smacked his thick lips, striking his chest with a curled fist. "Manouya am I!"

Had Terk's mug paused midair? He must have imagined it, for the enforcer buried his face in the froth, slurping loudly in a demonstration of Human manners.

"Morgan."

" 'Morgan.' " The bartender bent forward, rolls of blubber settling on the bar, small eyes oddly intent. "This is not a common name, on Auord. Should I know this name?"

The question set off alarm bells. Or was it the look? "I don't think so," Morgan said easily. "I only go to places like this when my little brother visits."

Terk wrapped a heavy arm around his shoulders. "Mother worries he doesn't socialize. All those children."

The Brill reared back. "Humans," it rumbled, going to serve another customer.

The arm tightened, drawing Morgan close. "That's no bartender," Terk whispered, low and urgent. "I've heard that name—"

Before Morgan could do more than tense, the music stopped.

The Humans, like everyone else, turned around to see why.

Drapsk.

The little beings poured down the stairs like a waterfall. At first glance, they resembled toys, the sort preferred by Human children, with round bodies of soft white, covered in what wasn't quite bare skin, but not quite fur, and paired stubby arms and legs. But instead of a Human face, or a doll's, a Drapsk had only a small round mouth, ringed in short, bright red tentacles. No nose. No ears. No eyes.

No need, Drapsk ably sensing their surroundings. Trade Pact xenospecialists longed to analyze the capabilities of those expressive, feathery antennae, a pair of which sprouted from each Drapsk head.

Plume color varied with tribal allegiance. The blue-green of these meant Heerii, but that was to be expected. When Morgan had last been on Drapskii, the Heerii had risen to "ascendance" over all others, including the Makii, who'd willingly taken on their coloration. It worked for Drapsk.

Antennae erect, the Heerii came down the stairs two by two, leaving room for the predictable stampede of customers vacating *The Raunchy Retian*. It wasn't that Drapsk were known for violence, though each of these wore a belt with a blaster, holstered, to their left side.

It was how they filled a room to capacity.

Within minutes, the bar contained dozens of Drapsk, a solitary Ordnex snoring in a corner booth, and two Humans.

The Brill hurried around the bar, lifting the bottom of his apron in a shooing gesture. "Time to be gone," he said briskly. "Closing up, Gentle Homs."

"'M not done." The enforcer added an eloquent belch as he leaned back and made himself comfortable.

"Why close?" Morgan picked up his mug. "Drapsk are excellent customers."

Manouya's cheeks puffed, squeezing his eyes into unreadable slits, but he didn't press the matter.

As the rest of the Drapsk settled at tables and booths, easing the comatose Ordnex to the floor to make room, two of their number stepped to the bar, antennae aimed at those waiting. To Human eyes—most ocular types, for that matter—the beings were identical, but something familiar in the bearing of the right-most caught Morgan's attention.

Could it be? If so, the last time he'd encountered this particular Drapsk, its name had been Levertup, and those plumes the bright yellow of a Skeptic. Skeptics were Drapsk scientists and researchers; more importantly, they were an impartial judiciary, being—apparently—tribeless.

The opposite was true, as he and Sira had learned. A Skeptic underwent *gripstsa*, the switching of roles between pairs of Drapsk, until he had experienced every task important to a tribe. Following that, he would commit *lar-gripstsa*, to become a member of each tribe and learn their uniqueness. Only then was a Drapsk ready to reproduce, a process requiring the Scented Way, their planet Drapskii, and all other Skeptics: *su-gripstsa*.

A life cycle surely unique to Drapsk, though few sapient species willingly shared the details of theirs. Had the Drapsk not needed Sira's help to reconnect Drapskii to the Scented Way—which had, coincidentally, made the Rugherans and their world, White, equally happy—theirs would still be a mystery. And remain unsuccessful.

Morgan, now overly versed in the intimate ways of Drapsk, had to admit their offspring—tiny balls with transparent antennae and those stubby limbs—were adorable to Human eyes, too.

If this individual was the Drapsk he'd known, however briefly, the being was learned, stubborn beyond his species' norm, and they'd a shared history. Levertup had been Rael di Sarc's Skeptic, assigned to watch over her as she'd tried to heal Drapskii.

One didn't acknowledge a previous life role, but he'd been curious—long ago—and researched all he could about Drapsk, including their naming conventions. Taking the chance, Morgan bowed. "Captain Heevertup. Thank you for coming."

All five tentacles popped into the Drapsk mouth, then out again, glistening with moisture. "I would not refuse your invitation."

So he was—had been—Levertup. The tacit confirmation should have been gratifying; instead, it robbed Morgan of speech. This Drapsk had known Sira—worshipped her. Would expect her here, or involved.

How did he begin to—

"I arranged this meeting." The Brill struck his chest. "Me!"

Not a bartender, Terk mouthed triumphantly.

The Drapsk on the left sucked a single tentacle into its mouth and chewed—reviewing facts, possibly. Or distracted. Heevertup oriented on the Brill. "You provided the location. By your clothing, you are its keeper. Please provide refreshments."

Manouya tore off the apron, throwing it aside. "Help yourselves," he boomed. "On the house."

"This oughta be fun," Terk commented under his breath.

No doubt having witnessed or contributed to his share of bar raids, Morgan thought, amused, but Drapsk weren't typical spacers.

Hooting happily, the roomful of Drapsk organized themselves in a smooth flowing stream to go behind the bar. On passing the beverage shelves, each chose a container. Taller shelves were accessed by Drapsk lifting one another. Nothing was broken or disturbed. As they came away, their choice affixed to their mouths by their tentacles, the hooting changed to a satisfied gurgle.

The captain and the other who, at a guess, should be the *Heerala*'s first officer, waited in polite silence for the others to return to their seats.

Morgan collected himself. They'd a job to do. He exchanged looks with Terk, the sort of nonverbal intraspecies' exchange unlikely to be interpreted by other sorts of being. Not that there were guarantees between any two of the same species, but they knew each other by now.

Well enough for Morgan to see Terk's outward calm covered a

rising excitement, one he guessed had nothing to do with an absent box of Clan crystals and everything to do with a new hunt: this Manouya.

The Brill, whomever he was, had to wait. Must wait. Morgan risked a quelling frown.

Terk grinned, all innocence.

Meaning they were no longer here for the same reason.

∗ ✳ ∗

"Please begin, Gentle Homs."

Captain Heevertup had commandeered a table, inviting the Humans and Brill to sit with him. The Brill had done so with the care of someone who'd learned not to trust the furnishings made by the less dense. The first officer stood beside his captain, still sucking that tentacle, as yet unintroduced. Heerii manners, Morgan reminded himself. The tribe tended to secrets.

"If you would," the Drapsk captain indicated Terk.

The big Human spread empty hands. "Ask him." With a nod at Morgan.

Morgan assumed a confident air, smiling at the Drapsk. The smile was for those with eyes; the little beings would detect whatever chemical signaling accompanied it. "My colleague and I—" he wasn't letting Terk off that easily, "—are here in search of a particular item, honored Captain. One we believe you may be able to acquire for me. I've brought a sample." He brought forth the crystal and put it on the table, holding it in place with a finger.

The upper third of Heevertup's antennae bent toward the crystal, blue-green plumes drooping down. They fluttered, sending a tiny breeze to raise the hairs on the back of Morgan's hand. On impulse, he rocked the crystal back and forth, fascinated as the antennae of both Drapsk waved in gentle synchrony.

The beings were sensitive to the Scented Way, or rather to any change in it. They'd reacted involuntarily to what the Clan, or he, did there. Could they confirm what, or who the crystals held? "I've heard there are more, on Auord."

The tentacle, now pale, popped out of the first officer's mouth with a spray of saliva. "Such items are unavailable. They were acquired for another client."

"Who?" Terk demanded.

Subtle he wasn't. Before the assembled Drapsk did more than stiffen with offense, Morgan intervened. "My colleague and I know the Heerii would never reveal such confidential information. We are curious why you'd come to this meeting, if your goods are spoken for."

"To gauge the market," the first officer said at once. "One must set a price reflective of demand."

And, no doubt, to identify who was in the market. Traders, indeed. About to continue, Morgan paused. Heevertup's antennae struggled to stay erect. He didn't agree, that suggested, but wouldn't overrule the other. About the pricing—or why they were here?

"I can't imagine you would waste our time. Surely there's room to negotiate," Morgan suggested, looking at the captain. "It's possible, is it not, your clients would be amenable to selling a portion, for the right price. You'd be acting, as Drapsk are famed to do, in their best interests." Drapsk prided themselves on knowing what customers wanted before they did—and obtaining it. Until today, he'd assumed legally, though the Drapsk he'd known would consider liberating cargo from Scats a public service.

"We think of our clients first, it is true, Gentle Hom," the officer agreed, tentacles spread in a pleased ring around his small mouth. "We Heerii are the very best—"

A discontented rumble from the Brill. "This jabber wastes my time. BAH!"

Like an echo, a chair toppled in the distance as a single Drapsk rolled into tight ball of white, done with the meeting. *Eopari*. The so-not-helpful Drapsk response to stress.

The captain stiffened. "We decide the use of time, not you," with unDrapsk-like sharpness.

"It is also true, my good Drapsk," Morgan pressed, "that no trade ends until delivery is made and payment exchanged." He kept it calm, composed. "When you hear my offer—"

"'Offer'?!" Manouya interrupted again. "This Human lies to

you. Look at him. Shipcity dregs with nothing but the rags on his back." His voice dropped an ominous octave, rattling the table. "My business is the only one worth your consideration. Send them and their scrap away. Then we will discuss what I want."

"We're all friends here," Terk advised him, his tone like ice.

"I am 'friends' with no Human."

The enforcer leaned forward, the angles of his face harsh. "That so?"

Morgan's boot found those bare, orange-painted toes and pressed, not gently. There was a card to play yet on the board. Paying no attention to Terk's glare—or the Brill's—he spoke to Heevertup. "I do not come empty-handed," stated with the certainty provided by Bowman's unlimited Travel Voucher, sewn inside his coveralls; perhaps not the use she'd anticipated, but if it retrieved the crystals? No question she'd honor it. "Let's discuss terms, good Drapsk. If you remember me at all, Captain, you know my word can be trusted."

"We could never forget. Jason Morgan. The Human Mystic One." The captain stretched out a hand. Morgan met it with his, startled when the rest of the Heerii, except for one white ball, rose to their feet. "Beloved of She Who Brought Drapskii to su-gripstsa."

As if they'd been waiting for that signal, the Drapsk—all of them—rushed to the table with a drumming of little feet. They pressed to get as close to him as they could, and when Drapsk pressed, others gave way, including Terk and the Brill.

Morgan endured the crowding, mouth firmly closed as rosy tentacles patted his cheeks and jaw, and stroked his lips. Tasting what they offered would be the Human version of lar-gripstsa; he'd rather not become an honorary Heerii at this or any moment.

More Drapsk and more, their antennae dipped until the Human found himself engulfed in blue-green warmth. He didn't dare move: the plumes were fragile as well as exquisitely sensitive.

All at once, in shattering unison, they spoke.

"We grieve with you."

He'd dreaded telling the Drapsk about Sira.

Why had he thought they wouldn't already know?

Interlude

Plexis

PLEXIS SECURITY was responsible for the thousands of sapients who lived and worked on the immense station, as well as the multitudes who came and went. Responsible in the sense that none of those watched by security better mess with station operations—from safety protocols to the collection of air tax—nor do anything to impede the ample flow of business.

Plexis being, above all, a living entity of its own, as fragile as only a metal-and-plas egg in vacuum could be. The station would choke and die if starved. First, though, would come riot and panic. Without the dedicated beings of Plexis security, dressed in however much sturdy gray fabric as their particular body form could accommodate, anarchy was a dropped parcel away.

These were not thoughts Tayno Boormataa'kk entertained as he crouched anxiously in the waiting area assigned to "those we haven't arrested yet." The decor and fixtures were pleasing, and a counter displayed a variety of beverages informatively labeled regarding their potential addictive or poisonous nature depending on species.

On Plexis, individuals were responsible for their own failures in judgment.

He was, Tayno worried, here for such a reason. Not that he knew which of his failures had attracted this unwelcome summons—

A door opened. There were two in this room. One, the exit, had locked behind him. This was the unfortunate other door. "Hom Huido." The security guard beckoned. "This way, please."

His "uncle" considered the inability of most other species to tell them apart as the only reason to let a second Carasian male in his territory live, it being convenient and entertaining to have a stand-in for his magnificent self deal with station bureaucracy and tedious customers.

Most of the time, Tayno was delighted to oblige.

Not this time, but even had he wanted to try, there was no arguing with security. He rose. "What's this about?" As Huido, after all, he should be daring.

"The deputy inspector will explain." The guard—a nondescript Human-ish creature with a large weapon at his/her hip—regarded Tayno's girth, then hit a control to widen the door, stepping aside.

Courtesy was promising, Tayno thought hopefully. The last time he'd had to turn sideways and squeeze through, leaving significant marks on his beautiful carapace. And, to be honest, the doorframe.

The last time, he'd been interrogated by that unpleasant Inspector Wallace. Not a problem today. Wallace had been encouraged, rumor had it, to take a post on Kimmcle, a world of regrettable reputation. Judging by the glee with which that rumor spread, others hadn't enjoyed Wallace either.

"In here, Hom Huido."

As Tayno entered what he was relieved to find a simple office, he made sure his eyestalks were erect, eyes oriented ahead. To a Carasian, the display was aggressive, almost rude, but Huido had assured him—often—that he tended to slink as if about to hide as a rock and that wouldn't do, not to pass as his mighty self.

When Tayno saw the image displayed on the wall-sized screen behind the desk, he couldn't help but slink a little, withdrawing his eyestalks until only a row of shiny black beads showed along the gap in his head disks. Even he could tell it was Mathis Dewley. His new Human friend.

"I'm Deputy Inspector Jynet, Hom Huido. Thank you for coming."

"I didn't have to?" Tayno blurted.

"Of course not. You're an upstanding citizen of Plexis—and a busy one, with the work being done on your valued establishment. I appreciate your time."

Tayno dared unslink a trifle, a dozen eyes sliding back into the open. "I am busy," he agreed. "Very busy."

"Indeed." The Deputy Inspector of Plexis Security was an Eima. Though a theta-class humanoid, her cheeks were covered by loose dewflaps hanging from eye socket to jaw edge. It gave Eimae what Lones called a doleful look, but to Tayno, Jynet's face bore an uncomfortable resemblance to the splayed lobes of a crushed *atar*, he once having leaned—accidentally—on a bowl of the expensive fruits.

For which Huido had made him pay.

The resemblance grew uncanny as her flaps turned shiny green. "Then I won't delay," Jynet continued. "Can you identify this individual, Hom Huido?"

It didn't appear a trick question. "Yes. That's Mathis Dewley. A worker at the restaurant. Human," he added helpfully.

She made a note. What had he said? It worried him when they made notes.

"When did you last see Mathis Dewley?"

"It wasn't yesterday," he said with confidence. She waited, pen poised. Not the right answer, then. It had been a while. He twitched a handling claw as he counted breakfasts to himself, or more precisely, breakfasts with the Turrneds, who served a delicious syrup every five days he did his utmost not to miss. "Five syrup—I mean twenty-five station days. Is there a problem? I hope there isn't a problem." He fought the urge to crouch. "That was the first time I saw him, too. Twenty-five days."

Another note was made. "I can't say, Hom Huido. But if you see Hom Dewley again, please inform security at once."

That was all? Tayno expanded with relief. "I will," he promised.

"I'm always glad to assist. Being an upstanding citizen," he added, in case she'd forgotten.

Another flash of color below her eye sockets. He began to fear it indicated amusement. Ever-so-slowly, he backed toward the door.

"There is one other matter I wish to bring to your attention."

He stopped.

The deputy inspector held out what looked like a piece of plas. The sort that had words on it. "Take it," she told him, when he didn't move.

Tayno extended a handling claw, seizing the thing gingerly between the tips. "What's this?"

"It's an apartment."

His eyestalks collided trying to examine the plas. "It is?"

That color again. "Your pardon. Let me explain. This is the address and access code for an apartment rented under the name Jason Morgan. Your friend, I believe?"

He spared three eyes to stare at her. What would Huido say? "More than friend," he replied, doing his utmost to add a firm boom to his voice. "My blood brother!"

"Excellent. Then you'll assume the lease. The terms are there," she pointed to the plas hanging from his clawtips. "It's in arrears, but my colleagues assure me the *Claws & Jaws* regularly covers Morgan's debts."

Debts. Tayno knew all about those. Debt was why most of his pay vanished, going to cover some completely coincidental damage to the plumbing—Huido couldn't expect him to put the rest toward this apartment?

He could and would. There was another source of funds, but— "We aren't open yet," Tayno protested weakly.

"We understand the situation, Hom Huido, and have no wish to add to your burden."

That sounded good.

"I'll take your guarantee to pay in full two station days after you reopen," the deputy inspector finished. "The going interest rate will apply, of course."

That didn't. "Of course," he echoed weakly, then realized the rest of it. They'd wait to be paid. Tayno almost shook with relief. They'd wait!

All he'd need was for Huido to return by then.

And to be, the Carasian decided, well away from Plexis before his "uncle" saw the bill.

* ***** *

It wouldn't be so bad, Tayno consoled himself as he made his way home along the concourse. Others made way for him; some hastily, a preoccupied Carasian akin to a walking avalanche.

Yes, he'd planned to build a new pool—his own pool—but to be realistic, his new word, what was to stop Huido from trying to take his wives?

The wives he didn't have yet.

No, he was better to go. Start a new business, in a new place.

He paused outside the restaurant to admire the refurbished sign. *Claws & Jaws: Complete Interspecies Cuisine.* Much classier than the neighboring: *Skenkran All You Can Eat Chow.* Which was in a terrible font, making the word "chow" look more like "claw" which might, come to think of it, be intentional. They were, regrettably, open for business; taxes and fines paid, or the right bribe found.

The Carasian sighed, making a rain-on-plas sound, then brightened. If it were his sign, it could say *Tayno's Fabulous Food.* Or *Tayno's Treats.* He liked that one. Short and tasty. Wait. "*Tayno's Tasty Treats!*"

"Hom Tayno?"

Caught! As he flinched, he belatedly realized the voice came from his right elbow and was familiar. Bending eyestalks, he saw Lones, who'd taken Ansel's job, caring for the household behind the restaurant. "You aren't supposed to call me that," he complained. "Not outside."

"You need to come inside quickly." The smaller-than-most Human actually put two hands around a handling claw and tugged. "Now!"

Alarmed, Tayno settled himself on his balloon-feet. "What's wrong? Is there a problem?" If so, it wasn't fair, not twice in one day, and he refused to have anything to do with it. Then he had a truly terrible thought. "Tell me Chef The Righteous SeaSea doesn't want to be paid in advance." Yesterday, he'd been thrilled to have a chef of such repute apply to the *Claws & Jaws*. Yes, it had to be a mistake—not that he'd say so. Ever. Why, SeaSea's desserts were famous! Not that he'd tried one yet.

The point was, he'd hired her on the spot, without asking Huido. Now, with the apartment—

"It's not about the chef. We've a—guest. The workers won't go into the kitchen until it's gone." Lones swung on Tayno's claw, bracing a foot against another. "Please. You have to come."

Passersby had noticed. Some were pointing. One hooted. Another cawed loudly.

That was laughter. Yes, no doubt about it, laughter. Huido's reputation was in danger! Tayno weighed the consequences of that over what might be in the kitchen. If only Hom M'tisri hadn't taken a vacation—though they'd no work or pay for the Vilix, making it less a vacation than a forced leave-of-absence—but the Vilix had a gift for dealing with awkward guests.

One he must aspire to, if he were to ever have his own establishment.

Besides, how bad, he decided, could the situation be?

"Show me."

* ✳ *

It was worse than he could have imagined. Tayno stalled in the doorway, feeling Lones run into him from behind and utter a muffled string of incomprehensible words.

Where there should be a shiny countertop, featuring a sink and two grills, was a gooey black *something*, squeezed to fit beneath the ceiling. The pots from above the sink lay strewn over the floor.

Long fibrous arms poured over the counter to join the pots. The tip of one was stuck inside a lid handle; it flexed, making a fretful noise.

Lones snuck under Tayno's great claw. "I think it's a Rugheran," the Human told him. "Just popped out of thin air, like I've heard they do."

Would the shocks never end? "The air is thin?!" Was the station at risk?

"It's an expression. The air's fine," Lones reassured him. "Anyway, the Rugheran's been talking. Keeps saying one word."

/~MORGAN~/ the mad creature obliged.

"That's the one."

It wasn't speech so much as a feeling of wind, blowing over his carapace. No, not wind.

Grist. Fear forgotten, or at least pushed aside, Tayno took a hesitant step closer, drawn by what was more than scent but less than full comprehension. All he knew was that this thing, this unlikely mess, had the second most magnificent grist he'd encountered in his lifetime.

After Sira's.

"Morgan isn't here," he told it, sorry to bear that news, for the grist held a tang of *NEED* as well. "He's been gone a long time. That's why I have this, you see," Tayno waved the plas still in his clawtips, then stopped, realizing the Rugheran might make less sense of it than he had. "How can we help you?"

Another ineffectual tug at his claw.

"What is it?"

"Is that wise?" Lones whispered, his face very pale. "We don't know what it wants with Hom Morgan."

/~!~MORGAN~!~/

"No need to shout," Tayno told it, resisting the urge to slink just a little. "He's not here and that's that." Summoning his courage, he went on. "I can act on his behalf—"

The arm twisted, sending the pot lid flying into a wall.

The kitchen *warped* . . .

Inside that *twist of space,* the Rugheran shrank to the size of a pin, then vanished.

A moment Tayno admittedly missed, his head disks firmly shut.

He opened them slowly. Seeing nothing untoward, he gave himself a shake, hoping the ensuing rattle covered the tremble he couldn't stop. "Well . . . well. Well, then."

"Hom Tayno."

He bent an eyestalk to regard Lones, presently hiding behind his claw. "Don't worry," he boomed. "It's gone."

"I know." An arm lifted, a hand rose, a finger pointed. "Who's that?"

His eyestalks converged.

A figure lay among the pots as if dropped there. Paired arms, legs. Human—

No. The flavor of, yes, her grist, betrayed the truth.

Clan.

* ✳ *

Snosbor IV

They were no longer Clan, but Destarians. Seven adult pairs.

The first requirement of empire, Wys di Caraat thought, stepping down the ramp. The next spread in front of her: Snosbor IV.

The system itself was nothing special: within the sparsely settled Fringe of the Trade Pact, off most lanes. That of itself was a recommendation for a people who'd soon have no need of starships.

Snosbor IV itself had everything she could ask. When the Omacrons had been among the First, they'd colonized this verdant world, only to be decimated in recent times by a sequence of plagues. Abandoned by their kind, a remnant population had managed to survive.

Say rather, a pliable workforce. No more would they need to acquire Human telepaths, with their vulnerable minds; that path had led the Clan to disaster. The Destarians would be more prudent.

Wys smiled. Besides, according to the Scats, Humans might become hard to find.

She waited as the group assembled to greet the ship settled into their tasks. Most were servitors, Omacrons mind-wiped into a biddable state, who went without a word to assist with the cargo the Scats had put outside. Scats, she'd discovered, would go to significant effort to avoid Omacrons, charging more for landing on this world. Aliens.

Two were her people, faithful from the start: Lyta di Kessa'at and her Chosen, Odar. The loss of their pregnant granddaughter, Ruti di Bowart, had been a bitter blow, her offspring carrying as it did at least a trace of Sarc lineage. The pair bowed deeply, shields lowered in respect to her greater Power, unmoving until she gestured acceptance.

The di Kessa'ats would retrieve her personal luggage, including Erad di Caraat, her Chosen, long past tiresome. He'd traveled in confinement; would live that way here. A burden, that her continued existence depended on his, but at least she didn't have to look at him.

I'm HERE, witch.

Wys sent a flash of *pain* along their link, gratified when her sense of him faded.

To one side on the pad stood a solitary Retian, Talobar, who bowed clumsily when he noticed her attention; a presence, if not welcome, then necessary. Leaving the rest to their duties, the elderly Clanswoman walked down the ramp. She gathered the Retian with a nod.

He fell in step beside her. "You traveled without incident, Most Honorable?" The Retian continued to try new titles on her; this one, even to her, didn't fit and she frowned. His breathing was a labored wheeze, suffering in what to her was a pleasing warm climate, with the right touch of humidity. To Retians, it was a desert, and every so often he'd raise a mask to obscure his toad-like face in fog, inhaling deeply.

Never a complaint, not while his goals were linked to hers. Goals, she thought with pleasure, closer than ever to fruition. "The—shall we say, key components—are on their way," she told the creature.

"Not by—you know my concerns—"

Tedious creature. "They travel by starship, as agreed." Wys discounted its dread of the M'hir and their Talent, as well its incomprehensible prattle about "stress" on the "key components" should they have been 'ported here. What she took seriously?

Maintaining the belief in the Trade Pact that there were no more Clan, a belief that suited her very well, indeed. Oh, the moment would come when they'd reveal themselves again—when the Destarians would rise to their rightful place.

"Good. Good." Talobar took a gasp from his mask. "Highest One, I personally assure you all is in readiness. Might I ask when will they arrive?"

"Soon, Talobar," Wys di Caraat told him. Bored, she formed a *locate.*

Concentrated . . .

. . . to stand on a broad tiled balcony, wreathed in flowers, hers now, overlooking the central square of Caraaton, her new city. She grasped the rail with gnarled hands and smiled. "Very soon."

Her smile faded as words formed in her mind. *First Chosen.* As their link formed and strengthened through the M'hir, the greeting was tainted with a worrisome *fear,* as shouldn't be. Merin di Lorimar was her niece and powerful; she'd be high in the Destarian leadership.

Once Wys deemed it time to relinquish any of it. *Report.*

Aliens intercepted the final loading. They made off with—the *image* of a list formed behind Wys' eyes.

The elder Clanswoman absorbed it. Gone was a substantial amount of what she'd wanted here, for her people. Infuriating, but not a crisis. These aliens would pay, eventually, but mere belongings could wait, even her own: those "trophies" taken from the House of di Caraat when the Council declared it forfeit. Jarad di Sarc's trunks, filled with pre-Stratification parches inscribed with the genealogy of their kind, were crucial if they were to rebuild properly, but their absence wouldn't slow the first steps.

She would have them back. Once unloaded, *Ikkraud* would go to Auord; its new mission far more to its captain's taste than transport—

Then Wys reached the final item on the list. *Tell me you've arranged to retrieve it.*

Our allies have gone offworld. They have—

I know what they have. Half of what she would have—they must have. They were too few and vulnerable. Talobar had taken germinal material—their future—from every Destarian, beginning with her and her unwilling Chosen; had combined the results not according to the dictates of Choice but by some formula of his own; had produced sparks of new life.

Life that flickered and failed in his machines. He'd switched to living incubators, but the Omacrons died shortly after implantation. The Retian claimed he'd a solution, one requiring a ripe female body of their kind. If they'd one to spare, which they hadn't.

Not yet.

Wys added a sting of *disappointment* to her sending. *You are Destarian. You do not need allies to do what you must.*

Merin didn't shield her *doubt. Talobar said we shouldn't risk moving it with Power.*

Intelligent, Merin; her willingness to question a course of action was occasionally useful.

It was not now. *Recover what is mine. NOW!*

And if that sending *hurt,* well, her niece would take it for the promise it was.

Of worse, should she fail again.

Your will is mine, First Chosen, with a hint of *pain. First, I've something more to report. The servant the Scats provided us isn't Human, but Assembler. Allow me to drop it in the M'hir.*

Oh, and the *hate* behind that request. Wys smiled. *What's done is done,* she replied almost gently. Her people didn't see what she did, didn't appreciate how the Assemblers had been a force of nature, sweeping away obstacles. *Watch it for treachery. Learn what you can, but recover what is mine. That is your duty.*

A sense of *acquiescence,* then nothing at all.

Chapter 7

"YOU WILL COME to the *Heerala*," Captain Heevertup announced briskly. "We will contact our clients about this item on your behalf."

The moment of intimacy had ended as suddenly as it'd begun, Drapsk scattering, Terk and Manouya returning to their seats without a word. Having dealt with the dear little aliens before, Terk looked resigned. The Brill, on the other hand, hadn't taken his gaze from Morgan.

Morgan, for his part, didn't care. Let Manouya speculate. He hadn't realized how isolated he'd made himself, inside and out, until the Heerii. Hadn't imagined words could still touch his heart.

Being grateful didn't mean he'd let down his guard. "I am honored by your invitation, Captain," the Human said carefully. Drapsk interpreted what was "best" for their friends in their own disconcerting fashion. Going on the *Heerala* might net him the box of crystals as a gift—or find him whisked away to their world, locked in a luxurious prison of Drapsk good intentions. "I will double my offer if you could contact your clients directly. I need to acquire the items I mentioned as soon as possible, then conduct other urgent business."

Terk made a strained noise.

Antennae dipped in sequence from the captain to the first

officer, Drapsk talking to Drapsk, then the first officer turned, fluttering his antennae toward others. The silent communication spread along a path to the Drapsk nearest the door. Three leaped to their feet and dashed up the stairs and out.

"Our esteemed clients instruct us to put these items in your possession, Jason Morgan," the captain announced smugly. "The Consortium agrees you know how best to handle them safely."

What in the hells did that mean? Morgan wondered furiously. Who or what was this "Consortium?"

"To prevent further delay, I've ordered delivery to your home. We'll discuss compensation—"

And how did they know where he lived?

Before Morgan could ask those and other urgent questions, the Brill roared. "Enough nonsense! Deal with me now, you little thieves, or I'll report you to the authorities!"

Terk covered his mouth with a hand as though holding in a laugh; his eyes were anything but amused.

The Brill ignored him, busy trying to skewer the faceless Drapsk captain with a truly intimidating stare, only to fail as so many had before him. "Well?" he shouted instead, thudding both fists on the table.

It cracked.

Several crew rolled into balls.

Captain Heevertup twitched antennae, and blasters appeared in every small, steady hand, pointing at the same large target.

"You might want to reconsider your approach," Morgan said mildly, knife hidden but ready.

Manouya bellowed out a scornful laugh. "They are do-nothings, these Drapsk. Show and bluster. I—" fist thudding into chest, "—am no Scat to run and hide when they rattle! Those who fail me pay. You need not, great captain of do-nothings. All I want is the Brexk. Your "clients" can name their price."

Captain Heevertup gave a tiny hoot of derision. "We do not respond to threats."

Smiling, Terk leaned back, hands behind his head. The position looked harmless, but Morgan knew what was hidden down the other's collar . . . and the smile?

Anticipation.

Perfect. They were surrounded by angry Drapsk whose eyeless aim wasn't in any sense reliable, hence the blasters, and Terk itched for a bar fight. Bowman'd better hope Two-Lily Finelle could handle him.

All over Brexk, the Retian version of large, ill-tempered bovines? The meat was exported, and expensive, but Huido claimed it wasn't worth the price and only served it in the *Claws & Jaws* if a customer placed a special order.

Morgan doubted the clientele of *The Raunchy Retian* ordered Brexk steaks; didn't mean its bartender wasn't looking to score a prize here. There was a thriving "tax-free" market on Auord for luxury foodstuffs, no questions asked. Manouya could be part of it.

Still, something wasn't right, Morgan decided, curious.

Manouya raised his arms, hands shoulder-high. "Forgive my passion," he rumbled. He leaned his head from side-to-side, the cracking of his neck joints audible in the hush. "I am in a dire predicament. Please, gentle beings." The Drapsk holstered their weapons at some cue from their officers. Terk scowled his disappointment. "Sit. Hear me out, as graciously as you've heard this Human."

Even more curious. This might have been an entirely new Brill, slick and unflappable, with a more cultured use of language. Could Drapsk hear the change as he did? Detect that subtle twist to the word "Human?" There were those sapients in the Trade Pact who detested humanity, but even they found getting along more useful than conflict. Especially as the majority of those who crewed starships—and admittedly worked as bartenders—were Human.

Human, Morgan thought with a chill, or their mimics. Assemblers.

The Clan.

Had some Clan wronged this Brill? It was possible. They'd done their share of damage across the Trade Pact, damage left without repair or acknowledgment.

Or, simpler, Manouya just didn't like his species. Fair enough. Morgan didn't like him.

He smiled agreeably. "It is his turn."

"No reason for you to linger." Manouya didn't look at Terk. "Either of you."

"Then we'll take our leave." Curious he might be, but the crystals were what mattered—wherever the dear Drapsk had sent them. Morgan rose to his feet, bowing to the captain. "We'll settle our business tomorrow, Captain Heevertup. Fair Skies."

Terk appeared to plant himself at the table. Fine. He could stay and watch the aliens negotiate over raw meat.

"Stay, Jason Morgan. Please." Antennae tips bent toward the Brill, Captain Heevertup sucked in a pensive tentacle, then spoke around it. "We welcome the presence of neutral observers."

Ones they trusted, in other words, and why hadn't he seen it coming? The Brill brought this on himself by behaving unpredictably; the ever-cautious Drapsk responded by having known quantities at hand. Morgan sat back down; out the corner of his eye, he saw Terk hide a grin. Poorly.

"As you wish." The Brill remained on his feet. One ivory-tipped finger traced the crack in the table. Stalling?

Planning, Morgan decided. The loud bluster of moments before had been a show. This methodical, icy patience was the true Manouya, and the Drapsk were right to be wary.

The finger stopped. "I've said I've a predicament. I am the victim of a grievous act—a theft. What was stolen is both personally precious and priceless. The bulk, I freely add, of my considerable wealth."

Not a bartender, Terk mouthed again.

"You accuse us?!" exclaimed the first officer, who promptly inhaled all five tentacles and rocked furiously. Around the mouthful, he mumbled and sputtered variations on "How dare you!?"

"Peace." Manouya's false smile split his face. "I do not." Another neck-cracking shrug. "I concede Drapsk could have found my three well-hidden vaults, but you do not have the means to empty them of all validated Hoveny artifacts without a seal cracked or alarm triggered."

Terk stopped breathing.

Only for an instant, but the Brill caught it. Morgan saw the shift of his attention.

Felt it come back full to him like a blow. "Those who do have such means," Manouya continued, "appear Human."

The Clan. He knew what they could do. Knew they still existed. How?

"Not these Humans," Terk chuckled, spreading his hands. "If we were that rich, would we pick this dive for a drink?"

A slow blink dismissed the enforcer. The Brill's gaze returned to the captain. "The cargo the Scat assembled was destined for these thieves. Things they value. The Brexk, above all. I've been following that cargo as my best hope of finding them and recovering my property. Until," smoothly, "you changed its destination for your unnamed clients."

It had the ring of truth, but why? Did he really think his "predicament" mattered to Drapsk who already had buyers?

No. Morgan's blood went cold. The Brill gave them the truth because he didn't care if they knew it. Because it amused him, as giving his true name had amused him earlier. What was Manouya? A harmless investor, albeit in the rarest antiquities known in the Trade Pact, shouldn't have the skills to trace a cargo tagged with the latest enforcer tech—or know how to access those who did.

Tech happening to fail when Manouya was in place to take over in person. Disguised as a bartender to meet the beings he knew had taken what he wanted—

Manouya. Terk had reacted to the name.

Another snicked into place, and Morgan's blood ran cold: the Facilitator.

If so, here, at their table, sat the smuggler mastermind who'd eluded discovery or capture, who operated on a level that had Deneb's Blues and Grays envious and authorities chasing their tails, those who had them—

Who'd helped the Assemblers reach and destroy the Clan, along with his life—and Sira's.

Morgan schooled his expression to bland interest. If Manouya was the Facilitator, he'd come to this meeting with resources. Odds were Terk's recorder and tracer hadn't worked since they entered *The Raunchy Retian.*

By chance, they'd caught Manouya in what must be a rare

moment of vulnerability, needing the Drapsk's cooperation, enough not to care if two Humans suspected his identity or knew his goal.

Two Humans, Morgan decided grimly, who'd be lucky to survive the night. They had to find out what the Drapsk had that the Clan wanted so badly—and why they hadn't simply 'ported it away with them.

Captain Heevertup conferred silently with his officer, plumes twitching, for a long moment. The Brill waited.

Terk shifted in his seat.

Nothing, Morgan could have told them, guaranteed the Drapsk were even discussing the present situation. The featherheads were prone to leaps of logic unfathomable to non-Drapsk.

Not this time, it turned out. When Heevertup was ready to speak, he put his stubby fingers together and pointed them at the Brill. "You do not require any items we possess."

"I've just told you why I do." With menace.

"You've told us what you ultimately desire: your property. We can tell you where your Hoveny artifacts are now. The information will cost—" The amount named was astronomical.

Terk whistled.

Manouya's eyes narrowed. "Half now. Half when I see my property again."

"You won't see it again," the Drapsk explained in a reasonable tone. "Why would we agree?"

For all the reaction he showed, the Brill might have been a statue. His mouth moved. "Then you'll see none of my credits."

The Drapsk conferred again, Morgan tempted to test the effect of tossing beer over their antennae. Whatever they knew, or thought they knew, about the disappearing artifacts wasn't to be shared, especially not with someone as unprincipled as this.

Could they be aware who he was? It wasn't out of the question. Drapsk didn't, as a rule, volunteer information outside their tribes; for all Morgan knew, the Heerii considered the Facilitator more useful specialist than criminal. An opinion that would change once they learned his involvement in the deaths of their treasured "mystic ones."

"Transfer half." A stubby hand gestured, and one of the crew brought forward an ordinary contract pad.

Manouya spat on it without hesitation, eyes locked on the captain. "Done."

"Very well." Captain Heevertup rocked back and forth. "Instruments on Drapskii detected a disturbance reaching throughout the Trade Pact. It was later determined this disturbance affected only materials known to be from the Hoveny Concentrix, a civilization that—"

Morgan felt the hum first in his teeth, then inside, reverberating through his rib cage. Low. Loud.

Reverent.

Brill prayer. They'd a bewildering—to non-Brill—pantheon of gods and were as prone to pray during stress as Drapsk to commit eopari. Admittedly, the prayer was less debilitating.

Giving them something, he thought fiercely. The Brill were members of the First, leaders in the search for the answer to what had happened to the Hoveny, their predecessors in space. There was a superstitious fringe who preached the Hoveny Concentrix had angered their gods and been destroyed by Divine Intervention. Close enough, Morgan knew, to the truth.

Was Manouya a believer?

The hum ceased as the Brill collected himself. "Your pardon. What do you mean, 'affected'? Where is my property?"

Another Drapsk committed eopari.

" 'Where' is impossible to determine," the captain said, chewing a pensive tentacle. "The Hoveny materials were drawn into the Scented Way. The Scented Way has—" he added a little too helpfully, "—dimensions corresponding to this one, but none we can link to what's within it."

Manouya grunted twice, then leaned forward on his elbows. "Make sense."

"Our best scientists give no clearer answer. The last remnants of the Hoveny were removed from this space at 15:14:34.345 standard."

There was a disturbing gleam in the Brill's eyes. "Confirming who did this. I know who has taken this revenge on me."

Antennae shot erect. "You do?" Captain Heevertup's voice quivered.

"Yes, and they want what's in your cargo hold. I'll be—Grasis' sucking Hells!"

With a clatter of falling weaponry, every Drapsk, including the captain, curled into a tight ball. The ones who'd been seated bounced gently to the floor, several—including the captain—rolling under tables.

"Shame." Terk lifted his sandaled feet to let that particular ball continue its motion. "Seen them do this for most of a day," he commented, eyeing the Brill. He stood, mug in hand. "Guessing you don't mind if I help myself?"

The Brill looked incredulous. "What?"

"Wait for me." Morgan took his own mug, following Terk to the bar as if they were nothing more than spacers out for the night. Every step, the skin between his shoulders crawled, expecting attack, but the enforcer had the right of it. They'd one chance to convince Manouya they weren't a threat.

They made it to the bar and walked around, Terk heading for the taps. He wrapped his hand around a pull, glanced down—

Then lunged for Morgan, dragging him to the floor.

Together, they stared into the bulging eyes of the real bartender. Her body had been jammed between the kegs, fitting only because her arms were cauterized stumps.

The stunner with the digester appeared in Terk's hand. As he tensed to jump up and shoot, Morgan grabbed his arm. "The Drapsk."

Realization darkened the other's face. Working quickly, the enforcer began to assemble another weapon from parts from various pockets.

"Wait." Manouya should have reacted by now. Morgan put his hands on the bartop, then rose to his feet. "He's gone."

Terk sat back, banging his head against the keg as he swore with vicious creativity.

Leaving the enforcer to vent his frustration, Morgan went around the bar to confirm they were alone—other than the balls of comatose Drapsk. Throwing knife in hand, he fell into that unconscious stealthy grace he'd learned long ago, on another battleground, checking booths and shadows.

Behind, Terk kicked in the storeroom door, still swearing.

They met at the table. "This mean anything to you?"

Manouya had written an address in the warehouse district. It was the word beside it, larger and underlined, Terk meant.

" 'Brexk,' " he read aloud.

"Still on that?" Terk shook his head. "All right, what's it mean? Other than the obvious."

"The meat is a popular export," Morgan ventured, the corner of his mouth deepening. "Smugglers like the density."

Terk gave that "thought you'd know" snort, then shook his head. "Could be code for something else entirely. Bet the Drapsk know." He used his sandal to nudge the ball of first officer.

"I wouldn't," Morgan advised. "Any movement during eopari leaves them disoriented when they wake."

The enforcer desisted. "Can't have them make less sense than usual." He looked up at the door. "You stay here. They like you. Find out what the Brill wants."

"The Facilitator."

"Yeah, him." A flash of cold eyes. "Bowman caught a Split under Norval. Named Manouya as the Facilitator, but it was a dead end till now. Trader trick, huh, getting the Brill to admit his real name?"

Trick? Knowing how to show courtesy to customers of differing shapes and cultures was an essential tool, but— Morgan moved his hand in a throwaway gesture. "I doubt Manouya gave a thought to his true name having meaning to us. He doesn't think much of Humans."

"I got that." Terk eyed the table, then rapped it with a decisive knuckle. "Can't let the Port Jellies get their paws on this. Stand back." Producing a vial the size of his thumbnail from inside his jacket, the enforcer carefully squeezed droplets over the table-top, concentrating his efforts on the writing and the crack. It sizzled and popped in an unmistakable manner.

"Scat spit?"

Terk grinned. "Happens in all the best bars."

He was Bowman's second for good reason, despite the occasional lapse of caution. Morgan eyed him. "You're cheerful for a being with a limited life expectancy."

"Part of the job." Terk's unhandsome features clashed in grim angles. "If Manouya wanted us dead, Morgan, we'd be that way. Suits him to have us run around loose a while longer. You got his attention. My guess? He knows you've a connection to Clan. Me? I'm just the pisspot." He stooped to collect the Drapsk contract pad. "The pisspot who'll see if Bowman can pry an ident out of the Brill Board Member, while you get whatever Manouya wants from the Drapsk."

Morgan frowned. "Don't underestimate him."

"Don't spoil the moment." That grin again. "We're ahead."

＊ ✳ ＊

Morgan carried a chair up the stairs, using it to prop open one of the doors. Damp air pushed in, redolent of the alley beyond. If he was lucky, the stench would penetrate *The Raunchy Retian* and wake the Drapsk.

Until then, they were his responsibility. He sat in the chair, stretching out his legs, and crossed his arms over his chest, prepared to wait.

A Drapsk blaster in each hand.

Interlude

THEY WANTED ME TO RETURN. To search the Trade Pact for Acranam's exiles and bring them home.

In Rael's body.

"You need do nothing more, Sira. Your connection to that flesh will end," the projection of my noncorporeal sister promised, as if making sense. "Remember, you mustn't scan Between— the M'hir—for them."

"They'll be shielded anyway," Yihtor added unhelpfully.

Not from my Power, not if I knew to *look*. I didn't bother arguing with him. "Assuming this—" I waved my hand between Rael and my admittedly not-real body, "—is remotely possible, why can't I?"

<<*WE'LL KNOW*>>

That hadn't, as I recalled, stopped me before. But Rael's face paled. "Sira, any use of your Power in the M'hir affects it. For all we know, a single heart-search could cause it to—to fail." Her cupped hands flew apart.

As if that dreadful, life-filled Dark could crack like a Skenkran egg, an image I didn't need right now. "Then it can't be done." In the Trade Pact, my kind had been notoriously unable to comprehend the distances involved in space travel. I saw no sign Singers were any better at it, but I tried. "No one person could travel the entire Trade Pact, let alone search for hidden Clan. I don't even have a starship!"

"You have friends who do. Allies who can conduct such a search." Yihtor's mutilated face seemed to float. "As do I."

"That's why I can't do it," Rael insisted. "I would, Sira, but there's no one left in the Trade Pact I trust."

It wasn't bitter. It was the truth. The Clan hadn't those connections. Most of them. I stared at Yihtor, who'd dealt with any being willing to pay his price. Mind-wiping. Memory theft. Trust wouldn't be a factor for him either, but he could rely on extortion.

"Yihtor will be himself," I said. "I won't, by any measure."

Rael's eyes glistened. "You'll find a way to convince them, heart-kin."

"There's one who'll know—" Yihtor began, but whatever he sensed from me stopped him. Wise.

"Will we?" I lifted my hands, turned them to study the calluses left by my keffleflute—what I remembered of those calluses and flute—looked up. "For this to work, Yihtor and I must keep our memories—" of what? being less dead? "—when we enter the Trade Pact. If we start fresh again, as Stolen do? We'd be useless."

"Our bodies still hold ours," Rael said. "I will guide you, Sira, along that binding. I'll ensure yours are put in place."

This kept getting better, I thought grimly. "Our previous lives are only half of it," I reminded them. "You and I, Yihtor," I directed my gaze at him, "aren't enemies here. The problem we're to solve comes from here. How do we remember AllThereIs there, when no Stolen ever has?"

<<WE WILL.>>

I closed my eyes, briefly, then opened them. "Watchers are coming?"

An actual voice answered, as hollow as space, but oddly familiar. <<The Great Ones do not touch that which has purpose and place. We will hold the way through Between.>>

Taisal Sarc, Aryl's mother. I'd met her, her Watcher-self, before. Powerful, yes, but Between wasn't in any sense forgiving of intrusion. I doubted that had improved with this rot they feared. "How long can you hold?"

<<*Until the last of us fade.*>>

From every existence. As Watchers. As Singers. If I'd doubted the dire urgency to those here of what Rael had come to tell me, if I'd cared, selfishly, more for Morgan and the Trade Pact?

I couldn't now.

Offering a hand to each projection, I bowed my head. "Take me back."

Passage was akin to this—this *velocity* through the Dark. M'hir life startled and moved away. Others, hints, glimpses, swam close. Hungered.

Fell behind.

Never before had hands *held* mine. Hands that held other hands. I envisioned an infinite string of Singers and Watchers stretched across the universes and for an endless time that wasn't at all—

I belonged.

Abruptly, the M'hir reacted, its smooth, almost peaceful depths becoming a tumultuous, raging ocean . . . no, not an ocean, for that I'd *seen* before. This was wind, howling and full of debris and grit . . . we were tossed up, let fall, helpless . . .

Only one thing offered safety . . . Vessels, those rare havens . . . but where?

I glimpsed a dire truth: a Singer could be lost here and never be found.

Watchers took hold, and we who were lost were guided, herded, *RUSHED* . . .

Not *Stolen*—

Saved.

＊✳＊

I'd a pulse.

I'd forgotten the small steady beat. Hadn't needed it. Hadn't missed it. How easy, to forget flesh and be mind.

How numbingly strange, to be flesh again, and wonder why . . .

Chapter 8

MORGAN KNEW WHY he was sitting in a chair in the entrance to a seedier-than-most dive in Auord's All Sapients' District, his backside well past numb. He just wasn't sure why he was still there, given the sun was climbing behind the spires of the shipcity, its rays making him squint, and he'd better things to do, surely.

He sighed and stretched. No help for it. He couldn't leave the dear little balls of Drapsk, for balls they remained. The only disturbance had been a chittering from behind the bar late into the night that proved to be a pair of larger-than-usual vermin, quarreling over the unfortunate bartender's corpse. They'd paused to stare up at him, teeth gleaming, eyes a wicked red, then gone back to their feast. The Human had made himself watch until he was confident the Drapsk were in no danger. Besides, he was sure they had some type of internal alarm; a nip or two might have roused them.

No such luck. No sign of Terk either. He pulled out his com, regarded it morosely, then tucked it away again.

Standing watch wasn't new; sleep didn't tempt him. The waking illusions had ended, not those disguised as dreams, and when he had the choice? He'd rather think of Sira as she'd been.

Not relive their final moment, over and over and over.

Morgan shifted position, changing his grip on the Drapsk blasters. They suited a smaller hand than his—a hand like hers. Not that Sira had willingly picked up a weapon. There'd been that time she'd rescued him brandishing the ship's sealer—

Gods, it hurt, as though her loss scraped out his insides, leaving him empty. Leaving him hopeless.

Empty, he wasn't. Sira was gone, but he'd fill the hollows with her memory no matter what the cost.

As for hopeless? Well, Morgan thought wearily, what use would hope be? She was gone. It was done. He'd a job. Live and do what he could for his friends.

What he was willing to do. There were minds around him, waking to the day, and some would be sensitive. Minds he could *reach*.

And would not. Bowman hadn't tried to persuade him; she'd understood.

When he'd first felt his ability, Ren Symon had taught him not control, but how to give strength to serve another. He'd tried but failed to draw a young Morgan to darker places, to wield his mind as a weapon. From the Omacron, Morgan learned to keep out other minds and believed he was in control, using his ability to do useful tricks. Work locks that required the Talent. Spook those who feared telepaths by the merest hint of Power. Scan for ill intent.

Stay safe within his own mind.

Sira had taught him to move beyond it. Even as his shields became impenetrable, she'd uncovered his gift for repairing damaged minds. Even as he'd learned to *push* objects in the M'hir, she'd shown him the living links within it, Clan to Clan, mother to child. Between Chosen—

They'd dreamed in harmony—

A waste canister toppled in the alley.

The Human was on his feet before the last echo, easing into the shadowed doorway.

Another canister went down. All at once, a trio of shapes hopped past Morgan, skidding in refuse as they fled for the alley's exit.

A massive shape followed, low and fast, claw snapping viciously

in air. The clang and clatter of weapons against hard shell was sufficient to terrify any being not yet in full flight, ending only when
the apparition came to a rattling halt at the bottom of the stairs.

Stepping into the sunlight, Morgan found himself reflected in
a row of gleaming black eyes. "Huido."

"A fine morning, brother," the Carasian boomed in great high
spirits. From the stains on that claw, not everything had eluded
its grip. "Friend Terk said you had a problem." A hopeful snap.

Morgan smiled slowly. "Don't tell him I said so, but the man
has moments of genius. Come in."

There being nothing more likely to wake a roomful of Drapsk
from eopari than Huido.

* ✳ *

There was nothing more likely to delay and distract a roomful of
Drapsk than Huido. The Carasian stood in the middle of *The Raunchy Retian,* holding perfectly still while cooing, smitten Heerii
climbed all over him. A few were cuddled—there was no other
word for it—against his balloonlike feet. Including the first officer.

He'd either forgotten the depths of their infatuation, Morgan
thought, grinning, or Huido's chase through the alley had added
something spectacular to his natural body odor.

Though it wasn't Huido's odor, exactly, charming the Drapsk.
They possessed a sense similar to that of Carasians, able to detect
what the latter called grist. Grist could be pleasant or not, according to Huido, depending on factors ranging from mental health
to emotional stability. Grist could be highly admirable or not, and
that was trickier to explain. Good versus evil was too simplistic,
but part of it.

The M'hir was part of it, too. Drapsk claimed there were elements in this space that were simultaneously components of the
other, some alive, some less so. These elements helped make the
M'hir what it was: connected, dangerous. Beautiful, that as well.
All meaning what, Morgan couldn't begin to guess. When Drapsk
tried their earnest best to explain such matters, the result was
always confusing.

Not so the Drapsk presently fluttering their plumes over the scarred shell of a heavily armed and armored alien. They had, Morgan thought with a sudden rush of warmth, excellent taste in friends.

But time wasn't one. "Huido, you big oaf," he called fondly. "Stop fooling around. We've work to do."

Starting with a visit to the *Heerala* and an order of Brexk.

* ✳ *

There were strictures governing the design of starships. Physics led the way, of course, it being needful to separate radiation, vacuum, and random particles from atmosphere and flesh, not to mention build engines to burrow through subspace enclosed in shapes to escape gravity and friction. Right on the heels of incorruptible nature came the deep desire of all spacefaring species to limp into an alien port and be able to leave again, repaired. The success of the Trade Pact owed as much to the development of common standards for mundane machinery as it did to the unceasing diplomatic efforts of its members.

Or more. Then, Morgan thought, looking around with interest, there were species like the Drapsk, who found a way to bury any commonalities beneath the requirements of their biology.

The interior of the *Heerala* was a maze of doorless curves, with wider spaces budding left or right at seeming random. A drafty maze, whiffs of air conveying chemical information throughout the ship. The ceilings were higher than those in a Human design, presumably to allow more targeted communications to travel unimpeded.

Something not happening to them, unfortunately. Huido remained a living magnet; whenever they passed crewbeings hard at work, they'd stop with a twitch of their antennae, then join the throng behind.

Or in front. Each time they rounded a bend, a cluster would be waiting. There'd be a momentary pause to allow these new Drapsk to flutter at the Carasian, then they'd whirl and join those already out in front, as happy to lead the way as to follow.

If, as seemed probable, they acquired the entire ship's complement, Morgan thought wryly, at least the *Heerala* couldn't take off with them on board.

Captain Heevertup walked beside him. When Morgan broached the subject of their "clients," the Drapsk would interrupt to point out this feature or that. As suited a tribe in ascendance, it turned out, the Heerii had the latest and finest ship in the Drapsk fleet, incorporating a host of improvements. "We are much faster now," the being said modestly. "It is a secret how much, you understand, Jason Morgan."

The Human raised an eyebrow. "Until you put into your next port."

A hoot of a laugh. "We are observed, that is true, and envied. But we would never use our full potential on ordinary passages."

Implying the *Heerala* was something other than a trade ship. All Drapsk ships were armed, something they freely admitted, it being impolite not to inform those who might otherwise contemplate a violent interception in a quiet corner of space. Morgan hadn't heard they'd begun to actively pursue conflict. Making this a courier, perhaps.

Making these "clients" more interesting than ever. The Human took a long step to put himself in front of the Drapsk and stopped. Huido did the same.

That forty other Drapsk collided softly into the Carasian couldn't have been an accident.

"Captain Heevertup. Is there anything you can tell me about your clients—this Consortium you mentioned? It's important." Morgan lowered his voice. "I wouldn't ask otherwise."

"I understand." The Drapsk touched the bracelet on Morgan's wrist. "All I can tell you, Jason Morgan, is that they trust you, and they trust very few." His antennae fluttered. "As I hope you trust us."

So the mystery deepened. He hadn't the remotest idea what trust meant to the Drapsk or their clients. Whether based on knowledge of his actions or his reputation, did their version of trust translate to confidence in him?

Or in his predictability?

In either case, this faceless Consortium had a use for him. The crystals. It would help if he'd a clue whether they knew the danger they posed, or didn't and were content to dump that part of the cargo on a foolish Human willing to pay handsomely indeed for rocks.

With Bowman's voucher.

Just once, Morgan thought, he'd like to go into these things with all the players labeled: good, bad, don't bother us we're busy.

"I do," he said with a small bow and waved the captain onward. "My thanks."

✳

Shortly afterward, they arrived at a curved, featureless wall. The Drapsk spread out along it, leaving a section open. When the captain approached, the section folded itself into the floor and disappeared.

A door unlike any Morgan had seen. Judging by the thickness of the wall now forming its frame, a blast-capable door.

Sized for Huido.

"Fancy," the Carasian commented, eyestalks spinning as he lumbered through. "Why don't we have these?"

"Because we don't have a ship," Morgan reminded him.

On the other side was a spacious, relatively standard cargo hold, with plas crates and bundles prepped for lift with ample tie-downs and nets. Oddly, those appeared to be of the same material—and pink—as the walls. Because they grew from them, he realized, impressed. No other doors, but having seen one appear, Morgan supposed the Drapsk could open their hold anywhere that worked for the task at hand.

As opposed to shifting mountains of cargo in order to access the one crate you hadn't expected to ever sell that suddenly became the deal maker—if you could get to it in time. 'Porting had, Morgan recalled, significant advantages in such situations.

Drapsk spilled into the cargo hold after them, stopping before crossing a line the Human couldn't see. The captain and another

Drapsk, wearing a harness supporting a variety of tools and presumably the hold supervisor, continued on with Morgan and Huido, their goal a stack that looked familiar, indeed.

"This is it," the supervisor stated, tapping a bar against what was, this close, a Retian-made stasis box, the extra-large sort they used to export fresh Brexk, complete with a broker's seal of inspection.

"It's not meat. Yet," Huido observed pragmatically.

Morgan crouched to study the control panel. Standard, as it had to be. "From this, the system's up and running." Straightening, he regarded the box thoughtfully. "Doesn't make sense." True, as he'd told Terk, smugglers liked using Brexk, but who'd use a living one? Revived, it would do its utmost to gore and trample whatever was in reach.

"Tastes better fresh," his friend offered. "If you like Brexk." What Huido had been hoping for, reasonably given the decor of *The Raunchy Retian*, were Retian eggs. He'd been hinting about food ever since.

"Brexk wasn't on our clients' list," the captain volunteered. "They expressed no interest in it, making this item available for purchase."

Morgan nodded absently, his fingers trailing along the top of the box. The tech was no different from the tripboxes used to transport the ill or by recruiters to ship their unwilling cargo. The Clan were involved, with all that implied. If he used his *other* awareness, what—who would he find?

He lifted his hand away. "We have to open it."

Tentacles popped into mouths. The cargo hold filled with the sound of sucking Drapsk.

The Human looked down at the captain. "Trust me, Captain. This is no ordinary cargo. Whatever's inside is wanted by very dangerous individuals." Manouya. Acranam's renegades. A tossup who was worse. "We need to know what it is."

One set of tentacles popped out again. "It looks ordinary. If we don't open it, it stays that way. We'll keep it safe," Captain Heevertup proposed. "Or you can buy it—" suggestively, "—and keep it safe yourself."

Drapsk logic, Morgan noticed, but to find the Clan, they needed to move ahead with Bowman's plan: trace an item the Clan wanted.

With a modification, he decided, glancing involuntarily at Huido. Several eyes swung his way. Suspicious, that was.

Rightly so. The Carasian wasn't going to like this, at all.

"Manouya left an address. We'll substitute something of our own for what's inside, then reseal the box, well enough to pass a smuggler's inspection—not a Port Jelly's, mind you, but someone who knows the work. When you deliver it to Manouya, it mustn't appear to have been tampered with."

For everyone's sake.

The captain turned to the tool carrier as if to ask a question.

Instead, they stepped close, tentacles disappearing in one another's mouths.

Gripstsa. The change of place. Morgan glanced around quickly, relieved to see none of the other Drapsk had paired.

When these two were done, however, the *Heerala* would have a new captain.

"Couldn't have waited," Huido grumbled.

"We can start without them. Keep watch." They were, after all, surrounded by Drapsk who were alert and paying rapt attention.

A claw rose. "For them or an angry Brexk?"

"Anything."

Huido easily split his attention, but most of his eyes remained on Morgan. "What are you up to?"

Before answering, Morgan keyed the box to revive its contents; otherwise fail-safes would prevent any attempt to open it. A display showed a sphere rapidly diminishing in size. "Manouya can detect Bowman's toys. That leaves one way to follow this shipment to the Clan."

"No."

Morgan raised an eyebrow. "Yes."

"You want to be put in there?! In stasis?"

" 'Want,' no." The Human shrugged. "I don't see another option."

"That isn't an option. You can't be serious. I am not—" Huido's voice rose in a crescendo, sending several Drapsk into eopari. "—putting you in there!"

The Human rapped a gentle knuckle on his friend's carapace. "I can climb in myself, thanks. You'll set the auto-revive, so I'll be awake and ready before the box is opened."

"Or awake too soon, and you'll use up the air and die. This is—" with an offended rattle, "—the worst idea you've ever had. And what about the crystals?"

"You know where I've been living," Morgan grinned. "Take care of them for me."

Huido stared as if lost for words.

The sphere flashed: the halfway point. Morgan used the tip of his force blade to slice the inspector's seal, making as straight a cut as possible. Mist ghosted out along the incision, sliding cold down the sides of the box. He kept his hands clear of it; the chemical was potent until reacting with air.

The sphere vanished, the screen going dark. Cycle complete, the lid cracked. With a sigh of mist, it rose, swinging up and away.

"Stand clear!" Weapons hummed, Huido prepared for a charging Brexk.

When nothing large and hairy heaved itself out, Morgan stepped forward, peering into the box. A form lay inside, human-oid. Tubes connected it to additional boxes within the cavity, ex-plaining the need for so large a box.

He'd fit. First, though, who was this? He waited impatiently for the last of the cloying mist to evaporate.

Then the features became clear: eyelids and lips sewn shut. Hair shaved. None of it disguised a face he'd known both in nightmares and awake. The name escaped his lips before he could stop it.

"Yihtor."

"He's back?!" Huido pounced, claw raised.

Morgan jumped in his path, holding up both hands. "Wait!"

The serrated deadly claw snapped a hairbreadth from his nose as the Carasian shuddered to a stop. Eyes converged, perplexed. "Wait?! Why?" Deeper. "We hate him."

"This isn't him." Morgan waved behind at the box. "It's what's left: an empty husk." The mind was gone, wiped by Jarad and the Clan Council. Sira'd believed Yihtor—what was left—had been dropped in the M'hir. They all had. "The Retians must have taken the body and kept it alive," he said, gorge rising in his throat.

The species had no pair bonds, reproducing in an instinct-driven mass event. Perhaps that was why the complex strategies of others held such fascination for them; for some Retians, verging on obsession. Baltir was the Retian who'd worked with Jarad di Sarc, their plan to use material from Yihtor to produce viable offspring from Sira. He hadn't known—who could—that Clan reproduction required the M'hir as well.

If the remaining Clan wanted Yihtor's still-living flesh, odds were they hadn't learned any better—

"Jason." Huido's eyestalks shot erect, staring over his shoulders. "It's no husk."

Morgan turned slowly.

Despite the tubes, impossibly, the body was sitting up. Its blinded face moved as though sniffing the air. A frustrated groan erupted from the chest, then—

—a *scrabble* at his mind!

Jumping back, Morgan slammed down his shields to rebuff the attempted contact.

No—it couldn't be.

But was. He knew the foul *taste* of Yihtor's mind. The Clansman had attacked his in search of Sira, using pain and fear to rape his memories. To save them both, he'd *retreated*, hiding so deeply inside himself he'd needed Rael's help to return.

"What is it?" Huido boomed anxiously. Then, angrily, "Let me end this!"

Breathing hard, Morgan shook his head and managed not to shudder. They needed answers—he did.

He spoke to the box. "You were gone."

And oh, the horror of that blinded face nodding.

Then the wreck uttered another groan. Softer. Despairing.

A plea.

Yihtor gone—and back again. From what little Sira had been able to tell him about the Clan and AllThereIs, this wasn't how it worked. "Your body," Morgan guessed, his heart pounding with dread. "It brought you back."

Another nod. With that effort, Yihtor slumped over the edge, blood from his abused arms drawing lines down the side of the box.

They'd been enemies. But what had been done to him— Morgan went close.

Huido's protest was loud and nonverbal.

"He's no threat," the Human said. "If I'm wrong, take care of it."

His fingers brushed skin, chill and clammy, then Morgan released a cautious tendril of thought.

Only to be seized by uncountable *hands!*

Interlude

An Undisclosed Location

A FOOT FIDGETED.
It wasn't alone.

A hand twitched. Nearby, more amorphous shapes paced on their cilia bases, while what was—or appeared—a Human head moved its lips. "Not fair. Not right. Not fair. Not right."

Whomever thought a box was a good way to travel hadn't been cooped up for days with the most disagreeable company.

"Hate you, too," a "knee" subvocalized, for not even the head could make sound alone. "Always uppity."

"I have to be up," the head snapped back.

Five other Assemblers subvocalized a chant of "Uppityuppity hadagreatfall." It being an undisputed drawback of the topmost position.

"Bah." The head formed eyes just to close them. They'd arrive soon. Choiola wanted Mathis Dewley back on Plexis. To set the trap for the First. They would be he. He would succeed!

Let others group with failures and lesser ambitions. They would learn the news and swarm to this nexus.

The prospect was enough to make the head want to smile.

"Uppityuppityhadagreatfall!"

Almost.

Chapter 9

*...H*ANDS PULLING HIM into the M'hir!
Somehow, he tore himself free. But this wasn't
where he belonged . . .

. . . before, he'd seen the M'hir as though standing on a beach
bordered by an unending ocean of black. An ocean at times wild
and deadly; at other, rarer moments, smooth as obsidian.

Always, before, an ocean touched by her light—for Sira had
been that, here, so brilliant it was hard to look at what she was,
keeping him safe with her presence.

No longer. This version of the M'hir was a tidal bore, dragging
him through the *DARK*, stealing what wasn't breath but was life . . .

Hands gripped him again, *pushing* him forward . . . and what
was that?

Did they sing?

* * *

. . . Morgan gasped, feeling air fill his lungs again.

"What happened? Did that crasnig hurt you again?"

"No," he whispered, holding out his hand to keep the frantic
Carasian in place. "I don't know what just happened, but it wasn't
Yihtor. Not—alone."

"Danger—"

"No. I think—I think he's a messenger," he concluded softly. Morgan laid his palm flat along the other's forehead. *I'm listening.*

Morgan. The powerful, overbearing mindvoice he'd known was whisper-thin, almost desperate. *Find Rael.*

Sira's sister? *She's dead. Here.* No telling what the Clansman understood in this state. *You're in the Trade Pact.*

Find Rael. Find HER—

Morgan removed his hand. Yihtor was unconscious; he knew better than pry into such a well-schooled and protected mind. He roused himself. The Drapsk had moved closer, drawn by the use of Power. The last thing they needed was for them to take an interest in Yihtor's future. "Contact Terk, Huido. Our friend here needs the medbay on the *Conciliator.*" A ship crewed by those with implants, not that Yihtor posed that type of threat.

"Shouldn't we let him—ah—go where he belongs?" the Carasian questioned, eyes aimed at the Drapsk, too.

Without treatment, the Clansman would die. As Rael hadn't, it seemed, not yet, despite Sira being touched by her sister's mind from AllThereIs.

Not dead enough, then.

"We need him," Morgan stated, numb inside. To learn what else, if anything, he'd come to say. A guide, if they were lucky, to the Acranam Clan.

Most of all, to help Rael, heart-kin to him as well as Sira. He made himself grin at the Carasian. "There's good news. I won't be going in the box."

Huido gave a suspicious rattle. "Where will you be going?"

To do what Yihtor asked. "Hunting." He'd find Rael di Sarc's body.

And end it, setting her free at last.

* * *

Morgan pretended to stagger, using the motion to sweep the alley with keen eyes. Now, more than ever, caution mattered.

Once certain he was alone, he shifted the boards covering the basement access he'd found and eased through the gap. The building above was a Turrned Missionary, busy only at mealtimes. Neither the Turrneds nor those they fed appeared to know there was a floor beneath.

He replaced the boards and waited in the dark, listening. Once sure he hadn't been followed, Morgan activated a small hand-lamp and made his way down. There weren't stairs, not anymore. A previous tenant had left a rickety ladder propped in the stair-well, a ladder Morgan stowed away before daring to sleep.

Uninvited guests were welcome to fall. Not that he'd had guests.

Morgan took hold of the rusty door handle and lifted before pushing inward. The door moved without a sound. Someone who didn't know the trick to it would find the door shrieked like a Skenkran launching from a height.

Ladders. Hinges. Sometimes the lower the tech, the better.

Door closed, he ordered up the portlight. The room was five paces wide and twelve long, walled in old stone and plaster, its low ceiling cluttered with abandoned plumbing and dusty webs. A threadbare mattress leaned against one wall.

The only other furnishing was a crate he'd used as a table, presently home to a box that hadn't been there when he left.

The Drapsk, ever capable, had known where he lived after all.

Costly work, the box; almost as long as his arm, made of real wood with inlays of semiprecious stones. He'd seen it before, in Sira's memories, and expected what he found inside: cloth-lined compartments, sixteen of them. Nine housed crystals, similar but unique in color and wear. Reaching into his pocket, Morgan drew out the one Terk had liberated and dropped it into a slot.

From what he'd learned from the Om'ray, these housed the Adepts of a Clan, their knowledge preserved as well as the indi-vidual. Or they could be empty orbs, waiting for use.

Or were, as Terk succinctly put it, junk. Morgan closed the lid and prepared to 'port the things into the M'hir and be rid of them.

Only to pause, fingers curling together in midair. He didn't know; that was the problem. Acting out of ignorance was a guar-antee of trouble.

He put the box into his carryroll with the rest of his belongings. He'd never unpacked, not here, and it was time, now, to go.

First—

Morgan grabbed the top corner of the mattress and pulled it from the wall, easing it to the floor. The portlight came to hover, as it had many times before, at his shoulder, illuminating the wall beyond.

A figure in spacer coveralls floated there, as though suspended among stars. Her hair was adrift, eyes closed; sleeping, it seemed. If not for the way she'd been drawn with charcoal rubbed almost faint, if her arms hadn't been left trailing, limp . . .

She might be about to roll over and smile at him, again.

Morgan traced the sweet face he knew best of all, the rough stone dragging at his fingertips. "Good-bye."

Then took out his force blade, to erase every line.

There was no going back.

Aside: The Thremm

"IT IS OF CONCERN, I agree, but—"
Not that words were spoken. Among Thremm, communication involved directed pulses of electromagnetic force, their innate understanding of such fields making them sought-after mechanics as well as stage magicians. The emotional content of their eloquent language resided, however, in another sense entirely.

For the Thremm were empaths, requiring no more than proximity to share the emotions of like beings. Thus, the speaker of "It is of concern, I agree, but—" also and accurately conveyed: *anxiety/concurrence/doubt*

"Others within the Consortium report similar findings." *concurrence/support/purpose* "For our part, we've long observed the lesions within the span of the Emotive Deep corresponding to the Human inner systems of the Trade Pact. This is new, my worthy partner-third, and I cannot overstress the significance of such concentrated disruption if it continues." *intenseworry* "We will be silenced. And worse."

Sparks danced along exposed skin. *terror/terror/terror* "You view this as an extinction level event."

concurrence/support "As does the Consortium."

terror/determination "Then we must act."

agreement/agreement

Chapter 10

THIS WAS, in every way, a problem. Morgan leaned against the wall, his arms folded, and half closed his eyes. "You're sure?"

"Look who's asking." Thel grunted, fingers flying over controls. "Of course, I'm sure. Scats put their cargo through the warehouses same as everyone else. Who do you think checks manifests on this rock, anyway?" She continued to mutter.

Confirming that in the days before their hurried departure, the Scat ship had taken on sixty cages of the squeaky pink fluff that was their version of spacer rations, three tons of raw nicnics—there was something for the books, a legit cargo—and a registered stasis box, by the size and weight Trade Pact standard, classified benignly as "Transplant Materials."

Or not so benign. Trade in body parts was taxed on Auord, not regulated. The only barrier to a full-fledged business in bits? Auordian cells were incompatible with Human, the largest close market. They remained touchy on the subject.

They should consider themselves lucky, Morgan knew. There'd been others who'd found their parts worth more to strangers than their lives.

A medical seal would speed a solitary stasis box through customs, fewer questions asked. Obtaining that seal? Beyond the Scats. "The *Worraud?*"

"Still parked in high orbit," she assured him. "As long as they pay the fee and stay clear of traffic, no one down here cares. Mind, I've a complaint from a Whirtle freighter, but they're such easy targets I dunno why they leave their home system. Told them the Scats claim to be waiting for passengers and a final bit of cargo to be shuttled up. Don't imagine the Whirtle believed it." Thel chuckled.

If that final cargo was the Brexk box, Manouya hadn't wasted any time making sure it resumed its journey. Morgan had left the delivery to the newly minted captain of the *Heerala,* Henerop; Terk promised not to follow it, which had more to do with his belief in Bowman than in the Drapsk.

A shuttle, though? Before what Bowman grimly referred to as the "purge," he'd have been surprised if any Clan knew what a shuttle was for, let alone bothered with one. Now? Keeping their survival secret could be worth the loss of speed.

Whatever the reason, the delay worked in his favor. "I'll need a ship."

"To go up there? I thought you weren't crazy." Thel paused. "What about the enforcers? Their big brute's insystem. It'd make filets out of that Scat."

"They'd need a reason," he reminded her. More than his instincts drawing a pattern from a second stasis box and the ravings of a Clansman back from the dead. After all, unimpeded, the *Worraud* was Bowman's best lead on the Clan and the Facilitator.

"Shame."

The shame would be in failure, Morgan thought darkly. Failure to help Sira's sister. "A ship, Thel." Whatever it took, he'd cut Rael's final tie to this part of space and set her free. "Nothing flashy. Reliable and no questions asked."

"You? Afford a ship? I fired your skinny self."

"I quit, remember?"

Thel grumbled, but busied herself on the com. Morgan closed his eyes, snatching what rest he could.

"Got one."

Too fast. Morgan cracked an eyelid. "What's wrong with it?"

"As if you can be picky," she sniffed. "The owner's good people. Been having a run of bad luck, that's all. Can use the work and won't ask your business. Cousin of mine." As if that were all there was to say about it.

His lips quirked. "A cousin." Thel Masim had a plethora of them, each owing her for something or other. In a way, wasn't he one, too? "Fair enough. Here." He tossed her the voucher stick.

Thel turned it over to check the chip, then whistled. "You nick this from the pretty lad?"

"Just take off the fee. Keep it reasonable." Morgan tilted his head back, closing his eyes again. An owner, out of luck? He knew that drill. "Add a twice again contingency for parts. I don't want to be stranded up there because your cousin couldn't stock spares."

"She does her own work—takes pride in it."

He'd done the same, once. "A lift to orbit, Thel, and back in one piece. All I ask is it holds together for that."

"*Wayfarer.* That's her name." Sharp with disappointment. "Not that you asked, I notice."

She'd loved the *Silver Fox.* Loved the free traders with their quirky, cobbled-together ships full of family.

Morgan pulled away from the wall and gestured apology before remembering Thel was the wrong species—and so was he. "Good name," he said instead.

Now to see if the *Wayfarer* could get him up to the Scat ship.

He'd worry about the rest on the way.

* ✳ *

"Thel's cousin, huh." Terk shaded his eyes to study the waiting starship. "Looks like high-fashion scrap."

"It was designed by Zetter Byi, the vid producer." Huido rumbled. "*Sles'* private yacht. Before our time."

Morgan had expected an inner system trawler, not a ship with these sleek, fluid lines. Five times the size of the *Fox,* the *Wayfarer* retained a certain shabby glory, though what she was now was debatable. Her once-elegant fins had been thickened and modified to handle less accommodating landscapes. Not the best choice; he'd have gone with adjustable gear, rather than risk the cheaper one-size-fits approach. Terrain could be a trap. Ivali of *Ryan's Venture* had a Thremm who was a—

Not his ship. Not his problem.

A cargo port had been cut into her curved belly beside the main air lock. The air lock retained most of its ornate original frame, a tiled mosaic gleaming blue and gold in the midday sun. Dull black marred it: lost tiles replaced with patches. The skyward thrust of her nose offered a glimpse of the ship's former beauty, but a hasty network of cables had been attached to hold it straight.

Terk pointed wordlessly.

Huido, who'd gone ahead to check out the ship, dipped carapace to shoulder in a shrug. "I'm told it's been windy."

Rivets marked the outline of what would have been an observation deck, its transparent panels swapped out for a ring of pitted gray metal. A mistake, that. Passengers would pay more if they could see outside the ship—

—and Sira would have loved it.

Morgan gave himself a shake. "Let's not keep the captain waiting."

* * *

"The captain's busy, Gentle Homs. Occupied. In the midst." The Whirtle blinked its oval eyes as it spoke. A sign it wasn't comfortable giving such news to three, admittedly, intimidating beings. Impatient ones.

Though Morgan was doing his utmost not to glower, Terk's glower being far nastier, while Huido? Didn't appear perturbed in the slightest. Seeing that, the Human modified his tone. "Do you expect the captain to be long?"

"It could be long or not. Longer, maybe." The indecisive Whirtle shrank into itself, increasing its resemblance to an upright sausage. The being had squeezed its soft torso into spacer coveralls meant for a humanoid, a trio of tentacles writhing inside each sleeve with only the tips showing. "Would you like a refreshment?" it asked hopefully. Dropping to the floor, it humped quickly to what had been, once, a bar.

They were standing in what had been, in the *Wayfarer*'s prime, a reception area. The carpets were gone, but the bar—real or replica marble, though he'd bet real—stretched the length of one wall, complete with the original vidscreen that had filled the space behind, now dark and cracked. Loose boxes filled most of the bar's countertop, but a space had been cleared for a tray with three bottles of water.

The Whirtle rocked up on its toes and stretched out a flare of tentacles, but couldn't reach the tray. "A moment, Gentle Homs."

It tried hopping.

Terk growled under his breath and snatched a bottle for himself.

Nowhere near ready to lift, not with all this loose. Morgan frowned. "I'm certain Thel Masim conveyed the urgency of our need to her cousin. I ask again. Will she be long?"

Eyes regarded him, then the Whirtle uttered a truly sorrowful sigh. "I can never say, Gentle Homs. Never at all. It's the engines, you see. The captain takes such a personal interest. Sometimes I don't see her for days and days." Realizing this may have sounded negative, it hastened to add: "The captain works very hard."

Morgan lifted a finger, stopping Terk's outburst. He should have guessed. "You've no ship's engineer."

"Oh, but we do." Eyes blinked. "We do! Our engineer is, ah, the captain. She's very good. And works very hard."

Support from one's crew was a positive. The rest? "I'm sure," Morgan soothed, then asked innocently, "The engine room's on the fourth deck?"

Eyes blinked. "Goodness, no! The fourth is for passengers. Paying passengers," wistfully, as if those had been in short supply. "The engines are on the eleventh, well away."

Morgan smiled. "Thank you."

※ ✳ ※

Leaving Terk and Huido to keep the Whirtle occupied, Morgan strode down the gloomy corridor to the lifts. He counted steps as he went, checking the distance between operational lights. A deliberate shutdown, he concluded, relieved. This captain, like others facing Auord's shipcity's costs for downworld services, conserved power.

The lifts? Two had little warning ribbons affixed to their old-fashioned panels at Whirtle-height. The third looked functional. Morgan stepped inside. Another panel waited, this one gleaming with polish—or use, and he sent the lift down. Smooth and fast.

Without thinking, the Human reached out to pat the wall. "Not bad."

Old habits, he chided himself, and hoped the lift com wasn't live. Though it was true. Outdated as the *Wayfarer* was, her original construction had been no-expense-spared. He'd a sense of her owner/captain/engineer now. Someone who'd seen past the years and quaint details to what this ship could be.

Not that she was close to there yet. When the lift came to a not-so-smooth halt, Morgan stepped through the opened doors. He sniffed and had to smile. Oil. That way.

On this floor, the layout was more direct: a corridor went around the ship's heart, accessing all sides. The doors he passed were vacuum-capable, ovals set inside heavy frames, with manual as well as servo locks. He looked into the viewport of one, nodding unconscious approval when it proved to be an internal air lock. No freighters were built like this, however much those who called them home might wish for the protection. It wasn't economical. Engines failed and vented their poison; people died and it was the risk you took, being a spacer.

The door ahead was larger than the rest—and ajar. A steady beat came through it, as well as the scent of oil and, yes, sweaty Human.

What did it say about his life, that this combination made him homesick? With a wry grimace, Morgan stepped into the *Wayfarer's* heart.

Captain Usuki Erin wasn't in sight, unless he counted the bottom of a boot presently wagging in midair, the person presumably attached to it swallowed deep inside an open pipe. Morgan took advantage of her preoccupation to wander around the engine room.

Engines. To his surprise, the *Wayfarer* boasted two, one with a translight drive and the other without. The latter was a third smaller and had been, from the look of it, scavenged for parts. Smaller and—he went closer, absently grabbing a rag to protect his hand as he took hold of a flange and leaned in—odd. Some sort of coil was connected where he'd expect a—

"A prototype SDIW49 power converter." The figure in filthy coveralls leaned in beside him. "See there?" A wrench aimed at the coil. "The notion was to capture the dump velocity and use it for a boost insystem. Fast as a greased—fast."

"Captain," he acknowledged, dipping his head in salute. "Was it ever activated?"

The wrench flipped in the air, caught as the other backed out. "Sure. Byi ran it during a race. If it hadn't been completely illegal—" with admiration, "—the record would still stand. You're Morgan." She wiped a hand on a marginally cleaner bit of clothing and thrust it out. "Usuki Erin. Call me Erin—on *Wayfarer* we don't do formal."

He took it, feeling calluses matched to his own. "Erin."

"You captained the refurbished patroller, didn't you? The *Silver Fox*. I saw her once—how did you—" Her round cheeks flamed red. "I'm sorry. Word went out. She was a good ship."

"As is this," he replied, somewhat bemused. How young was she? His height, with the strong build that came with doing her own work, black hair cut to her ears, a short, upturned nose—and those cheeks; all within Human norm. He could make a reasonable stab at her heritage and be wrong; traits in humanity tended to resurface.

Maybe not so young, by the experience etched into the skin around her sparkling brown eyes and at the corners of a generous mouth. She'd lost an eyebrow—recently, from the gleam of medplas—

The other eyebrow rose. "Know me later, will you?"

"Stitts VII."

Now a frown. "What else Thel tell you?"

"Don't worry," he almost smiled. "I like to guess. I crossed paths a few times with some traders from there." A pleasant-enough world. "I saw a resemblance."

"The *Casini*? Or the *Triverse*?"

Hung around the shipcity, had she? It had been the *Triverse*, all hands lost a few years ago in a tragic accident. "I don't remember," he lied. "How soon can you lift?"

Another, fainter blush. "As to that—glad you thought of parts." Gesturing him to come along, Erin led Morgan to where she'd been working. "I'm half through replacing the compression coils, but there's the rest. Be faster if you help."

"Often ask your passengers to work for you?" he asked, but was already pushing up his sleeves, fastening them above the elbow. Whatever got it done, and he'd not mind this. Her eyes caught on the bracelet. Morgan pulled it off and tucked it safely in a pocket. "What else?"

Erin' eyes lifted. "There's some stowage to be dealt with," she admitted. "Noska's a diligent little chit, but not the fastest. He has some trouble with shelves." A shrug. "I tell him to carry around a stool, but he won't. Says it's demeaning for a real spacer."

"I've seen what's lying loose." Morgan frowned. "Crew safety's the captain's responsibility. You should have taken care of it before playing in here."

" 'Playing?' I'll have you know—"

"I do know," he interrupted, his voice low and harsh. "Better than you think. You work on the engines because it feels like progress every time you put something back together, because machines don't argue. They don't dictate terms you can't meet. And they don't try to take your ship from you. You've been hiding down here, Captain Erin, letting debts pile up around your fins, when you should be out there—" his arm swung wide, "—making the trades that will save you, your crew, and the *Wayfarer*."

He ducked the wrench she threw at his head, but didn't stop. He couldn't. Here was such opportunity—wasted. "Tell me you're worth my time," he dared her. "Tell me there's the faintest hope this ship gets off the dirt."

"Least I have one." Her face was hard.

"Do you?" Morgan asked, suddenly gentle. Gods, he knew her, inside and out. Knew *this*, as he did so little these days. "You've a gift for machines and an eye—a good one—for starships. I'm not doubting that. But the moment one of your creditors demands to be paid, this is gone. All of it."

She didn't like it, but listened. Finally, "You got an answer to that, *Captain* Morgan? You got more to say than what I'm doing wrong on my own damn ship?"

No one had told him, those long years ago, what to do. He hadn't asked, was the sorry truth, too consumed by his own problems. Certain he was alone and should be.

Until Sira. Who'd not only asked for his help, but insisted he teach her to be crew on the *Fox*. Who'd come to love the ship, despite those moments when her lack of knowledge threatened the plumbing and worse.

He'd no time for this—

"And I have made trades," Captain Usuki Erin informed him. "Just—Auord doesn't have the right customers, is all, and without the ship ready to fly, how'm I supposed to find them? Tell me that?"

He should find another ship—

Unless—

Jason Morgan took a deep breath. "Show me what's in her hold." If there was hope for the *Wayfarer*, it was there.

Interlude

I'D GIVEN UP HOPE.

What replaced it now was purpose and not all of it was mine. There was a *presence* close. Another, nearby. Innumerable those who waited Between, *holding* us in this instant. Wanting me to do—what?

Sister. Heart-kin. You must accept where you are. You must feel the reality of it. Breathe. Trust me.

So I did. It felt strange, to have to think of it.

Sira, trust nothing. Taisal's advice.

I found myself inclined to giggle with my new breath, but managed to not. They didn't appreciate how they sounded in my head.

I had a head?

Do you remember—remember—re—

"Waking her wasn't in our instructions."

I certainly didn't remember that voice, if that's what they meant. Really, I thought, growing annoyed, disembodied helpers should be, well, helpful.

"Your arguments-sss are tediouss-ss."

Breathing? I'd have stopped if I could, remembering too much all at once. The sibilance, the hiss and spit around words?

Scat.

I breathed, had a head, and was helpless in the presence of a species that viewed any weakness as invitation. Not good. Not good at all. Panic would be the right response. At the very least a forthright stand.

Did I have feet?

There. That's it, sister. Quickly. Take hold and bring the rest!

Take—

HOLD! I was wrung out and emptied.

Then *FILLED!*

"She'll need time in a med cocoon."

"Why would we have one of thos-sse?"

Memories rushed into place. I knew my past; was grimly aware of my present. The only thing not quite settled?

What I was. The body I remembered wasn't *this* body. Rael's— my—arms and legs felt like ill-fitting shoes. The rest—oh, dear.

Without bothering to open my eyes, I vomited. Violently enough to produce a satisfying shriek from someone too close followed by the drum of feet as he/she/it moved out of range.

While not the "hello" encouraged by my Human for appropriate first contact, at least I'd made an impression.

* ✳ *

With the irony I'd come to expect from the universes, the first voice I'd heard in NothingReal—in the Trade Pact—belonged to an Assembler. Her name for one-minds was Argyle Touley, and she was afraid of Scats.

Sensible, yes, and common ground of a sort, but having Touley— my assigned caregiver—fragment whenever a Scat entered the room? Wasn't helping, other than to amuse the Scat. When we were alone, as now, she came back together and did.

"I will close the remaining holes now. Are you prepared?"

Had I a choice? I nodded, counting stains on the ceiling as she applied what had been a package stapler and was now an impromptu medical device. The only advantage so far to being in a body other than my own was a lag in sensation, but as that was growing shorter, it wouldn't be long before I'd experience the stapler in real time. "How many are left?"

"Six," Touley informed me. *Snap.* "Now five. It is better not to leak."

In our brief times together, I'd noticed this Assembler's fondness for tidbits of the obvious; we'd covered that vomit stank, naked skin lost heat, and Scat—although her employers—were bad. I'd come to the conclusion that, far from being simple-minded, Argyle Touley merely lacked experience conversing with one-minds.

She was practicing with me. *Snap.* "Four."

Fortunately, she'd used dabs of glue to seal the ranks of small holes lining my arms and legs. As each set, the surrounding skin puckered, and I knew I'd be in for some serious itching—once my brain worked out where those limbs were. I supposed in a way I was experiencing myself the way Touley did: as disassociated parts.

Snap. "Three."

"Ouch." There, the first staple making itself known. More to come, I thought dourly.

"Do you want me to stop?"

"No," I said, though it was more of a grunt. The thing stung. On the plus side, now I was well aware of my left breast. The one with a staple in it.

Snap. "Two."

And there was Rael's—no, my—right breast, complete with staple. I refused to pity myself; Yihtor would have no gentler reacquaintance with his body, given the damage done to it, though with any luck, he'd arrived to proper medical care.

Not an Assembler with a stapler.

Snap. "There is one left. You must roll to the side."

I tried, managing to turn my head to face a blood-splattered apron. "Not enough. I will arrange you." She did, then waved the, yes, bloody stapler in my field of view. "This the biggest hole. It will take several. Do not move."

Snap. Snap. The one on my belly announced itself with a sharp bite. "Touley—" I gasped more than said, "—why are you doing this?"

"You were leaking." *Snap.* "Stupid Scat wasn't to wake you," she elaborated. "You were safe in the box. Out of the box, you leaked. You must not die."

This, from a member of the species who'd done their utmost to eradicate mine? It wasn't, in any sense, what I'd call compassion. I had a value.

No, Rael di Sarc's body had a value, but it wasn't to Touley, not directly.

Snap. Snap. By the sound of it, she was stapling my entire hip. That was going to hurt far more than the burning spots informing me of the rest of my new abdomen.

Better questions, I thought suddenly. Targeted. Species-specific. "What is the gain to your—" amalgamation? collective? "—assembly?"

Snap. "Group."

I felt a ridiculous sense of triumph. " 'Group.' How does my survival benefit them?"

She paused to stare at me. "Success."

My triumph evaporated. If we were going to move forward word-by-word, I'd faint before understanding anything at all.

"My group," Touley said then, her body expanding so I could see the cilia connecting her parts. They locked back together with an unpleasant meaty *snick.* "Good bits. Most," she gave her right hand a sour look. "Touley group succeeds, others take us as nexus, follow as one. Everyone happy. Makes more success." She applied the stapler. *Snap.*

Morgan hadn't known this about Assemblers. Had anyone, before? "Who can join a group?" Could I?

A one-shouldered shrug. "Release from group, easy. Follow nexus, easy. Latch to better group? Only if can make success for the rest. Each nexus must decide. Touley group? Scat today. Clan. Best group." With a chilling smile. "Others pick foolish Humans. Brill. Others— You ask too many questions for someone with no group at all."

How wrong she was, I thought, letting myself be *aware* of the uncountable Singers and Watchers binding me across universes. Overwhelming, that sensation, and I pulled back, but with something of my confidence restored.

Snap. "Finished." Touley tossed the stapler over a shoulder that twitched as if trying to duck. She bent to stare into my face, dark eyes gleaming. "You need to eat now. One-minds use so much energy to be alive. It is hard to imagine being one part so big. So alone."

But I wasn't alone, not *there*.

Here? In the Trade Pact?

I'd a hip again, tracing itself in fire. That pain made tears slip out, crossing over my nose in a maddeningly immediate tickle— it wasn't loneliness, wasn't longing, please let it not be what I mustn't imagine—

Touley drew back in alarm. "You are leaking again!"

"No! It's normal." I was terrified she'd try sealing up my eyes. Was that what had happened to Yihtor? "My eyes clean them-selves. Leave me be." The last came out more like begging.

The fingers of her left hand ran up her right arm, then back again. Thinking? Arguing? They stopped. "I will obtain suitable food. Stupid Scat didn't think of that, either. Wasn't to wake you. Bah."

She turned to leave me. "Wait."

The head rotated on the shoulders, giving me another unset-tling glimpse of the thick cilia holding it in place. "Why?"

Because any company was better than my own? Because I no longer trusted my heart?

"I want to know why the Scat woke me, if it wasn't supposed to."

A toothy grin. "Maybe you are suitable food."

After that, I was happy to see her leave.

* ✳ *

I grew numb, then calm. I couldn't waste this opportunity.

First, I used my privacy to take stock; a sign, I supposed, that my mind was settling into its new home. My eyes told me I was in a small metal-walled room with an open drain in the floor, pre-sumably to relieve myself if and when I remembered how. My fingers found a plas sheet beneath me. It felt—strange.

No, it was the fingers, with their exquisitely sensitive tips. No calluses, no thickened spots from playing the keffleflute, hauling cargo, or climbing the canopy. Rael's short life had been gentler than mine.

Till now.

I focused on the sheet. Unlikely that it protected the table or countertop presently my bed. My guess was they'd used it to carry me here from the stasis box.

Having it ready to wrap my corpse if I'd died in the process was a bonus. Kept the ship tidy.

I was thinking like a spacer again, my ears attuned to the low hum of engines. A hum that indicated—I knew this—a ship using her own power, but not underway. We could be linked to a station like Plexis.

That hope faded as I remembered this was also how a ship felt when dropped out of subspace to hide, the likelier scenario.

Hiding, or waiting.

The hard surface beneath me was abruptly worse than the hurts to my skin. "Going to try sitting," I warned my new body, and did.

While the resulting contortion did raise my torso, my feet and legs skidded on the blood-slick sheet and the rest of me followed.

To the floor. Almost. As the sheet fell, I clung to the table with both hands, arms outstretched over its surface, its edge digging into my abused stomach. "Missed the staples," I said breathlessly. "Has to count."

I kicked one foot, then the other free of the sheet but had to pause before attempting to rise. Why was I weak? Stasis kept a body ready to move, unharmed.

If the body was healthy.

Rael had been poisoned—had died of it, only to be brought back to life. Her body, that was. Which I was in.

I shook my head and was immediately sorry as the room spun. "Think it through," I told myself. There could have been lingering damage. Maybe they'd had to flush out the poison, explaining the holes and punctures, but these were crude, hurried.

I'd had my own experience with field surgery and it had been better than this. Not that I was one to talk, being held together at the moment with staples and glue. Glue that was, thank you, starting to itch like a thousand little bites.

Bites, I thought, growing still, left by teeth. For I was no longer alone.

Pairs of small red eyes watched me from the hole in the floor. The sort of eyes that implied teeth.

A dainty foot clawed thoughtfully at the rim, as if gauging the effort required to come out all the way.

Dinner, on the loose? The Scats favored live prey. Or the ubiquitous vermin that snuck on at every port—

A distinction hardly of importance as one yawned, its very pointed teeth catching the light.

Climbing back on the table was beyond me. Instead, I heaved myself to a shaky stand, then used my feet to push the sheet along the floor. The eyes blinked in unison. Deciding my behavior was alarming, the owners of those eyes whisked away and were gone.

I made myself keep going to the floor drain, made myself toe the disgusting sheet to stop up the opening as best I could without toppling over to join it. "Chew on that," I told the vermin.

A door I hadn't noticed opened, revealing Argyle Touley with a tray in her hands. She made no comment about the sheet. "You are up. Good. Here is suitable food." She put the tray on the table.

My stomach objected; I ignored it, focused on what else she'd brought, draped over an arm. "Is that clothing?"

"Yes. Do you wish it first? Naked skin loses heat."

What I wanted first, I thought desperately, was to feel clean again, but I'd take being dressed.

I'd known pirates to acquire wardrobes of species-specific belongings, but what Touley held out for me was more basic. The enterprising Assembler had taken a blanket and cut openings for my head and arms. She did most of the work getting me into it, securing the result with a length of wire around my waist. "Better?"

"Yes. Thank you." The blanket was black issa-silk, light as air, and smooth enough not to snag on the staples. I looked down at myself—

—at Rael—

—at me. I fought the urge to *disconnect* and remember. While I remained here, this was my body, and I needed to believe it.

I was taller, that gain from long legs, tattooed in the Denebian fashion. My sister had worn clothing to display them. The blanket did a good job of that, too, ending mid-thigh; at least, what it did cover was warmer.

"Now eat suitable food."

I risked a glance at the tray. It held a bulb of water and a handful of— "E-rations," I said, my lips dry.

"Human food," Touley reminded me. "Eat now." She grabbed one and unwrapped the end, thrusting the tube into my hand.

E-rations.

I brought it to my mouth and took a bite. The stuff was as tasteless as I remembered, requiring a serious effort to chew. While you could soak them in water, they'd turn to a slimy gel and stick to your teeth and be that much harder to swallow.

Morgan liked e-rations. He kept a couple of tubes in his pocket, insisting they were for emergencies. Shipwrecked on a world without restaurants. A failure of the kitchen replicator—which had happened, so that wasn't a good example, and we had, it was true, shared e-rations beside a crackling fire in a jungle without restaurants—

Closing my eyes, I heard a voice cry out in such anguish I wanted to weep, yet it was my new voice, wasn't it, and I'd done so well, I'd tried, I had, and managed until this instant and taste not to think of—

Him.

Chapter 11

"—SHOULD HAVE TOLD HIM."
Deep in thought, Morgan tuned out the voices. Whether Huido had appreciated the state of the *Wayfarer* or not was irrelevant. Either they could get her off the ground, soon, or he'd find another way up to the *Worraud*. Once there, well . . .

. . . part of the answer could be stacked in front of him.

Bone. It filled the hold; first up, neat rows of pale skulls, each with three empty sockets regarding him with all the baleful intensity of the original owners. Yabok weren't hunted so much as they were battled, and big ones—like these—won often enough to make such hunts irresistible to risk-junkies.

Beyond the skulls were racks of ribs and hips, crates of vertebrae and horns, while along the walls hung the vastly elongated finger- and wrist bones that were the Yabok's most lethal weapon. In life, they supported a transparent membrane inhabited by microscopic stinging organisms, symbiotic partners. Once touched to skin, they'd fire. Prey—or a hapless hunter—would die in silent agony, paralyzed and unable to scream.

He walked down the rows, Erin a step behind, and her silence held an agony of its own. The bones filled the *Wayfarer*'s main hold. On an inner system world, Yabok bones would be a high-ticket prize, especially if you knew how to arrange an auction. Get a bunch of grandies in the same room, show some hunt footage, and they'd climb over one another to acquire a danger-free trophy.

On Auord? Lucky if portcity maintenance would take the lot away for road filler and not ask for a disposal fee. She'd been taken, plain and simple. Knew it, too, by the way none of it was secured for lift. No wonder she'd been hiding in the engine room.

Bone, however, had other uses. Morgan stopped by a scapula as tall as he was, and ran his fingers over the bone, feeling its pores and hardness. He stretched out his arms. The shoulder blade was wider.

He stepped around it. Thick enough.

"I'll take this one," he announced briskly. "How much?"

Erin stared at him, then threw up her hands. "Take it. Hells, I don't care."

"Huido will buy the rest."

The color drained from her face. "Pardon?"

"Yes, pardon?" The Carasian's eyestalks swirled in all directions, as though trying to count the giant skeletons.

Morgan carefully didn't smile. "If you don't have a price in mind, Captain, allow me. You've my word it'll be fair."

Huido rattled. "No need to be hasty."

The Human tapped twice on the nearest bit of carapace, their signal for "play along." "Don't be shy, my friend. We both know time is of the essence, but I'm sure, with immediate transport to Plexis, you'll have these in place in time for the grand reopening of the *Claws & Jaws*."

Erin looked from one to the other with growing hope. "Hom Huido? Is it true? You'll want them all?"

A trio of eyes surveyed her expression. "It is . . . I do . . . because . . ." a worrisome pause, then Huido gave himself a shake, ". . . I've been looking for dramatic new decor for the entrance. How wonderful you have these. And so many. And—" The eyes returned to Morgan, a pleading in their depths. "—that I can afford them."

The Human grinned, picturing Bowman's reaction. "I'm sure you can."

The Whirtle hugged itself, crooning in delight, but Erin smiled and grabbed hold of Huido's great claw with both hands. "Done. And thank you, Hom Huido. If you need more," persuasively, "I know a source."

Eyestalks bent. "These will suffice," with utter conviction.

Morgan lost his grin, his attention back on the bone. Terk stepped up beside him and spoke in a low whisper. "Tell me you aren't thinking what I know you're thinking."

"Even Scats don't disable the safeties." In particular, those that gave a chance, albeit minuscule, to a hapless being blown from a ship in space. "A hatch detects complex organics, the autos unlock. That's my way in."

"Your way dead, you mean," with a glower. "Still have to manually open the hatch. How're you going manage that without taking off your suit? Which would be—" as if he was hard of hearing, "—the 'dead' part. Before the Scats can shoot you."

"I've a better idea." Morgan put a hand on the other's thick shoulder. "I'll need something—things—from the *Conciliator*'s cryobrig."

The enforcer shook it off, growling. "No. Not happening. No way."

"I'm doing this with or without your help," he said quietly. " 'With' would be preferable."

Terk swore under his breath. Then, louder, "Bowman'll skin me—for starters, mind, then she'll get creative."

"Probably."

"You're scum, you know that? Pure scum."

Which was yes, no matter what cost, and Morgan didn't attempt to offer thanks.

No need, with a friend like this.

* ✳ *

"Hom Huido's cargo has been loaded," the new captain of the *Heerala* said with pride.

As he should, the *Wayfarer*'s hold having been emptied in record time, though Morgan guessed Henerop's immediate background as cargo supervisor hadn't hurt.

"Will—will Hom Huido be coming soon?"

Good question. The Carasian stood in the open hold door, an ominous cloud blocking most of the sunset. The final group of Drapsk edged past, staying as close as they could to the far side. "Give us a moment," Morgan asked.

"I don't want to go," Huido rumbled at his approach, his voice deep with anger. "I won't."

The Human leaned on the bulkhead by the door, taking an appreciative sniff of sea-scented air. Auord's shipcity's one grace, that switch at early evening; soon, of course, to be followed by rain. "Can't make you," he agreed.

A suspicious eye aimed his way.

"Besides," he went on easily, "Tayno's there. I'm sure he'll know what do with a shipment of Yabok bones."

Another eye.

"As I recall, there's room in the corridor behind the kitchen. Not to mention Plexis will have replaced your quarters—"

"My pool?" With a clatter of outrage. "You suggest my fool of a nephew would pollute my new pool with those—those—filthy scraps?!"

"Only if he ran out of space," Morgan assured the distraught Carasian. "It's not as though—" he pretended to hesitate.

All eyes converged.

"—you have wives for a pool. Then again, Tayno might have been lucky—"

Huido loomed larger. His great claw rose and snapped, the stub bent as if eager to do the same. "LUCKY?!" The word echoed through the hold.

A ball of Drapsk rolled down the ramp.

"Could happen."

"It could NOT! Wives do not choose based on chance. They study and compare their options, make reasoned, thoughtful— you're laughing," with outrage.

"Bone dust." Morgan made a show of coughing. "If you're certain Tayno won't attract wives of his own, then I don't see the problem. He can put the cargo anywhere he wants. You left him in charge of the reopening, after all."

His friend shrank to normal size. "I left to care for you."

"I know." Morgan turned serious. "You saved my life. Now I'm asking you to take care of yours."

A sullen rumble. "No, you're asking me to abandon you before battle."

The Human went to lean companionably against that hard shell, neck bent to meet the gaze of uncountable unhappy eyes. "There won't be one, I promise. A quick stop and switch play, Huido. Thel delays their shuttle till we're in place. Terk'll be on the *Wayfarer*, pretending the ship's off course with mechanical trouble." The real possibility of that something his friend didn't need to know. "The *Worraud* distracted while they're trying to dock their shuttle. I'll slip over, find Rael's body, and end her suffering. They'll never know I was on board."

Huido's sigh rocked a blaster onto Morgan's shoulder; eyeing the weapon, he didn't dare move. "Could be worse," he said lightly. "I could have gone up in the Brexk box."

Delivered, according to Captain Henerop, with seals restored, to Manouya's address. He hadn't been forthcoming as to what was now inside—a still-comatose Yihtor having been transferred to the *Conciliator*—and Morgan hadn't asked.

"If you're worried about the Scats?" he hazarded. "This is civilized space. If they find me, they'll call in the Jellies and have me arrested." If they decided otherwise, well, with Terk involved, Bowman would be watching; not that Port Authority, whose jurisdiction extended to orbit, would be pleased by enforcer intervention. "I'll be fine."

"You can handle Scats." A small handling claw shifted the weapon from his shoulder, then closed over Morgan's arm to demand his full attention. "Yihtor's back in his body. What if Rael's inside hers?"

He should have known Huido, with a heart bigger than his head, would go straight to the crux of things. "I'll do what must be done. Rael deserves to be with those she loves, not trapped here."

With Sira, but he couldn't say it out loud.

"No matter what happens, that is her fate. What troubles me is now. Why they're here. Yihtor hasn't told us. We don't know."

"We know," Morgan said heavily, "the Clan can't be in Trade Pact space. Sira—she made a deal. That's the only way I can explain it. Her part was to ensure those who belonged in that other universe returned to it; theirs, to stop harming worlds to find them." Sira had saved the Hoveny, along with the Oud and Tikitik; species neither of them had known existed before. She'd expect nothing less of him now, with the Trade Pact at risk. "Yihtor. Rael. The Clan I saw yesterday and any others still hiding here. They must go back. They die, here, or we do." Morgan hardened his voice and his heart. "Rael first, by my hand. I owe her that."

The claw released his sleeve, straightened it with a fussy little movement. "It's going to rain, isn't it?" Huido said dolefully. Louder, "I hope the aircar has a roof."

"It does, Hom Huido, it does. A wonderful roof." Hearing his cue, Captain Henerop hurried up to the Carasian, antennae tipped forward. "It waits outside."

Morgan reached up his hand, felt the pinch as Huido's needle-tipped jaws closed on it. "Take care of yourself," he told his friend, when they were done.

"Bah. I shall take care of that wretch of a nephew!" Huido boomed. More quietly, "Take my excellent advice. Don't die."

The Human raised an eyebrow. "That's it?"

"I'd give you better," with an amused rumble, "but we both know I'd be wasting my time."

Interlude

An Undisclosed Location

THERE WAS A ROOM in Trade Pact Board Member Choiola's living quarters, be that her apartment or on board a Brill ship, no one else was ever to see.

Which wasn't strictly true, given the room had inhabitants with eyes, but this being her first and firmest rule it was obeyed by servants, crew, and tradesbeings without question or speculation. With fear, yes. Brill were a volatile species, physically intimidating, and known to apologize, too little and too late, for their acts of temper.

Choiola apologized not at all.

The room was furnished in bright colors, not all of which a Brill eye could detect, but she wanted everything to be exactly as it should be. Little chairs were pulled up to little tables. Cups the size of her fingernail sat waiting. There were rugs shaped like flowers and puffed pillows resembling fish. Not the sort with teeth, of course. Happy fish. Happy flowers.

Having time before her next meeting, she crouched awkwardly and cooed. "How's my little preciouses?"

The toddlers—a boy and girl as Humans referred to their get— looked up trustingly from the sand. They'd eyes of disproportionate size and charm; a species' trait. Brown, on this pair, as was their skin and hair. Siblings. Naturally born twins, in fact.

Adding horrifically to the cost, but the supplier knew her tastes. She hadn't liked her last set as much, not even as "gifts." They were gone now.

These were new and special. She quite liked their eyes. And their toes, too. She let them wrap their chubby little fingers around her smallest, discouraging with a tap the boy who tried to fit the tip of her polished nail in his mouth.

Both paused at that, their eyes round. Their mouths opened, but no sound came out. The girl had learned Choiola would not abide the mewling noise they made.

The boy had not. A simple matter, to remove the tongue. At this stage, they healed with remarkable speed.

A shame they aged quickly, too. Developed awareness. Discovered the darkness in their nursery.

It was all over so soon.

The Brill lifted a curl of hair, softer than issa-silk it was. She could use another blanket—

Chortle-chirp!

The toddlers leaned together at the cheery interruption, not daring to move. Choiola rose to her feet with a displeased grunt. Her vidcaller was early. Anyone else, she'd make wait.

But the Sector Chief of the Trade Pact Enforcers mustn't be given cause to wonder where she was, or what she might be doing. Oh, no.

Not yet.

Choiola activated the servos. One would rake the sand. Another was equipped with nipples to dispense authentic Human milk, it being important to the continued health of her precious guests.

She did like their round cheeks.

* ✳ *

Plexis

"I don't like the look of her," Lones said. "She's too thin."

The Carasian relied more and more on the small Human for guidance. Lones had told the rest of the staff he had a "guest." They took this as a welcome return to normalcy, Hom Huido housing aliens in the living quarters of the restaurant so often, the biological accommodation had extra porcelain whatevers. He'd only broken two. So far.

His lot, to be burdened by another's inexplicable whims.

Huido's, alas, to arrive home not only to the bill from Plexis, but a potential—surely minor—lawsuit filed by Chef The Righteous SeaSea. She hadn't taken being fired well at all; hardly fair, since every chef on Plexis had been fired from the *Claws & Jaws* at least once.

" 'Thin?' " Tayno regarded the figure on the bed from the safety of just inside the closed door. She looked normal to him. "Are you sure?"

"I am." Lones gently lifted her wrist. A hand with six nailless digits hung languidly from it, knuckles prominent, blue vessels beneath the skin. Paired green rings wrapped fingers and opposing thumbs below the outermost joints; she'd arrived wearing nothing else. "You shouldn't see a person's bones. And look how pale she is!" He eased the wrist and hand back down.

Her eyes had followed the movement. Now they drifted back to puzzle at Tayno, much to his discomfort. Deep-set, those eyes, in a face without eyelashes. Sparkling dots inset in her skin—or the bone beneath—marked where there should be eyebrows; her head bore a short fuzz of white that flattened or rose of its own accord. A face within Human or Clan norm; a face he wouldn't confuse with any other. It might have been carved in ice, like the ornaments they put into a bowl of prawlies to keep them cold for customers.

She moved when required. For their care, to use the fresher. Had consumed food, though only when they weren't present. She'd yet to speak, but she wasn't, to Tayno's relief, deaf. Whenever he said "Morgan," her face changed.

He didn't do it often; the change wasn't nice.

"We need to bring in a med-tech, Hom Tayno. She could lose the baby."

Tayno wasn't entirely clear on the details, but had grasped that "baby" referred to the only thing round about her, a growth distending her abdomen. He'd have gladly arranged a shower, like the one for Ruti, and make another gift.

Something about their guest told him neither would be welcome. "The Rugheran left her in our care," he said, not for the first time. Well, Morgan's, to be precise, but the Human wasn't here, and no one knew where he was if not. "If only she could talk."

"About that." Lones went into a bag Tayno hadn't noticed before and pulled out an ominous clutter of disks and wire. "It's a sleepteach set with Comspeak. If our guest—" He held out the device.

She turned her head on the pillow, closing her eyes briefly. No, that meant.

Lones lowered his hand. "I don't know what else to suggest, Hom."

"Give it to me." The Carasian took the thing with a small shudder. Technology, in his experience, existed to create embarrassing problems that other beings would have to come and fix, beings who considered anyone having such problems to be problems themselves. He waited for the thought to finish, sighed, and draped the wires and disks over several eyestalks.

Eyes he aimed at her.

"Hom?" Lones tried not to laugh, then did.

Tayno lowered his eyestalks, careful not to lose the device, then wiggled them.

The corner of her mouth deepened. The start of a smile?

"Put them on yourself," Tayno ordered, lowering himself so the Human could gingerly retrieve the sleepteach. One wire refused to leave an eyestalk and it was all the Carasian could do not to flinch and snap his claws while Lones untangled it.

The Human demonstrated how the disks rested neatly against the sides of his head, with one on the forehead. Then he closed his eyes, resting the side of his head on a hand, and made that noise Humans did when sleeping.

He'd inspired Lones by example, that's what he'd done. Tayno swelled with pride.

After two snores, Lones opened his eyes, and began to speak, gesturing as if to wave the words outward.

"I don't think she'll—" Tayno began.

Their guest beckoned imperiously.

"I think she does," the Human said with a smile as he obeyed, fitting it with care on her head. She touched the metal as though curious, then gave the Carasian a somber look before she lay back and closed her eyes.

Tayno watched uncertainly, then leaned toward Lones. "Can she understand me now?" he whispered, disappointed when the other shook his head.

"It'll take the night. If it works. Hom Tayno?" He was holding the door open. "We should leave her in peace."

Lones knew best about many things, Tayno thought as he went out and let the other close the door.

But their guest wasn't here for peace.

Chapter 12

THE DEAFENING RACKET didn't bother Morgan, though, he winced, that high-pitched grind? Not good news. He touched Erin's arm to gain her attention, then shook his head.

She released the manual throttle to end the test. "How's that?" she shouted over the engines.

Waiting for the noise to stop, Morgan eyed the bank of gauges, comparing them to the specs in his hand. "We need to boost the field integ thirty percent if we expect to get close to nominal."

Her grimace matched his feeling on the subject. They'd been in the *Wayfarer*'s engine room most of the planet night. Progress, yes, but each step forward opened a new can of toads.

None they hadn't handled.

The rest of the ship was, hopefully, close to ready as well. Noska, the Whirtle crewbeing, had been put in charge of stowing everything loose, with the help of some of the *Heerala*'s Drapsk who—at his request—discreetly whisked away what couldn't be managed. Most, Morgan hoped, would end up in a recycler. He couldn't blame Erin; Whirtles were prone to hoarding.

Perching on the edge of a crate, Morgan pulled two tubes of e-rations from his pocket. "Here."

Erin shot him a harried look. "There's no time."

"Sit. Eat. We need fuel, too." He made to toss one to her.

"Got my own. For emergencies." She grabbed a rag and cleaned the worst of the grease from her hands, then dropped cross-legged on the deck. Pulling out a tube, she opened it with her teeth, then took a good-sized bite, regarding him thoughtfully as she chewed.

"Go ahead," he invited, amused. "Ask."

"Huh." She swallowed, then squinted as if to see through him. "You could have found another ship. One ready to lift without all this—" a gesture to the tools and parts strewn around them. "Why stick with us?"

Because she referred, without thinking, to the engines and herself as "us." Because he was as sentimental in his way as Huido and wanted to believe the *Wayfarer* and her captain had a future.

Neither being reasons the hard-eyed engineer would accept, Morgan swung his e-ration in an echoing sweep. "I've missed this." Whether she believed him or not, it was true.

A second noncommittal "Huh." Erin took another bite and chewed, her attention drifting to the exposed core of the engines. "Could raise the intermix a notch. What do you think?"

"You're the expert." He'd recognized at once how much her theoretical knowledge surpassed his—what he had to offer were cheap fixes, the creative workarounds that had kept the *Fox* moving longer than she should. One occurred to him now. As he described it to the *Wayfarer*'s captain, her eyes gleamed with interest.

No more new problems, they just might make it.

Morgan checked the time.

Where was Terk?

* ✳ *

The answer arrived with the Whirtle. Noska burst into the engine room, tripping over a pipe, tentacles flailing. Morgan caught it short of a puddle of oil, steadying it on its feet.

Erin hurried over. "What's wrong? Is it Russo? That—"

"No no no. We paid the bill and the interest and you have to listen! There's a LEMMICK trying to get in!" The Whirtle's eyes were rimmed in urgent red. Its voice gained a second component, a rapid ear-piercing tremolo. "A LEMMICK!!!" Warning the rest of its kind, that sound, Whirtles being painfully sensitive to airborne particulates—and odors.

"That'd be Finelle," Morgan said with relief. At Erin's incredulous look, he added, "Terk's new partner, Two-Lily Finelle."

"A LEMMICK!!!"

Erin tried to pat Noska on the head, doing her best to reproduce the species' soothing hum. The being dodged back, stumbling again. "Seal the air locks!" Noska demanded. "Call the authorities!!"

"She *is* the authorities," his captain shouted at it, losing patience. "Calm down!"

Noska's nostrils, wide and lined with fine white hairs, snapped shut. "'On't cob down! DEBBICK!!"

"You'd better go," Erin told Morgan, eyes glinting with determination. "The two of us will finish what's left."

"You're sure?"

"DEBBICK!!!"

She mouthed "GO!"

Morgan eased by the pair and out the door.

* ✳ *

Terk and his temporary new partner were standing on the ramp in front of the *Wayfarer*'s functioning air lock, the tow line to a loaded grav sled in the latter's hand. The Human was making rude gestures at the vid lens.

The Lemmick? Seeing what she wore, Morgan swung the port wide, smiling in welcome. "You must be the new partner. I'm Jason Morgan." Habit made him hold his breath; manners dictated otherwise.

This was no ordinary Lemmick. Finelle was encased, from boot tip to her elegant, rear-aimed *pororus*—the flexible organ extending the head other species were not invited to touch—in what looked to be a skin-tight pink balloon. Flat clear globes revealed her dark lidless eyes, while a grid covered her mouth, located beneath where a Human would have a chin.

Instead of her enforcer uniform, over the body balloon Finelle wore a version of Terk's disguise—correction, Morgan thought, smile widening—she wore part of Terk's disguise. The crustacean-covered shirt worked as dress, coming down to her knobby knees. It barely fit around her waist, Lemmicks being significantly wider there, and would have made wings at her narrow shoulders but she'd tied the excess into a pair of lumps framing her oval face.

Completing the look, her weapon belt wrapped the middle of her chest, the holster a thick strap secured by a band around her thigh. It put an unusually nasty-looking needler in easy reach of her three-fingered hand.

Terk's lack of shirt exposed his neck and hairy chest, both improbably roped with muscle, both a network of scars.

Suffice it to say, no one would trouble the pair.

"How's the ship?" Terk asked. He lingered to eye their surroundings as Finelle brought the cart through the air lock, stepping quickly through.

"Ask me in an hour." Morgan leaned back, his hands out to the sides, their palms aimed at the Lemmick. "May your day be free of incident."

Finelle passed her partner the cord in order to free her hands to echo the gesture. "And may your evening be memorable. You have fine manners, Captain Morgan."

"Yeah, he's a charmer." Terk glowered. "And gonna cost us our commissions."

Finelle tittered, the laugh of her kind almost soundless. "Surely just yours, Partner Russ-Ell." She made his name into a little song. "It wasn't my thumb on the release order."

"Terk." Low and clearly frustrated. "Call me Terk."

"You know I will not, Partner Russ-Ell." Another titter, to put the big Human in his place, then the Lemmick grew serious, putting her hand on the crate. "We must deal with these promptly, Captain Morgan."

No use telling her he was one no longer; Lemmicks liked their aliens labeled by function. "This way."

Morgan had set up a workspace near one of the emergency

escape hatches. A line of dark red spacesuits, varied in size and body shape, hung on the bulkhead beside it. One hook was empty.

Terk pursed his lips in an appreciative whistle. "Pretty. Do they hold air?"

"This one does." The suit fit well; he'd expected no less given the original cost of these. "I've stripped the beacons and alerts." Along with anything else liable to *ping* on basic sensors, but he had to trust the *Worraud* boasted the usual Scat tendency to focus on what was big enough to shoot at—and might shoot back.

On another table, the antithesis of a spacesuit: the Yabok scapula, the pitted pale bone looking as out of place as the creature itself would have.

Finelle lowered the grav sled to the deck. The crate affixed to it was sealed with scraps of black tape. She set about removing those; under each was a sophisticated enforcer palm lock. "Tell him, Partner Russ-Ell, as I do this. My condition." Finelle placed her palm on one after another, springing them open.

At Morgan's sharp look, Terk ran a hand over his head then grimaced. "You have to ask their permission."

"I don't need it." He pushed forward the pail of vacuum-stable glue with one foot.

The Lemmick stopped with two locks left, on opposing corners. "I do."

Morgan gazed at her, reconsidering many things, including why Bowman had picked a Lemmick for her staff. This Lemmick. Finally, he gave a slow nod. "You've brought the means?"

"I have." She slapped the remaining locks simultaneously. Terk helped her remove the lid, setting it on the deck.

Inside was a carnal house of disembodied parts, with a head squeezed on top. The eyes opened to give a baleful stare, the mouth moving without sound.

"You're still in custody," Two-Lily Finelle told it sternly. "Secure the doors, please, Captain Morgan."

In case the Assemblers made a break for it.

* ✹ *

The torso came first, four shapeless lumps seizing one another's cilia and giving a pull. The head walked itself over what was now a chest, falling more than climbing into position. Another bout of writhing cilia, then a neck connected the two.

The chest heaved and the mouth opened to spit out a curse. "Not my group, Stupid One-Minds. Not my group. *TASTE BAD!*"

"Then let's get this done," Finelle told it. "We have a job for the rest of you. If it goes well, your conditions will be improved."

The eyes acquired a sly cast. "All to be in their right groups. ALL!" When Terk growled, the eyes slid his way, then back, unimpressed. "Need us. Do."

Smug, that was.

"Need them," Morgan countered, waving toward the crateful of assorted hands. Some waved back. "I've glue."

The hands cowered, fingers clenched. No problem with their hearing.

"Scary Human." The eyes found him. They were bloodshot, but passably blue. Cold. "We know of you. Know of your group."

"And you know Chief Bowman," Finelle stated, stepping in front of Morgan, her pororus pulsing. "Who is scarier?"

The mouth worked a moment, then, very quietly, "What offer, one-mind?"

"You stay warm. You get to communicate with one another. Captain Morgan's pleased with your work, you get a visit from—" a sac enlarged below Finelle's lower jaw, then shrank.

Nothing audible to Human ears, but the hands wiggled fingers in response. Even the head looked impressed. "Bowman's guarantee?"

"Do not question the chief's integrity." Two-Lily Finelle said, her tone as deadly as the needler on her thigh.

Catching Morgan's eye, Terk actually winked. The prospects of this partnership were improving.

The torso flexed, sending a sigh out the head's lips. "We accept. What are we to do?"

Morgan told them.

* ✳ *

The Assemblers in agreement, and safely locked back in their prison until needed, Morgan took the two enforcers on a quick tour of the *Wayfarer*. Their plan didn't include having to fight inside the ship.

Plans had been known to change.

So far, theirs was on track. He'd used the com to check in, shouting over Noska's continued alarm call. Erin had assured him the ship would be ready in time. She'd take care of the engine room, and would he please keep his guests as far away as possible.

As they walked briskly over each deck, Terk and Finelle didn't take notes, memorizing the ship's layout in quick glances, assessing choke points and potential ambush. At least Terk would be, but Morgan took it on faith that Bowman's Lemmick wouldn't miss a thing. A third of the ship was inaccessible: to them or an enemy. With no foreseeable use for staterooms, recreation center, dance or dining hall—nor with the crew complement the *Wayfarer* would have required at her peak—Captain Erin had sealed the majority of those sections, shutting down life support and gravity to conserve resources for the rest.

"Last stop, crew deck," he informed them as they rode the lift.

"What about command?"

Morgan eyed Terk. Not an idle question; the enforcer's preferred strategy was to seize control if a situation went sour, and apologize—maybe—later. He spread his fingers in a sign the other knew. *Someone listens.* He'd leave the coms alive with strangers roaming his ship; he gave Erin credit for the same caution. "The captain's secured the bridge while she works in the engine room."

As she should, with her ship full of strangers.

Instead of signing back, Terk rested a forefinger on the blaster hanging from his belt: his favorite lock opener.

Morgan shook his head vehemently, but he needn't have worried. Finelle snapped a finger, stinging Terk's ear. The enforcer jumped and whirled to stare at her. "What the—"

She waved at the opening lift doors. "Let us see the crew deck,

Partner Russ-Ell. If Captain Morgan will show us the ship's galley, you can eat something. Food is calming."

The Lemmick walked out first. Terk turned to Morgan with an aggrieved expression, rubbing his ear. "Did you see that?"

"See what?" Morgan inquired, keeping a straight face.

"Very funny. She's on trial with me, remember, not you." With that, Terk shoved his way into the corridor after his erstwhile partner.

* ✱ *

By the number of furnished but empty quarters along the outer curve, each larger than his and Sira's cozy cabin on the *Silver Fox,* the *Wayfarer* could house a crew of nine, providing three shifts on the bridge.

No one passing out exhausted and alone, as he'd done more often than not, Morgan thought enviously, reliant on autopilot and luck to get to the next world.

It had been a decade, Erin had told him, since the *Wayfarer*'s corridors had echoed with the sounds of a full crew; today these rooms were advertised on Auord's boards as passenger accommodations. No takers—yet.

Captain Usuki Erin's quarters were located on the command deck, attached to the bridge, as were those of her second in command—and entire crew—Noska. For the *Wayfarer?* Autos helped, but two? Not enough. They'd have to stick to safe insystem routes or risk joining the *Triverse.*

Not his ship, not his problem.

But Morgan lagged behind Terk and Finelle to collect the wrapped candies delicately placed in welcome on each cot—a certain Whirtle had a future in the hospitality trade—tucking them safely into a zipped pocket pre-lift.

Finelle opened a door on the inner wall. Terk put his hand on the frame and leaned in. "Not the galley," he dismissed, and pulled back out.

Making it the medbay, the enforcer notoriously unfond of such places, or what passed for emergency first aid given the

Wayfarer's state. Morgan wasn't interested either. A lift to orbit, his excursion to the *Worraud,* and back down. If anyone needed care, it'd be him, and he'd no intention of getting it here.

Yihtor waited on the *Conciliator,* Bowman waiting with him. For their return, with her prisoners, yes, but most of all for answers: the course to set for the rest of the Clan high among them.

He growled under his breath, disgusted at himself. Bowman, wait on anyone else? Wasn't happening in this universe or any other. "Terk—"

"Galley!" the enforcer announced gleefully, disappearing through the next door.

Morgan followed him inside, cursing inwardly. She'd sent these two as her proxies, that's what she'd done, to report anything of value a former starship captain and telepath might uncover. He was slipping, not to have seen it coming.

Slipping, he thought abruptly, not to know Bowman would expect him to figure this out and use what she'd sent to the *Wayfarer.* Two of her best staff, that secure conduit for information, weren't minor gifts. Meanwhile, she was—where?

Another element not his problem.

"You were saying?" Terk asked, busy programming the kitchen replicator.

Morgan nodded to himself, then pretended to sigh. "Just remember what you eat goes on my tab."

"Oh, I will." With a wicked grin.

* ✳ *

It wasn't only Lemmick exhalations that quickly filled the air around them, but the many and varied hard bumps on the skin were scent glands. The material containing the pungent result was, Two-Lily Finelle told them, called *Allura Nine.* "I can't tell I'm wearing anything," she said proudly. "Here, try to pull it off." She offered each an arm.

The Humans declined. "You made this?" Terk asked. From his tone, he wasn't happy to contemplate a partner capable of invention.

"No, Partner Russ-Ell. My fourth-over-sixth uncle is the genius of the family. With the chief's permission, I'm testing this prototype on his behalf. My uncle owns a large and successful retail business," she continued. "When I retire from being an enforcer—assuming I have not been killed in the line of duty—" with a disturbing titter of mirth, "—I have vowed to join him. We will sell very many of these and be rich. Our people long for a means to work with those who are—" a pause for thought, "—challenged."

A balloonlike fabric; a Lemmick entrepreneur? "Is this uncle on Plexis?" Morgan asked, leaning back.

"Why, yes, Captain Morgan. He's famous. Do you know him?"

Terk, back at the replicator, quickly put a finger over his lips and shook his head.

Making Finelle's famous fourth-over-sixth uncle the balloon seller whose "large and successful business" consisted of a collapsible table whisked away at the first sign of security. "I bought some of his product," Morgan replied truthfully. Balloons inflated with Lemmick breath. If an accident with a larger-than-most balloon had led to this invention, Plexis would be the first to invest. "May you both be successful."

"What I really need is a Whirtle. If one of them can remain in a room with me, with witnesses, it will be a true test of the Allura Nine." Finelle tilted her hand, palm-down. Disappointment. "Partner Russ-Ell informed me there's one on board. I'd hoped our paths might cross, Captain Morgan."

"I made sure they didn't," he confessed. "With apologies, but Noska has work to do." Work it had hopefully resumed, though from what he'd seen in the engine room, Erin might have tossed her Hindmost into a closet to calm down.

He'd opted for water, as had Finelle. Terk brought his second bowl of a hot spicy concoction to the table. The *Wayfarer*'s crew galley had space for several more. Stowed, or sold. The table and its surrounding stools were properly bolted to the floor. A floor, like the walls, stripped back to underlying gray metal, without a token coat of paint. Hardly welcoming, but they hadn't much longer to wait. Dawn was here.

With it, tugs were on the move. Thel would send theirs ahead of the shuttle booked by the *Worraud*.

"Chief took a runner to Ikita Sert for a meeting," Terk suddenly announced around a mouthful, eyes on Morgan. "Depending how things go, she'll join us soon or not."

A briefing, by the gods. "And my cargo?" Morgan asked, careful to keep it nonchalant.

"In the hold and secure." A tip emptied the bowl. "Up to you to deal with all that."

Bowman left him in charge? "Not—" he began, then stopped. Who else? Yihtor and any other Clan had to land in his lap. Hadn't he been the one to tell her about the entities? While she . . . ?

Would do what she did better than anyone he knew: hunt. "Some things don't change, do they?" Morgan said ruefully.

"Nope." Terk tossed his bowl and spoon into the recycler set in the wall, then stretched, joints cracking. "Typical. We do all the tough stuff, officers take the credit."

"Partner Russ-ELL—"

Bending toward Finelle, Terk covered his ears and stuck out his tongue.

Stunned speechless, the Lemmick reared back.

Morgan laughed.

The galley com crackled to life. "Tug incoming. Please meet me on the bridge."

"You heard the captain," he said.

It was time.

Interlude

THANKS TO THOSE *linked* to me, I kept my sense of how time passed in AllThereIs, marked by events on a celestial scale, less so by immediacy, not at all by heartbeats or breaths.

Or tears. I'd run out, so they weren't much use either, except to warn of limits. To my strength, to my ability to function here, to the time I had to finish my task. Not to my pain, but I'd known that.

What I hadn't? How it would feel, to be here, standing in the same universe as Jason Morgan. I could do a heart-search and find him. Bring him to me, bring me to him.

I'd the Power.

It would be that easy, and to every Sapients' hells with the M'hir—

—then what? Give Morgan up again, before the Great Ones thundered through Between to shatter the universes?

The *DREAD* I felt wasn't mine alone. It eased, fading back and away. They trusted me, those who held on, who'd sent me here and stayed.

Should they? I let out a shuddering breath and hoped.

"I thought you were done," Touley muttered, mistaking the sound. The Assembler had taken refuge from my little storm in a corner. She stood there now, arms tight around her middle as though insisting her parts stay together.

I used the edge of my not-a-dress to wipe mucus from my face, letting out a second of those shuddering breaths. "No," I said, uninterested in deceit. "I won't do it." Whatever the alien thought I meant didn't matter. I wouldn't lose control again, not here.

Spotting the tube of e-rations, I picked it up and made my way to the table. Somehow, I climbed up to sit on it; Rael's body protested in ways I vaguely remembered. I bit and chewed. Swallowed. Bit and chewed.

Maybe it was the taste of the e-rations, but my brain started to work again, fastening on a question. Trapped in this room, with an Assembler between me and the door, what would Morgan do?

Meanwhile, slowly, Touley edged out of her corner. She gave the drain—or was it the bloody sheet?—a wide berth and neared the end of the table. "I asked the stupid Scat one-mind for you why he woke you against orders."

I kept chewing.

As I expected, the Assembler came a little closer. "He said you were protection. You barely stand. How are you protection from anything?"

Scats seized or abandoned notions with bewildering speed, assessing each on the basis of personal gain for personal risk, but they weren't xenophobes. Meeting other species, Scats had quickly realized they were influenced by different motives. What they thought of those didn't matter; they had use.

One, in particular, succeeded with a multiplicity of victims.

"I'm a hostage," I guessed, more to myself than her.

"What?"

"The Scats believe they can control those who want me if I'm threatened with harm."

"Harm taking you out of the box."

Point taken. "Out of the box, I'm easier to move or hide."

"Those who want you will be angry, not controlled."

Chewing, I shrugged, inwardly alert. Any new information could be of use. "Maybe the Scats want to offer me to a wider market." Use her words. "To a different group."

Her hands gripped the table beside me, the left white-knuckled, the right resting. "Bad. Bad. Not do!"

"Why?"

Her mouth clamped shut.

No matter. She'd come within reach. I swallowed my last mouthful, surprised to find I'd finished the tube's contents. Rolling the wrapper neatly, I made a show of looking around, as if hunting where to put it, then set it on the table. Touley's eyes followed the wrapper.

I threw myself forward, pushing off from the table, managing to grab her by the wrists. We both fell to the floor, but she hit first. I rammed a knee into her torso, a move Morgan had taught me.

She fragmented. Shoulders burst from arms; wrists pulled in opposite directions; the torso split and ran for it. I turned my face in time to protect my nose as I dropped through what had been Touley to land on the floor.

The head laughed without sound as it backed away.

I showed my teeth at it, then maneuvered to my knees, still holding the wrists. Losing its smile, the head began to frown. As if summoned by mutual need, the legs and feet rejoined. Other parts scrambled to follow.

"Too late," I assured them. Rising to stand, I staggered gracelessly to the door and whipped one of the hands through the air. The fingers went wide to protect themselves, leaving the palm flat to press against the lock.

As the door whisked open, I stepped through, then let it close, smiling as I heard the lock snick into place. Scats liked that sort of effect. The hands wriggled in fury, and I tossed them down the corridor. They were welcome to try and climb the wall to unlock the rest of their group.

I'd no intention of arriving at our destination as a hostage or helpless. Scats could be negotiated with—hadn't I done it before? The trick was to find the right Scat.

Which meant finding the bridge.

Chapter 13

THE BRIDGE OF THE *WAYFARER* was unlike any Morgan had seen before, and he'd seen his share. Curved he'd expected, not this steep ribbed funnel cutting through two decks, facing a blank wall of equal height. Stairs led down one outside edge, with a handrail. A tube offered a quick ride down the other. Between, attached like pods on the funnel's ridges, were a dozen traditional consoles with padded seating for crew. To reach them?

"You swing. Like this." Captain Usuki Erin slipped her hand through a strap attached to a colorful cable, one of many looped against the outside walls, and launched into the air.

Not quite. The cable let her walk—bounce—along the funnel's side to reach her command post; she tied it off once there. "*Wayfarer* was designed for racing in null-grav," she explained, her voice carrying flawlessly. Augmented. "Pick a seat and strap in. Any console can assume the full range of ship functions, but don't worry. Nothing's live but mine."

Two-Lily Finelle took to the air, a sight to chill the heart of any Whirtle, but Noska would ride out the trip in its quarters. A well-deserved rest, Erin had explained, a twinkle in her eye. The Lemmick's landing was more a collision that landed her in a chair, presumably the one she'd intended. She gave a cheerful wave.

Terk turned sickly green.

Morgan, after a quick study of the nearest rib, took pity on him. "Here," he said in a low voice, tapping the rib with his boot. It expanded outward to offer a comfortably wide path, a pulsing light marking the way. No, a countdown. "I'd hurry," he added.

With Terk safely at his console and strapped in, Morgan chose a cable that would bring him to one behind and to the right of the captain's, keeping his feet in contact with the ribs. Once there, he pressed the cable against the mechanism that gripped it for later use, then perched on the edge of an exceedingly well-contoured chair. Leather, by the texture and wear. The *Wayfarer*'s builders had style, he'd give them that. The console itself? A glance reassured him. If the need arose, his hands knew such controls—

Not his ship.

Rigged for racing, was it? His gaze traced channels in the wall, dropped to assess the layout of the consoles. Morgan nodded to himself. The *Wayfarer*'s bridge was designed to slide into another, more typical configuration. He leaned forward, pitching his voice for the ship's captain. "Showing off?"

Erin grinned up at him, not bothering to deny it. "Did you see your friend's face?" she chuckled. "Admit it, it's a fun option. Noska's plan is to charge a bit extra to let passengers ride through lift."

"Sitting like flies on a wall?"

"No. Like this." She stretched out a hand and operated a switch.

The bridge went dark, except for tiny telltales on the consoles.

Then the far wall opened, letting in the dawn.

Framed in starships, the ocean stretched to the horizon, painted in reds and orange. An atmospheric freighter floated by overhead, dimming the light for a moment, while below, in the lane between ships?

A tug approached, great arms wide in welcome.

This wasn't a viswall, like that in the galley of the *Fox*—or not only one—but a window two decks high.

Theatrics. Part of him disapproved on principle. You were a trader or an entertainer, not both, and space travel had better be predictable, every check done every time, or you were dead. Boring was safe.

The other part of him—the part that thrilled to the roar of engines and the chance to see new worlds—thought Noska a shrewd business-being and this? The best bridge ever made.

So would Sira.

"Whaddayou say, Captain?" Erin asked. "Like the view?"

Not without her.

An irrational decision, maybe, but Morgan lowered his eyes, refusing to look. He felt the familiar shudder as the tug took hold, the lurch as the ship was plunked from the ground, the vibration as the journey to the field began. He'd missed this, too.

"Thel confirms the shuttle's away," Terk announced, his voice booming through the bridge.

Erin swore and twisted in her seat. "You've accessed my coms? How!? Stop!"

"I've skills," the enforcer said modestly. "Oh, and Captain Yo'lof from the *Paradigm* sends congratulations."

Morgan met Erin's outraged glare with a half smile. "He's a decent comtech. Might as well put him to work, too."

A look that could melt plas. "Nothing goes out without my—"

"Pardon, Captain?" from Terk. "Missed that. Busy updating shipcity control with our status. Thel advises any dents to her tug will be on your bill and to enjoy the flight."

"Acknowledge," Erin said icily, turning back to her board.

"Incoming from the *Eaky*: 'Thought you'd grown roots under those fins, pumpkin.'" Innocently, "Do you wish to respond, pum—Captain?"

Letting the two spar, Morgan settled back in his seat and closed his eyes.

The *Heerala* had lifted before dawn, on course for Plexis, with Huido and the Yabok bones.

As well as the box containing Cersi's last Adepts. Or rocks. Whatever they were, Huido would keep them safe until Morgan could deal with them. If need be, the Carasian would destroy them. Better that, than—what? What they didn't know loomed like a chasm.

Keep it simple, Morgan reminded himself. The potholes would tell him when they'd arrived at the field; Auord's attempts to fix the junction between the shipcity's firm laneways and the more fluid nature of the field being a long-standing joke. He'd exit the bridge once suborbital; no sense leaving the comfort of his seat until the quick and dirty work on the *Wayfarer*'s engines proved to either work—or blew them to particles, annoying Thel and melting a good portion of the landing field.

Even odds which.

* ✸ *

Lift-off achieved, he set to work. The *Wayfarer* had decent-sized air locks, but Morgan had to tilt the scapula to fit it inside. The Assemblers—hands only—wiggled a protest, but kept hold. Whatever the head had told them continued to work.

He'd have felt safer gluing them down.

"We're in position, Captain Morgan. The shuttle has lined up to dock with the *Worraud*."

He shifted to aim his visor at Finelle, her large eyes visible through the inner window. "Terk?"

Her voice could smile. "Partner Russ-Ell makes a convincing idiot. He has the Scats as incensed by his clumsy work on coms as they are terrified by the nearness of our ship. Captain Erin has helped by making our engines appear to falter."

Morgan hoped "appear" was all it was. "Good. Ready?"

"Yes. I'll extract the air at your command. The interior lights will go off before the hatch opens, again at your word. May your journey be— I'll wait here," the Lemmick finished with a confidence he wished he shared.

The return trip, at least, he planned to make under power. "Do it."

The suit fit better than any he'd owned, but the tang was the same: metal on the back of the tongue; the redolence of confined Human flesh. Recyclers never got it all. Homey, that. Breathing and pulse, steady, but they should be. Some trips in the *Fox*, he'd spent as much time outside as in.

Morgan angled the bone to check on his cohorts. As the air thinned, the Assembler bits were losing color, their flesh tone becoming gray. At the same time their skin thickened, exchanging flexibility for strength. The species didn't advertise its ability to resist vacuum and hard radiation, but free traders were well aware, faced with scouring hulls of such hitchhikers or face fines. The red-eyed vermin were among the worst, working their way into any crevice or hiding place, tolerating with ease what etched away at a ship's hull. Assemblers preferred not to hang on the outside of starships and, able to pass as Human, rarely did.

As if aware of his scrutiny, the hands bent toward the hatch.

Impatient to get this over with, were they?

Morgan steadied the bone. He wasn't. There'd be new nightmares to follow, without any surety he'd done the right thing.

For Rael.

"Open the hatch."

Interlude

"I WILL HAVE YOU blown out the hat-ssch."

Being nose to snout with an enraged Scat was an experience I'd planned not to repeat in any lifetime, let alone go looking for it. Yet here I was, again.

Black foam edged the serrated teeth lining the jaws. Scales covered the skin, delicate on the throat, sharp and overlapped over the cheeks and head. A frill rose behind each large yellow eye, frills pulsing with emotive color.

As now, red with fury.

"You can't," I told it, calmly, not sure which gender I'd encountered. I did know this was a member of the crew, not an officer.

The sweeper being a dead giveaway.

The head reared back in offense. "Why can't I?"

"Because the captain's expecting me on the bridge. If you delay me—" I left it there, not daring to ask directions.

"The captain?" The Scat angled its head to bring its right eye to bear. If the other was flawed, that could explain its position in the crew—while making it inclined to seize any chance to promote itself at the expense of others. You really couldn't win with the species. "Are you one of them?"

"What do you think?" I countered, possibly too clever for my own good.

Luckily not, for the frills lost their red and flattened, and I saw its claws tense on the sweeper. "Mindcrawler. They told us-sss you would arrive on the ss-shuttle."

"And so I have." Clan, here. With a shuttle, docked and presumably about to leave. I spared a moment to sigh inwardly. A reasonable chance to escape captivity, but I couldn't take it. Not until I dealt with whomever it had brought and discovered where to find the rest.

At least my task looked to be easier than I'd thought.

Tempting, to lower my shields and *search* for minds like mine, but I'd been warned against it. Besides, I'd no need, having spent time on a Scat ship. Shuttles docked with the big hatches on the cargo level. That's where I'd find the Clan.

"I need to go back to the shuttle, come to think of it," I said, as if the creature with its predator focus locked on me wasn't at all unnerving. "I forgot my gift for your captain."

The eye glistened, its slit pupil widening. Something wrong with my appearance, or smell, was making its way through that long skull.

The moment it arrived, the Scat's jaws began clattering in the laughter of its kind.

I leaned back to avoid the inevitable spittle. "Get out of my way!"

"You will—"

The corridor lighting flashed red, then white, then red. A klaxon screeched a warning that didn't need to be in Comspeak to be understood: collision alert. As the Scat Hindmost hesitated, I hit the power reverse on the sweeper and held my breath.

The creature disappeared in a cloud of filth.

Who knew my shifts as Hindmost would prove useful?

As the creature clawed at its good eye and spat, I dodged low through the cloud, still holding my breath, and ran down the corridor for the lift. The flashing light turned my steps into terrifying slow motion and at any instant I expected claws to rip into my skin. I couldn't hear pursuit over the unceasing alarm, but the Scat would be after me, if only for its own sake.

I got the lift door open and threw myself inside, closing it at once. I gasped for air, this body—my body—shaking so hard I could barely stand, somehow managing to send the lift down.

Danger!!! The howl from the Watcher—more than one—locked my muscles. Just as well, or I'd have dropped to the floor. *HARM!!*

What's wrong? As well ask a storm for sense as pry an answer from them mid-drama, but I tried. *Tell me!*

An unlikely *calm.* Suddenly, in a dire echo of the past, another howl began, one I understood all too well.

Names.

Clan had died, and it was too soon and wrong to feel anything but grief at their passing. I shuddered, closing my eyes.

It was only then it occurred to me to worry about the collision alarm.

What was happening outside the ship?

Chapter 14

ONCE OUTSIDE THE SHIP, Morgan walked along the *Wayfarer*'s hull. Where his mind insisted was down, Auord spun, a jewel on velvet black. Glints marked other ships in orbit or on approach. The distant Port Authority station was blindingly white, rings caught by the rising sun.

Their lights were off. As instructed—with a reassuring lack of questions—Captain Erin brought her ship within the large shadow of the *Worraud*. The distance between the two continued to close, albeit very slowly. Alarms would be sounding throughout the Scat ship and in the shuttle limpeted to her far side.

Morgan kept the bone between him and the Scat, taking a step at a time until he reached the spot he'd determined beforehand. He was, at this point, supposed to activate the display in his helmet to verify his position.

Where was the fun in that?

The Human bent his knees, hit the mag release, and launched himself—gently—into space. It wasn't as though he could miss the *Worraud*. The pirate filled his sky. The trick was to arrive with as little momentum as possible. He had what the *Wayfarer* provided already. With any luck, he'd added just enough to reach the other ship before it moved. A possibility reduced by the docking shuttle, but as soon as it was secure, the pirate could—likely would—take evasive action.

Especially with Terk on the coms to keep up the panic.

Unable to feel his passage, the bone blocking the forward view, Morgan counted his breaths. Ten. Fifteen. Nothing but hull in view now.

Nineteen and the bone shifted in his hands. The Assemblers were active, reacting to the nearness of their target. He could see the outermost ring of the escape hatch beyond the bone and braced himself.

Contact.

The hatch autos would respond to the touch of life. First to unlock—the bone vibrated, then pulled him forward.

Morgan found himself inside a Scat air lock.

The hatch closed itself, air immediately blasting through the floor grid. The Assemblers abandoned the bone for the grid, cilia holding tight. He stepped around them as he removed his helmet, clipping it to his belt as he headed for the inner door. It couldn't open till the pressures matched. He pulled a stunner and braced himself.

There.

The second the door unlatched, hands scampered past Morgan to squeeze through the opening, climbing over one another in their haste. By the time he stepped over the sill, the corridor beyond was empty.

Should have used glue.

He shrugged, dismissing the escaped Assemblers, and headed left at a jog. Terk hadn't been able to produce a scan of the *Worraud*, but Morgan knew his way. He'd made a point, last year, of studying Scat ship design; every edge helped when dealing with beings liable to switch from ally to predator without notice.

The chaos of the alarm and shuttle bought him moments, if that, before someone on the bridge noticed an unanticipated Human on sensors. The *Worraud* had a single cargo hold, one deck below this. The stasis box, and Rael, had to be there.

So would the shuttle, but the proximity of the *Wayfarer* should keep its doors locked tight till the all-clear.

A lift could be recalled from the bridge, so Morgan entered the first ladderway he came across. Ignoring the steps, he gripped the null-grav railing with a gloved hand and slid down.

Short of the next deck, he swung around, catching a rung with both boots. The alarm had stopped, and his lips thinned. They knew they had an intruder.

The hunt was on.

Gloves off, force blade loose in its sheath, Morgan eased to the floor. About to exit, he froze, the *taste* of change filling his inner sense. Hardly surprising, given he was sneaking around a Scat ship—

—but he hadn't *tasted* such a warning since—

Didn't matter. There was no time to figure it out and no guarantees he could.

He pushed the door open with his shoulder, hard, and jumped into the corridor beyond.

To find himself face-to-face with a stranger.

Interlude

HIS FACE MUST BE A STRANGER'S. It was impossible we'd meet again, here, like this.

Neither of us moved, even to breathe, and all at once my resistance crumbled and I believed. Jason Morgan was here. He'd appeared time and time again at the end of hope and beyond expectation, so how could I be surprised now?

But this wasn't the Morgan I remembered. This version was thin, worn from inside. His dear face was marred with lines carved by grief, and I felt my heart give a single, heavy lurch of despair. I understood. Accepting, I took a slow breath.

I wouldn't do this a second time. Couldn't. Not to him. I opened my mouth, not to reveal myself, but to hide.

And that's when Jason Morgan seized me by the throat and brought up his knife.

Chapter 15

MORGAN RAISED THE KNIFE. "You were in stasis," he heard himself say. Protesting—as if it was Rael's fault she stood there with his hand tight around her throat, watching him with eyes alive and aware.

Her mouth moved. Trying to answer; fighting for breath. Cursing his own weakness, he eased his grip. "Sira sent me," she gasped.

Morgan released her, his resolve crumbled. He put away his knife. "Why?"

"To find the Clan." Hand trembling, Rael reached up to touch the bruise blooming around her white neck, but all she said was, "The shuttle."

He gave a curt nod. "This way."

* ✳ *

It wasn't far, but they couldn't go as fast as he'd have liked. Rael kept herself on her feet with a hand on the wall. Seeing that, Morgan moved to put his arm around her waist. She flinched aside, eyes wide.

"Rael, let me help you," he urged gently, despite a deep, growing anger. She'd been badly treated, that was plain. They should head back to the *Wayfarer*, get help. "I can give you a locate—"

"No! No. I can't 'port." She pulled aside the blanket serving as clothing to show him the ugly wound on her hip. "There's more, here." A gesture to her front.

Staples held her together, the sort he'd use to attach a cover to a cargo crate. Around them, the skin was red and swollen. Every step must be agony.

He handed her the stunner. "Hold still," he ordered, unable to keep fury from his voice. Coming to her other side, Morgan placed an arm behind her shoulders and bent to put the other behind her knees. "Tell me if I hurt you." He rose, cradling her against the suit.

"It's all right," she said, whether to him or not he couldn't tell, for the words were oddly breathless.

"Good."

Careful not to jostle her, Morgan strode down the corridor to the next junction. There, he put his back to the wall and eased his head around for a look.

An Assembler hand scampered past.

He felt Rael start. "It's okay, they came with me."

"Really?" she murmured. "I thought it was one of mine."

Something to sort later, the Human decided.

Granted they made it that far.

Interlude

I'D MADE IT THIS FAR, I told myself. As nightmares went, I couldn't complain. In Morgan's arms—though the spacesuit was every bit as unyielding and uncomfortable as I remembered—not dead, yet—though technically I was and Rael wasn't, and the part where Morgan had been about to kill me—her—required explanation—but if I turned my head, so, and gave the tiniest sniff?

The scent of him filled me.

Plus, we were about to reach the shuttle, and the Clan I had to find. It didn't take much to guess Morgan had come for them, or why. "Yihtor," I whispered.

A nod. "He told me to find you. I thought to—doesn't matter."

To end Rael's misery. My heart ached again, this time for my dear Human, faced with such terrible duty. We'd brought him nothing better. "Is he still alive?"

"Yes. Shh."

I tightened my shields, but Morgan didn't offer mindspeech. He was moving again, slipping around the corner as though I weighed nothing. I readied the stunner, glad of a weapon.

Only to find I didn't need it.

Morgan set me on my feet in the open door to the cargo hold, holding out his hand for the stunner, then used the weapon to gesture sharply to the shuttle's air lock. "Go."

I edged my way along the wall, it being the route free of corpses.

Three had been Scats, their bodies lying where they'd crumpled, snouts aimed at the floor. A different body was nearby, this one crisped and still smoking above the waist. I covered my mouth and nose, aghast to see Morgan squat beside it to check pockets. But he'd known battlefields, my Human, and what was this, if not another?

A fifth dead, facedown in front of the air lock. Luck beads were braided into her lanky brown hair, and she wore spacer coveralls with Auord's Port Authority logo on the shoulders. The pilot. I stopped because I could go no further, staring down.

Morgan reached by me to key the inner air lock, then helped me step over the body and move through into the shuttle. After that, he became a blur, sealing doors, taking the pilot's seat, hands flying over the controls. "Do you know how to strap in?" he checked, over a shoulder.

Of course, I . . . it was Rael he doubted. "Yes," I replied. Choosing the bench as the least painful option, I sank down on my good hip. I secured the straps as best I could without crossing any staples; now the action had paused, each seemed intent on reminding me I was vulnerable flesh.

"Final warning. Breaking dock," Morgan announced, not to me, but to the coms. The air filled with outraged sibilants and hisses. "I wouldn't, if I were you," my Human said next, cold and sure. "Port Authority's on their way, and you've quite the mess in your cargo hold." A pause, more hissing, then, "Us? Didn't see a thing. Shuttle out."

He slammed a fist to close the connection.

"What didn't we see?" I asked quietly, unwilling to ask: Was it you? though I'd watched Morgan kill a Scat with his mind before. Not, surely, the shuttle pilot.

Having set our course, Morgan spun the chair around to regard me, his expression grim. "Two Clan—a female and a male—rode up on this shuttle with a stasis box. They'd reason to believe it contained Yihtor di Caraat's mindless body. The Clansman's dead, back there, courtesy of the Scats. The other?"

The Scats had killed two, but I felt no urge to correct his count.

The names the Watchers howled, greeting the Stolen returned, had been of a Chosen pair. As for the Clanswoman? I'd seen no box, but I'd heard the Watchers' protest. "She 'ported himself and the box safely away." A 'port tearing another wound in the M'hir. This had to stop. "Where did she go?"

"Good question. Any idea what set them at each other?"

"The captain woke R—me from stasis against orders. He feared the Clan. I think he wanted me as a hostage. It wouldn't have worked. My kind," I grimaced, "don't understand negotiation." Or other species, but that was old news. "By the time the Clan arrived, I wasn't where he'd left me."

The corner of his lips quirked in that half smile I knew. "Bravely done."

I gestured gratitude, stopped as something *hurt*. My breath caught.

Morgan's expression changed, and he left his seat, coming to kneel beside me. To my chagrin, he undid the straps I'd managed to fasten. "Can you lie down?"

Rather than waste breath answering, I toppled sideways, feeling warm hands lift my legs onto the bench. "That's better." He lengthened the straps, placing one around my shoulders, the other at my thighs, then found something soft to put under my head. "Rest, Rael," Morgan ordered. "There's a medbay on the *Wayfarer*—the ship I hired. We'll be there soon."

Light as a feather, familiar as love itself, fingertips brushed my forehead, taking with them the worst of the pain. His gift, freely given.

It was all I could do not to weep.

Aside: The Goth

THE CASUAL VISITOR to the portcities of Iktia, the Goth homeworld, would encounter a typical theta-class humanoid species, with safe-for-most food choices and technology blandly similar to any Human inner system. The Goth were famed for a refined love of the ridiculous extending from abstract art to Goth politics, said to have the most entertaining parliamentary system in the Trade Pact. No one was sure if their sense of humor was a quirk of Goth biology, or a defensive response to the gloom of perpetual cloud cover over the planet's fertile landmasses.

But what lived in those clouds had nothing to do with humor.

Clear of starship lanes, thousands of platforms floated out of sight, each containing a small number of residents. Monitors, they were called, living as far from the world below as possible. The surrounding press of cloud granted a mystique to the work that helped new arrivals cope with its wearing blend of dread and boredom.

That it discouraged premature departures without exhaustive interviews and psych evals was a bonus, the monitors' task too important to diminish with failures. Those below could go about their business, secure in the knowledge that should any Hunters *escape* the Black, they'd feast on those above first and hopefully be satisfied.

Goth compassion being of a practical nature, most monitors were those about to die soon anyway.

It hadn't always been this way. Once, all Goth had embraced the Black, drawing it close when ready for sleep, to dream in harmony; inviting it near those about to die, that they enter a realm of peace.

Then Hunters had come through, and Goth learned these bitter truths: that the Black wasn't peaceful—

That it wasn't theirs alone—

And in it, they were prey.

Goth fled, *pulling* themselves as free of the Black as their nature allowed, making themselves *smaller* there. Hiding, in sight.

Though all missed the dreams, and those who couldn't bear their loss applied to be monitors, to expose themselves to the Black. To dream and die in the clouds. And yes, Hunters found them. And yes, Hunters took one here, and one there, but overall, the population below felt protected and safe.

Until the moment every monitor over the northern pole went silent.

Two reports were sent automatically: an alarm to those below, for what good it might do.

And one to the Consortium.

Chapter 16

"I TOLD YOU it was a terrible plan." Terk paced as though the entire ship were too small to hold his frustration, stopping only to point a thick finger to where Morgan sat by the med cocoon. "But I was wrong. You came up with a worse one."

"I couldn't let her die."

"That was the idea! What are you going to do now? Kill her after supper? Maybe after a good night's sleep, because we all know it's so much easier to murder a friend who's looking you in the eyes."

Morgan waved a listless hand. "Peace, will you? I was wrong. Rael and Yihtor are here for a reason—"

"And you know what that is because she told you, and you believe every word." Terk threw up his hands. "Do you hear yourself? You were about to kill her. She'd say anything. I should do it," flat and dark, taking a stride toward the cocoon.

He stopped in his tracks when Morgan rose to his feet, hands loose and at his sides. "Like that, is it?" the enforcer said in a different, too-quiet voice.

"Sira sent her." There. He'd said it. "I know how it sounds—"

Terk hissed between his teeth. "I'll tell you how it sounds. Like you're not yourself. And if I'm to guess why? It's the reason a surgeon cut into my head. The one that makes Finelle a good, safe partner because no telepath can touch the weirdness in a Lemmick's head. You've been *influenced,* Morgan. She got to you."

His shields had been proof against the most powerful of the Clan. Now Terk doubted? Morgan fought back bitter laughter. The other was serious—deadly serious—and for Rael's sake he couldn't let this go. "Terk—"

The enforcer held up his hand. "You convinced me. Convinced the chief the presence of Clan in the Trade Pact endangers the rest of us. That they belong in some heaven of their own, and sending them back is the right thing for them as well. Has any of that changed?"

"No. Will you let me finish?"

Terk crossed his big arms.

"Finally." Morgan sat back down, glancing at the readouts. The cocoon had enveloped Rael the moment he'd laid her on the diagnostic table. Modern equipment, the best a trader could afford. Erin planned a future on the *Wayfarer.*

He'd put that at risk, returning with—with whatever Rael was now. No help for it. "The deal between the Scats and Clan was falling apart before we showed up. I retrieved Rael—" because she'd stood there, covered in her own dried blood, and faced him with a courage he'd seen in only one other person. "—because she isn't the enemy. We can't trust Yihtor or anything he says. I can't. I do trust Rael. Sira's sister, Terk. My sister. A known ally. If I'm being influenced by anything, you great lummox, it's common sense."

"Huh." The enforcer possessed a full vocabulary of monosyllables. That "huh" reserved the right to knock that sense into Morgan's head.

He tried not to look relieved. "Agreed."

With another "huh," Terk grabbed a stool and sat, legs outstretched. He lifted a sandaled foot and wiggled his orange toes. "Gonna miss these," he complained, the change of subject deliberate.

A peace offering, of sorts. Morgan smiled to himself. "You don't have to change."

"Nah, I do. Finelle's a stickler for regs." The foot dropped.

"Besides, she's bringing back my uniform. If I don't put it on, you watch, she'll stun me and do it." With grudging admiration.

Deserved, Morgan thought. The wily Lemmick had appointed herself to deal with Auord's pricklish Port Authority. Giving her credentials, she'd summarily dismissed any suggestions the *Wayfarer* or her personnel were involved in the deplorable events on the *Worraud,* other, of course, than being ideally situated to recover the drifting, empty shuttle.

Which she offered not only to return, but to bring in person, willing to assist—personally—with their investigation. Although theirs was patently a local matter, she'd an interest: specifically, an anonymous tip that Assembler criminals wanted by the Trade Pact Enforcers could be hiding on the Scat ship.

Faced with the horrifying prospect of a Lemmick in their shuttle, let alone sharing confined space with one, Port Authority acted swiftly, politely declining both offers. In the spirit of cross-jurisdictional cooperation, they would watch for the Assemblers. As for the shuttle? Please keep it for her personal use while in Auord orbit. It was the least they could do.

Unsaid, they'd vent it to vacuum when she was done.

After scolding Morgan for letting most of her prisoners escape, despite such clever arrangements for their recapture, Finelle had loaded the crate with the rest of the Assemblers into the shuttle and gone to the *Conciliator.*

Morgan suspected she'd wanted to take Rael as well, but the unconscious Clanswoman had been in the midst of having the staples removed by servos, her wounds properly sealed with medplas before the cocoon did its work.

Or had Finelle, willing to use her species' reputation to sway the local Jellies, surmised something of his?

Morgan gave himself a shake. They expected Finelle back shortly. Rael? Could wake within a few hours or need more. He should have a plan, he thought wryly. If only to give Terk something else to mutter about.

Noska came into the medbay. "Captain Erin's compliments, Gentle Homs. She'd like to remind you staying in orbit wasn't our agreement. Port Authority will charge a fee."

"Add it to the tab," he told the Whirtle, who crooned happily to itself and left.

Terk's eyes narrowed. "What's up your sleeve now?"

Morgan rested his hand on the cocoon's blank gray top.

"I wish I knew," he admitted.

Interlude

Snosbor IV

"THE OTHER BOX?"

"The Scats opened it. We'd no chance to find the—the contents, First Chosen."

The arm of her chair was fine wood. Wys stroked the carved whorls of it with a finger, focusing on the sensation instead of her fury. It wouldn't do to kill the messenger.

However satisfying.

Merin di Lorimar stood very still, shields down; her fear palpable but under control. She'd accept any punishment. A believer, this one, who'd made a difficult decision to salvage what, yes, mattered most.

"Go." The finger lifted and the Clanswoman bowed, disappearing from her sight.

At last. Wys rose, going to a chest against the tapestried wall. She removed a package wrapped in soft tissue and took it to the wide table by the window.

The Retian knew not to start without her.

She opened the tissue, tossing it aside to drift to the carpet, then spread out what it had protected. Clothing, the latest fashion from the inner system worlds, the finest materials. Human-made, to her order. She knew her son. His size. These would suit his fair coloring.

Not that he'd know. *FURY!* Wys indulged herself in it for a moment. Two. Dismissed it. What mattered was the potential in her son. Dressing him like this would showcase that potential for the others, remind them why Yihtor di Caraat was their future.

There should have been two to dress, two to reveal. Her gnarled hands clenched on silk. She'd have the hide of that Scat for a seat cover.

Wys released the silk, stroked it. Her people would find Rael di Sarc again.

Hadn't they already located a second consort for their king? The more, Wys smiled, the better.

"Exalted! Exalted!" The Retian ran in the door, chased by one of her personal servitors. His mask hung around his neck, spewing fog.

Waving the Omacron away, Wys regarded the alien benevolently. "I applaud your enthusiasm, Talobar, but I'll come to your lab when I'm ready."

"You can't!" The creature was shouting—at her? Wisely, he mollified his tone. "Don't come. It's a disaster."

"What?" She felt her face tighten. "You weren't to open the stasis box without me."

His eyes blinked, one at a time. "I couldn't help it," he confessed. "The readout made no sense. I feared something might be wrong. Something was, Highest High. Terribly wrong."

Belatedly, she noticed the blood on his hands, dripping on the carpet. "My son—"

"His body wasn't in the box, a Brexk was. A large, angry female. My lab's a ruin!"

Steeling herself, Wys sat down. "Make sense, fool. You're telling me Merin brought the wrong box?"

"No, it was the right box. I tested—there were traces. Your son's body was inside. Alive. Someone replaced it—him with a Brexk." The Retian held up his bloody hands. "That's dead."

"Well, then," she said calmly.

Talobar's ugly eyes stared at her. "But it isn't well, is it?"

"Clean yourself. Repair the lab and keep it ready. Oh," the Clanswoman smiled, "have the kitchen collect the meat. I do enjoy a nice steak."

The poor thing was beyond confused. " 'Steak?' "

"See to it."

The Retian turned and ran from the room.

"No one touches my son," Wys murmured, her voice almost peaceful, stroking a shirt embroidered with stars.

No more dealing with aliens.

No more wasting time.

She sent an urgent *summons*.

While all around, the M'hir *burned* with her hate.

* ✳ *

Plexis

"I do not hear you. You are not-real."

Tayno sighed. As quietly as he could, he tightened every joint. His guest didn't like the noises he made.

She didn't like, he thought woefully, very much at all, though he'd had a promising report from the kitchen. "Would you like more prawlies?"

Her eyes flickered.

"I'll get some," he said, heading for the door with some haste.

"Wait."

Holding another sigh, the Carasian stopped and heaved himself around.

"I—" She licked thin lips. "You've been an—improvement— over those who took me. I will make an exception for you, not-real, and hear your words."

Tayno maintained his cautious crouch, a recent habit in her presence. Once she'd regained her strength, she'd taken to throwing things. At him. Oh, the sleepteach had worked. She could speak and understand Comspeak.

Just not comprehend where she was. How she'd arrived. Any part of it.

She'd been angry ever since.

"Hello," he ventured, as if they'd just met. It seemed safer. "My name is Tayno Boormataa'kk." Instinct warned there was no pretending to be Huido here, not with her. "I'm glad you're feeling better."

" 'Better.' " She appeared to contemplate the idea. "Than when I arrived here, yes, but not—not better." A long pause.

Her fingers played with their rings, and he'd a startling thought. Was she afraid? Of him? Surely not, but Tayno gentled his voice. "What can I do to help?"

Her eyes lifted. "Can you find my people? For I am alone, as I've never been, as no Om'ray should be. The world—this—it has no shape to me without them. Nothing makes sense."

Tayno gave a doleful little *ring* with an upper claw. "Things here don't always make sense to me either," he confessed. "I find it best to stick to what I know."

"Wise advice."

It was?

"What I know, Tayno Boormataa'kk? My name. Tarerea Vyna. My world is, was Cersi. I watched it die from our Cloisters. Was being carried up to safety with my kin until—" Her face darkened. "Until the rumn shaped themselves as the Living Dark. Until they came and stole us away. For time without measure we were imprisoned together, unable to move, hearing only the wails of the dead. Then we began to die."

Tayno's eyes tried to hide.

"As Keeper, I called upon Vyna Cloisters to save us and something did happen. Its shape changed. I believed we would escape." Tarerea's hands cupped air and made a tossing motion. Dropped to her sides. "It may be the others did. I have to hope so. The Living Dark were angered. I thought they'd kill me, but instead, they rid themselves of me. Left me here. That, Tayno, is the sum of what I know."

Huido'd told him worth was measured by what someone gave of themselves. By that, Tarerea was very worthy. Hers was a terrible, marvelous story, like the ones he'd read late at night, and wasn't this Vyna like those heroic characters who suffered to save others? Nothing so grand, the young Carasian thought enviously, ever happened to him.

Though wasn't he, just a little, part of her story now? He found he no longer felt like slinking. "They are the Rugherans. What you called the 'Living Dark.'"

She took a step back. "Your allies?"

"No!" His claws raised defensively and Tarerea flinched. He lowered them in haste, tips to the floor, so she wouldn't be afraid. "Rugherans are—they have a tangy grist, it's true," he explained, "and that's—interesting—to be around. In small amounts," quickly, in case she thought he was the sort of person who was influenced by his senses. Which he was, Tayno admitted deep in his hearts, having rather enjoyed the grist of the Rugheran in the kitchen, but he did know better. "Yours is nicer," he concluded. Especially since she'd started talking about the rest of her kind. He wasn't sure why that would be, but it was.

"I don't understand your words." With returning frustration.

"I can explain—my uncle is," not that much larger, Tayno reminded himself, "very good at talking to aliens. He says we— Carasians, like me—sense the truth of others beyond this." He tapped the floor with a clawtip. "Grist comes from what the Clan call the M'hir, but that's just a name they made up."

Tarerea came close, moving around him, touching his shell. His eyestalks followed her, making him dizzy. "I've heard that name before," she told him, to his relief coming back to stand in front. "We call it the Great Dark."

"We call it—" focusing, Tayno produced a long, low rumble, then hunched in embarrassment. "Forgive me. It's rude to use words others aren't equipped to hear properly." Among the many lessons Huido tried to knock into his shell.

"I am not offended. Sit with me. Can you—sit?"

He collapsed to the floor with a noisy clatter.

Her lips stretched. "I see you can." Tarerea sat in the stiff chair they'd found for her room. She hadn't cared for the easi-rest. "Tell me more, please. About the Great Dark and those who touch it. About the—Rugherans."

How could she be so calm? If inexplicable aliens had stolen

people he cared about, he'd be—well, he'd be in a closet, hoping not to be next.

Though a tiny part of him hoped he'd do better than that. Here was a being with the courage he lacked. An example of how to do better.

He began to grasp why Huido valued his friendship with the Human, Morgan.

"I will tell you what I was taught when I came from the Mother Sea," the Carasian said with a rush of pride. "There are those who are only here and cannot be *there*. There are those partly *there*, but mostly here, and those mostly *there* and barely here at all. Then there are those—" his voice lowered and eyestalks bent to look over his shoulders, though they were alone. He hoped. "—those who are only *there* and should not be here. Not at all."

She swallowed, but nodded. "I've seen—what shouldn't be seen. There were *things* in the Dark. They tore Fikryya Vyna apart."

Tayno dared reach out a claw. After a moment's hesitation, she touched her fingers to it. It made him feel brave.

Braver. He wished never to see what hunted *there*. "The Tide pulls on every being, *there*—here—*there* again. The froth of their lives washes over us as grist." It sounded as perplexing now as when his instructors first spouted it, but that's what happened when males ventured too close to the territory of females. "You're female, aren't you," he deduced. "You understand such things."

"I understand these Rugherans trespass wherever they go."

"Not everywhere," he corrected. "They have a homeworld. It's called White. S—" Tayno stopped himself. If Tarerea disliked hearing "Morgan," a cautious being would avoid "Sira" at all costs. Added to that, he wasn't entirely sure he was supposed to know about their time there. It was never easy to tell if others forgot he was there and said things they wouldn't if they remembered, or if he was part of conversations that quickly soared past his understanding. He settled for a neutral, "I've friends who—"

She'd leaped to her feet. "My people will be there. Take me at once!"

"I'm sorry. I can't," Tayno cringed. "I don't have a starship." Or a budget, for that matter, so tickets were out of the question. Could one even get tickets to White? "I wouldn't know how."

"Your mind is a scramble," with some disgust. "Is there anyone who can give me the locate? I can go myself. If it isn't too far." She sank back down, hands resting on the arms of the chair. "How would I know?" as if to herself. "They could be waiting."

He couldn't help but shudder. At the thought of "they" and her question, for Tayno was well aware what a "locate" was: how the Clan chose a destination for their travel through the M'hir. He'd overheard Huido worrying such travel might affect his performance in the pool.

Making it something to avoid at all costs.

Though, as it happened, he did know someone who could give Tarerea Vyna the locate for White. Someone who'd been there. Was still here, as Sira wasn't.

Jason Morgan.

Chapter 17

BEFORE MORGAN COULD SETTLE on a course of action—or a course, for that matter—Constable Two-Lily Finelle rejoined the *Wayfarer*, in a hurry, via one of the *Conciliator*'s launches.

Bringing Yihtor di Caraat with her.

Terk, at a low boil since they'd received the news, launched to his feet when the pair entered the medbay. "What's he doing here?"

"It was here, Partner Russ-Ell," Finelle said calmly as she steered the grav sled with its med cocoon, "or see him leave with the *Conciliator*."

Her partner swore creatively, ending with, "—that twisty Ordnex dumped us."

Morgan helped guide the opaque cocoon into place beside Rael's, wordlessly making the connections. The ship's med unit took over; a display activated, showing the Clansman's condition. Unconscious, but the readout looked normal. Better than he'd expected.

"That is the case. Captain Lucic professed itself 'uncomfortable' with the chief's last order, to bring a civilian on its ship to be in charge of an undisclosed Clan situation. It refused to grant us access to this listed criminal. My return without most of my prisoners did not strengthen my argument on your behalf, Captain Morgan. Not that I blame you."

"Sure she does," Terk said.

Her regard shifted. "Partner Russ-Ell signed for the Assemblers' transfer from the cryobrig. The captain noticed. You are, I quote, 'asreliableasalways.'"

"I answer to the chief." Grimly.

As would the "uncomfortable" captain of Bowman's cruiser, once she returned to take charge. "Doesn't matter. We need Yihtor with us," Morgan declared.

If only so he could send him home with Rael. Easier, now; med cocoons had a mercy function.

"I assumed so," Finelle replied serenely. "Which is why I put Partner Russ-Ell's name on his release, too."

* ✱ *

Terk changed into his uniform, then came back, taking a stool to park his bulk at the door, blaster unholstered and across his lap.

"I'll be on the bridge," Morgan told him. He'd set the med units to sound a warning when either of the sleeping pair were ready to awake. It wouldn't be soon enough. "Call me."

A grunt. The enforcer wouldn't be happy until he had a chance to use that blaster.

The Human went on his way. Terk was well aware their guests were helpless and the servos could be trusted. That wasn't the point. The enforcer knew the Clan. He didn't stand guard over Yihtor; he watched for those who might arrive to claim him. Unlikely, that any would have a locate for the medbay of the *Wayfarer.* In that, they'd done better than planned.

But a heart-search? That did pose a threat, should any be able to *reach* this far.

A stronger possibility was what might lurk in the ship. The former yacht had no internal sensors and ample space for Assemblers or any other stowaways. Not a concern when they were making a quick trip to orbit and back; now, they'd take no chances.

Morgan rubbed gritty eyes. When had he last slept? Running

on nerves; that was the truth, and he'd need to rest soon. Not yet, he told himself as he rode the lift to the command deck. He marshaled his thoughts. Captain Erin had shown remarkable patience through the past hours, keeping off the coms. He owed her for that as much as her ship.

A ship he needed again.

Finelle had returned with more than Yihtor—she'd obtained the *Worraud*'s scheduled ports: Kuraly, Wingels 20A-Orbital Station, Snosbor IV, then on to Plexis. While Scats weren't known for respecting their posted list, the *Worraud* played the honest trader, right to nicnics in her hold. If she'd left Auord without incident, a good bet they'd have stuck to that course, making one of those four stops?

The Clan.

The *Conciliator* was listed as en route to Plexis, implying Captain Lucic had reached the same conclusion. Did the captain hope to find the Facilitator for Bowman? Lucic had, according to Finelle, confiscated the shuttle as evidence. Auord Port Authority had filed a strident protest.

They could get in line. Terk was halfway convinced the Ordnex officer wasn't after Manouya, but working with him. Admittedly, the enforcer's default in every situation was to suspect those around him, but he could be right this time. If so, Morgan decided, Bowman could deal with Lucic, and would.

Plexis was a waste of time. Since hearing the list, he'd known where the Clan must be: Snosbor IV.

The port he and Sira had been going when everything tipped sideways, starting with Bowman. The first blow against the Clan had been a ploy to discredit her, their greatest ally; she'd run rather than be jailed. When he and Sira diverted the *Fox* to try and help, a missed shipment had been the last thing on their minds.

The shipment, he'd learned later, had been a ruse. Someone had tried to lure them to that planet, someone capable of *influencing* Ruti di Bowart to divert the *Fox* back to Snosbor IV when they didn't come on their own. Morgan hadn't forgotten—he'd merely tucked the puzzle away, assuming it no longer mattered.

Until now. He expected Rael and Yihtor to confirm his belief.

The Acranam exiles were on Snosbor IV. Wys di Caraat. All of those who'd wanted Sira from the beginning.

They'd hated him then. They'd hate him now.

He'd need Rael and Yihtor on his side, recovered, before that confrontation, but they'd time to heal on the way.

If—a big if—the *Wayfarer* had it in her.

* * *

When Morgan stepped out on the bridge, he raised an appreciative eyebrow. Gone was the racing configuration. The floor was now level, lines marking where the funnel ribs had locked into place. The consoles for on- and incoming crew were connected into practical working clusters, with the captain's chair and console between.

The window had been sliced in half. It didn't make the view of the world spinning below any less breathtaking.

Noska sat its station at the console to the left, running coms. Captain Erin swung around to look at Morgan, a finger along her jaw and a question in her eyes.

Before she could ask it, the Whirtle spoke up. "Enforcer Finelle reports she is secure. All's safe. Am I to be sure of this? Are we? Can we?"

"Yes, Noska. Relax." Erin grinned at Morgan. "The enforcer's quarters have a one-way flow. Finelle's idea," she added, in case he took offense. "She wanted a break from her suit."

"Suit!? I'm to trust a balloon?" the Whirtle muttered to itself, tentacles fussing at the boards. "Could rip. Could tear. A pinhole! Then what?"

Erin ignored it. She waved Morgan to a seat. "We're ready to descend. I'll request a med transport for your guests once we go."

"That won't be necessary." He sat, resisting the impulse to relax into its comfort. "They're doing fine as they are, thank you. I'd like to extend our arrangement."

"Stay in orbit?" She made a face. "Don't take this the wrong way, Morgan, but much as I enjoy your credits, I've better things to do with my ship."

"Is the *Wayfarer* translight-capable?"

Erin's mouth fell open. Closing it, she stared at him, hard, then swallowed. "You're serious. To go where, exactly?"

"Can she fly," he countered, "or not? Simple question."

Instead of a glib answer, the *Wayfarer*'s captain—and engineer— turned back to her console, calling up information she hadn't expected to need. Morgan waited, trying not to close his eyes.

Hoping.

"You look about to fall over."

He opened his eyes to find Erin standing nearby. "The ship?"

She leaned a hip on the nearest console. "We'll need to take on supplies, if you're all coming." At his nod, she gestured to the Whirtle. "Start the math." Back to Morgan. "We can get those and top up the tanks at Auord Orbital. It'll cost."

He shrugged. "The engines?"

Erin bared her teeth. "Now that's where it gets interesting. *Wayfarer*'s good to go, my guarantee, but we'll have to install that pretty new sequencer while in subspace. Unless there's time to hit a dock and do it first? Thought not," at his look. "Makes it a mite risky."

" 'Risky?' " Noska echoed worriedly. "Why?"

"Because without one," Morgan answered without turning around, "we don't leave subspace. Ever."

The Whirtle hiccuped.

"Yeah, that'd be why. On my own, I wouldn't do it." Erin's gaze was frank and open. "But I've seen your skills, Morgan. Daresay we could swap out in the bridge, too, for that matter. Terk for Noska. You for me, if you're willing. I don't usually have a sub."

"Captain knows I am not a very good pilot," Noska explained, eyes blinking. "I don't like to fly. I don't ever want to crash." With emphasis. "Ever."

Morgan liked them. Well enough to wish he could give an-other answer and not pull these two into dangers they couldn't imagine and didn't deserve.

Without them, he'd fail and so might the Trade Pact.

"Agreed."

Her face lit. "Hear that, Noska? We're leaving this hole of a system!" She stood straight. "What's our course?"

"Take us to Plexis Supermarket, Captain Erin."

Her eyes went round; that was all. She gave a short nod and went back to work. The Whirtle, having no dignity to protect, bounced up and down, crooning and hugging itself.

The pair would be anything but happy when he changed that course, his first shift as pilot, but for now, to get them motivated? A course to Plexis would definitely do.

Interlude

I'D NO COURSE, being adrift and dreaming.

I'd no pain, no fear. A respite, this moment, my first since— Ever?

Memory stirred, but I wasn't ready—

Sister, see this.

I wasn't ready.

See what we do. How we wound. Why we harm.

Like the opening of an inner eye, this growing awareness. Peevishly, I tried to deny it, but Rael wasn't alone.

LOOK! cried the Watchers, in their harsh mad voices.

So I must obey.

At first, the M'hir appeared as it always did. Dark. Unstable, where living minds *touched* it; dangerous, where their passions *roiled* it into storm. Never a place to linger.

LOOK! LOOK!

I glimpsed ribbons of light through the black and knew them. Passages, where Clan had traveled, following the bond etched between mothers and their distant children. Spotted a faint network, like a web strung with dewdrops, and knew that as well. Connections, for Clan had existed here, as well, their minds woven through the Dark.

Still did, for some of those lines were brighter.

Teeth *flashed,* and vanished into the depths. I wasn't their prey, not at the moment, merely of *interest.*

What do you expect me to see? I asked, wishing to be left alone. Adrift. Dreaming.

SEE!

A howl, that echo, able to freeze blood had I any.

I waited, unimpressed.

There, sister. As if Rael took my head and aimed it—had I a head or eyes—I found myself looking into the utter black. A pale *streak* burned across my view, then vanished.

Behind it, the Dark of the M'hir *stiffened.*

I watched it *crack.*

And through that *crack* I saw—

Stars.

* * *

Between was failing!

I opened my eyes to find myself back in NothingReal, in a box.

Before either—or both—or all—could cause me to panic, the top of the box split open and moved aside. Staring down at me was a Whirtle in a helmet. A Human-sized helmet. A helmet that stayed put because the Whirtle had stuffed the opening around its slender neck with socks. Colorful socks.

Some had stripes.

It was impossible to panic, even about the end of the universes, faced with a Whirtle in a helmet held on by striped socks, so I did the only thing I could. I smiled and said, "Hello."

"Hello." Its voice was muffled but clear. Tentacles appeared in my view, slipping with care behind my shoulders. "Would you like to sit, Fem?"

"Please." The tentacles were stronger than they appeared, though I found it odd to see them spring from sleeves meant for arms like mine.

I was in what had been a med cocoon, now quickly turning itself back into a cot topped with a comfortable mattress. My cleaned skin was free of staples and glue, both replaced by medplas matched to the healthy flesh around it. The only area still red and sore was my left hip, though I discovered, as the Whirtle helped me, I could move it without an added twinge.

Clean felt wonderful. Everything did, leading me to suspect the med unit had administered a stim along with whatever else it detected this body required.

The Whirtle hugged itself, a sign of happiness as I recalled, then one tentacle freed itself to point at my chest. "Orchids."

I looked down. Rael had flowers tattooed around her nipples. My nipples. While the effect was artistic, I felt myself blush for no reason. "Is there clothing for me?"

"Yes," another voice. "I took the liberty, Fem di Sarc."

The name was as much a shock as seeing, while not smelling, the Lemmick standing at the end of the cot, though it did explain the helmet on the Whirtle. Rael was di Sarc as well, I reminded myself. "Thank you. Constable," I added, for she wore an enforcer's uniform. And was covered in what looked suspiciously like a balloon. "I could be dreaming," I announced, the truth being important.

"I can assure you, you are not. My name is Two-Lily Finelle. I'm partnered with Russ-Ell Terk, who is also on board. You know Captain Morgan."

And I'd orchids on my now-enthused nipples.

If there was a hint of desperation in my reach for the clothes in her arms, I'd excellent reason. Rael was exquisite, with or without tattoos, and the last thing I wanted in this life or any other—

—was to watch Morgan respond to her beauty.

Petty, I scolded myself. Worse. Ridiculous. To be jealous of my own body, borrowed or not; one I'd inhabit no longer than it took to find the remaining Stolen and guide them back to All-Therels.

None of it stopped me pulling on the clothes as quickly as possible.

To my relief, they were blue spacer coveralls, used but mended and clean. They almost fit, for a bonus. I rolled up the too-long sleeves and pressed the fastener in place.

"If you wish," Finelle said, holding out a small square mirror and comb.

I hesitated, then took them in my hands. I raised the mirror.

Chosen, Rael's hair had been a waist-long mass of gleaming black, full of life and opinion, if more mannerly than mine. Mine? Red-gold and a thorough nuisance. I'd left its memory behind with Morgan, remembering the shoulder-length wisps I'd had before my Commencement.

Better that than dwell on how my hair would wrap warm around his neck and arm, and fall like water over his bare skin.

Rael's hair had been butchered for some reason while she was in stasis. I'd seen the remnants in her projection: a coarse stubble, stiff and motionless.

I looked into the mirror.

Green eyes looked back, not gray, though our shared lineage showed itself in their width and shape. The eyes should have sparkled with youth, not be aged by pain and grief, but in that much, the mirror showed me.

The hair—Rael had misremembered. What I saw wasn't cropped short. It'd be ear-length if clumps hadn't stuck out in all directions like so many bent feathers and, instead of black, it was dark brown, verging on red at the tip.

I reached up to touch the strange stuff, forgetting the comb in my hand until it struck my forehead. "Ow."

Morgan appeared in the doorway. "You were to call me when she woke!" he said angrily.

"I assumed you'd want to finish your time in the fresher," the Lemmick replied, unflustered. "I see I was incorrect."

She had a point, given the Human was shirtless, with drying foam in his hair and sliding from his shoulders.

Bones showed, as though he'd starved for weeks. Ribs and arms. At the base of his neck, around the soft hollow filled with his pulse I'd—

I stopped there to focus on the face in the mirror, attempting to use the comb. Not something I'd done lately and, as if to complicate matters, my hands wanted to shake—

—wanted to hold Morgan. Care for him. Take away the pain. Then double it, I warned myself, cruel but true.

"My apologies, Finelle," he said with better grace. "I'd set an alarm on my com as well. I thought something was wrong. Noska, you're here."

"I am in charge of the medbay. Why would I not be here?"

Because of the Lemmick? Out the corner of my eye, I saw how Noska kept a firm hold on its helmet. Brave, that. "I appreciated your care, Noska," I said warmly, giving up on the hair to gesture gratitude with mirror and comb. "It was a relief to wake to a friendly face."

A dusky color rose up Morgan's throat. Before he could apologize to me as well, there being that business with the hand at my throat and—oh, yes—the knife? I found a smile. "And a relief to be rescued from the Scat. My thanks." Putting aside the bothersome grooming tools, I added respect to my thanks. "I'm sure you have questions. I'll do my best to answer them all." I looked up.

And found myself trapped.

Jason Morgan had remarkable blue eyes. They darkened at the stir of his Talent or, as now, with emotion he couldn't hide. The times I'd fallen into their depths were the happiest of my life, and I couldn't break their hold now.

He glanced away first, going to a still-closed cocoon. "Yihtor's doing well. He should wake soon. Shall we wait for him?"

No. I wanted this done, to stop struggling against myself.

The better part of me remembered my Human's subtle ways. To ask Rael such a question, in front of the constable and Whirtle? It wasn't about waiting at all, but his way of asking the urgency of the threat we faced. Without alarming one or both. Without revealing why I'd come.

Between had *cracked* because someone had 'ported where it had become brittle. Someone? The Clanswoman on the *Worraud*, fleeing the conflict with her prize.

I'd watched the *crack* seal itself again. We had time.

"Yes," I answered, putting *confidence* under the word though Morgan's shields were like smoothed stone. After all, if that time started to run out, I could count on the Watchers deafening me with howls of despair.

"While we wait, I could use some boots." I lifted a bare foot and wiggled my toes, unintentionally flexing the delicate vine tattooed around the ankle. No sign he'd noticed, but I put the foot back down. "And is there a chance of something to eat that doesn't come from a tube?"

A smile transformed his gaunt face, disappearing as quickly as it came.

Still, I thought stubbornly, he'd smiled. Maybe if I were here long enough, I could ease his life in some other way. Help him move beyond me.

The pain of that thought cost me a breath. Fortunately, Noska chose that moment to bustle close, a tentacle securing its helmet. "Fems. Hom. The *Wayfarer* took on supplies at Auord Orbital and her galley is well equipped once more. There are choice selections, I promise. The captain knew to leave the ordering to me." Its mouth continued to move, but I couldn't hear a word. Was it whispering? In a helmet? Seeing my blank expression, the Whirtle raised its voice to a near shout. "If I left it to her, we'd eat those disgusting e-rations all day!"

I slid my gaze to Morgan, and decided I wanted to meet the *Wayfarer*'s captain.

* ✳ *

Captain Usuki Erin was on the bridge. We'd meet later, I was assured. First, Morgan wanted to talk to me, alone.

The prospect made me unaccountably shy.

Terk was off-shift and presumably resting. Knowing the Human as I did, I thought it more likely he was stalking through this unusual ship or sampling the galley, but that room proved empty when we arrived.

Finelle stayed with Yihtor, to Noska's relief. The Whirtle accompanied Morgan and me to the *Wayfarer*'s galley, closing the door behind itself, then struggled to free itself of the helmet.

Taking pity, we helped pull out socks until the being could extricate its head.

Three eyes blinked in a face beaded with yellow sweat. "My thanks."

"You don't need to wear this around the constable," Morgan told it. "Her shield works."

"For you." Its nostrils flared so wide, I could see the textured folds within. "Human chemoreception lags a thousandfold below a Whirtle with a sinoidal infection. Underwater. An old infected Whirtle underwater." Noska gave its analogy a moment's thought, embellishing it with a decisive, "Wearing noseplugs."

"Granted," Morgan said, somehow keeping a straight face in the presence of such outraged dignity. I hid my smile with a hand. "But for the sake of Whirtles of all kinds," he continued, "should you not embrace this opportunity?"

"What 'opportunity' do you mean?" The load of suspicion in the Whirtle's tone implied it had dealt with conniving Humans before.

"To be the one to prove—or disprove—this new technology. If you, with your excellent senses, test Finelle's new shield—"

"She's a LEMMICK!" The nostrils slammed shut. "DEMMICK!"

Sternly. "Be careful how you speak of the constable, Noska. Constable Finelle is a passenger on the *Wayfarer*. As a member of her crew, your duty is to your ship and her passengers."

Morgan had been able to bend my brain around species' prejudice, too. Most of the time. I could almost see the anguished thoughts tumbling through Noska's head, but when its nostrils finally eased open, all it said was, "As crew, I should be on the bridge. Please enjoy the galley, Hom Morgan. Fem di Sarc."

The Whirtle humped away, a mode faster than walking.

Chagrined, Morgan ran a hand through his hair. "That didn't go well."

"You tried," I reassured him. "Who knows? Noska could come around. Some do. Some don't."

"So long as we get the trade, Witchling," he finished automatically, the saying one we'd used, often.

The endearment one I'd never thought to hear again.

Morgan's face lost all expression. "Your pardon, Rael. That was—inappropriate."

I'd sounded like myself. How could he not react?

"How so?" I asked softly. "It's what you called my sister. Never apologize for remembering her. You were partners as well as Chosen. Now, let's find something to eat. We both need it."

He dropped into a chair rather than sat. "I'm not sure I can. I'd—" The uncertain pause wasn't the Morgan I knew. He turned the bracelet—a legacy of so much—on his wrist. "I'd wondered—do you—did she—" Words failed him. He stared up at me, hope burning in his eyes.

Careful, I told myself. To buy time, I went to the ever-present pot of sombay and poured two cups. "How do you take it?" I asked before turning, pleased my voice was steady.

"Straight, please."

I brought the cups to the table, pressing his into unresisting hands, and took the seat across from him. "Jason, I won't mislead you. I'm not here to deliver a message from Sira. There's nothing she could say to ease your grief or hers."

"Then—she lives." His dear face transformed with joy, tears spilling down his cheeks. "She lives," a whisper.

Was that what I did?

Steadying myself, I took a sip, unable to taste what I'd remembered. "Sira—" use the name, no matter that it coursed through his body like a visible shock, "—sent us back to ensure you keep living. She helps us keep our memories of here, as well as All-ThereIs." Not a lie, I thought, and covered my lapses. "She's not the only one. Yihtor and I are supported by others of our kind."

"Hands." Curiosity sparked in his eyes. He didn't bother wiping the tears. "I felt them, when I entered Yihtor's mind."

How had he— Morgan had the courage, I reminded myself, and perception. Not least in Power, my Human. Far from it. I had to warn him to avoid the M'hir—not to 'port—but first, "They held us while we waited Between, in the M'hir. We couldn't enter these Vessels," I put a hand to my chest, "until they were freed from stasis."

"As I woke Yihtor," my Human said with a nod. "He sent me to find you. He knew you'd need help."

Yihtor expected me to provide it, once in the Trade Pact. "What else did he tell you?" I asked, uneasy.

"His exact words? 'Find Rael. Find her.' Then he passed out." Morgan raised his cup, drank. His eyes puzzled at me over the rim.

Flustered, I rose again, setting the kitchen servo for the first thing I remembered. Some kind of bland stew, sure to disappoint Noska, but I was consumed with my own puzzle. How could the two of us be sitting to supper? It seemed more incredible than my being in my sister's body.

"How did you find me? Find us."

As we ate, Morgan explained. About Bowman's hunt. The dear little Drapsk and how they'd complicated matters. The surprise of finding any Clan had survived. "Yihtor will know who they are," he said ominously.

"Acranam's exiles. Sira's aware," I replied, when he raised an eyebrow. "But we don't know where they are."

"Snosbor IV." He came close to smiling at my surprise. "That's my guess," he qualified.

Where the *Fox* had been heading, on our final voyage as honest traders. I managed not to nod in agreement. "Something Yihtor can confirm. When he wakes."

His face turned grim. "I hope so." He eased back, deliberately lightening his expression and tone. "Till then, Rael, we get to rest."

I didn't want rest. I wanted to drink in the sight of him, his voice, this place. To learn everything that had happened while we were apart. To him—to others. "What of Huido?" I asked, trying not to be as anxious as I felt. "We'd left him in that terrible place. There was the explosion."

Morgan grinned. "On his way to Plexis to reopen the *Claws & Jaws*."

I stared at the stew, blinking hard.

"He was waiting for me. On Ettler's."

I looked up. The grin had been replaced by something tight and pained, telling me the rest. Huido had seen Morgan through other dark places. None like this. Without thinking, I reached across the table and laid my hand on his. "I'm glad he was there."

Our eyes locked. This time I looked away first, pulling back. I put my foolish hand below the table, curling the fingers.

"I'm glad Huido's going where he belongs," Morgan said more briskly. "Tayno does his best, but he'll molt on the spot when he sees what's coming."

He told me about the Yabok bones he'd had to buy in order to get this ship out of debt, and I laughed more than once. Despite everything being dire and fraught, in these precious, stolen moments something was healing in us both. Not enough, I thought, never enough.

But so much more than either of us could have dreamed.

When Morgan finished, I wiped my eyes. "Tell me about this ship," I urged. "The *Wayfarer*."

My Human did just that, with a very familiar enthusiasm for detail, stopping only to pour us more sombay and find something sweet to nibble.

I committed every word, every inflection, to treasure in memory.

In case this was the last time we sat like this, and talked.

Chapter 18

HOW LONG, since he'd sat like this, relaxed like this, and
talked about nothing at all. Not that the *Wayfarer* wasn't remarkable, Morgan thought with a twinge, but she wasn't his ship.

Rael wasn't Sira.

Yet—

There was a familiar grace to her, an ease within Rael's company he hadn't felt in too long, and if the Clanswoman was merely
being kind, encouraging him to eloquence about new coils and
retrofit fins, would her eyes sparkle with such interest? To his
surprise, Rael had questions, ones showing she'd some knowledge of starships.

Sira's knowledge. He'd faltered on realizing that; covered
what might have been an awkward pause with a search after Noska's promised treats. Pleased her with the result, which pleased
him, too.

After that, it was easier. It helped to look at her very different
face, so he did, anxious to avoid a repeat of that embarrassing
"Witchling." Her wild scruff of hair was another good distraction,
except for what it implied: like Yihtor's, Rael's body had been
used—

"What's wrong?"

He gestured apology. "Nothing."

Rael had a generous mouth. It rose to one side, a dimple appearing in her cheek. "You were staring at me," she countered, "then all at once you—" Her long fingers fluttered in the air. "—weren't here. Where did you go?"

The truth with her, he thought suddenly. As with Sira. Nothing less.

"It struck me, what had been done to you. Before. After." His grip had left purple blotches on her slender throat, fading with treatment, but still visible. He tried to lighten the moment. "Then there's your hair."

"This?" Rael reached up to give the stuff a tug and grimaced. "I look like a Vyna Chooser. I've never heard of a Chosen being shaved. I can't imagine our hair putting up with it." She drew a lock down over a green eye and squinted. "Oh, dear. I think it's growing."

"Is that bad?"

"Not if it behaves." She released the lock and batted it with a finger, going cross-eyed to watch the result. "I don't need complications," as if to herself.

The com panel came to life. "Hom Morgan, this is Hindmost Noska with the captain's compliments. The *Wayfarer* is prepped for her journey and ready. The other passengers have been notified."

Morgan rose to his feet. "Tell the captain I'm on my way to the engine room."

"She thanks you. The internal alarm will sound. Noska, out."

"We're getting underway?" Rael had stood, too. "To Snosbor IV?"

"Plexis."

Oh, the question in the arch of that eyebrow.

Perceptive. He had to smile. "We'll talk about our course later. I need to get you somewhere secure."

Her safety mattered. In that instant, Morgan realized he couldn't think of Rael as though she'd borrowed her body as she had the coveralls from ship's stores. Not anymore. To him, she was back, someone he cared about, a person he'd fight to keep alive at all costs.

How Human of him, he thought with some irony, well aware the feeling, instinct, whatever it was? Was going to be a problem.

Later. "This way." With a bow, he indicated the door. "Thanks to Noska, you've your choice of quarters."

Rael's face developed an unexpectedly familiar expression: Sira's, when she suspected him of concealing a risk to spare her worry. Sure enough: "Why do I think the *Wayfarer* hasn't gone subspace in a while?"

Fairly caught, Morgan answered with the truth. "First time with this rebuild," he said smoothly. "We're on something of a test flight."

Her brow furrowed, and her eyes flashed with displeasure. "And you talked her into this, didn't you? Risking a trader's ship and livelihood—not to mention lives."

"It's not as bad as that," he replied, startled to find himself so quickly on the defensive. The sisters were more alike than he'd remembered. "The ship's ready. Captain Erin knows I'm here if there's any problem."

"To repair the engines." Rael looked relieved. "Of course."

His turn to frown. "Well, and swap out as pilot. What else did you think—" Morgan took an involuntary step toward her, lowering his voice. "Sira told you. What I did with the *Fox*." He shouldn't feel betrayed.

How could he not? She'd left the dangerous memory intact in his mind, believing he had the will and strength to keep it secret. To never use it. "I thought she trusted me."

Rael closed the distance between them, her eyes searching his face. "Sira does," earnestly. "As do I, Jason." Her hand reached for his, hesitated, curled to a light fist, and dropped to her side. "This isn't about your will. It's your Talent. You mustn't use it. For the ship—for anything. Not now. It's too dangerous."

Explaining the powerful Clanswoman's strange reluctance to 'port them from the Scat ship—why she hadn't escaped on her own. His mind raced. Was this about the entities from AllThereIs? Could they detect those entering the M'hir? Was that the real reason the Acranam exiles had avoided using their Power until desperate?

The last thing they needed was a new threat, the Human

thought grimly. Didn't mean one hadn't just landed in his lap. "Why?" he dared ask.

Her gaze was bleak.

"The M'hir is breaking."

* * *

With impeccable timing, the strap-in alarm sounded, ending his chance to learn more. Morgan swept Rael into the first empty quarters, delaying to be sure she knew how to use the cot's auto-safety and com link. Again, her expertise with such systems took him aback. He'd have to get used to it; Sira had prepared her sister well, even filling in history she'd missed. How else would Rael, who'd died in the Trade Pact, know of Vyna's Choosers, with their bizarre shaved heads?

How else . . .

Morgan shook his head. For all he knew, in AllThereIs, everyone shared memories; hardly the most comfortable thought, that.

He jogged to the lift—no need to check on the enforcers or Yihtor—and hit the button for the eleventh deck. The *Wayfarer*'s lights had changed their warm daylight hue to the warning glare of imminent departure from normal space. In the final five seconds, they'd flash red.

If you hadn't reached safety by then, that meant grab hold and good luck.

Once at the engine room, Morgan closed and latched the two main doors, sealing the air lock and isolating the compartment from the rest of the ship. He walked past the spacesuit hanging on the wall and took his post at the engineering console, shrugging the straps over his shoulders. "Engine room to bridge. Ready here."

Captain Erin answered. "Don't break my ship if you don't have to, Morgan."

"Understood, Captain. Morgan out."

He keyed in the code she'd given him to open the left armrest, exposing its contents. Without hesitation, the Human wrapped his fingers around the fail-safe stick. Erin would do the same on the bridge. He hadn't lied to Rael, simply omitted a detail. He wasn't here, now, to make repairs.

Starships flouted the speed of light by traveling in subspace, where the laws of physics could be cooperatively bent. Ships had one chance to burst from the fabric of normal space intact: their engines must initiate a solid bubble of subspace to receive them. If that initiation failed to occur, the autos shut down the engines, saving the ship.

If the initiation was flawed so the bubble couldn't be held, the autos ejected the engine compartment, saving the ship.

For this "test flight," they were betting the *Wayfarer* could complete initiation and get them into subspace. That, inside the bubble, he and Erin could complete working on her engines before they needed to exit. That they'd all live to celebrate.

Making it necessary to disable the autos, designed to stop any such gamble.

Putting Morgan where he could watch the readouts live. Hear the engines. Smell, as it were, trouble. If he did, or if Erin saw something amiss developing on her boards, the first person to clench their hand would blow this compartment and himself into space, saving them all from a horrible death.

Not that anyone had ever reported on the process of dying in a collapsed subspace bubble, but horrible likely covered it.

He'd tumble helplessly until Auord Port Authority showed up to tow the ship and her errant parts to dock. The fines would be beyond Bowman's Voucher. The *Wayfarer* would be, to all extents and purposes, scrap.

Not his ship, but definitely his problem. Sira would have—

Lights began to flash, their red in time with his heartbeat.

The engines' hum took on a throaty roar of power.

Morgan's every sense tuned to the ship. He was the ship, for a glorious instant, and *felt* her engines as the machine took hold of the fabric of space—

—and punched through.

They'd done it. The *Wayfarer* had done it, leaving Auord behind, sailing the stars as she'd been built to do.

"You beauty!" he praised, releasing the stick to throw up his arms. Next stop, according to their posted course? Plexis.

Which it wouldn't be. They'd go to the exiles' world and remove the Clan from this universe. It would be over.

And Rael would be gone.

Morgan lowered his arms to press them over the hard knot in his stomach. "You fool," he acknowledged, his voice less than a whisper.

Interlude

Plexis

TO MANY, Plexis security was a joke.

Mathis Dewley wasn't laughing. Most of him. The left foot was amused, but that had more to do with the pink shoe it insisted was suitable despite the brown boot on the right. There was never accounting for taste.

If all of him could have fragmented inconspicuously to scatter in the station's depths, he/they would have, but Choiola had given him specific instructions.

The first being to locate Gryba, who'd traveled here in one piece, meant walking around on two legs, pretending to be a one-mind. For that, even an Assembler needed an airtag on Plexis. Hence shuffling along in this achingly slow line—he'd picked the shortest, as always, but the sensible strategy had yet to pay off—to have one of the things slapped on his cheek.

The second being to awaken the surprises waiting throughout Plexis, foremost the one in the *Claws & Jaws*.

To be free to follow those instructions, he mustn't attract attention, especially any from the disturbingly large and robust clot of security guards around the exit to the station proper. Dewley tried to see what they were doing or if they'd a particular interest, but the Oduyae in front of him were a group of sorts, clinging to one another in the face of so much strangeness.

He'd show them strange.

No, he wouldn't. Dewley bumped the annoying elbow bit against the counter.

The Oduyae grunted and wheezed their way forward, a process complicated by each of them pulling a small three-wheeled box by a string, said strings tangling around their tails as well as one another. Really, this was the joke, and he mimicked the laughter of the Humans around him when the largest Oduya tripped, falling into the rest.

Laughter quickly turned to shouts of alarm as several of the carts overturned and were crushed, releasing their buzzing contents into the air.

Fools. Even he knew Oduyae traveled with their pollinators, Dewley thought with disgust, moving around the mess. The buzzing swarm was intent on reaching Oduyae armpits, the Oduyae equally intent not to be pollinated in front of strangers, thank you, while everyone not biologically engaged exerted themselves to get out of the way.

The Assembler spotted an arm waving a tagging hammer and changed direction. An Ordnex had opened a new line. "Overherepleasegentlebeings.Hereplease!"

Security thundered past as Dewley stepped up for his turn, nets in more than a few hands or equivalents. "DoyouacceptresponsibilityfortheairyoushareonPlexis?" the noseless creature droned.

More shouts. Dewley resisted the shoulders' urge to turn around and watch. "Yes, yes."

Multijointed fingers made quick work of tapping the waxy patch to the skin of Dewley's head. The rest of its parts snickered but held their grip so the Assembler could walk briskly through the exit.

Unchallenged.

But as Dewley stepped on the moving ramp to the station's interior, a slim figure left a shadow to follow.

✳ ✱ ✳

Plexis Supermarket, as befitted a shopping and entertainment destination of such magnitude, had hundreds of lodgings for those inclined to linger—or unable to recall their parking space. The quality improved spinward, which was why this meeting place was in the opposite direction, the *Best Slumber Inn* being popular with patrons of some standards, yet stingy with their credits.

Dewley spotted Sept Gryba in the octagonal lobby, coiled near the free sombay dispenser, a matched pair of fancy carryalls at sept's feet. He hurried over. "I'm here."

"Were you followed?"

"Were you, Waste Of Time?"

This time the elderly Omacron did not curl away. "Mind your manners, Split. I'm your better."

Wasn't true, but Dewley couldn't help but be impressed by the other's uncharacteristically firm voice. That, and sept's clothes. Gryba, far from attempting to avoid attention, had elected to wear a brilliant red flowing cloak over a glittering flexible tabard proclaiming sept to be the *Galactic Mysterioso*.

"We're late. Come along," Gryba ordered, adding a brusque, "You're my servant. Bring the bags. And be careful!"

Dewley, about to grab the matched set of luggage, set his hands around the grips with care. The left, anyway. The right wavered before reluctantly taking hold.

"Wait. Take these." Gryba began tucking slips of shiny plas into every pocket of Dewley's jacket.

The Assembler twisted and hissed. "What these? What!?"

"Free passes to my show. Hand one to any gold tag we pass. Only gold, mind you."

One-minds went mad, Dewley reminded himself. "Why?"

"To make us invisible. No more questions. This part of the plan is my doing, mine to achieve. If you get in my way, I've this." The cloak twitched aside to show the hilt of a needler.

Nasty Omacron, Dewley thought with an inner shiver. Nasty needler, doubtless set to spray and catch all its bits. Good partner for the First.

Good partner for success.

Not that sept was overly observant. The Assembler lifted the bags. "Not enough hands."

Gryba went another color, then sighed. "I'll carry one."

The right hand moved first, releasing its burden.

＊ ✳ ＊

Invisible they were, Dewley discovered. It was a trick, but a wonderful one. He'd only to wave a pass at anyone who looked their way and they'd flinch aside. Hardly promising for the Omacron's show, but since there wouldn't be one?

The Assembler began to enjoy himself.

"They've put the sign up," Dewley noted with a sense of the rightness of things. Using the reconstruction crew as cover had entailed a distressing amount of actual work, but he'd gained the access necessary to set Choiola's trap. What a treat to have the crew finish before they destroyed the *Claws & Jaws* once and for all.

Others were at the restaurant's entrance, their attention on the door and the being blocking their entry, not the sign. Typical grandies, thinking posted dates didn't apply to them.

With surprising strength for sept's age, the *Galactic Mysterioso* pushed Dewley into the nearest mass of plants and slithered in after him, bag tight to a curl of abdomen.

The Assembler kept together, barely. What appeared lush and groomed from the outside wasn't in here. Rotting vegetation squished underfoot, dead sticks poked at him, and everywhere, little red eyes appeared.

Then disappeared.

"The restaurant isn't allowing beings to enter."

Dewley subvocalized his opinion of his companion. The rest of him offered their own versions, each guaranteed to get them needler-sprayed had they been heard. However satisfying, this didn't get him out of the rot. "The opening is in eight days," the Assembler whispered.

"I know that, you revolting bag of bits. The Brill's cook was to offer the *Galactic Mysterioso* an advance tour of her kitchen. A tour we can't take while there's a commotion at the door. They could have already called security. Is there another way in?"

Considering what the left hand gripped, the Assembler was reassured the Omacron had had a plan. Of sorts. "Follow me."

It being impossible to exit the planter without being noticed, or smelled—the rot clinging to their footwear—Dewley jumped out waving a handful of show passes. Those around obligingly looked away.

His turn to lead. His turn to be important.

A slim figure lingered a moment near a teashop window. Then followed.

※ ✳ ※

The Assembler instructed the *Galactic Mysterioso* to leave sept's cloak and tabard behind a waste canister, to be retrieved on their way out.

"Why?" sept demanded, shivering and naked. Sept's exposed flesh was an unappealing beige, part scaled, part squishy skin. A weak thing. Stupid waste of time.

With a needler tucked in a belt. Trying not to stare at that, Dewley explained. "Eyes watch us. Everywhere on Plexis. Less here," grudgingly, but those garish colors would catch the attention of the most jaded ocular watching the screens. "Leave what we don't need."

Gryba folded over one case, doing something to open then close it. Sept straightened, a small metal orb in one hand, then pretended to drop it.

The right foot tried to run. The left held firm, but a wrist let go, heading for an exit.

"It can't hurt you, fool," Gryba told him with scorn. Holding up the orb, sept regarded it with pleasure, by the flare of yellow green under sept's skin. Or lust.

All the same to the Assembler. "Not a game," Dewley hissed, retrieving the wrist.

"Oh, but it is. The best of games. That's why our leader's coming for the show."

Dewley pulled out a pass, regarding it dubiously. "This?"

"No, fool. *The* show. The moment we reveal ourselves and our glorious purpose. She wouldn't miss it."

Oh, he would, if he could. Quiet was better. Sneaky was best. Traits he'd admired in Omacron, but this sept wasn't normal. Or, scary thought, Gryba was normal, and all of sept's kind were playing their own game.

Games. Shows. He did not approve. His approval wasn't required, of course, but Dewley glared at the Omacron. "This does waste time."

"True. Lead the way."

The pair entered the tunnel. Servos rumbled by in both directions, messengers zoomed overhead, and the Omacron cried out when a servofreighter brushed by, too close.

Horrified, the Assembler dared grab the other and give sept a shake. "No. Nothing loud," he scolded in a strained whisper. "In here, the machines block us from vids, their noises cover our steps. Not shouts."

"Don't touch me," as the Omacron jerked septself free. "Mindless mechanicals." But the words were properly quiet.

His importance restored, for now, the Assembler picked a servo towing a tall stack of crates, then showed his companion how to walk close behind it. They'd entered not far from the belly of the *Claws & Jaws*. Soon—

Gryba was gone.

The Assembler looked around frantically, then left the cover of the servo and rushed to the side, pressing himself against the curved wall. There was the usual ledge for waste canisters and waiting deliveries behind.

Gryba was there. At least sept was hiding behind a canister. But why? This was, Dewley thought anxiously, not the *Claws & Jaws*, but the nearby Turrned Missionary. Turrneds were to be avoided. They had weird eyes and would, if allowed close, pat his parts with their soft hands as if they could tell exactly who he was made of—a shoulder argued about the food, and that was the only plus—

The Omacron waved.

Reluctantly, Dewley eased his way to sept's curled side. Before he could chastise the other for failing—again—to follow his lead, a hand raised, a digit pointing.

Someone else, coming down the tunnel.

Gryba had been followed, Dewley thought. Which wasn't a good thing, he realized, his triumph at the other's failings turning to dismay. What were they to do?

Hum?

For that's what the Omacron was doing. *Humming.* A quiet little sound that nonetheless *itched* along Dewley's many parts and wasn't, he decided, a nice hum at all.

Though too far to hear over the machine noise, the figure slowed, shaking their head as if pained.

More *humming.*

The figure moved to their side of the tunnel, leaned against the wall. Dewley could see her now. Human. Common size and shape. Her clothes proclaimed her as one of Plexis' customer-assistants. The stunner now out in her hand, wavering as she tried to aim it at them, suggested otherwise.

More *humming.* Annoying, that *itch,* but Dewley didn't dare complain, didn't dare move, for the Omacron was doing something.

The stunner fell. She slid down the wall, helpless.

Only then did Gryba move, sept's walk more like a dance, torso curling from side to side, sept's eyes wide open to expose that ominous black ring.

Humming.

The Assembler followed at a distance, not because he wanted anything to do with this, but he had to know, didn't he, what was happening.

What an Omacron could do.

When Dewley reached the Human, he saw blood streaming from her eyes, ears, nose, and mouth, which wasn't so bad—

Until the brain followed, oozing out like melted jelly.

The *humming* stopped. The Assembler gasped with relief, the *itch* ended. "What did you do to her?"

"Nothing I didn't enjoy." At Gryba's chuckle, Dewley came

close to fragmenting in terror. Then, "Search the body, but don't remove anything. I want to know who tries to spy on us."

Empty pockets. Her com must be an implant. Dewley glanced at the ruined head. Not touching that. His hands resumed running themselves over the body, quickly finding what was pinned to the inside of the short, brain-soaked jacket. "Plexis security," the Assembler announced, showing the badge.

"Bah. Following you, no doubt. Your face is known."

Dewley, hearing his doom in that, cowered by the corpse. "I belong to the group," he protested. "I will stay hidden. You need me." And hoped the Omacron remembered who was guiding sept to their targets as he saw red eyes under the nearest canister, vermin lined up for the feast.

"You could be a useful distraction, should I require one."

"I could," Dewley agreed glumly.

"Come. I want to be done and out of here."

They made their way to the *Claws & Jaws* without further incident. The Assembler hurried past the service corridor to the restaurant, though the right foot was tempted to run inside and seek help.

But it was too late for that. Dewley stopped where an innocuous bulge in the tunnel wall made a shadow. Without waiting for orders, he pried off the piece he'd cut while working, exposing ordinary plumbing.

And something else: a new connection, with a plain pump and valve, leading to an upright funnel with a lid. Nothing unusual, nothing to trigger sensors or alarms. The Assembler removed the lid, his fingers clumsy with a growing excitement. After all, this would be the start of their success.

"Move aside." Gryba cracked sept's metal orb like an egg, pouring its contents into the funnel, waiting while Dewley replaced the lid.

"That's it?" the Assembler asked, rather disappointed and having forgotten, for now, his dread of the Omacron. Explosions, now. He preferred explosions.

"Appearance deceives. What is here will spread, one to another to the rest. There will be no escaping it."

"And the Humans? You need my help." That being their next task, Dewley wanted to be sure. Needed, urgently, reassurance his group was ascending, or his bits would scatter for good and then where would he be? A head, in a tunnel? "We need success!"

The Omacron must have understood for sept paused to consider him, then said carefully, "The First has promised. Yours will be the only such shape in the Trade Pact. To you will belong what now is Human. But we've work to do, much work, before Choiola arrives."

"Yes. Yes!" They would seed each of the surprises he'd placed throughout Plexis. He'd placed many many surprises, hidden in all the places, including many only bits could reach. His bits! First, the *Claws & Jaws*.

Then, the show. Dewley grasped the reference now. Their surprises would open all at once and release what the Omacron had brought into the "airweshare."

The show would start when the one-minds began to fall.

"Why not all?" the Assembler asked with new eagerness as they made their way back along the tunnel, this time clinging to the back of a wide servocarrier.

"What we would do requires testing." The Omacron's skin flushed yellow green as they passed the corpse. Red-eyed vermin paused to stare.

The Poison Makers. Those who knew the Omacron—what they were—called them that. They were rumored to test their concoctions on themselves, their own worlds. Poison and guile were their weapons of choice, though they themselves were deadly. He'd seen it, Dewley had, and knew himself fortunate above all other Assemblers to grab hold and belong to sept's group.

"Plexis is past due for catastrophe," Gryba whispered cheerfully. "Whatever they suspect, they will believe this one is natural. We will have severed the head of the Consortium—who knows, they may be blamed for what comes next! The First will continue unopposed. The Trade Pact will end in agony."

The Assembler could hardly stay together for joy.

Chapter 19

A STREAK OF GREASE across her forehead, engine parts strewn about her where she sat cross-legged on the floor, Captain Usuki Erin radiated delight. "I've been wanting to do this since getting the ship," she confessed.

"Take the engine apart in subspace?" Morgan chuckled. He measured the remaining width of an ignitor tip, then tossed it in the bin with the other rejects. "Can't say it was one of my ambitions."

"You know what I mean." Her fingers didn't stop their busy, efficient motions. Dismantle and clean, determine what remained in good order, was the starting point. They'd leave undisturbed what kept them in subspace, moving translight, until the time came to exit the bubble.

"Hand me that." Once he'd passed her the tool, she applied it to the next assembly. "Thel refused to let me do a thorough stripdown." A grin flashed. "Something about putting a hole in her precious shipcity if I made a mistake."

"There's that." Though he didn't see a mistake being likely. As he'd suspected from the start, Erin proved equal to any ship's engineer he'd worked with—and superior to most—making Morgan curious. "You know you could write your own ticket, doing this."

"Could, yeah." An offhand shrug. "Turns out I don't get along with know-nothing captains." She shot him a glance. "You're different."

Morgan smiled. "High praise."

She laughed, stretching for another part. "Don't let it go to your head. Haven't seen you take the controls yet. Could be," she teased, "you're a lousy pilot."

"Could be," he agreed equably, getting back to work.

* * *

The rest of that day they took breaks in turn, Morgan insisting. Noska and Terk traded off on the bridge, not that there was anything to do but watch coms, Finelle keeping watch in the medbay. Rael slept.

Best estimate on the refit, no surprises? A standard day and a half. Make that two. There were always surprises. Toward the end, they'd be catching naps in the engine room.

Two and a half days to Plexis.

Double that to Snosbor IV.

The *Wayfarer*'s aged autopilot could accept trip tapes with a predetermined course had it not been, in her captain's words, gunked up. Chiseling out the now-hard remains of what had been Noska's breakfast hadn't been high on her list, finsdown on Auord.

Lacking tapes, you entered a destination. The ship's navsystem would compute the most direct route available, accessing the latest star charts to avoid close proximity to posted hazards such as, but not limited to: novas, comets, space stations, intersystem blockades, and reported piracy.

Morgan picked up the sheet of plas with the coordinates for Snosbor IV, doing the math. If he made the switch now, assuming Erin didn't notice the *Wayfarer* heading in a direction negative to the one she'd input—a safe bet, given her preoccupation with the engine?

By the time they were supposed to exit subspace, they'd be two and half days from Snosbor IV; four and half from Plexis.

Plexis, where there was always outbound cargo to be had, if you knew where to go. He'd dangled it, bait to Erin's ambition to be a trader at last, knowing she'd bite.

Faced with being nowhere close to a destination, they'd have to keep going. Closer was safer, with this old ship and her cobbled-together engine. Despite Snosbor IV having nothing worthwhile to fill the *Wayfarer*'s holds, surely Erin would agree to continue on—

He wouldn't. Morgan leaned back with a frustrated sigh, staring up at the ceiling of his quarters. Like him, she'd think of her ship first—no, second. The urge to space him would come first, but he read Erin as getting past temper. As thinking.

Of her ship first. The future.

Not part of his mindset. His lips twisted. Ahead lay darkness. Unless the Clan on board could send the rest of their kind home without, as Rael warned, using the M'hir, it'd be up to him. To become an executioner—a murderer—defending those who didn't know against what they couldn't believe.

Then, watch the life fade from Yihtor's eyes. That, he thought coldly, he could do.

But from Rael's?

Morgan slammed his feet down and stood. The plas he tucked decisively in a pocket.

His future and theirs might be set.

The *Wayfarer* and her crew deserved a choice.

* ✳ *

"Hasn't budged," Terk said, jerking a big thumb toward the med cocoon.

Morgan scanned the panel. Many of the readings were outside his rough-and-ready medical expertise; a sufficiency were not. "He's improved. It won't be long."

"You changed our course yet?" Terk grinned at whatever showed on his face. "We fixed the coms. No more listening."

"To us, you mean," Morgan said dryly. "Tell me you don't have ears in the captain's quarters."

"Me? Spy on our good captain?" The enforcer spread his big arms. "I'm wounded."

"Huh," he replied. Easier to talk Huido into a sandpit than Terk out of surveillance. "We're still heading for Plexis. I've the new coordinates." He patted his pocket.

"And?"

"I need to be sure."

A scowl. "Now you've doubts? After dragging us into subspace in this decrepit scow?"

He ignored the slur. "When Yihtor wakes, he can confirm it one way or the other. Don't you think we owe the captain that before sending her ship off her legally posted course?"

Terk's face attempted astonishment; the result was a pained collision of angles that eased into a smirk. "I win. Bet Finelle you'd be smitten."

Unable to believe his ears, Morgan stared blankly. "Pardon?"

"You heard me." Smug, that. "Smitten. Attracted. Our Captain Erin not only owns a ship as much a pile of fun dregs as your old one, she's got your kind of attitude. And don't tell me you haven't noticed that smile."

Someone had, apparently. "I'm attempting to do the right thing here," Morgan said pointedly.

"What's wrong about an attraction?"

"I can wake him." Morgan, relieved at the interruption, turned to see Rael in the doorway. "If you wish," she added, walking into the room.

Her movements were easier, and her high cheekbones glowed a healthy pink. As for her hair, it was noticeably longer, though had yet to stop its defiance of gravity. As a result, she looked like a ruffled Brassard chick. The childhood memory surprised Morgan.

No, the ruffling was real. She'd overheard them and was disturbed. "The situation—" he began, stopping at her gesture.

"Is clear to me." Rael walked to the cocoon and rested her fingers lightly atop its hardened surface. "If the Clan are on Snosbor IV, the sooner we get there, the sooner we'll be done. The sooner," with stress, "heart-kin are together." Her eyes found Morgan's. "You want to ask the captain. What if she refuses?"

His "We get a ship at Plexis," overlapped Terk's gruff "Not an option." The two glared at one another.

"I see." Rael closed her eyes.

The instant Morgan sensed Power *flowing,* he tightened his shields, dividing his outward attention between the Clanswoman and the medpanel.

Rael's eyes opened.

Interlude

I OPENED MY EYES and stepped back. "He stirs." An unnecessary announcement, as the med unit chortled and beeped to itself, the top of the cocoon folding aside to the accompaniment of flashes on the display panel beyond, but I felt on edge.

In this skin, in this place.

Touching Yihtor's mind, that most of all. He'd been close to waking on his own, my *nudge* all he'd required to reach consciousness. I withdrew at once.

The tension between Morgan and Terk was an odd thing to find a comfort, but I'd witnessed it before. My Human could handle the other's bluster. The two respected one another's strengths and, usually, had similar goals, though I'd realized long ago what Terk never would.

Morgan was more dangerous.

It showed now, I thought, watching him prepare for Yihtor. I saw what others couldn't: how his eyes gained their watchful focus, how his body aligned itself, deceptively relaxed but ready to act. Inwardly, he'd prepare, too. I dared extend my *awareness,* finding *nothing* where Morgan's thoughts should be.

If I probed deeper, I'd rediscover the shape of his shields, those he'd had and those I'd taught him. Their shape matched—

had matched—mine, Chosen enclosed within each other's protections, not excluded.

I'd severed our Joining. Was no longer Chooser or Chosen or—alive, I reminded myself.

Not so Yihtor di Caraat. He sat up on what was now a cot, his bare chest rising and falling with breath, his gray-green eyes open and aware.

Eyes that found and dismissed the Humans, locking on me. *Rael di Sarc. What's happened to you?* With all his old arrogance. *Why am I here? Why is* he? Morgan. With too-familiar malice. With *intent*—

"Something's wrong," I warned, leaping forward to stop whatever he planned.

Morgan was faster, hitting a control on the panel. A fine mist enveloped Yihtor's head and with his next breath, he fell back, unconscious again.

I took hold of his limp hand, a hand I'd never wanted to touch, and *reached*.

. . . *finding Yihtor, alone.* His shields, down at first, were reforming. Behind them, I found what I'd feared: the unChosen Clansman of the past, filled with ugly ambition and worse, the urge to hurt Morgan, to make him pay for taking *her* away.

Me. Yihtor no longer remembered I was here, knew nothing of AllThereIs or our mission. Was exactly who and what he'd been before Council erased his mind. Had being back in his physical mind broken his link to the others or—

/anxiety/~StopGo~/urgency/

A Rugheran?!

Or more than one. If I *opened* to the M'hir, I'd see them, their sinuous bodies traced by light—

"Rael!"

—summoned, I opened my eyes and there, most improbably, was the Rugheran: in the medbay, crowding a very pale Terk against the wall. Morgan stood in front of the mass of gooey black, hands out in a valiant, if useless gesture to keep the thing back from me. Tentacles, long and fibrous, clung to the floor and ceiling as if gripping the ship was important. It spoke again.

/ *identity*/~*help!*~/*urgency*/

Next, a wave of sorrow and longing filled me, a wave I'd felt before, in the amphitheater on Drapskii when the dear confusing Drapsk had presented me with a covered lump of dying *something*, and I'd sent it swimming off into the M'hir.

"It's all right," I told Morgan, easing around his tense form. I hadn't thought of Rugherans as individuals, but I knew this being. I'd saved it—or at least thought I had at the time. "Hello. Again."

Morgan was staring at me now, not our visitor, but I'd no time to worry about that.

/ *identity*/~*help!*~/*urgency*/

"I got that," I said. It knew me as well. Wonderful. "What help do you need?" I asked warily. If more interplanetary sex, now wasn't the moment. If ever.

/*anxiety*/~*StopGo!*~/*urgency*/

"Stop what? Who?" Morgan. Our eyes met. "It's shown up before," he told me, quick and low. "Wanting Sira."

My poor Human, beset by my leftovers. "I suppose I'll have to do," I said as calmly as possible. "Answer us. Explain."

/ *anxiety*/~*BADGO!*~/*urgency*/~*STOPGO!*~/*DREAD*/

I winced at the force behind the message; Morgan doing the same. "Who?" I demanded. "Stop who?"

Then, chilling me to Rael's bones, an answer:

/ *DREAD*/~*US*~/*DREAD*/

The Rugheran vanished, as though scaring itself. Terk landed on the floor, bouncing up with a curse and a weapon in both fists.

Morgan looked to me. "What's happening?"

I hugged myself, not that it helped. "I don't know. I'll ask. Keep him—" a nod at Yihtor, "—out."

Going to an empty cot, I lay down and *invited* the Watchers.

＊✳＊

Taisal answered.

<<*Between suffers.*>>

Harsh, that voice. Distant, yet not. We'd a connection on this side of Between as well as the other. Family. *Yihtor's link has been lost.*

<<Hunters came.>>

I knew *what* the Watcher meant. There was an abundance of M'hir-life; none of it, in my experience, was friendly or comprehensible. Some were predators, and I'd felt their *teeth* in what was me, in that Dark. If the Rugheran's arrival had somehow aroused them, there was nothing to be done about it. I'd greater worries.

Or did I? *Were Singers harmed?* Been consumed, trying to hold Yihtor? Could that happen to me? Would I forget, too, and the Trade Pact be lost?

<<Some were startled and let go. We protected them.>> A pause, then, disquietingly: *<<this time.>>*

Time wasn't an ally—I knew that as well as any Watcher. It was my turn to be harsh. *I need Yihtor to remember.*

<<Do you?>>

She posed a potential strategy, Taisal being who she was and what she'd been; I made myself consider it. Could I use Yihtor-that-was to find his mother and followers? Possibly, but he, too, was a predator.

One I refused to allow near Morgan.

I need him to remember. Restore the link.

<<Send him back.>>

＊ ✳ ＊

I sat up quickly, jarring my hip. The pain was a welcome reminder of what was flesh—and what wasn't. I looked for Morgan.

Finding him sitting, too close, on the cot. At my flinch, he stood at once, gesturing apology. "Are you all right?"

I was, and wasn't, not with what I had to ask of him. "We have to kill Yihtor," I said, my mouth dry, "then bring him back to life."

Terk swore under his breath. Morgan sent him a quelling look, turning his gaze back to me. "There's no other way?"

"For this, no."

"It can be done," he said, no expression in his face. "Why?"

"If we don't, he'll be what he was." I searched his face. "You remember."

Without another word, my Human went to Yihtor's cocoon. Terk met him there, as if to intercede, then stood aside, throwing up his hands.

I'd be of more use Between.

Reclining once more, I closed my eyes.

Chapter 20

HER EYES CLOSED, her head on the mattress haloed by an unruly mass of red-tipped brown hair, and it wasn't her.

Wasn't Rael . . .

Or wasn't . . .

No. Morgan stopped the thought. She'd given him a task, to protect them from a terrible enemy, however bleak the means. Without Sira—without her Power, Yihtor was too strong for either of them.

The med unit would revive the Clansman, if reactivated in time. As for ending Yihtor's life? He reached for a pillow.

Terk got there first, pushing two fingers deep in the flesh beneath the unconscious Yihtor's chin. As the body flexed, trying to survive, the enforcer looked detached, almost clinical.

Not the first time, that said.

The body stopped moving. Terk checked for a pulse, then gave a grunt and moved aside. "All yours."

Unsure if he should be queasy or grateful, Morgan took over, reactivating the unit. Alarms blinked, and servo hands fussed. They waited, the moment full of question.

A pulse registered on the panel, then another, along with slow, steady breaths.

Leaving the machine to finish its job, the Human went to the other cot and looked down. Expressions flickered across Rael's face: determination, effort, then a fear so pronounced he clenched his fists and made himself remain still. Finally, calm.

Her eyes opened. Warmed, seeing him, and it wasn't fair, wasn't right, he thought, repulsed. They should be gray, not bright green, with that look.

"We killed him for you. Did it work?" Morgan demanded roughly.

She blinked, and the warmth was gone, replaced by caution. Rael sat up. "The Watchers guided him to the Vessel—brought Yihtor to his body, that is," she corrected and stood. "I'll wake him again, and we'll know."

Morgan stepped farther back than necessary to let her pass. Rael acknowledged the distance with a tiny frown, but focused on the Clansman. Instead of whatever she'd done before in the M'hir, this time she simply walked up to him and pinched his arm, hard.

Yihtor's eyes opened. "Ouch," he said, a hand reaching not to the pinch, but to where Terk had pressed his fingers, shutting off the flow to his brain.

"You're welcome," that worthy said, though it had to be a first even for him, conversing with a former victim.

"Yihtor," Rael urged gently. "Do you know why you're here?"

He nodded. This time, when he sat, it was a struggle. Rael put her arm around his shoulders to assist. "Morgan found you." With wonder, looking between them. "I knew he would."

There was, Morgan thought, something new about his face. Then he realized what it was: the underlying hunger was gone. This Yihtor was content, fulfilled by whatever he'd found in that other universe.

Seeing he could sit without help, Rael sat on the nearby stool. "We've an urgent question," she said quickly. "Remember, you mustn't *reach*. Where would Wys and her followers go?"

"Back to Camos," Yihtor replied. "To our former home."

Terk shook his head. "We'd have known."

"The Assemblers attacked Camos," Rael said, adding, "It must be part of the Song, now."

"Ah, yes." Yihtor looked down at his legs, under the blanket, then rapped a knuckle on the device where his knee had been. "This isn't. I'm glad I missed it. The Retians, I suppose. They were eager to get their paws on us."

Terk met Morgan's look, nodded, and pulled out his com, moving off to speak in a low voice. He'd have Finelle contact the *Conciliator*—presumably not her captain—and start a query down those lines.

"Would she go to Ret 7?" Morgan asked, while this went on.

Eyebrows rose over those scar-lined eyes. "No. We all knew better than to trust Retians in numbers. She'd wanted to go to Omacron—liked working with them—I'd disagreed. I found Human minds more useful." A gesture of apology. "I don't like remembering that. I don't like being here."

Terk would add Omacron to Finelle's instructions.

"What about Snosbor IV?" Rael asked as though just thinking of it. Clever, he thought, approving. "Its population is Omacron." She glanced at Morgan. "Janac knew. My Chosen."

As if he needed an explanation for her knowledge. Why?

"Why ask these questions?" Yihtor frowned, moved uneasily. "I don't like remembering. Let me do a heart-search." His eyes lost focus.

"Stop." Rael snapped her fingers under his nose, claiming his attention. "Remember this, unChosen, like it or not. Here we were property, of our parents first of all. We were never trusted."

Morgan hadn't known Rael took their father's betrayal so personally, but he should have guessed, given how close she was to Sira. Heart-kin as well as sister. And hadn't Rael been the one to step up and help them be together?

"I was. My people were loyal!"

"Would your people go to Snosbor IV?"

Brow furrowed, Yihtor's lips moved without sound, as though trying to find words. Finally, he gave up. "I can't remember."

She gave him a pitying look. "Because your mother didn't want you to."

"You think she blocked my memory?" Yihtor accused, a hint of his former self in its heat. "Impossible! I was the leader."

"Of her empire, not yours."

His face crumpled. "Sira—"

"Was never yours, Yihtor," Rael said quickly. "You know that," with emphasis. "You remember now."

"Yes," faintly. "But how can I help, like this? What good am I except as bait?"

For Wys di Caraat wanted her son back—his body at least, Morgan thought with pity of his own. It might come to that, but first?

"I can remove the block," he heard himself offer.

Rael whirled. "No!"

"We need the answer. So does Yihtor." He made himself be calm to counter her alarm, feeling enough of his own. "It's my skill. Sira must have told you."

"She told me you were reckless!" Fire in her eyes as she half-rose, her *fear* pressing against his shields. "That you'd need protecting from yourself!"

Yihtor found her hand; Rael stared down at him. Whatever passed unheard between them, Morgan couldn't know, but she gave a shuddering sigh and nodded in defeat.

"Please try, Morgan," the Clansman said to him, lying back down. "I must rescue my family from this life and have them, as they should be, in mine."

The word "rescue" was deliberate, an appeal to what were more Human instincts than what he'd known of Clan's. "Very well." Morgan waited for Rael to leave Yihtor's side, but she moved back, not away.

While Terk, weapon drawn, went to the end of the cot.

His protectors, Morgan thought, touched. Not that either were a match for the Power waiting for him, but he chose to believe this Yihtor.

If he was wrong, they'd know soon.

The Human pulled the stool to the head of the cot, careful of Rael's toes, her worried nearness a distraction he put aside. Steepling his fingers, he focused, then laid his left hand on Yihtor's forehead, closing his own eyes.

Clarity. His first impression was of passion, controlled, organized, driven. The potential here astonished.

Appalled, knowing it had been wasted, but none of these thoughts helped, Morgan knew, and he dismissed them.

Usually, he needed to penetrate shields, at least the minimal layer healthy or ill minds kept as a last resort, but Yihtor's mind lay open to him. Trust?

Need. A word, simple and direct. *Find what we need, Human. I hide nothing.*

Morgan didn't hesitate, plunging deeper.

He'd expected the worst, in this mind, and wasn't wrong. Speed was his only defense, moving through and past the faces of Yihtor's many victims, a panorama of lives destroyed for profit, for the Clansman had specialized in the theft of knowledge.

Leaving ruin behind.

He'd expected to find himself, here, a memory of when Yihtor had almost defeated him and won. Instead?

Morgan found Sira.

. . . *in a room, no, their cabin, on the* Fox. *She wore the coveralls he'd found for her; they didn't fit, but she'd rolled up the arms and legs.*

. . . *she sat on the bed, their bed. Her hair was short, as when he'd first met her, short and dripping wet.*

. . . *her fingers traced a vine he'd painted on their wall. Over and over. As gently as breathing, but she didn't breathe.*

. . . *which wasn't right. And the painting was the last he'd done, of a vine they'd seen together, his gift for her. And her hair was a glory of fire and gold, down to her waist.*

. . . *yet she looked as she had when she'd first arrived on the* Fox. *When she'd given him the name Kissue, unable to recall her own. He'd named her that day. Sira.*

She stays like this.

. . . *the voice didn't belong here. He resisted.* Sira. *He tried to call her name, but she didn't turn, didn't breathe, kept tracing the memory of a vine with those fingers he'd kissed, over and over—*

Morgan. HUMAN!

And it wasn't just Yihtor taking hold of him, pulling him away from her; there were hands beyond number, and all of them cried out with sorrow and regret:

She stays like this.

✳ ✳ ✳

Morgan found himself on the stool beside Yihtor, his hand a fist trembling in midair. He eased it down to his thigh, pressed it into the muscle, focused on that. The rest?

"She stays like that," Yihtor said, his voice coming from some great distance. "Did you expect any less?"

"I expected more. I thought she lived!" The Human twisted to look at Rael. "What I saw isn't life."

"Sira has made her choice. She abides in it." Rael drew herself stiff and tall. "It is not for you or any Singer to question. Nor for Yihtor to share." Pointedly.

"I was her Choice," Morgan said, reeling with grief. "Is that all she does now? Pretend our lives haven't changed? Pretend I'm there? Forget—" Forgetting the pain, he'd grant Sira in a heartbeat. But to reject it? To live trapped in a lie? "—forget what happened to us?"

"'Forget?!' How dare you, Jason Morgan." Twin spots of red appeared on Rael's pale face. "She stays like that because she chooses, as she did here, to have you in her heart. Sira cherishes what you had together over any other life. Forget?" Her voice lost its fury. "She knows what happened better than anyone. She knows the price you both paid and accepts it, gladly, knowing you're alive. Knowing she never can be."

So soft, those last few words, they were barely audible.

"While I appreciate there are feelings going on," Terk broke in dryly, "we need a course. Morgan?"

He gave himself an inner shake. "Understood." This time, when the Human put his hand on Yihtor's forehead and dropped his shields, he kept his eyes open. The Clansman met his gaze, his own guileless.

Let's do this.

Aside: The Tidik

"IS IT TRUE?" The *ors* trembled. "Can it be?"

The *wef* raised milky eyes. "All things end."

"Journeys end," the *ors* protested. "A story. A life. Not the universe."

"Why?" she asked gently.

Because it was too big a thought, the *ors* wanted to admit, but felt ashamed. "I wish it wouldn't. I wish to finish my work. To see this cycle's *tweels* fix their paths and become *wef* or *ors* or *wefors* or *orswef* or something new. I wish a full life, so I may weave the dark and light within me into peace. Must the universe end before I'm ready?" Too small a thought, perhaps, but *ors* wished most earnestly to live and was an honest being.

Her *nessems* glistened with approval. "The question we all ask, *ors* of my family and heart.

"Let us hope the Consortium finds an answer."

Chapter 21

"SLOW DOWN. Stop!"

Morgan shortened his stride but didn't stop. Rael caught up to him at the lift. "What do you want?"

"To meet the captain."

The reasonable request, after all else, muted his protest. "Come, then."

They rode the lift in silence. Though he felt her eyes on him, the Human concentrated on his argument. Yihtor had had a block in his memory, not only smothering his knowledge of Snosbor IV—now confirmed as where they had to go—but the scope of his mother's plans. Those plans presented a new and dangerous hurdle to overcome: a local population certain to be under Clan control.

The Omacron he'd known were curious about other telepaths. Gentle beings. They didn't deserve this. Terk and Finelle were to contact Bowman to arrange reinforcements and begin some hasty diplomacy.

While he asked a captain to take her ship into what boded to become a small war.

The lift stopped. Morgan waved Rael through the doors. "Left to the engine room."

"Destarians," she said abruptly, then gave an odd laugh.

Morgan looked at her. "What?"

"Clan, naming themselves after a Human starship? I'd have thought Wys less—" her lips thinned, "—whimsical."

He halted. "Rael. We need a way to resolve this, quickly and without casualties." Other than the Destarians.

"I know." Her face filled with determination. "Get us there, Jason. By then, I hope we have an answer for you."

* ✳ *

Captain Erin's face was all frown when they arrived, and Morgan's heart sank. "Fem di Sarc," Erin greeted, giving a nod. "I'm pleased to see you out of medbay."

No, she wasn't. At least, she wasn't pleased to have a passenger—even one in the ship's coveralls—walk in on a problem. For problem there was. Morgan's experienced eye had spotted it immediately: the carefully reassembled sequencer housing, with its "pretty" new core, was in pieces. Again.

Rael, for a wonder, saw it also, or recognized the mess didn't bode well. "Forgive my intrusion, Captain. I see this isn't a good time."

"Few are," Erin said, then added with better grace, "I'll have Noska dig out some entertainment vistapes."

"A pleasant way to pass the journey, I'm sure," the Clanswoman replied, a glint in her eye. "Thank you." With a last look at Morgan, perhaps wishing him luck, Rael left.

"What went wrong?" the Human demanded, joining Erin to look down at the parts.

"Ran a test, and it blew the last high-limit statcontroller." She puffed out her cheeks, letting out a long slow breath. "That's it, then."

Morgan half smiled. "Only if we worry about having one. Let me show you." The result was ugly and broke regs, but when he made the final connection and Erin connected the power?

The sequencer glowed blue, its new core spinning free and

clear. Erin checked it twice with her scanner, then again. "This shouldn't work," she told Morgan half angrily. "The statcontroller has to be in there."

"That's what scoundrels like Big Bob's would like us to think," he replied, wiping his hands. "They burn out faster than any other part—and cost more than they're worth." Her pride being what it was, Morgan didn't bother telling her most free traders figured that out in their first year of operation. "The bypass? Just a trader trick."

"Any more tricks I should know?" with a calculating look around the engine room. He wouldn't be surprised if she'd developed a few of her own; sometimes all it took was knowing rules could be broken.

"It'd take a while," he answered honestly. "We need to talk, Captain."

Disconnecting the sequencer's core, she stood with it in her hands. "So talk."

"Maybe you should put that down first."

In case she broke the new one, throwing it at him.

Interlude

I WALKED DOWN THE CORRIDOR to the lift, seriously tempted to throw something. If I'd anything to throw. Starships—ideally—lacked loose objects. "'Vistapes,'" I growled under my breath.

Who'd this Erin think she was?

The captain, I reminded myself. A captain faced with a passenger in her engine room. An engine room full of fascinating bits. I hadn't seen that light in Morgan's eyes since my return.

Which would be why, I sighed to myself, I chafed at being summarily dismissed. I'd been his crew—his shipmate. Not that Morgan let me near anything that could be damaged by willing but ignorant hands, but I'd passed tools. Cleaned. I'd graduated to monitoring the plumbing—the safest part of life support, if hardly glamorous—and hadn't always messed that up.

There'd been, occasionally, more cleaning.

Above all, I'd made sure the most important "part" of the *Fox*—Morgan—ate and slept.

Bury my face in vistapes during my last voyage in a starship? With him?

Arriving at the lift, I stepped inside, then reached for the com panel.

We'd see about that.

✳ ✳ ✳

The Whirtle humped over to a cupboard, opening it wide. "If you're sure about this, Fem—Hindmost Rael—here are the supplies."

Who'd have thought I'd smile to see a sweeper? "I'm sure. I don't enjoy being idle. Thank you, Noska."

By the look on its face, I'd grown a second head. "Do you need instruction?"

I pulled the device out of the cupboard, turned it on, and checked the status of its container and filters.

"I see not." The Whirtle sighed happily. "All the decks, any deck, whatever deck you like. I haven't been able to keep up, you see. Not and prepare for lift, and now I've bridge duty while the captain is working very hard. With Morgan. Very hard. They don't come out," woefully. "They keep eating those revolting e-rations when I've just restocked the galley."

Not overly subtle, our Noska, but as this fit my own inclination, I nodded obediently. "I'd be happy to take them suitable meals."

"And sweep."

"And sweep." As proof, I swung the sweeper to face the corridor with what I considered definite flair. "Anything else?" I asked, all innocence.

"More?" The Whirtle crooned and hugged itself. "Oh, yes."

Then assigned me enough tasks to keep three of me usefully occupied until Snosbor IV.

Interlude

Enforcer Battle Cruiser *Conciliator*

THERE WERE CERTAIN TRUISMS accepted throughout the Trade Pact, regardless of species. Scats weren't to be trusted. Lemmicks stank. And Sector Chief Lydis Bowman wasn't, in any sense, a fool.

Given some Scats could be as trustworthy as their natures allowed, and Lemmicks, some, aspired to less olfactory impact on their neighbors, eventually someone would test the last item of the list.

Not that it ever ended well when they did.

This being a thought no doubt of benefit to Captain Lucic before embarking on its own attempt, it came much too late at this juncture.

Given the being waiting at its table.

"YoutooktherunnertomeetwithBoard!"

Bowman lifted a brow. "Apparently not."

The Ordnex chose bluster. "Howdidyougetin? Thedoorwas locked!"

The brow lowered. "Apparently—not. Sit, Lucic."

Somehow, the captain found its behind planted in a chair.

"Let's put aside, for the moment, the tracer specialist you

provided for me when I went to Norval. Who is in custody, by the way."

Lucic's fingers tangled in one another. "Icanexplain—"

"Oh, allow me." Bowman took out a noteplas, flipping slowly through pages, each flip making Ordnex fingers tighten a little more. She paused. "Ah, yes. *Troudor 3. Silcil 48.*"

"Pirates. Iwastheonewhotoldyou."

"Yes, you did. Fine intel, that. Earned trust." Somehow, her mild tone gave the last word a threatening emphasis. "You also informed me these pirates did some work for the Clan—for Clan I happen to be interested in now. Care to tell me where they might be?"

Fingers went white and a knuckle popped with a sound like a snapping stick. "Iwouldn'tknow. I'mabusybeing. Captainofthis ship—"

"Apparently not," Bowman commented idly, flipping more pages. "Here we are. Another interest of mine. Manouya."

Three pops. "Iwasinpursuit!"

"So I noticed. Without me or my staff. Interrupting a mission of significant import while you were at it. Doesn't inspire confidence in you or your motives, Lucic, let me tell you. What I want to know?" She put down the noteplas and leaned on her elbows to regard the other being, chin on her fists. "Why. You've done well by the *Conciliator,* according to the bridge crew. An unblemished record. I've no complaints—till recent events. One chance, Lucic. Why?" Bowman waited, her patience a terrible thing.

Fingers slowly untangled. "Tofindhimfirst." The flaps over its nasal cavity flared with a long exhalation. Shoulders sagged. "Toaskmyquestionfirst. Beforeyoulockedhimaway."

She lowered her fists to the table between them. Opened them, palms up, fingers spread in the Ordnex offer of reciprocity. "What question?"

Lucic's hands hovered in the air, shadowing hers. "Can'ttell can'triskit."

"One. Chance."

The Ordnex set its hands above hers. Larger hands, probably stronger. They trembled at such proximity, and avoided contact.

Offer acknowledged—and refused. "Itisofnoimportancetoany oneelse." Regret, in that tone, and dignity. "Therearegreatmatters underway."

Bowman's eyes didn't leave Lucic's. "You've sent my ship to Plexis. That part I get. If you were guessing, I'll confirm. Manouya's there, all right. Showed his ugly face, bold as a Scat." She raised her hands, touching palm-to-palm. Insisted, by that. "Here, it's you and me, Lucic. What would you ask first?"

Fingers wound, with care, over hers—acceptance—then: "Whohasmybabies?"

Chapter 22

"SNOSBOR IV. Snosssborrr IV. Snosbor IV."
In lieu of throwing parts of her ship at him, Captain Usuki Erin elected to repeat the planet's name to herself as if tasting it.

Or questioning his sanity. "I've the coordinates," Morgan interrupted.

"Doesn't surprise me," dryly. "What does is you asking permission. You could have entered those. I wouldn't have noticed till too late."

Had Terk failed to keep their conversation secret? No, Erin was smart, too smart for games or tricks.

"It occurred to me," Morgan admitted. "I changed my mind."

Her wrist turned in invitation.

Morgan sat on the bench. "We're on a mission. Terk and Finelle—"

"Who are what: Enforcers or Port Jellies?"

Smart, indeed. "Constables under Sector Chief Lydis Bowman." Her eyes widened at the name. "Rael and Yihtor were kidnapped." He kept it simple, stuck to what truth he dared give her. "With Thel's help, we were able to rescue Yihtor before the *Worraud* could lift, but they still had Rael. We needed a ship to follow them. Yours."

"Huh. Thought Thel was cagier than usual." Erin studied him, then sat on a stool. "Spoke well of you, Morgan."

"And of you."

"So what are you, exactly?"

He spread his hands. "What you see."

A sardonic look, but she let it go. "That spacewalk?"

"I had to—" some things he hoped she'd never know, "—free Rael before they could harm her."

"Do more, you mean." The captain'd seen Rael carried in, the blood smeared over staples, the filthy blanket for clothes. "Scats." She spat over her shoulder.

"They weren't working alone." Morgan leaned forward. "We've a chance to catch those responsible, Erin, if we can get to Snosbor IV in time. I'll pay for your time and the ship."

"Deviating from a posted course is an offense."

"Our posted course will remain Plexis till the last minute. Bowman will take care of any charges." He hoped. "She's covering our costs."

Erin looked surprised. "The voucher's real?"

His turn. "You came this far without checking it?"

"We're cousins, remember?" With complete confidence. "You don't pay up, in full, for what's done and this new course of yours? Thel'll strip your hide from your bones."

There was that.

And there was this. "We don't know what's waiting for us," Morgan cautioned. "The plan—if you agree—is to get us to Snosbor IV. Bowman will be there," not that they had confirmation, but it was the plan, "we'll transfer over to her ship, and the *Wayfarer*'s free to go where you will."

Erin frowned. "If there's no ship?"

"A quick land and dump, the *Wayfarer* to wait for us in orbit."

The frown deepened. "What good are we up there?"

Finelle had asked the same question. Morgan shook his head. "Whatever happens, planetside isn't where you want to be, Erin." Especially with Clan involved.

Especially these Clan.

"Huh." She rose to her feet.

Bad as Terk for those says-it-all-grunts; he understood hers, too. He could try to protect the *Wayfarer.* Her captain would decide how.

∗ ✳ ∗

Course set. Three days till exiting subspace, but neither Morgan nor Erin slowed the pace in the engine room. As long as the *Wayfarer*'s bowels were spread over the floor, they were at risk. One emergency—something as simple as a fire in the galley—and there'd be nothing they could do but die.

Not that they thought in such dire terms. You didn't, that was all, fear being the shortest path to error. Leaving Terk and Finelle to take care of plots and plans—along with their guests—Morgan plunged into the work, concentrating completely on the ship.

He tried to, anyway. Whenever he paused, the dreadful image of Sira, sitting alone in the cabin of the *Fox,* swam up behind his eyes. It wasn't what he'd wanted for her; shouldn't be what she wanted for herself. Oh, he understood. Who better? Her mind held such Power, such will. She'd had enough of being what others wanted. Where they wanted. That their life together was her choice now?

Said it all, didn't it?

If he could be with her, in that unending dream, he would. He'd share it, share anything. Free her, that most of all. Hear her laugh.

Morgan worked harder.

Worse, something niggled at him. A feeling as though he'd missed a step. Double-checking himself became triple-checking, but it wasn't the mechanics. He could—and had—worked on the *Fox* half-asleep.

No, this had to do with—

"Hello."

Morgan raised his head, startled to see Rael enter the engine room, a steaming tray in her hands.

"It's suppertime," she announced briskly, looking for a place to put her burden.

Erin tipped a crate free of what covered it and patted the top. "Here you go. Thanks, Rael."

"My pleasure, Captain."

A slim figure in spacer coveralls. A tray brought to where he worked, because he forgot more meals than he remembered. Morgan's heart threatened to choke him, and he looked down at his hands, unseeing what they held.

A bowl and spoon appeared in his view. "If you let it get cold," Rael said quietly, "I'll be cleaning the freshers." She took the tool from his numb fingers; delayed, eyes on him, till he took the bowl. "Thanks."

"Didn't know I was starving," Erin said around a mouthful. "Noska told me you'd volunteered to help him. Appreciate that."

"You're working as crew?" Morgan asked, incredulous. Rael di Sarc had many fine qualities; a willingness to exert herself wasn't one of them.

In proof, she held out an elegant hand. Red marked blisters, the largest shiny with medplas.

"And doing a fine job of it," the captain praised. "Noska does his best, but with four passengers—suppose you don't count, Morgan—three, he's close to frantic."

"It's the least I could do," Rael replied. "How goes your work here?" As if the real question wasn't: are we going to die?

Hearing it in her voice, Morgan roused himself. "The *Wayfarer* will be ready ahead of time. We've finished the teardown."

"Putting her back together's the fun part," Erin contributed. "This is delicious. Are you a cook, too?" Wistfully.

"Not at all." Rael smiled. "Credit goes to Noska's shopping and your replicator, though being hungry helps."

Morgan paused, spoon halfway to his lips. "We missed a meal?"

Her smile grew soft. "Just one. I'll keep track from now on, but don't miss sleep. That I can't bring on a tray."

Erin laughed. "Well put, Rael. I'll kick him out later. Thank you again."

"Yes," Morgan said quickly. "Thank you."

After the Clanswoman left, Erin grinned at him. "And much becomes clear."

"What?"

"You. That crazy stunt, breaking into a Scat ship. Rael, bringing a tray." She pointed her spoon at him. "You've history."

That they did. Morgan gave a slight nod. "We're family. Rael's sister was my lifemate. Sira." And if it hurt, saying her name, Rael had been right, the memory was what mattered. "Sira was attacked by those behind Rael's kidnapping."

"So it's personal. I get that."

They ate in silence, then Erin added, "Thel taught me personal is one step from stupid."

Morgan's lips twitched. "I believe I've heard it from her myself once or twice. I promise—" and there it was, Sira's voice as if he could hear it now, what she'd asked of him, "—I promise to keep living. Which means we fix this engine."

"Deal," Erin told him with satisfaction.

As if she'd heard far more.

Interlude

Plexis

H E'D BE SATISFIED, decided Tayno Boormataa'kk, if his life contained a single station day in which he arose in the morning to find only what he expected to happen, happened. No less and, emphatically, no more.

Surprises being, in his experience, unpleasant at best. Ever since he'd agreed to impersonate his "uncle" to beings unable to tell them apart, Tayno thought woefully, the surprises hadn't stopped coming.

To be sitting in the waiting room of Plexis security, the one for "those we haven't arrested yet," for the second time? Was worse than a surprise. It was dangerous.

He was harboring an alien. An alien without an airtag. Somehow, they'd found out. They being the faceless beings who existed to cause surprises to happen to him.

Life, as he'd grown to enjoy it, was likely over. The urge to slink was nigh overwhelming.

"Why are you afraid?"

Opening the disks of his head with an effort, Tayno elongated an eyestalk to regard Tarerea Vyna. She'd learned to read his body language; admittedly, slinking was a bit obvious. He'd have to try harder. "I have legitimate concerns about the reason for this invitation," he said.

When the summons arrived, he'd panicked and run into a wall, it was true, but the wall had been in the way of escape and—there was none. Lones had calmed him. Had told him what Huido would do. Go forth in outraged dignity and virtue, bring his guest, in case she was the issue, and prove he'd no secrets. No obvious ones. To that dubious end, Lones had quickly coached Tarerea in her role, starting with calling him Huido in public. He'd explained it as Carasian manners, to use a different name for strangers. She'd seemed oddly pleased.

The Human had hurried to a consignment shop run by a relative of one of the kitchen staff, who'd collectively taken a great and amused interest in their guest's transformation. The relative had loaned them—there being no funds left in any budget to buy—an outfit worn by a Human grandie to the five hundredth showing of *Hamlet the Scat.*

Apparently, you couldn't wear something that expensive twice.

Tarerea Vyna was, Tayno thought with some pride, resplendent. Soft rich fabric enveloped her from chin to crystal-encased toes, its color shifting from blues to subtle reds with her movements. A collar flared behind her head, framing her face. If it was still too thin by Human standards, who would notice? A slim jeweled band wrapped her nearly bald head; from it hung gems that winked blue and red. They weren't real, but who could tell?

The appropriate gold airtag was affixed to her cheek, also not real. The restaurant had authentic blue ones for staff, but Lones had insisted only gold would do. Tayno studied it anxiously. Had it started to slip? He'd so many doubts about this, it was a wonder he wasn't shaking.

"You're shaking," she whispered, ending that hope.

The clothing emphasized the protrusion of Tarerea's abdomen, something Lones had assured him was a good thing but that, Tayno knew, was Humanocentric. There were many sapient species on Plexis with vastly different reproductive cycles and all the oddness of manners that went with them. Why gravid Ott required the private dining room and their food provided before arrival, lest hungry offspring burst from their pouch and attach to the nearest non-Ott, which was truly disturbing when it was you—

A door opened. The unfortunate door that wasn't the exit. "Hom Huido." The security guard beckoned. "This way, please."

As before, the guard—non-Human this time, though the species' name escaped him in his distress—adjusted the door to fit a Carasian's width, then stepped aside. "The deputy inspector will see you now."

Tarerea Vyna rested her hand on Tayno's great right claw. "Together," she stated, her tone admirably imperious.

"Of course."

* ✳ *

"Hom Huido. Thank you for coming."

Last time, she'd claimed he'd a choice; this time he'd known he hadn't. Still, Deputy Inspector Jynet's courteous greeting deserved a response.

Having none, Tayno blurted, "I can explain!"

She hesitated. "What is it you wish to explain, Hom Huido?"

"My accompanying him here without advance notice, Inspector." Tarerea Vyna had taken a seat. Now she gestured, her rings catching the light. "I am Tarerea Vyna. My host, the magnificent Huido Maarmatoo'kk, wishes to enlist Plexis Security on my behalf." She smiled at Tayno. "I've assured him I need no special treatment while shopping your wonderful station, but he fusses over my condition."

The paired flaps under Jynet's eyes flared yellow. Interest? Curiosity? Suspicion? Tayno wished the Eima came with a manual. They all should.

"Deputy Inspector, Fem Vyna. My superior is offstation. Please accept my welcome and regards on behalf of Plexis. Is it acceptable to inquire if you are imminent?"

"It is." Gems glittered as Tarerea bent her head. "I am not, which is why I've come. I must find what my child needs."

Not the words Lones gave her to use, but close enough, Tayno hoped. A wealthy mother-to-be was their carefully chosen lure, Plexis Security's first through fiftieth mandates being to encourage consumers to spend. Keeping them safe from pickpockets, mugging, and spoiled food was, of course, implicit in that lofty goal, but facilitating such a shopper as Tarerea? They'd be crawling, Lones said, over one another to help her spend her credits.

An image Tayno tried not to envision.

"And you require personal assistance," with—yes—that was pleasure. "I'd be delighted to arrange whatever you require, from unobtrusive security to expert item identifiers."

Security to follow them around? Tayno's shudder made a rain on plas noise. "She has me!" Finding himself once more the center of attention, he went on weakly. "I've agreed to accompany Fem Vyna while she is here. Until the *Claws & Jaws* reopens, I am without occupation."

Or funds. Would the Deputy Inspector, as Lones insisted, conclude he'd been hired as a bodyguard?

"In that case, Fem Vyna, added security would be redundant," Jynet replied. "Hom Huido's reputation is well known. In this office and Plexis in general."

Was that good? It had to be good.

"However, if I may? You might require assistance in specific stores, Fem Vyna. There are some in which Hom Huido will, ah, not be fully comfortable."

Wouldn't fit, the Eima meant. A deplorable fact he'd discovered while hunting for his gift for Barac and Ruti's baby-to-be. The owner had used a winch to pull him out, its hook leaving a hole in his carapace. Only visible from the rear, but still. The shelving, Tayno recalled, had been in worse shape.

Tarerea inclined her head again. "You are most kind, Deputy Inspector. I will not hesitate to contact you, should the situation arise."

They were done. Cheerful again, Tayno rose from his crouch. "Thank you, Deputy Inspector, for your time. We won't take any more of it, will we, Fem Vyna?"

"A moment more of yours, Hom Huido, if you please."

"Oh." He sank down again, morose.

The screen behind Jynet came to life with a face. "Mathis Dewley has been sighted on Plexis," the deputy inspector announced, flaps washed with white. "I felt you should know."

Who? Oh. "The worker in the restaurant. My restaurant," Tayno elaborated. "I haven't seen him." Not that he'd looked, but he wouldn't—

"I will tolerate no threat to me and mine," Tarerea Vyna declared fiercely.

A new color appeared below Jynet's eyes: a deep purple, almost black. "Why do you think Dewley is a threat, Fem Vyna?"

"Fem Vyna speaks out of instinct," Tayno offered, aiming a handling claw as tactfully as possible at the bulge. "Her condition, you see."

The Vyna remained tense. "What is that creature?"

She'd seemed to grasp their firm admonishment to treat every being as sapient and real, though Tayno personally doubted some of those he saw on the concourse were either, but to have Tarerea launch into her "not-real, not-Om'ray" tirade now would be bad.

Very bad.

The deputy inspector didn't appear surprised by the Vyna's question. "An Assembler."

An Assembler, on Plexis. Of course, there were Assemblers on Plexis, Tayno told himself, Assemblers were everywhere, like vermin. *The* vermin, the ones able to cling to starships like those horrid mites that clung to sand grains, waiting their chance to attach to a passing shell and burrow inside to succulent flesh—

"Hom Huido? Fem Vyna, is he all right?"

Like pox, that other dreadful combination of fluff and teeth. He'd—

"Huido!" A knock on his head, firm and demanding. "This is no time to—to—dream."

He must be brave. Maybe not as brave as Tarerea Vyna, but as brave as he could be. Tayno peered out, discovered the other two peering back. He gathered his courage, then gave a great noisy shake and rose to his full height. "Dreaming," he announced boldly, "happens when necessary for a Carasian." Rude, to invoke species' distinction, though for all he knew others did it to him. "You were saying, Deputy Inspector?"

The purple of her flaps had grown red edges. Those faded with his attention. "I said, Hom Huido, one of my best constables has been following Mathis Dewley since he showed at a tag point. I anticipate her report shortly, but in the meantime, the Assembler went directly to meet with this being."

Another image appeared.

"The *Galactic Mysterioso?*" Tayno read aloud, relieved to his core it wasn't another Assembler. The lettering was in a striking font. One he'd like to use for his—

Tarerea was on her feet, studying the image. "Old, this one. Dangerous."

"An Omacron?" Tayno chuckled. "If any come to the *Claws & Jaws,* my—I must provide a private chamber and the gentlest of servers. They bolt, otherwise." His sort of customer, truth be told. Never a problem, always quiet and cowering—

"That is their reputation, Hom Huido." The deputy inspector spread her short fingers on her desk, flaps now a softer mauve.

" 'Reputation?' " The Carasian's eyestalks converged on the Eima. "You know differently?" He'd cancel the advance reservations for the dance troupe at once. No, have Lones do it. That'd be safer if there were objections—

"I know Scats refuse to dock in the same section, which has always made me curious." Jynet's flaps eased to yellow. "Are you certain you don't recognize this individual? Sept entered Plexis under the name you saw, claiming to be an entertainer, but we've no listed booking for sept. Please take a close look, Hom Huido."

Tayno obediently swung every eye to the screen. If Humans were hard to tell apart, he thought, frustrated, Omacrons were impossible. Their thin bodies curved this way and that depending on mood. What passed as a face had small eyes, smaller nostrils, and a mouth with thick lips, but those features were stuck within ridges and not always visible. Those ridges were wrinkled and soft over the *Galactic Mysterioso's* face; was that why Tarerea judged sept old? She could be right.

Regardless, this was a face he couldn't be sure he didn't know. Or did.

Feeling less than adequate, Tayno concentrated on the clothing, with the glorious lettering on the midsection. No help there, but the cloak? Where had he seen its like before? *"Kapenen's Unusual Rentals!"*

The Eima's cheek flaps developed a hint of purple, a color he was beginning to suspect meant impatience. "I'm not familiar with the establishment."

"It's in the back of *Boyle's Repair Shop*—they do excellent work with faulty stasis units. You ask for Kapenen, say 'I'm here for my glass slippers,' and they escort you through a curtain." Was that a secret? Unlikely, since Boyle would loudly demand Tayno to repeat the phrase, laughing each time till his round belly shook and he ran out of breath.

"I—see. And this is important because?"

The Carasian quivered with excitement. "Before the Regrettable Event," that being how he'd come to think of the attack on the *Claws & Jaws* by those wretched Assemblers, "there was an actor from *Hamlet the Scat* who came for the prawlies special." Actors, far from being glamorous goldtags, he'd learned, lived on appetizers. Huido, in another of his whims, insisted actors receive an extra large helping if they came in costume, which seemed to attract others to the restaurant simply to stare, though they had to order to sit at a table.

"Prawlies are delicious," Tarerea Vyna offered.

"Hom Huido?"

Tayno forced his mind back on track. "Once the actor got sauce on his cloak—" His fault, as it happened, having been thoroughly flustered by the Ott offspring, which hadn't wanted to let go, so he'd had to carry the things around the restaurant. "—but it wasn't a problem because he rented it from *Kapenen's*." The cleaning charge hadn't been as painful as Huido's response to being thought the one who'd flung sauce. "The cloak looked just like that." With a triumphant thrust of his claw at the image of the Omacron.

When this didn't elicit a reaction, Tayno repeated the gesture, putting a little more force behind it in case the Eima had missed it the first time. "Like that."

"I grasp your meaning, Hom Huido," the deputy inspector assured him. She lifted her hand high, then brought a finger down on her desk as though showing him something he'd missed. "Jesper will see you and Fem Vyna out. Thank you for your assistance."

They were done? Tayno hesitated. Should they be done?

Tarerea Vyna took firm hold of his claw. "Thank you, Deputy Inspector, for yours." She urged him toward the now-open door, with its waiting guard.

"Oh, and Fem Vyna?"

They stopped as one, turning to look back at the Eima whose flaps had gone white, the color Tayno was beginning to associate with a daunting focus. "Jesper will replace your airtag for you," she announced. "Yours is slipping."

This time it was Tayno who steered them to the door, and quickly.

＊ ✳ ＊

The *Infant Emporium* was, Tayno had been assured, the finest source of unnecessary items for offspring of the rich. It should be, located on one of the uppermost levels of Plexis. If not for Tarerea Vyna's now-valid gold airtag, security would have stopped them two below this one.

The *Emporium* itself consumed so much space, was so impressive and grand, the Carasian began to seriously rethink the restaurant business. Unfortunately, Tarerea wouldn't go through the glittering doorway. "I don't understand. Why must we do this shopping?"

Lones had explained "shopping." Tayno sent eyestalks in every direction. No one was close, so he dared answer with the truth. "We want the deputy inspector to believe you're here to buy things for the baby."

"What I want I take."

Could the Human have missed a crucial component of the

process? "It's not important," Tayno said hastily. "We won't buy anything—" having no credits, and taking was out of the question, "—but it's important to appear interested in these things." He waved generously at the opening.

Almost decapitating a Neblokan, who grunted rudely and rushed inside, followed by three living attendants, each struggling with a load better suited to a grav sled.

Tarerea Vyna didn't budge. "Why?"

"Because—" Best not mention the potential difficulty posed by failing to impress the deputy inspector and so Plexis itself—he'd seen Tarerea's reaction to imagined threat and had no desire to see her truly upset. Again. In public. "—aren't you curious?" Plaintively. "I've never been inside, myself. I hear it's remarkable."

"I have no time for curiosity or this shopping, Tayno. My people languish in captivity. Let us go."

"Wait." People were approaching. People as in Humans. A small horde of Humans, meaning courtesies and curiosity galore, Humans being drawn to those pregnant like blowflies to stranded jellies. He had to get the Vyna out of sight. The Carasian gathered his guest within an irresistible claw and drew her into the store.

"I'll 'port us both," she threatened, but didn't, to his relief. Instead, Tarerea Vyna opened her eyes wide and stared.

The *Infant Emporium* was, Tayno thought with amazement, bigger on the inside.

A bewildering complex of racks rose overhead, messengers at the ready to deliver an item of interest. On the floor surrounding them were the merchandise displays suspended at adjustable viewing heights. The babies in each looked so lifelike, Tayno worried at first they actually were. Which they couldn't be, so he followed Tarerea to the nearest.

In it, three small Humans sat playing. Each wore an exquisitely detailed outfit, a miniature of what an adult would wear: a spacer, a dancer, and yes, that one was a chef. Each played with an array of themed toys, though the Carasian wasn't entirely sure one should be gumming the business end of what was undoubtedly an expensive replica needler. Still, the infant looked blissful.

They went to the next display, where six little Papiekians hung in ornate sleeping bags, their tendrils clutching jeweled rattles. To the next, where a group of Whirtles were rapidly building a bridge from candy. The next, where a Human baby younger than the others slept in a bed made from a Norsenturtle shell, which must be a replica also, Tayno decided, trade in the iridescent shells being illegal. The market for shell and, not coincidentally, soup stock had led to Trade Pact restrictions on the export of fellow sapients for consumption.

That said, the soup, Huido'd assured him, was exquisite—

"Are Human babies born without minds?" Tarerea asked abruptly.

"I don't think so. Not that I know much about other species' reproduction," he replied, though "nothing" would have been more accurate, "but they play with toys at this size—and say words."

"Ah."

The syllable held such sadness, Tayno's eyes converged on his companion. "What is it?" It seemed inherently dangerous, to grow inside another body and be inflicted by all that could happen, and Tarerea had suffered hardship. Carasians, as was proper and rigorous, swam the warmth of Mother Sea until large enough—he shook himself, getting back to the point. "Are you afraid your baby will come out—wrong?"

" 'Wrong?' " she echoed softly, her fingers stretched toward the baby on display. She brought them down over her swollen abdomen. "Within her should be the mind of a Glorious Dead, an Adept full of wisdom and Power. Solina Vyna was lost when the Rugherans took us, as all were lost. I am empty and will die of it."

" 'Die?' " No. This was terrible, impossible. How could she be so calm? Overwhelmed, the Carasian crouched and came as close as he could, using the tip of a handling claw to stroke her arm. "There are medical staff on Plexis," he offered without so much as a thought of the budget. "I'm sure they deal with babies—full ones and empty ones. I could take you. Save you."

"The only thing that could resides within the crystal orbs of

Vyna Cloisters. I accept my fate. So must you." Tarerea touched a finger to his claw, a look on her face he hadn't seen there before. "You have become real to me, Tayno Boormataa'kk."

A profound admission. He'd have been exceedingly happy to be "real" except that how could he be, knowing this brave and special being was in such danger? It was enough to make him slink, but he wouldn't. Not before her.

It was enough to make him long to touch her skin with his jaws, but Huido'd warned him innumerable times the tender gesture terrified non-Carasians and he mustn't, ever.

Though Jason Morgan wasn't Carasian, and he never looked terrified—

He'd take no chances. "I am honored, Tarerea Vyna," Tayno told her.

Her lips curved. "No more being serious. Those around us will notice. Is this not a beautiful child?"

Tayno dutifully scrutinized the sleeping Human. Chubby fists. The eyes were closed, long lashes on the round cheeks. The little mouth worked in and out as though sucking on a memory; probably a toe, by its moist glisten.

He'd take the Vyna's word for the appeal.

"She is, indeed." The Brill had been standing at another display. Now, she moved closer. "How old, do you think? Six months?"

Half again Tayno's bulk, the creature, though he trusted the gauzy robes added to her size. The Carasian felt the oddest impulse to stretch to his full height and raise his greater claws, which would not be considered polite at all. "I wouldn't know," he replied stiffly.

"Well, it's the best age. Take it from me." The Brill tipped her big head toward the display, making a cooing noise.

Tarerea appeared taken aback. "It is not-real."

Tayno hoped she meant the baby.

"These, no," the Brill agreed. "Yet fully representative. This *is* Plexis." The other's savoring of those words reminded Tayno of a food critic they'd had to let gorge at the *Claws & Jaws*. No review, Huido'd said afterward, was worth the slobber. "But I see you're making your own, Fem. When are you due?"

Tarerea Vyna's hands went to her abdomen, as if protecting what was inside. "It is impolite to inquire."

A second Brill, smaller than the first, arrived. "Excuse my colleague's curiosity," he boomed. "We rarely meet a—" was that hesitation real or feigned? "—Human in your happy condition."

Tayno could tell Tarerea was anything but happy at the moment. He made a show of rattling his carapace. "Enjoy your shopping, Fem, Hom." He suffered a momentary pang, aware he should invite richly dressed, gold airtags like these to the opening of the *Claws & Jaws*. No, the Carasian decided. They weren't right, neither of them. Huido would understand. "We must go."

"No need to hurry off," the male objected, his deepset eyes fixed on Tarerea. "Join us for a drink. We'd enjoy knowing more about you."

He shouldn't be afraid of this being, the Carasian told himself. Wasn't he bigger? Didn't he have claws and a body encased in shell? Though come to think of it, a Brill's thickened skin was akin to body armor, bulging over bone and muscle. Heavy gravity beings, Brill, and fond of physical self-expression.

They weren't to be given the nonrecyclable porcelains.

He shouldn't be afraid, yet it was all Tayno could do, all at once, not to pick up Tarerea and run.

"No time, no time," he blurted.

"My turn to ask your pardon." The female Brill clutched her companion's arm, ivory nails digging in. "We can't always indulge our hobbies," she told him, then smiled pleasantly at Tayno. At least, the Carasian thought the expression on her face was meant to be pleasant, though it wasn't at all. "We know you're a busy being. Huido Maarmatoo'kk. You are, aren't you?"

Much as he'd rather not be at the moment, Tayno managed a weak, "Yes."

"Such a shame about your fine establishment. We're all looking forward to the reopening. Please accept a token of our esteem." She held out two strips of plas, the sort that were used as advertisement.

He'd no choice but to take them, though he did so gingerly, with the tips of an extended claw. "Thank you."

To his discomfort, the Brill put her ivory-nailed hand on his claw, with weight behind it as though testing his strength. Before he could pull back, she did, smiling. "We'll see each other again soon."

Not if he saw them coming, she wouldn't. "Fair skies," he said firmly.

It felt like an escape when they were finally out of the store.

"No more shopping," Tarerea said vehemently.

"No more," Tayno agreed.

* ✳ *

They'd gone down the ramp to the level below and were walking through a zone of plantings and promotional waterfalls, the latter with a stream of words enticing passersby to seek the virtues of *Beneficial Massage for All Bodies, Group Specials Available* when Tarerea spoke again. "What did the not-real give you?"

"What? Oh." He'd forgotten the strips. Tayno brought them in range of his nearest eye and read. Without noticing, he came to a halt beside a group of tall pots containing taller clumps of grass. He didn't notice the grass rustled despite the lack of wind, moved by those inside who peered out with curious red eyes.

Nor, truth be told, could he have remembered his own name at that instant, seeing what was on the strip. He'd reached, he decided wearily, his limit for surprises in a lifetime.

"What is it?" the Vyna asked finally. "What's wrong?"

"She gave us passes to a show," Tayno replied. "A show by the *Galactic Mysterioso*."

An Assembler posing as a Human? It was what they did. An Omacron in disguise working with that Assembler was admittedly stranger. But a connection to the sinister pair of Brill—who'd paid too much attention to Tarerea—who'd seemed to know she wasn't Human at all?

"We have to get back," he said, shifting into motion. "Quickly." The Vyna reached for his claw, and Tayno skittered frantically out of reach. "Not that quickly!"

They'd get to the *Claws & Jaws,* lock all the doors, then he'd call the deputy inspector.

Or have Lones make the call. Yes, that's what he'd do.

Because something, Tayno feared to his shaking core, was very wrong on Plexis.

Chapter 23

SLEEP WASN'T GOING TO HAPPEN. Not while his thoughts whirled like this.

"Lights."

Not when he couldn't settle on why.

Morgan crossed his arms behind his head, ordering his body to relax. The refit was going well; Erin had insisted he take the first rest period. Insisted he did rest, which wasn't the same thing. The *Wayfarer*'s captain had him pegged, or so she thought.

What she didn't know, having lived a life free of anything worse than a few overeager debt collectors and some less-than-pleasant employers?

How a life could be empty.

That wasn't, however, what made sleep an impossibility.

Something was wrong. No, he corrected. Something wasn't right. There was no *taste* of change. No imminent threat, that implied, though they were as prepared as possible for another surprise Rugheran.

Just that niggle. What was bothering him? Frustration became annoyance. What was he missing?

In his experience, unsolved mysteries were dangerous. This one? If he didn't know better, he'd think he didn't want the answer.

Which made no sense.

Morgan kicked off the sheet and rose. He'd spent too much time alone, in bed, facing a universe that refused to make sense either, to start again here. He'd enjoy ship life while he'd the chance. Enjoy this peculiar, fascinating ship, the *Wayfarer*, while he'd the run of her.

Dressed, he headed to the galley. He'd bring Erin a cup of sombay. Talk engines.

* * *

Shipnight. The corridor lights were dimmed, not out. Doors were closed: the medbay; where the others slept. Morgan rolled his head, easing a knot in his neck. Just as well he was up and moving. He'd have taken more care to move quietly, not to disturb those who could rest, but he wasn't the only one awake.

Any spacer would recognize the *whooshwhirrr* of a sweeper set to hush mode. Pricey new machines might be soundless, but the *Wayfarer's* was third-hand and its hush was more the polite "sorry to be making noise in shipnight, done soon" variety. A reassurance, that little noise. Someone was on duty; you didn't have to be. He might have been able to sleep, had the sweeper been outside his door.

Noska, Morgan decided, smiling to himself, avoiding the Lemmick. Maybe the Whirtle could be convinced to join him in the galley.

He lengthened his stride and came around the bend.

There was the sweeper. It wasn't Noska using it but Rael, her back to him.

Morgan stopped, for no reason.

For every reason.

In an hour, anyone could learn to use a sweeper. To maneuver the clumsy device without banging into walls in a day. But this economy of motion, this confidence promising to leave no section of floor unbuffed? Took months, if ever learned at all.

She'd known the Vyna. The Rugheran.

Knew ships.
Knew him.
This wasn't Rael di Sarc.
The truth left his mouth in a single breath.
"Sira."

Interlude

"SIRA."

His voice.

Nonsensically, I kept sweeping until I finished the oval I'd mapped out, turned off the sweeper—swallowed hard—then turned. My casual "Pardon?" died unspoken when I saw him.

Jason Morgan stood a few steps away in the night-dimmed corridor, his face unreadable, the blue of his eyes as dark as I'd ever seen them. Shock would do that.

The truth, would.

I dared feast my eyes on him as Rael never would, drink in the real of him, listen to breathing that was, admittedly, a bit ragged. So was mine, for that matter, and I wasn't sure if I should move or speak—or run.

Run, I realized a second too late.

Chapter 24

BEFORE—THIS *WRONGNESS*—could run, Morgan had his hands around *its* throat. He used the grip to shove *it* backward. Drive *it* through the open galley door. Push *it* hard against the table, so his arms could straighten while *it* bent.

Terk, there, half standing. Morgan lifted his stare from *it* long enough to meet the other Human's eyes.

The enforcer flinched and swore, then left the room, closing the door behind him.

Morgan shifted his attention to the *WRONGNESS*. He would end this. End this before his heart broke again, though he hadn't known it could break twice. And if tears splashed down on his hands, on *its* face—

His hands had *its* throat. He'd only to snap the neck. He glared down.

What looked back was love.

And it didn't matter, all at once, if the eyes looking up were green or brown or gray. He knew that look. Had lost himself in it.

"Sira."

Releasing her throat, he folded her in his arms and buried his face in her shoulder.

Interlude

MY ARMS, not Rael's, went around Morgan. My heart, not my sister's, pounded like something wild, something trapped, but if this was a trap?

Let me stay in it. I murmured such silly things in my Human's ear, though I doubted he heard me. Doubted, by the new burn around my neck, if I could speak louder than a murmur anyway. We'd have to talk about this novel tendency of his to choke me first.

We'd have to talk about so much, I'd no idea where to start.

This was good, though. Held tight; free to hold tight. Better than good. If I had my hair, it would be going mad about now.

Morgan took a ragged breath, then raised his head. Keeping one arm around me, he traced the outline of my face—my new face—as if discovering it. The rage and grief in his had turned to wonder. "A Vessel."

I had to smile. My so-clever Human. "Yes." My voice wasn't as hoarse as I'd expected, but Morgan's eyes dropped to my neck and he went pale. "I'm all right."

"You were nearly dead."

And was—while technically true, clearly not the right thing to say at the moment. "Could we sit down?" I asked brightly.

In answer, he brought me to one of the galley chairs, his arm around me, and sat, gathering me in his lap with possessive care. Aware of my injuries, my Human. Newly outraged by them, at a guess.

Part of me was as well, the part desperate for the removal of clothing and a meeting of skin. Not, I scolded myself, helping. And—unexpected. "It was Rael's idea," I said aloud, only slightly breathless. It might have been the fingers learning the shape of my ear. "She helped me get here."

Morgan's hand found my hair. Slipped to cup the back of my head. "Am I dreaming?" he said very quietly, and bent to press his lips to mine.

To Rael's. When I stiffened, he stopped, his mouth so close I inhaled the sweetness of his breath and felt the warmth of his skin on mine, and we stayed like that, as if in orbit around each other, suspended between hope—

And despair.

Until I could bear no more and turned away.

"Sira. Witchling."

"You weren't to know," I said, locking my gaze on the cup Terk had left steaming on the table. "You were never to know. I was to come and go. Finish my last duty to the universes and—go."

He captured my chin and turned me back to face him. "Go back to our cabin, chit?" Morgan shook his head. "You can do better than that," low and sure. "You've family there. Rael. Barac. It's your home."

No, it wasn't. This—I put my hand on his chest, the words trembling to be said. Words I mustn't ever say again. "So they keep reminding me," I told him instead, making a wry face. "What about a cup of sombay? We've some catching up to do."

Chapter 25

THE CUPS WERE WISE. Putting the table and cups between them wiser still. Knowing—*knowing*—Sira—was within reach made every cell in Morgan's body tingle with joy. With dread. The emotions confounded and confused to the point where, yes, sombay and conversation felt like a light in the darkness.

A conversation yet to begin. He'd no words; Sira seemed no more willing to speak. Maybe it was the need for words, between them, that held them in silence. They'd been Joined, their thoughts mingling without effort, emotions as intimate and real as physical sensation, memories exchanged when the moment called for it. Or held private, what should be.

To be together but separate wasn't new, the Human thought all at once. When Sira arrived on the *Silver Fox,* for their first journeys as a couple, they'd kept distance between them. So she didn't destroy him with her Clan Power-of-Choice, yes, but now?

Now it was to keep them safe from one another. He opened his mouth, hesitated.

"I should have practiced what to say," Sira said suddenly and her lips curled in that rueful grin he knew. "I've missed this." She lifted the cup and took a sip.

"I should have known it was you," Morgan said, pushing his aside. "That's not true. I did. I couldn't let myself believe it."

She didn't have to ask why. He saw the awareness fill those expressive eyes, more and more *her* eyes to him. Form had never been as important to him as what he'd seen of her *inner* self. Not that Sira's body hadn't been mind-bendingly beautiful.

Not, he thought with a rush of heat, that the shape in front of him was any less so.

A blush stroked pink over high cheekbones and Sira quickly pretended to sniff her sombay.

Had she *sensed* the feeling through his shields or simply knew his every expression? "We need to talk," Morgan said running a hand through his hair. His eyes found the com panel in the galley. The things were in the halls, in every room on the ship, including the freshers. If Erin wasn't eavesdropping, Terk most certainly was—and recording, too.

His blurted "Sira" in the hall would have been heard, though who'd understand it?

"This is ridiculous." Morgan held out his hand, palm up. An invitation.

She eyed it without moving. "The M'hir . . ."

"Human, remember?" They'd been able to communicate on his level before. Morgan touched thumb to forefinger twice. *Listeners*, that meant.

He saw the comprehension in her face, then Sira frowned. She signaled back: *Friend or foe?*

He traced a line across the back of his other hand, recalling a particular scar.

She nodded, mouthing a name. *Bowman.*

As to whether the sector chief was friend or foe? Sira would consider her friend, as he did; equally aware Bowman often had a different agenda—and would tell her friends last of all.

Morgan offered his hand once more.

With mesmerizing reluctance, her slender fingers came to rest on his palm. Words formed, her mindvoice as clear and right as it had ever been.

I'm not alone.

Listeners here, where he'd hoped for privacy? Morgan buried his disappointment. *Rael?*

Her lips smiled faintly. *Rael and everyone else, it seems. They make it possible for me to remember AllThereIs and why I'm here. To remember myself, here, as well. Without them, I'd be a Stolen and empty.* Her fingertips were cool, real, like anchors. *They risk themselves, holding Yihtor and me here.* With *regret. The M'hir—Between—is more perilous than ever.* Her eyes seemed to bore into his. *We don't have much time, Jason.*

That they had this—he pushed down a quite ridiculous joy. *What must I know?*

Warmth, then. *That whatever happens, I won't regret this.* Her fingers slid between his, gripped hard. *Though I've a confession, my captain. I've fallen in love with this ship. Think the* Fox *would forgive me?*

Morgan laughed, out loud and inside. *You aren't the only one,* he admitted. *The* Wayfarer*'s a beauty—could be a beauty.*

Then let's protect her, with determination. *This ship. The lives on her. One another.* Sira's presence seemed to grow, as if he glimpsed her shining in the M'hir after all. *The peril facing us is beyond belief or reason, but these things we can do. We will, Jason. Let the universes take care of themselves. They should anyway,* with a hint of asperity.

Gods, he loved her. Morgan brought her hand to his lips. *No regrets, Witchling.*

He'd cherish what he could. This moment, the softness of her skin, the look in her eyes, the *feel* of her mindvoice.

But this time—conviction settled around his heart like peace—he'd make no promise of after.

✳ ✱ ✳

Time flew and shipday arrived with a brightening in the corridor as well as a groggy captain. Erin grunted a greeting as she headed straight for the sombay.

Sira gave Morgan a lingering look, then gently tugged her fingers free. *I'm still here,* she sent, before he let go.

Here, but separate. They'd sat, thoughts flowing back and forth, for the past hours. He understood so much more; not all, and he wasn't sure Sira could either, not until she returned to

AllThereIs and became noncorporeal once more. There were concepts for which Comspeak had no words; some, he suspected, minds of flesh and blood hadn't evolved to grasp.

Some he could. Sira had shared how the M'hir had become brittle, let him *see* the crack through which the stars of this universe shone through, precious, vulnerable. No wonder she was loath to risk the M'hir again.

With the exiles 'porting at will? No wonder they were short on time.

"Breakfast?" Erin was looking at Sira—at Rael, Morgan told himself. He had to think of her by that name.

"Right up, Captain. Hearty or quick?" came the smiling reply. "Morgan?"

"Quick for me," he answered. "I'm off to the engine room. Anything I should know?"

"Hearty times two." Erin sank into a chair with a grateful groan. She grinned up at him. "Numnee'd cheat her own sibs for a cred, but damn, that Festor makes decent parts. For future reference."

"Noted." Morgan took the warmed tube from Rael. A thrill coursed through him when their fingers met, as if he were some brash youngling. "My thanks," he said, astonished by the effort needed to keep his voice steady.

From the gleam in a pair of lovely green eyes, his response hadn't gone unappreciated. Fortunately, the captain was more interested in her sombay than exchanges between her passengers.

"I'll bring you something more later," Rael promised, that look in her eyes, and Morgan wanted, urgently, to reach for her on the spot.

He would have, when the body Sira wore had been her own, when they'd been together on the *Fox* and had a future.

The thought was enough to quench what was, in the end, hopeless.

* ✳ *

Morgan shook his head in wonder as he passed the sweeper. The device had shut itself off, having done its part, and of all the ways he might have discovered Sira inside Rael this one had a certain symmetry. Sira, in a sense, had discovered herself—her true, independent self—as Hindmost on the *Fox,* where she'd battled sweepers and plumbing and doorlocks with equal determination. Such tech wasn't part of Clan upbringing, but she'd embraced it.

For her own sake, to make a new life, a new identity. For his, too. He'd have left his life as a spacer for her without a second thought, but Sira had fallen in love with the ship as well as her captain. Of course, she'd feel as he did about the *Wayfarer.* Was Sira not the other half of his heart?

The coming days, Morgan thought desperately, would be the best and worst of his life.

When he went around the bend in the corridor, Terk silently peeled his bulk from the wall to fall in step.

Been there since the galley, Morgan guessed. "I've nothing to say," he asserted, hoping to forestall questions.

The enforcer chuckled. "Finally figured her out, huh?"

He stopped. "You knew?" Impossible.

"Wasn't hard." Smug, that. "Those weren't sisterly looks, my friend. Finelle caught on, and she doesn't even know you two."

Morgan started walking again. "It doesn't change anything." He felt the other's eyes on him. "When this is over, Sira goes back." To her dream prison. To their life that wouldn't be. The hopeless knowledge filled him, shrinking the corridor to footsteps and the future to the lift panel—

When a hand blocked his, he was honestly shocked. "What?"

"Detour," Terk ordered, tipping his head down the curved corridor. "C'mon."

"Why?" Morgan didn't move. "What's going on?"

"You'll see."

* ✳ *

Of all the ways Sector Chief Lydis Bowman had appeared without warning in Morgan's life, she'd not, till now, done so standing on a Lemmick's outstretched hand. A gloved hand, filled with the latest comtech, but still. He'd have laughed.

Except you didn't, at Bowman. Especially at a Bowman backed by the wall of an arms locker that belonged in only one place he knew. "You're on the *Conciliator*." He should have guessed. She had the skills to hide anywhere—why not on her own ship? "After Lucic."

"Captain Lucic," she corrected, "has my full confidence."

Morgan couldn't help but glance at Terk. The enforcer gave a half shrug. Don't ask me, that said.

He looked back at Bowman with a frown. "Something's changed."

A tiny nod. "Manouya's on Plexis."

The *Conciliator*'s posted course. Lucic had known where to go—whatever that story, he'd no time for it. Morgan set his expression to neutral interest. "The Clan are on Snosbor IV." Where they needed the *Conciliator*—and Bowman—to deal with the Omacron.

That predator's smile. "Turns out—" deliberate repetition; reference to a network of informants not even her closest staff could tap, "—the Clan are why Manouya broke cover. A good number are on their way to Plexis to meet your ship. I need you there."

Not as bait—for reinforcements, Morgan realized. Bowman knew who was on board the *Wayfarer*—would know Sira was here, by now, thanks to her constables—and included them all in that "you." She had her prize in sight and what he'd told her of the entities would give anyone sane nightmares.

Given a chance to act on both problems at once? She wouldn't delay to consult. Not Bowman.

"You've altered our course." Morgan shot a look at Terk, who did his utmost to portray offended innocence, then glared at Bowman, who didn't bother. "Without checking with me."

"I wasn't aware it was necessary. Finelle?"

"We'll arrive at Plexis within one and a quarter standard days, Hom Morgan."

"Not without the engine, we don't!" Secrets and ploys. This one could kill them all if they ran out of time.

Incidentally ending the universe, which would serve Bowman right, he decided, beyond furious.

"What's the matter—"

In answer, Morgan spun on a heel, heading for the door. In the corridor, he broke into a full-out run.

Plexis?

On the bright side, Sira'd have a chance to see Huido.

If they made it.

Interlude

Plexis

TAYNO CLOSED and locked the door behind them, then checked the lock twice to be sure. "I've never been so glad to be—"

"Tayno, what are these?"

He turned, but eyestalks moved before his body finished, focusing on what now filled the hallway leading to the private section of the *Claws & Jaws*.

"Bones."

Very very large bones, not the sort used for soup at all, at least not in any pot he'd seen. They were stacked along one wall, leaving—thankfully—space for him, though he'd have to be very careful or he'd knock into them and then what?

"I know they're bones," Tarerea said in an urgent whisper. "Why are they here?"

"I don't know. They do," Tayno admitted, "arrange things without me." "They" being any of the restaurant's efficient staff, especially, he thought matter-of-factly, the ones who knew him best. "It must be for the opening." He gave himself a little shake. "We have to find Lones." And call the deputy inspector.

And tell her—what? Tayno's eyes converged on the crumpled

bit of plas in his claw, suddenly unsure. Had they uncovered a plot or would Jynet think him—Huido—a total fool?

"Tayno."

"I'm thinking—"

"Tayno!"

He bent up an eyestalk.

And froze.

He had to, because there, in the hall, black and glistening beside the stack of bones was another he. A magnificent he.

Not so magnificent as he, of course. Tayno swelled to his full stature and posed, dismissing the bone that tumbled behind, dimly aware of someone small beside him, shouting. There was someone behind the other he as well, also shouting.

Nothing mattered but this moment. This—appraisal. Previous acquaintance simply meant they'd no need to collide. Yet.

He would not budge.

Could not, truth be told, because whoever moved first lost, and losing meant being torn into tiny bits of he.

The other he wasn't whole. Where the right handling claw belonged was, to Tayno's consternation, a metal tool, like the hammer in the kitchen used to tenderize meat. Much larger. A hammer like that could shatter his head disks.

Making losing less palatable than usual.

The other he made a sound. One he hadn't heard since shelled. Tayno almost collapsed with astonishment, recovering to hold himself still.

The sound came again and continued. It came from the upper handling claws of the other, their tips vibrating together to produce that important low buzz.

The Bundle Call?

How confusing. How strange. They weren't in a pool and certainly weren't a mass of unshelled and barely shelled juveniles. While the Call was made by an adult male, this one was not his father. Though fatherhood was more a matter of who ruled a particular pool—

The buzz grew louder. More urgent. Those clawtips were the

only thing moving in the hall, with the exception of a second bone that happened to follow the first behind Tayno.

He was supposed to figure this out, Tayno thought suddenly. Not just stand here and pose, however magnificently. The Bundle Call meant gather, tightly, for protection. The Tide was going out, and those without shells would drown in air if exposed. Would be vulnerable to what hunted the shoreline. It was better, Tayno remembered clearly, to be in the middle of a bundle, which took a struggle, true, and some nipping.

That couldn't be it.

The Call translated, roughly, as "we die alone; we live together."

Well, then. Throwing caution and protocol to the winds, Tayno Boormataa'kk launched himself at the other he, clinging with all his might and claws.

"Too literal, Nephew," Huido Maarmatoo'kk rumbled, but kindly, extricating himself with ponderous care. "I intended to convey we must set aside our important but inconvenient instincts. It's time we battle, not each other, but side-by-side."

Tayno backed hastily. "Battle?!"

The ensuing crash would have been worse had not most of the bones fallen on him.

* ✳ *

Plexis

Fingers scrabbled, breaking a nail.

As the hand subvocalized a complaint, a foot and shoulder worked together to replace the piece of carpet over the conduit access, a task they accomplished just as a door opened, signaling the return of the room's legal inhabitant.

Bits became statues, pinned by portlights. Oblivious, the Festor chewed and belched its way to a set of drawers. The one foot in its path eased quietly aside. The one-mind found whatever thing it wanted, popped that into its maw of a mouth, then toddled back out.

The lights went off. The bits of Mathis Dewley fought and slapped one another, each striving to be first out the airduct.

Ten surprises to go.

* ✳ *

Snosbor IV

Our ship has docked, First Chosen. We have the locate, but our allies insist we wait for their contact.

Then wait. Wys worked her lips in and out, in and out, as she thought. A pinprick of annoyance: Erad, hovering as always at the edge of her consciousness. Futile, her Chosen's attempts to distract her; he expended so much energy to achieve nothing, she was tempted to ask him why he continued.

Asking would only encourage him.

Plexis was—problematic. Thanks to the interference of Sira di Sarc, their faces and idents were on a lamentable number of lists. And worse. Clan as part of the Trade Pact. Clan working with—instead of against—Human telepaths. Working with the Enforcers and their shields.

No longer. While their enemies lacked Power, the element of surprise must be on their side. On Plexis, others were too numerous, their spying tech everywhere. They'd weapons and perverse drugs.

But the prize, the prize was worth every risk. Her breath came quicker. This unnamed contact of the Scats had proven its use already. Whoever—whatever—it was. They'd known what was on course to the station.

Had sent a coded signal, hard on the arrival of the Brexk, concerning one ship in particular and its passengers, due to arrive shortly.

"Jason Morgan." Wys savored the name, its promise of the sweetest vengeance. The Human at the center of all trouble, past and present, would be delivered into her hands with what he tried to steal: Rael di Sarc.

She'd strip Morgan's mind of secrets, including where to find her son, as painfully, as slowly, as possible.

Then make what little was left of Sira's beloved Heresy a slave to her every whim.

Delicious as that prospect was, they'd more to sweep in their net. *Go with the contact, but be wary of the stranger. We don't know her capabilities.* Beyond sufficient Power to warrant caution. They'd drugs themselves, to use if she proved—resistant.

Another pinprick.

Old fool, Wys replied cheerfully. *This is what victory looks like. You should beg to be part of it.*

His *despair* was delicious, too.

Chapter 26

TO A SPACER, silence was trouble. Morgan shrugged off the notion, and kept working. They either woke the *Wayfarer*'s heart and exited subspace at Plexis—

—or stayed where they were as the great station kept moving away, that being the problem non-spacers didn't grasp. You didn't travel to Plexis, you planned an intercept course with something able to nip in and out of subspace according to a schedule of its own. Hence the importance of a posted course: Plexis would inform you, not particularly politely, if it wouldn't be where you thought it would, when you needed it to be.

Miss their moment? A healthy, whole ship could be sent on through subspace to the next window of opportunity, or to another destination. If there was one in range. This ship?

"You'll get wrinkles." Sira squatted beside him, the tool he'd need next waiting in her hands. "Frowning so much."

"Should have—known—better," he grunted with effort, shoulders working as he fought the recalcitrant bolt.

"Be fair. It's not as if you briefed Terk on this little—" she glanced around the cluttered engine room and settled for, "—project."

"Humph." The Human strained and finally, the bolt came free. He took the tool from Sira, pausing to squint suspiciously at her. "You're enjoying all this."

"Maybe." Her lips twitched. "A little."

"Wait till we're stuck in subspace and turn cannibal," he warned.

She leaned forward to press her lips lightly to his cheek. "You'll save the day."

Morgan closed his eyes. "Don't," he pleaded.

"What?" she replied lightly. "Be encouraging?"

Don't be as you were, he wanted to say. Don't make this like all our other times together, working to save the ship. Don't—

"Don't mix up the parts," he said aloud. "I need the transducer next." He pointed.

Captain Erin knew they were back on their posted, legal course. According to Sira, she'd blinked sleepily and then gone to bed, and Morgan hoped that was trust, but he feared it was inexperience. Plexis—it fooled you. Noska, on the other hand, hadn't stopped crooning over the renewed prospect of shopping.

"Here you go." Sira returned, resumed her squat. "Did you hear what happened on the bridge? Noska mixed up our enforcers and called Finelle for the shift change. They found themselves together in the lift."

He raised a brow. "And?"

Her eyes sparkled. "When Noska stopped screaming, it admitted even its superb senses hadn't detected anything Lemmickish. Finelle's now after Noska to record a statement for her uncle. That's going as well as you might expect."

"Small steps," Morgan replied. "Like this engine." To his eyes, what remained on the floor and bench had a sequence, a rightness. Erin had done a tremendous job. "So long as it all goes back together."

"That's what hammers are for." At his look, Sira laughed. "I learned it from you." Her face changed. "I won't forget, Jason. Don't ask me to."

"Understood." The darkness ahead was no further from her thoughts than his, Morgan thought. Sira was, quite simply, braver. As always. "We'll keep the hammer on hold for now, chit. This is going—I was about to say well, but let's see how the transducer fits first."

"Will you need me for that?" She checked the chrono on the wall. "Yihtor will wake soon—I should be there."

"I begrudge every breath we take apart," he said truthfully, then found a smile for her, "but no, I can manage. Erin will be down shortly."

Fingers brushed his. *As do I, Beloved.*

Aloud, "I'll be back as soon as I can."

When Sira left, the silence of the engine room wrapped Morgan like a vise.

He shrugged it off. " 'Save the day'?" he echoed, then grinned.

For her, anything.

Interlude

IF ANYTHING TROUBLED YIHTOR DI CARAAT, it didn't show in his face. Having dared *reach*, I knew better. His physical weakness horrified him; feeling trapped in the medbay made it worse. Which was why I'd wanted to be here.

"Breakfast is in the galley," I insisted. "No one's going to wait on you."

"I don't suppose you'll give me the locate." His full lips thinned. "I know what you're trying to do, Sira, but it's hopeless. I can't. You saw what they did to me."

I steeled myself. "What I see is a set of fully functional servo casts going to waste. You can stand, Yihtor, and walk." The *Conciliator*'s medtechs were trauma experts. I assumed getting the wounded literally back on their feet, quickly, was among their skills. If I was wrong, I'd apologize, but we were going to Plexis, to face those who were most likely his kin. We needed Yihtor whole and confident. Mobile, too, if possible; not all in the Trade Pact—or Plexis—would be glad to see us back from safely dead. I sneered, "You haven't made the effort."

Anger.

UnChosen, so proud. Feeling it, I smiled. "And once you're up, into the fresher. You smell worse than—old socks," I improvised, a Lemmick now in my inner circle.

I let Yihtor make the first tentative moves, stepping in to help him sit, then ease his legs to the side of the cot. His *fear* came through that contact, but so did a respectable amount of *determination*. I prepared to take some of his weight only to be waved off. "They work," he asserted grimly, "or don't."

"They" being smooth metal tubes encasing his legs from thigh to calf, looking less like knees than spare parts from the engine room. I made myself keep breathing as Yihtor swung his legs over the side.

We both stared as they bent with a fluid natural motion, as if the metal were flesh.

"We'll take it slow," I promised.

A breathless, almost laugh. "No, we won't. I want the fresher, then food." His feet, bare, touched the resilient floor, then he rose, tipping a little before finding his balance.

Yihtor had seemed to tower over me, but not my sister. As we stood eye-to-eye, my flinch was habit, nothing more, and I gestured apology.

"Never do so," Yihtor said quietly. "What I was here disgusts me. It cannot be forgiven."

"It can be forgotten," I reminded him. "When you Sing again, leave it behind."

His dark eyes swam with regret. "I must not, Sira. The Song must hold all truths, light and dark, not just the ones we want."

I wondered, watching Yihtor take cautious, then increasingly more comfortable steps, if he meant mine as well.

※ ✳ ※

In yet another set of used coveralls, the Clansman resembled a hero from a vid. Erin might be impressed, though it was the nature of our kind to feel sexual attraction at specific moments in life, to specific others. Looks weren't part of that attraction. We'd been bred to be beautiful, I thought with a rare flash of bitterness, not to have it matter.

"I've forgotten." Yihtor examined his plate dubiously. "Too long on tubes. Too long—" his hand collected air.

"Your body remembers," I assured him. "Put a small amount in your mouth."

I'd intended to chastise him for showing Morgan what I was, in AllThereIs; looking back, my anger was petty and undeserved. Yihtor had done it for me. He, like all the Singers, the ones who'd known me in NothingReal and the ones who'd shared their Song as well as mine, wanted me to be as complete as they were.

It troubled them I wasn't.

While sorry to cause them grief, I wasn't sorry about my choice. Explaining it, however, seemed impossible. My Human would say they lacked a frame of reference. They didn't understand love between physical beings. It had been bred out of us, out of the Hoveny, as an inconvenience to breeding for Power. Love itself, Singers comprehended and gloried in—I'd heard it, in their Song.

It was mine, for Morgan, his for me, they couldn't reach across the void to grasp.

Yihtor chewed and swallowed a few bites, though it didn't seem a pleasant process, before he paused and sat back. "How do we know my people will be on Plexis?"

"They chose Scats for allies," I reminded him, then told him what he didn't know. "Your mother's followers killed the *Worruad's* captain before leaving Auord. The Scats want revenge."

"That's their nature. Everyone knows it." Yihtor frowned. "Why would any Clan continue to trust them?"

"I doubt it's trust. If Scats are all she has left, Wys has to believe hers will stay bought. Unless she'd give up her plans." I raised a brow to make it a question for the son of the cruel and ambitious Clanswoman.

"She won't. Can't."

I nodded, unsurprised. "Bringing us to Plexis. The Scats have Clan on their ship—Clan they earnestly want dead, but are too smart to attempt to kill outright. They'll betray the Clan to anyone who'll do it for them." It wasn't safe to be a Scat who allowed an enemy to escape. As for enemies?

There'd been rare satisfaction in the report Terk had passed along to us. "The smuggler called the Facilitator is on Plexis. He was behind the Assembler attack on us. The enforcers believe he intends to finish what he started—that he's using this ship, us, as bait for a trap."

The source of Bowman's intel was irrelevant to its meaning: our kind had no friends in the Trade Pact; deserved none, with only Acranam's exiles left. It didn't make thinking of the plots against us any easier.

"I know the name. A client, of sorts. Efficient. Ruthless if crossed." From Yihtor, a chilling assessment. He took another bite, chewed as though deep in thought, then, "Why not leave these Clan to him, and go after the rest?"

He wasn't flesh—or hadn't been for much longer than I—so the carnage of an ambush gone wrong in a place as packed with beings and inherently delicate as a space station wouldn't occur to him. Or matter.

"They're ours to deal with, all of them," I said tersely. Perhaps Yihtor would assume my fleshself hungered for its own vengeance.

The truth? I believed I'd a way to send our kind home without blood on Morgan's hands, or anyone else's. My Human had shown me, however unwittingly. The flow of thought between us, be it mindvoice or shared memory, hadn't affected the M'hir. Taisal or any other Watcher would have howled if it had. I'd been halfway prepared, ready to protect Morgan, then so relieved to be left in peace with my love, the implications hadn't struck me until later.

The trick was touch, with its minimal need for Power. I'd experimented, finding I could *send* to Morgan without a reaction, but then, he was more than willing to *hear* me.

Acranam's exiles would not be. Physical contact would be necessary, that perilous intimacy Clan learned to avoid early in life, especially with the more Powerful.

I offered Yihtor di Caraat my right hand. "Let me show you."

And even he hesitated to take it.

Chapter 27

"I WANT YOU to take her through, Morgan." Without hesitation, Captain Usuki Erin planted herself at the engineering console and keyed the code to expose the jettison control. She glanced at him. "Best get your butt to the bridge."

The engines were as ready as could be; the room around them cleared of anything liable to move without warning, thanks to Sira. That this "test" would either pop them out at Plexis or strand them in subspace was a given, in the latter case with the added probability the engines' failure would be catastrophic, meaning he or Erin would have a decision to make. Push the button to save the rest, or die together. No question which would be a kindness.

Details. He nodded. "See you on the other side, captain. Rael, with me, please."

Sira looked torn. "I could stay." *'Port her back inside the ship.*

A risk she'd been willing to take for him, Morgan realized.

"I've all the company I need," Erin said, stroking the console. "Go on. Let's see if you're as good a pilot as Thel claims."

Morgan grinned. "I'll try not to scratch the hull."

"You'd be patching it."

✳ ✱ ✳

Morgan keyed in the bridge, waiting for the door to close before broaching what wasn't going to be a welcome topic. "You and Yihtor—"

Sira stared at the door, shoulders straight. "No."

The pair represented—something beyond comprehension—but they were here to help, that much he'd grasped.

And could be the Trade Pact's only hope.

Not the first time the slender figure standing next to him, the wondrous person inside, had stepped forward to be that hope, for her people, for him. The sheer injustice of asking Sira yet again wasn't lost on Morgan.

Yet—wasn't it her nature? With her unique combination of Power and compassion, Sira forged connections. Chooser to Human. Clan to the species of the Trade Pact. M'hiray to Om'ray to Hoveny. His universe to hers.

"You must protect yourselves," Morgan said bluntly. "You're here to save—" to say everything was an impossible weight, "—the day."

Her hair had grown; most still stuck out as though inflicted with static, but red-burnished tips brushed along her jaw. Through those, he spotted, of all things, a dimple. "I'm here," she said primly, "to sit third on coms." Then, with an underlying wave of *warmth* and *confidence*. "The ship'll be fine. I can tell Erin's better with engines."

"Different," Morgan mock-protested, as the lift doors opened.

The *Wayfarer*'s optimum bridge crew complement would be three. She'd double that seating to allow for the incoming shift, as well as ten more in this configuration, her previous owner having invited passengers to observe—prudently distant from any consoles.

At the moment, her bridge held a motley assortment of four, six with their arrival: Terk sat the second com seat behind Noska, while Finelle and Yihtor sat as observers. The Whirtle's helmet, stuffed with socks, was secured to its station. Perhaps it worried the Lemmick's protective suit would fail at some crucial moment. The species was known for its long-term planning.

"Captain Morgan," Noska announced. "You have the con."

Terk raised a brow. Morgan, heading to his seat, paused to say, firmly, "Captain Erin is overseeing the engine room."

"She's letting Morgan park the ship," Sira explained cheerfully.

Chit, he sent, receiving that too-innocent look as she strapped herself in—not, as stated, near Terk and Noska, but in the seat closest to his.

They'd history, here. He'd been the one in a med cocoon when they'd first set course for Plexis. He'd sent the *Silver Fox* there after refusing to comply with Bowman's order to bring Sira to her, knowing it could cost his freedom as well as his ship.

There'd been something about Sira then, as there was now. Had he fallen in love with her as he watched her efforts to fit in as Hindmost on the *Fox?* Or when he'd begun to grasp the courage that kept her going, despite her memories and Power being blocked? Had it been that moment on the bridge, when their hearts beat as one and he'd realized, with her, for the first time in his life, he'd no need for secrets and doubt?

Or when he'd gone into her mind, and seen himself as she did—

All of the above, Morgan thought, slipping the straps over his shoulders. "Bridge set," he sent to Erin. "Ready below?"

"As we'll ever be," came the cheerful reply.

He reached for the controls.

Interlude

HOW RIGHT IT FELT, to watch the *Wayfarer*'s controls lift to meet Morgan's capable hands. I settled back in my seat, which wasn't the copilot's couch of the *Fox,* nor was I in the body I'd worn then, but the feeling hadn't changed, nor the reason. My Human belonged at the helm of a starship. I'd give anything to make it happen—

But his future wasn't in my hands. That he had one, would be.

The ship's engine concerned me far less than Yihtor's state of mind. Morgan's urging for us to protect these bodies was well-founded. After all, I'd been willing to chance a 'port between a detached engine compartment and the ship. Children played 'port and seek across such minuscule distances, winking in and out so quickly, they barely skimmed the M'hir.

A 'port through it to Plexis wasn't a child's game. We'd leave a wound. Better we return to AllThereIs than further weaken Between.

Yihtor agreed, but I could sense his *unease* growing. He hadn't my experience with space travel. Instinct stirred within his physical self, telling him to 'port from danger. If the *Wayfarer* so much as shuddered, he could panic and he'd the Power to *move* to any remembered location, be it Plexis or worse, Acranam.

The Watchers sensed it, too. They were circling. Came so *close*, it was hard to remember to breathe—

Not helping, I scolded, as if they'd listen, turning my head. Yihtor's eyes met mine in a desperate plea. His fingers clenched the arms of his seat as though they could hold him in place.

I unbuckled my restraints and hurried across the bridge to take the seat beside him. Putting a gentle hand over his, I summoned Power. *Sorry about this.*

And *pinned* him.

His eyes shot open, but that was all Yihtor could do, constrained by my will. I'd held him like this before, when we'd been enemies, and the battle had taxed us both. This time, I felt him *test* the bounds I'd placed on his mind and then relax.

Problem, Witchling?

Not anymore, I replied, feeling the Watchers' withdrawal with profound relief. I let Morgan *feel* my smile. *Take us to Plexis.*

Chapter 28

THEY'D A COURSE set for Plexis—for where the *Wayfarer* had been told the station should be. Automatic, that inner "should." Like starships, information traveled subspace in bursts, and priority went to the needs of navigation; in Morgan's estimation, no starship captain worth the name believed the data stream infallible.

It having been touched, at some point or other, by living beings.

One of the less publicized but arguably most vital functions of the Trade Pact's Enforcers was to ensure that touch was in every-being's interest. Mistakes shouldn't happen. Willful tampering? The penalty, if caught, was to be denied further access. Exile, in other words, for who'd risk entering a busy system without data on what was there?

Mistakes were a fact of life, and no threat could guarantee good behavior—or even reasonable self-interest. Like all free traders, Morgan preferred to be in control when his ship broke from its subspace bubble, in case of one—or the other.

"Here we go," he announced, and pressed the waiting switch. His other hand was poised over the jettison button, but he hadn't decided what to do—

—when with a confident, throaty purr, the *Wayfarer* slid into normal space, answering any doubt.

"Scans live, Captain," Noska said at the same instant, throwing the result on the wall-sized screen. "Plexis Port Authority sends— EEK!!!"

Morgan didn't think; he acted, dropping the *Wayfarer* as proximity alarms shrieked their dismay.

The *Silver Fox* had been fast and nimble. Though much larger, the ship in his hands had been built to race by system rules, where speed wasn't the deciding factor, but maneuvering around obstacles was. The *Wayfarer* responded like something alive, diving along the z-axis, taking them below—what?

He silenced the alarms with the punch of a finger, rolling the ship to keep her "eyes" in line with that stunning shape. "Scan!"

"Reading now," Terk answered, the poor Whirtle likely under its console. "Bloody big, whatever it is," a grumble then, more useful, "Broadcasting a Trade Pact ident. Friendly, I repeat, friendly."

"Idents can be faked." Morgan sensed Sira's approach, felt her hand on his shoulder as he stared at the screen.

The starship was of no design he knew, of itself startling. What was caught in their lights resembled a ripple in water. Morgan flashed a look over the readouts: they weren't seeing all—or most of its mass. What they could see had no visible ports, no running lights of its own, nothing standard.

As if they'd startled it, the ship suddenly vanished.

Into subspace? If so, it should have dragged them with it, the *Wayfarer* too close to evade. "Report."

"It was there," Terk growled. "Just—not."

"There were minds aboard," Sira whispered. "None I could touch. They were—almost familiar."

Did it 'port?

I don't know—I don't think so.

"Plexis-com wants us in." The enforcer sounded incredulous. "We've been assigned a parking spot, priority one. They think we're a damn liner."

Morgan blew out a breath. "Then we park."

As he reoriented the *Wayfarer*, the great station came into view. An oblong cylinder, thicker aft than stern, her sides held ports and handles and scars aplenty, lit by an oversufficiency of lights. The screen went white, then reset. The "parking lot," in Plexis-com's quaint parlance, consumed the aft arc of what had been her material intakes, had she still been a refinery and in the business of swallowing asteroids whole. In recent years, more spots had been added, sprawled around her sides. The whole was a thoroughly messy, cobbled-together mass—

—that worked.

"I've never seen the outside," Sira said, then frowned. "Shouldn't there be ships?"

"Yes." Dozens in view. Hundreds. She knew it as well as he: an intricate, complex—occasionally jammed and disrupted—dance should cluster around the station, ships waiting to dock, ships departing, all needing to be done while Plexis was in real space.

The only thing moving was *Wayfarer*. And whatever had vanished, Morgan thought, unsettled. "Something's wrong. What's Plexis-com advising."

"Just the come-ahead, and be quick about it." Terk's grunt wasn't happy. "No other chatter. No complaints. Nothing."

"All good up there?" Erin's voice, on com.

"Priority parking, Captain," Morgan responded, unsurprised when the response was colorful. Station's prerogative, to choose their spot; the selection offered depended on how much the incoming ship was willing to pay, as well as species' concerns. Lemmicks away from Whirtles. Away from most, in fact. Scats near those able to defend themselves.

Free traders like the *Wayfarer*? You'd have to walk the length of Plexis before finding an airtag counter. To be swished into the zone used by goldtags, Plexis execs, and visiting heads-of-systems?

Either someone wanted a target on their backs, Morgan thought, or whatever kept ships nose into Plexis was ongoing.

And they'd arrived in the midst of it.

* ✱ *

"—the air you share on Plexis."

The waxy stamp connected with his cheek and Morgan stepped

ahead to let the others get theirs. Blue, of course. Under ordinary circumstances, the color would stir swift and unwelcome attention from everyone from security to wait staff, for this wide welcoming space was more entry lounge than tag point, complete with a three-piece band playing live music. The concourse beyond, the top level of Plexis, beckoned through archways—no congested ramps here—its tastefully muted lights and towering trees suggesting a retreat from the hardships of space travel.

Only the obscenely rich entered here.

The concourse was empty. The instruments hung on their stands, abandoned, and the only other person in sight was this airtag operator who'd come to greet them, an attractive *is-male* Skenkran young enough to be pre-flight. Its face-covering chitinous nose, a source of pride to the species, sparkled with inset gems, but Morgan was more interested in the ooze of yellow mucus. Tension could do that.

Or fear. "What's going on here?" Morgan asked.

"I have not been informed," the being said, its throat implant set to a melodic tenor. "Next?"

Waving aside the tag, Terk stepped close, chest out as if his uniform wasn't clue enough. "Contact your superiors. On my authority."

A sigh quivered along those not-yet-full shoulder casings, shimmering the hint of silk membrane beneath. "I would, Constable, but I've no way to do so. The internal coms went off before you arrived." Earnestly, "I'd hoped you could."

"On it." Making sure Yihtor, still uncertain on his casts, was leaning on the counter and Terk watched him, Finelle stepped away, raising her com.

Worse and worse, Morgan thought, glad he'd been able to persuade Erin and Noska to stay on the *Wayfarer.* "Where did everyone go?"

The Skenkran flipped a shoulder casing over its nose. Overtop, eyes peered down, blinking as though, having thoroughly hidden itself, they'd go away, too.

"It's all right," Sira told it. "You're not in trouble. Please. Tell us anything you know."

The casing lowered. "I was in the accommodation," it admitted. "When I came out, I was alone."

There must have been a mirror in it, Morgan sent. Is-males were desperately insecure about their appearance, fluctuating between obsessive vanity and anxiety. In the latter state, they'd rub their noses raw against hard objects to make them swell. He suspected the gem inlay wasn't so much ostentation but foresight on the part of the Skenkran's employer to prevent such behavior.

"What's your name? Mine's Jason Morgan."

Terk grunted. Morgan ignored him. Courtesy wasn't a waste of time. "You were intrepid to remain on duty," he praised warmly, pleased to see the casing lower further.

"My name is Pysyk Oes, Hom Morgan. I did not see what else I could do. This is my station."

"It's closed," Terk snapped.

The casing went up.

There were times— Rather than be frustrated with the enforcer, Morgan clapped his hands lightly twice, imitating the Skenkran encouragement. "Hom Oes, please come with us. We will see you to safety."

The casing came down. The youngster began to put down the tag hammer it had clutched fervently, only to stop midmotion, staring over their heads. Yellow mucus gushed forth. "No time!" Membranes spread for balance, the terrified Skenkran bolted into the concourse.

Morgan whirled, the others turning, too.

To see Carasians filling another, wider door.

Female Carasians.

They came through as a tight black mass, some turning to move sideways over the soft red carpet, all claws out in warning. The only sound they made was a soft *clickityclickityclickity*, as though fingers stroked a muted keyboard.

Larger by half again than any male, the chitin of their shells thicker and callused, their paired claws wider and serrated. No handling claws; females didn't need them. No dainty little mouths, able only to consume liquids. In the depths of those gnarled headplates was a set of criss-crossing jaws, able to macerate bone. Preferably while part of its screaming owner, females being obligate predators.

Their eyestalks were erect, gleaming black orbs aimed solely at the small group by the airtag station.

A year ago, Morgan thought, dry-mouthed, he'd have been right behind the Skenkran, though they likely wouldn't have made it. When motivated, Carasians moved with blinding speed. Back then, he'd believed females were mindless, confined to a pool by their male for the safety of others. A rumor his blood brother had cheerfully encouraged.

At his wives' insistence. Mindless? Carasian females were that species' thinkers, artists, and adventurers. At the pinnacles of their respective careers, each carefully selected the pool—and male—best suited to house what seemed a combination of shared meditation and violent debate. With sex, as Huido boasted, an essential and delightful inspiration to the females' intellectual communion.

Were these Huido's wives? If so, why enter Plexis here, and not through the docking bay he'd had built into the *Claws & Jaws*?

Though it did explain the empty lounge.

But where was Huido?

Sira stepped forward, and Morgan followed at once. The wives, towering like some nightmare cloud, clicked to a stop.

"You were right," Sira said to them, her voice clear and firm. "The Clan don't belong here. Yihtor and I have returned to remove the last of us."

As one, the giant creatures crouched, then rose.

Her cheeks the slightest bit pink, Sira bowed back. "We haven't done it yet," she warned. "There's still risk."

"YES!" Thunder, that disquieting reply.

The Human felt the word reverberate through his lungs.

Worse.

He *tasted* CHANGE.

Interlude

Plexis

FOR ONCE, a surprise filled Tayno with relief. Huido Maarma-too'kk was back. In charge, loudly. Rushing around. Knowing things. Capable. Staff jumped, happily.

There really was, Tayno decided, no need to bring up anything new. Huido's call to "battle" had gone mercifully unexplained, beyond the word; Huido himself continued to be in an unusually fine and forgiving mood.

A mood not to disrupt with unimportant items. The huge pending bill for Morgan's apartment could wait as long as possible, ideally until after he'd left to start his own establishment.

The arrival of a Rugheran in the kitchen, with Tarerea Vyna, presented a more pressing dilemma. Lones had introduced her to Huido as a "guest of Tayno's." Between the gold airtag, the glamorous clothing, and now-pleasant nature of her grist, Huido had accepted her presence graciously. Indeed, he'd compli-mented Tayno on his good sense, keeping the Vyna close.

Which, to be honest, had been a little confusing.

Having seen Tarerea to her room, Lones had hurried back, whispering to Tayno that her origin and the Rugheran were topics he, Tayno, must present to Huido as soon as the moment was right.

Maybe that could be after he'd—

"—leaving you in charge."

Tayno's eyes snapped to attention. He'd missed something, surely. "But you're back."

Workers carrying out those horrid—and heavy—Yabok bones eased around the two Carasians who, admittedly, consumed a significant amount of floor despite the generous proportions of the main dining hall. "Yes, Tayno," still with unusual patience, "however, I've other concerns. This business you've told me about, of Splits, Omacrons, and Brill together, must be dealt with—plus we're expecting company."

Three of Tayno's eyestalks swiveled to watch a tight group of Oduyae make their way into the restaurant through the workers and bones. Each towed a small sled. "Them?"

Huido bent an eye, then chuckled. "No, no. The Zibanejad Cluster are our new Master chefs. Excellent reputation. We're lucky to have them. Welcome," he bellowed.

The largest Oduya nodded gravely. "We arrive to serve." Or something like that. They were still too far to hear properly over the workers' din.

"They're serious folks," Huido confided. "You'll like them. I want you to give them a tour of the kitchen, make note of any changes they require. Anything," much louder, though the Oduyae were now beside them, "you need. Inform my esteemed nephew."

A nod to Tayno. "We will be reasonable."

Having known a chef or three in his life, Tayno doubted that. Touring the kitchen was easy, if the sleds could be parked outside, but a list of sure-to-be-costly changes? Now? He braced himself. "Perhaps, Uncle, you and I should go over the budget—"

"Nonsense!" A tender smack of the hammer replacing Huido's claw. "Anything these fine and creative chefs need, the *Claws & Jaws* will provide!"

He'd been afraid of that. "This way, please."

"When you're done, Tayno," Huido boomed, "oversee our new entranceway. I rely utterly on your good taste."

He couldn't mean— "The Yabok bones?" Tayno'd assumed

they were being removed by the workers, not— "You want me to decorate with them?" Huido snapped a lower claw in warning. Tayno altered his tone to a weak but enthused, "A privilege, Uncle."

"We arrive to serve," the Oduyae intoned, as if growing impatient. In fact, the entire mass of them were starting to edge, if slowly, toward the kitchen.

The tour. Tayno collected himself. "Wait for me. I'm coming." He hurried to get ahead of them and make sure the way was clear.

"Oh, and Tayno?"

He stopped and swung around. There couldn't be anything else. "Uncle?"

Huido waved at the sleds. "I recommend you escort the families to their accommodations before the tour. Carefully."

The boxes on the sleds weren't luggage, then. Tayno crouched by the nearest, eyestalks craned over. Little holes made decorative patterns on the sides and top. Through those holes emanated a *buzz*. A frustrated, angry *buzz*. And as he stared, the box seemed to grow, the buzz become louder, and there were seven of them, he realized, straightening in horror, all full of whatever buzzed and wasn't happy about being in boxes.

There was, Tayno thought numbly, a certain inevitability to disaster.

"I'll see to it, Uncle."

✳ ✴ ✳

Staff had prepared a suite for the Oduyae, the best other than Huido's own, it being the hope a well-rested and comfortable chef—or in this case, cluster of chefs—would shout and break things less often.

The Oduyae chefs seemed quiet and polite, following him with pleased-sounding murmurs in their own language. Wouldn't last, Tayno knew, and with more of them, the ongoing riot would be that much louder.

At least the "families" weren't the problem he'd feared. Yes, he'd bumped almost at once into a sled, tipping it, then tried to catch its box and missed, but an Oduya had made an impressive diving grab, so no harm done.

After that, they'd each picked up their box, hugged it to their chests, and insisted they needed no further assistance, thank you, to convey their families to their waiting accommodation. The last one in closed the door before Tayno could get more than a glimpse of what appeared to be sets of paired buckets enclosed within floor-to-ceiling nets.

Which didn't look restful or comfortable, but he wasn't an Oduya.

After a short wait, they reappeared. "We are ready to modify the kitchen," the largest told him.

To Tayno's alarm, all the Oduyae carried tools. The sort the workers had used to remove the wreckage after the explosion. "A list of your requests—"

"Is unnecessary." The Zibanejad Cluster, excepting the family members safely in nets, poured past him in a determined rush.

Tayno hurried to keep up. "Wait! Stop!" The kitchen was finished, counters gleaming, expensive cooktops ready to flame—hideously expensive, flame on a space station being one of those "control-or-die" fine prints in the lease, and Huido having been cited five times for his obsession with oil lamps—and they mustn't start breaking things before trying to cook a meal—

The chef stampede came to a halt in the kitchen door, reversed, and came at him, tools flung into the air. A curved bar hit Tayno on his headplate and he crouched, Oduyae climbing over him in their haste to return to their suite. Stunned, he aimed an eyestalk to follow.

The door closed behind them.

The Carasian took a moment to process, aliens a challenge at the best of times. Maybe the chefs, upon seeing the new kitchen, realized it was perfect as it was.

The budget was safe!

Unless they'd seen something in the kitchen. Say a gooey, scary Rugheran.

Not safe at all. Huido could well be unreasonable and expect to have been told about the first visit before a second.

Tayno sighed, rattling, casting three eyes in the direction of Tarerea Vyna's room. He was ever so much braver when she was with him, but Lones insisted she needed rest. She'd trembled, he recalled, after meeting Huido.

He stepped carefully around the discarded tools and went into the kitchen.

Nothing was wrong. Mystified, Tayno moved up one aisle, then down the next. He contorted to look under counters. Opened cupboards and drawers.

No Rugherans.

No surprises at all. Had he actually been right? Was the kitchen safe from its new chefs?

The door to the service corridor was open.

It wasn't, Tayno thought worriedly, supposed to be open. Well, yes, if there was waste from the kitchen to be removed or a delivery—the point was, with the restaurant closed and an Assembler on the loose, any access was to be locked. Or open and guarded. Better still, locked and guarded.

Against his better judgment, very slowly, Tayno went to the open door. The side, to be safe, keeping himself out of sight.

Two eyestalks curled around the doorframe.

Three more.

The rest of Tayno eased from hiding. There was nothing in sight, beyond a group of burping waste canisters. Methane collectors hovered above—

Red eyes appeared in the shadows beneath. "Off with you," Tayno said fiercely, rattling his shell. The eyes disappeared.

Were the awful things the problem? He closed the door. If the vermin had made it into the kitchen, if the new chefs had seen them, well, they could break their contract. The *Claws & Jaws* had already lost one chef—another tidbit of news Tayno didn't plan to share with his uncle—but that one hadn't demanded compensation.

There simply wasn't enough in the budget to send the Oduyae and their families home again, let alone pay penalties.

Filled with gloom, Tayno reached for the doorlock.

Only to have it *snick* into place before he touched it.

He stared. That was—odd.

He tried unlocking it, but the panel didn't respond. Hitting it wouldn't make any difference, he'd learned the hard way, however satisfying. He gave it another, firmer tap, just in case.

"Nephew! Stop fooling around," Huido bellowed from the door to the dining room. "Come quickly. Plexis locks her doors."

He couldn't slink with Huido watching; self-preservation, not courage, it being a guaranteed way to die, slinking before a larger male. In Tayno's opinion, station emergencies encompassed all the other ways to die, unless . . . he ventured hopefully, "Is it a drill?"

"They aren't saying. We aren't guessing. We must get your guest. Come!" Huido disappeared.

Tarerea Vyna? Wasn't she safer locked in her room? Technically, the Vyna couldn't be locked in her room, Tayno realized as he hurried to follow. She'd the locate for several places now, though he didn't think she'd go back to the *Infant Emporium* or the security office.

The hall was deserted, doors closed. "Why aren't there alarms?" he asked, catching up to Huido. The drills he'd endured thus far had included a cacophony of species-specific warnings, instructions, and skewed lighting, though the other Carasian was noisy enough, weapons and bags clipped to his carapace. Should he remind Huido he was supposed to don that padded vest? Maybe not. But why was the other's pitted and scarred shell polished so that his whirling eyes reflected at him?

"If it's an emergency, Uncle," he tried again, "shouldn't there be alarms?" Did Huido know something he didn't? Tayno brightened. Were the wives on their way home?

Huido didn't answer, busy keying in an override code, hunched so Tayno couldn't see, though it wasn't, he thought wistfully, as if it would help now, the rightful owner of the pool right in front of him.

"Bah." Huido backed a step, reared to his full height, then drove the business end of his metal hammer through the door control.

"You'll scare her," Tayno objected, pushing into the room first. "It's all right, Tarerea, it's me. Tayno."

"I know it's you." The Vyna looked more alert than frightened, though the blow must have sounded like an explosion. Had she never heard an explosion before?

He wished he never had. "Come with us."

She didn't move. "I won't go to him." Her head aimed up.

Tayno's eyes bent anxiously to study the ceiling. "Who?"

"Please, Tayno. Don't make me go. I won't Call this unChosen. I must not. He cannot be my Candidate." She stepped closer, gazed pleadingly up. The blue veins beneath her skin made it look like the finest porcelain—the sort liable to shatter. "He is not Vyna. Not Om'ray. He is kin to those who ended my world—"

"Tayno!" Huido had stayed in the hall. "We've no time for chatter. Come with us, Fem," he ordered, low and firm. "You don't belong here."

And there was something dark in how he said those words, and final, making Tayno feel as he never had before. Bigger. Meaner. So for both their sakes, he hoped Huido meant the room.

Because if he meant harm to Tarerea Vyna? To take her to this male she did not want? To send her away?

They would do battle.

And one would die.

When they came out in the hall, Huido reared as though taken by surprise, eyes converging on him. "Finally. I wondered when you'd start to grow up."

Tayno stood in front of Tarerea Vyna, posing just a little. "I'll permit no harm to my friend." Why, his voice was deeper— impressive.

Huido chuckled. "Good." His claw smacked Tayno without warning, sending him against the wall. "Just remember, Nephew, I'm not the threat. At the moment."

* * *

Plexis

The underbelly of Plexis was a maze of narrowed corridors squeezed through spaces originally designed to chew stone and

excrete wealth. Bulkheads crossed at intervals, making it necessary to step, hop, or whatever worked to get over them, and the
air here smelled over-shared. That these surroundings helped
make those forced to enter the station at this point feel unworthy
was a bonus, in the varied oculars of security, reserving glamour
and clean air to the upper levels for paying customers.

The lockdown on those levels didn't apply here. The doors
that mattered belonged to the starships nosed into the station,
and Plexis had, without warning or consent, attached explosive
clamps to every hull—

Having learned from a Scat what an unauthorized departure
could do.

By protocol, there'd been armed guards assigned to the junc-
tions leading to the sole Scat ship presently parked at Plexis, but
as such assignments were viewed more as a means to an unreported bonus than vital, those guards had taken it upon themselves to diligently search an adjacent area for suspicious activity.
One never knew where smugglers might be.

Or when the bought would return for more, so the Scats waiting with their passengers were eager to finish their business and
be away, hissing to one another, clawed toes clicking as they
shifted their feet. The section of corridor was poorly lit, several
of its portlights newly nonoperational. As a further improvement,
the few vids in evidence had been spat upon: corrosive saliva yet
another endearing characteristic of the species.

Most Clan had come late to a recognition of surveillance; not
so the five waiting with the Scats. Kero di Licor and her Chosen,
Taze. Denly and Nos sud Annk. Merin di Lorimar, her Chosen,
Tren, on Snosbor IV to be a living link through the M'hir. Once
underway, their Joining would *draw* her to him, as well as any
others in her 'port, for that was her Talent, to be the one to ferry
their prizes home.

Powerful, these five. Experienced. The Scats burdened themselves with weapons while any here could kill them with a thought,
and none trusted Scats or the situation. Necessity kept them together, and both species were impatient for that to end.

They were Destarians. Their future was here, claimed their

leader—worth any risk, and they were desperate to believe. Wys di Caraat had done as she'd promised, saved them from the Assemblers and found them a world of their own, but they'd *felt* the deaths of those left behind on Acranam. *Reached* into the empty M'hir. Knew they were the last of their kind. If Wys and her creature succeeded, a new generation would rise from the scraps of this one. If it was less than hope?

It was all they had left.

"Not long now," hissed a Scat.

"True." Merin looked up, her *inner* sense aware, searching. *They're here.*

Then let's 'port to them and get this over with.

Merin's Chosen followed her tendril of seeking thought. *A Chooser! The report was incomplete.*

Excitement sizzled, erasing any doubts.

Weapons lifted and whined in readiness, the use of Power alarming the Scats, not that they'd more than awareness. Merin held out her hands, palms out. "Peace." The tiresome aliens— their starship—would be required for the return journey.

The start, anyway. They'd 'ported to the Scat ship, already on its way to Plexis, in order to arrive like any other beings. Once safely away from the station, well, the aliens would no longer be necessary.

Taze di Licor, who tolerated Scats better than most, spoke up. "We apologize for the disturbance, Captain. We're eager—" unwise to reveal success, "—to find those we seek."

"You won't have to wait much longer," that individual informed them. For some reason, their jaws began chittering in their drooling laugh.

We can't trust them, Nos sent, an opinion he and his Chosen expressed with tedious frequency, having lost their only child to the species.

"We should wait in the ship," Denly suggested. "It stinks. There are vermin everywhere."

"Was-sste dissspos-ssal. We ss-stay—"

"Quiet!" Another Scat took a slow careful step from the others, tilting his head. "I hear ss-ssomething—" Unlikely, over the whines and beats of Plexis herself—

Then the Clan heard it, too. A little *hum.*

As one, the Scats, the most dreaded species within the boundaries of the Trade Pact, dropped their weapons and fled, clawed feet skidding on the floor.

"What—?" Merin frowned. *Be ready,* she sent quickly.

It's our contact, Taze replied as two figures came out of the shadows, walking toward them. Both were non-Human and, recognizing the species, he shared *relief* and *confidence. Foolish Scats.*

One of the figures was small and reassuringly familiar, the other a towering bulk, but physical threat didn't intimidate Clan—

*Wait—someth—*Merin's mindvoice simply stopped.

And the Clan learned—between the breaths just taken and the next trapped in their lungs, as they were *held*—what the Scats had known to fear and they had not.

For it was the small one, the discounted, the familiar, whose eyes were wide and ringed with darkness—

The small one who *hummed*—

"Look at that," the big one boomed cheerfully. "A mere Omacron—controlling the mighty Clan. Sept's about to do much worse than that to you, I'm afraid. Beg, if you like. Offer to use your Powers for us. To return our treasure—oh, wait." It raised its hands in feigned surprise. "You don't have any treasure. Just like you don't have any future."

The *humming* changed, became a drill, penetrating, searching—

—*finding* the door through their deepest shields, a trap set the first time they'd *touched* an Omacron mind, waiting for the one who would use it.

Merin tried desperately to speak. To *send.* To 'port. She felt Tren's Chosen's futile struggle, his terror.

Saw the others grow pale with fear.

—*going through!*

Saw what wasn't blood oozing from their noses and eyes. Felt it, warm and wet, then chill on her own face. *REACHED* outward—

"What's that?" The big one cupped its ear. "Who am I? Doesn't matter. I've a message for your leader and the rest of your kind. There's no room in the new First for Clan. Wait. Don't bother trying to send it. My colleague assures me there's nothing—not a single thing—you can do. I'll take it myself. Once we're finished with Plexis."

The small one stepped up to Merin, curling sept's red-cloaked body to embrace hers, and *HUMMED*. As the Clanswoman convulsed in agony, sept swayed as if to unheard music, skin glowing with ecstasy. Held tight as the body dropped, then began to rock rhythmically against it, pulsing toward climax as the life left—

The Brill kicked the Omacron loose. "Just do the job," the big one boomed with disgust. "Choiola's expecting us."

The Omacron's head whipped around in fury, to find septself facing a needler. Sept eased back, lids lowering. "I am of the First," thick with thwarted passion.

"You're a perverted lump of useful," the Brill informed it, threat in every word. Beneath, violence in every *thought*. The needler waved at the remaining Clan. "Make it quick, or I will."

"No! Quick I can be." The Omacron coiled to view those waiting. "There's more," sept whispered.

And *hummed*.

※ ✳ ※

Snosbor IV

Tren di Lorimar tried desperately to speak, to send, to do anything to warn his kind. Toppling over his desk, he fumbled to reach a stylo. His Omacron servitor came into view, long fingers picking up the implement.

Only to move it out of reach. Sept bent. Smiled.

The smile was the last thing Tren saw before his mind was *pulled* into the M'hir by his Chosen's, leaving a lifeless husk behind.

Chapter 29

NO MATTER HOW LOUD or varied the alarm, saving yourself on Plexis was assumed to be a personal choice, the station itself having two overriding concerns: to remain airtight and to prevent opportunistic theft. Make that one. If you failed to pay your taxes, shoplifters were given your address.

If the finite "air-we-share" was leaking into space, it was up to the individual to seek safety which was—not coincidentally—inside the nearest store or business, those protected by an emergency forcefield Plexis magnanimously supplied to all.

A hefty charge arriving once the emergency ended.

This wasn't a hull breach, Morgan decided. There'd been no alarm, according to the Skenkran. The great station had cleared its decks for some purpose—how he'd yet to discover, but why? That was the scary question.

Meanwhile, Plexis waited and they were on the move.

There'd been no question, the Carasians herding them into the main concourse with their combined mass, as unhurried and implacable as a docking servofreighter. Terk jumped out in front, taking point or to be as far ahead of that mass as possible. Morgan stayed with Sira, with Finelle and Yihtor shoulder-to-shoulder.

Behind them, the soft *clickityclick* of carapace to carapace, claw to claw.

The concourse was empty but not abandoned. The stores—here tastefully scattered throughout faux-forest glades—were encased in forcefield bubbles, distorting but not hiding the figures of those now held inside. On lower levels, there'd be some high-pressure sales underway; the entrepreneurs of Plexis unable to resist trapped customers—especially with the bill to come from the station.

On levels like this? There'd be soothing, efficient service. Entertainment. Nothing so obvious as *selling*. Credits would, ultimately change owners here, too, but with understated elegance.

Those on this level who hadn't, for their own reasons, sought safety with shopping took one look at Terk and made themselves scarce—prudent, given what followed them, though odds were the Whirtle family cared more about avoiding their Lemmick.

All at once, Sira tugged Morgan's sleeve and pointed, her green eyes wide with delight. "There's the *Bakka-Phoenix Reader Zone!*"

They were keeping ahead—barely—of a horde of motivated Carasian females, in a station under mysterious siege and—"You're shopping?"

"I'm observing." She grinned. "You know I've always wanted to see this level. No goldtags, remember? Sneaking up here's on our list."

"Our—" Morgan closed his mouth. The list they'd made in off hours on the *Fox*. Of all they'd do together. Large, small, didn't matter, Sira'd wanted to see everything, and he'd agreed, happily. Through her eager eyes, everything was made new for him, too. They'd time for it all.

Hadn't they a lifetime to fill?

He'd found the copy he'd sent to Ettler's for safekeeping. Destroyed what was now a list of nothing but regret.

Morgan watched realization cross her face, dimming her smile, only to see that smile brighten again. "It's bigger than I thought," Sira assured him.

"A recent renovation, Fem di Sarc," Finelle offered. "The entrances were enlarged."

Yihtor spoke. "Where are they making us go?"

"Down," the Human guessed, the rampways in sight.

"It's twenty levels down to the *Claws & Jaws*." Sira glanced over her shoulder. "Why enter Plexis here?"

No answer, but since their overwhelming "YES," the Carasians had been grimly silent. Nothing more to say—or nothing to say here.

Sira was right, though. If these were Huido's absent wives, they could have entered his pool in complete privacy. If they weren't, that still didn't explain why they'd entered on the upper level. Everyone knew Carasian females weren't seen in public—or, for that matter, out of water, which could have been their delight in ambush.

The same way "everyone knew" they were nonsapient as well as dangerous?

As far as Morgan was concerned, all common knowledge about the species had originated within exceptionally clever black head disks. Delayed sexual dimorphism, particularly when it included a dietary change to predation, might have made their neighbors in the Trade Pact a tad nervous.

Making this traipsing through Plexis—if by any stretch the females' ponderous movement was traipsing—that much harder to understand, since it gave a substantial cross-section of the Trade Pact's population their first, terrifying, look at what they'd let live down the hall.

"Why here? They're making a statement," Morgan concluded. "What it is, I've no idea."

* ✳ *

The backs of their hands would brush now and again, not quite by accident; neither of them were inclined to move farther apart. After all, this first ramp they took was spacious, with discreet hold-fasts for those with appendages other than hands and an easy slope. There was a ramp elsewhere for servos the Carasians likely should have taken, given the labored wheeze of this one as it descended, but it was too late now. They'd switch in another four or so levels to the usual utilitarian structures built to accommodate

grav sleds and whisk the blue tagged up or down with more concern for speed than safety. As those would be, at any time, jammed
with living things and luggage, falling was impossible, pickpockets
rampant, and being trampled imminent.

Ramps now deserted, like this one. Morgan didn't look forward to seeing what might be underfoot. Some things weren't
meant to be seen by the living.

Another brush, this time of fingers, though Sira looked straight
ahead. *Yihtor's scanned. The Clan are on the station, but we've a problem. There's a Chooser, too.* A hint of *puzzlement* he understood: Sira
had thought the exiles composed of Chosen pairs. *There's no
doubt. Yihtor feels her presence.*

Morgan understood that potential problem, too. The draw of
a Chooser was a potent lure to any Clan unChosen, let alone
Yihtor, who'd waited unnaturally long. *Will he go to her?*

No. Not yet, she qualified, the line of her jaw firm. *He's not fully
of this body he wears; what it wants isn't what he wants. This could
change.*

Morgan turned his hand so their palms met, his breath catching as her fingers laced through his. *Is that how you feel? What you
want?*

A thrill of *HEAT* answered, followed by a quenching wry *humor.
How I feel, inside and out, my dear Human, shouldn't be possible. We
are no longer Joined. No longer Chosen. This body was both, but not by
me. Do I really feel this?* Her fingers tightening, she met his gaze
with her own, sober and serious. *Can I? Or do I just remember how
we were?* "I miss you," a whisper, as if she didn't dare send it mind-
to-mind.

He didn't dare answer. If he did, he'd beg her to stay, to be
with him once more—only that, only once—but if his heart
ached now for the hope of it, that once would be more than either of them could bear.

Instead, Morgan brought his Witchling's hand to his lips, then
raised his head to look into her eyes—

Only to see what awaited them below.

"What is it?" Sira's head turned.

"Company." A line of Plexis security surrounded the base of the ramp.

Security in the eye-searing green of biohazard suits, usually employed for spills of noxious substances, particularly those found in spacer bars where anything could be considered drinkable by some being, and those inadvertent escapes from cargo holds or live food markets.

To see a full troop thus garbed was, Morgan admitted, a tad alarming.

"No wonder they were able to keep people in the stores." Sira murmured.

When they reached the bottom, Terk took a step to the side, scowling up at the wives. "Why don't we have suits?"

To his credit, he didn't back down, even as dozens of eyes scowled in return, eyes coming closer. The enforcer crossed his arms. When a female snapped a claw, he uncrossed them. "We need suits!"

"NO NEED!"

Staggered, the enforcer was undeterred. "Fine for you—you've shells. What about us?"

"You heard the Fems, Terk." One of those in green pulled off her hood. "Don't fuss."

It was Bowman.

Interlude

SECTOR CHIEF LYDIS BOWMAN.
      Her bright, miss-nothing eyes found me, though I held
back to let Morgan greet her first. My heart, still pounding from
what had and hadn't passed between us, however foolish and
fraught, tried to skip a beat then settled. From somewhere, I
found the ability to nod.

Bowman here explained a few things. I hoped.

Sira. We have to leave. Now!

Startled, I looked at Yihtor. *The Chooser*—but it wasn't a Call, I
realized, *hearing* Watchers *HOWL!*

"Now!" Aloud. He grabbed my hand . . .

I saw Morgan leap for us—

. . . then was somewhere else.

✳ ✱ ✳

This was the Plexis I remembered: like a dingy repair shop, cluttered with low hanging wires, damp collecting against the bulkheads. That and the stink helped, when nothing could have
prepared me for what was new here.

From the howls, I'd expected bodies. There were five—four, I realized. Yihtor used the wall to lower himself to the Clansman who improbably continued to breathe, oblivious to all else.

I couldn't afford to be. *Jason, we're on a sublevel. The Clan were attacked.* I sent what I could see, having no words for the ruin of their faces, for what had poured forth, for—I swallowed, hard, and looked around for anything more.

There. A weapon—a Scat disrupter—tossed aside as if useless. More than one. I picked up the nearest, though it wouldn't work for any other sort of being, Scat having their sensible side. Maybe I hoped whatever had done—whatever had been done here— wouldn't know any better.

No vid feed. With an echo of my own horror in his mindvoice. *Bring me down there.* An order.

One I couldn't obey, *feeling* the Watchers' continued turmoil. *We've done enough to the M'hir,* I countered, then tried to think. *We must be near the Scat ship.*

I'm coming. Stay put, chit.

Morgan vanished behind his shields, taking that bit of comfort. Shadows pressed in from every side, and I didn't want to stay here, not even to wait for him, but Yihtor was in no state to leave.

He'd made it to the floor. Put his hand gently on the fallen Clansman's forehead, the only part of the face not covered in what I very much feared wasn't only blood, and closed his eyes. Went still.

Power swelled; I kept my distance. Whatever he attempted, Yihtor was no Healer. Not that anything could stop this death and weren't we here, in NothingReal, to cause them?

A final soft exhalation signaled the end. Yihtor straightened to lean on the filthy wall, tipping his head back against it. His gray-green eyes found me, dull instead of bright. "The Watchers have Nos. Have them all."

"Did you—" I hesitated.

"Show him the way?" A pained shrug. "Yes, once I had what we need. Here." He held out his hand. Shoved it at me, when I didn't move right away. "Take it. The locate. The rest."

"The rest of what?"

"My mother's plan. I'd thought forcing myself on you the worst she could do—not that I was against it then." At something in my face, he dropped his hand. "Sira, she's working with another toad. Making us in tubes. Trying to plant the results in mind-wiped Omacrons." He shuddered. "You can't imagine how much she wants these bodies of ours." A limp gesture to me, to himself, then up. "And the Chooser."

Oh, I could. Yihtor had missed Faitlen's work with Retians— what I'd endured. It appeared they'd found another willing to let them tamper with us.

The Trade Pact's problem. "We'll leave the husks for the authorities," I decided, having a hazy notion of techs and devices gained, truth be told, from a few entertainment vids, but still. "They'll want to know who did this." And how, I shuddered. One body was contorted, as though the agony of her death had broken bones. I looked away.

Yihtor's gaze had followed mine. It stayed on the body. "My cousin and heart-kin, Merin di Lorimar. She *reached* along our bond as she failed. Merin's with the Watchers now," more briskly, looking up at me. "I know what did this. I've the image of those who came and who killed them."

He'd something else, I thought, mouth dry. The locate for Wys di Caraat and the rest of her followers. It could be over, that quickly.

Or bring disaster on us all. I felt the Watchers' *unease*; he would, too. Yet—I had to trust who he was now.

I sat beside Yihtor, my back to the wall beside his, the disruptor on my lap. They were, in the end, his people. His mother.

This was his choice. "What do you want to do?"

"I'm tired, Sira. Of being this. Of being here. That doesn't," with a glance my way, "make me heedless of why."

"I know." Morgan wasn't going to be pleased, I thought. Not at all.

For his sake, and all the others, I offered Yihtor my hand. "Show me."

* ✳ *

Vermin were scarcer than I remembered down here. A good thing. Better? Those who did creep close, giving the corpses an interested sniff, disappeared the instant they noticed me. Not that I'd seem any threat to such hardened Plexis dwellers; I credited the residual aroma of Scat on the disrupter.

What bothered me more than red eyes in the shadows were the faces in my mind. The Brill I could dismiss as Bowman's problem.

The old Omacron, dressed as any third-rate would-be entertainer wandering this station—this *Galactic Mysterioso*—was mine. The terrible power sept possessed, to kill with what wasn't only sound, but borne along by it, was beyond anyone else.

It could be beyond me. Perhaps. Among those horrific memories had been the shock of failed shields, as if some poison had eaten through what might have protected Clan minds.

Almost there, Witchling.

Glad to hear it. Glad? Morgan couldn't get here soon enough. Be where I could protect him, soon enough, and if I hadn't had vermin to distract me, I'd likely have given into instinct and 'ported to him.

Yihtor'd known those killed very well. They'd been adherents of Wys from the beginning, influencing Omacron minds to do their bidding. Something he hadn't done, a difference he believed would protect him.

By now he'd be in full command of the Scat ship. Plexis Port Authority would bluster, but they'd let the *Ikkraud* depart. Bowman would see to it, Morgan had told me.

Yihtor would take the ship back, as Merin and the others had intended, to Snosbor IV. The Scats would be afraid, but Yihtor had promised to let them live. I'd seen to that.

Scats who wouldn't leave their ship, not on a world inhabited by Omacron—how had we missed that clue?

Have they found the Chooser? I'd warned Morgan she—whomever she was—would be Manouya's next target.

Plexis Security's hinting some knowledge, but won't confirm over coms. With bite. Then, *stay clear of her, Sira.*

In case her mind was vulnerable, he meant. I'd shared everything I knew and guessed. We'd no guidance here except to assume the worst: that what exposed the exiles' minds to the Omacron could be latent in anyone who'd been in mental contact with them. I hadn't been. Rael's Chosen, Janac di Paniccia, had; he'd lived on Omacron III, doing to his servants and neighbors what Clan did to those weaker-minded—to Rael's outspoken disgust.

I trusted Rael's repugnance for any closeness to an alien mind to protect me now. Once we'd found the Chooser, I'd send her home to AllThereIs, then follow Yihtor. There were other ships. Fast ones.

After this Omacron was dead.

Docking now. In no mood to run down ramps or find a lift, Morgan had "borrowed" a Port Authority tug. My clever, precious Human.

Who'd been taught his first shields by Omacron telepaths.

We'd all believed the species harmless. Amusingly timid.

I wouldn't underestimate them again.

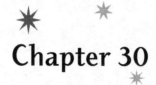

Chapter 30

"I DON'T UNDERESTIMATE HIM."

"I trust you won't." Sira's eyes were haunted. Little wonder, Morgan thought, having *seen* what she had. She'd come aboard the instant he'd opened the air lock and gone straight to the nearest viewport to stare outside, arms tight around herself.

Resisting the urge to rush into his. He'd covered his own impulse by closing the 'lock and going to stand on the control pad. A tap of his foot undocked the tug. A gentle lean forward sent it out and away. "We're to meet on Level Five, one quarter spinward."

Morgan moved his hand through the air above the pad, piloting the tough little vessel over Plexis as though skimming an aircar over dunes. The station's hull flashed below, and you got away with speed like this, as close as this, because all ships were stationary, including the rest of the tug fleet.

Unsecured debris would end them.

They passed over the sign few bothered to see: "Plexis Supermarket: If You Want It, It's Here." Those multicolored lights caught Sira. Band after band poured over her still, too-quiet form, then left her in relative darkness.

Morgan tried not to look. The trip to reach her had been a blur; he'd pushed the tug beyond its red lines, ignored its

warnings. This one he'd slow to a crawl if he could. Stop, if that
was at all possible.

Instead, he accelerated. "Almost there. You want to strap in?"

"It's a tug." Incredulous.

His lips quirked. "So it is." A spacer, hook into a station tug's
wall harness? This was his Sira, his crewmate. "I—"

"Stop! What's that?"

Morgan did the next best thing, dumping velocity with grabs
of his fist as he brought the tug, designed for quick, abrupt cor-
rections, back around in a slewing turn. The deck adjusted beneath them, servo dampeners taking hold, confounding senses
dependent on vision as the station swung overhead, then below.

Sira came to stand with him, clear of the control area. "There."

At first glance, what she'd spotted might have been a hole,
punched through the station to show the space on the other side.

But no hole *pulled* itself with long black arms.

One of which came free and waved.

At them.

"You're the master trader," Sira said slowly. "What do you think
that means?"

Trouble, that at the very least. "We're not waiting to find out."

Morgan sent the tug back on course with a quick flurry of
movements. One thing they both knew.

If a Rugheran wanted to find them, it would.

Anywhere.

As for finding— "What I want to know," he told her, "is what
Huido's up to—the big lug isn't answering coms. He's not at the
Claws & Jaws," Plexis kept a running total of the living mass presently within each establishment's forcefields, no doubt so they
could later add excessive breathing to the bill and adjust taxes to
penalize the popular. Security, at Bowman's pointed suggestion,
had grabbed those numbers. "The *Heerala's* docked, but they
don't have him."

"He'll go to his wives, won't he?"

"That'd be my guess." Unless, Morgan added to himself, the
arrival of females had Huido feeling heroic, a state of mind which
not only tended to leave dents in walls and smash servos, but

could very well send the Carasian hurtling joyfully toward dangers any sane being would avoid.

"We should find him." Sira knew Huido, too. "If he was the only Carasian onstation, I'd try a heart-search—his mind's hard to forget," with a small grimace.

"Save your Power, Witchling. It shouldn't be too hard," Morgan assured her. "All we have to do is find the biggest threat."

He surprised her into a chuckle. "How do we do that?"

"Easy." The Human slowed the tug as the telltales for Level 5, Spinward ¼ came in view. He aimed them at the row of waiting tug ports, then dropped his hands, relinquishing control. Theirs would find the first available slot. "It'll be whatever's caused Plexis to lock her doors."

"So we talk to Bowman."

"We get answers," he stated, determined on that point.

Sira's eyes seemed to see beyond him, then refocused, studying his face. "I wish—" She sighed. "It doesn't matter. Ignorance is its own danger—you taught me that, when I thought I was Human."

She could pass for one. Morgan tucked a stray lock of red-tipped hair behind her ear, lingering when a wisp caught on his callused fingertip. The stuff had grown to the collar of her coveralls and he knew better than leave his hand close—gods, he *knew* better than wait for her hair to slip around his wrist like warm, heavy silk—than hope—

Jason. When he didn't—couldn't—respond, Sira stepped inside the curve of his arm, putting her palm flat over his heart, and he'd happily die now, if the universe could for once be just, drowning in her eyes—

The air lock gave a too-cheery *ping* and whooshed open.

—forcing them apart.

Interlude

Plexis

"ARE WE TOO FAST?" Tayno slowed with Tarerea Vyna, eyes awhirl with worry. "Uncle! We're too fast."

It was all too fast. All too strange and he didn't like any of it. Didn't like the empty concourse, had never, truth be told, liked this part, where lights pretended to be stars and you had to watch your feet or step on what had been tossed aside. A considerable amount of tossing had taken place. Beings must have panicked—which could happen in the dark, which this was—before running for the interior of bars.

Though the music hadn't stopped and those he could see through the doors appeared to be dancing. There was no understanding aliens.

Huido looked back. "Do your best, Fem."

"I'm all right." She steadied herself with the claw Tayno offered and kept walking. "Is it much further?"

"One more ramp."

Did she nod? It was too dark to be sure. "It's not far," Tayno encouraged, though unsure of that as well.

Tarerea tired. He should carry her, but to do it gently would take both of his great claws. Claws he must keep ready.

It hadn't left, that restless mean feeling. If anything, this hurrying through the dark?

Made it grow.

They were heading to a starship, that much he knew. To Captain Morgan's ship, recently docked with the station, which was reassuring.

In secret, which wasn't. A courteous notification via comlink might have spared them this running around—and prevented surprises, always a plus—but Huido'd dismissed his reasonable suggestion, claiming "they couldn't be trusted."

Leaving Tayno to worry if "they" referred to the com system or to some mysterious enemy, this "threat" that wasn't his uncle at all. He glumly suspected the other Carasian enjoyed filling his head with such quandaries.

* ✳ *

Plexis' underbelly was a thoroughly unpleasant place; Tayno'd been grateful to avoid a return since arriving on the station, it unseemly for the great Huido Maarmatoo'kk to pick up his own shipments.

Plus, Carasians didn't fit very well down here. They had to go single file, Tarerea between them, and Tayno grew dizzy trying to spot all the wires and pipes before snagging on them, a process complicated by the need to keep some eyes on the floor, too. There were inexplicable bars of metal crossing their path every few steps. Tripping hazards! He should file a complaint.

Which Huido Maarmatoo'kk wouldn't do, not the Huido who moved confidently through this dreadful place without so much as catching one of his dangling weapons on a rivet; which was just as well, Tayno decided.

At least there weren't vermin in sight.

He'd his own burden. Huido had unclipped a bag, producing a box for Tayno to carry in one of his upper handling claws. The Carasian regarded it woefully. Each time he almost tripped, he couldn't help but squeeze it.

He'd almost tripped several times. The ends of the box remained intact, but the middle had become a splintered mass held to-gether by some inner lining. The lumpy contents hadn't come out—yet—surely that was what mattered.

He hoped they weren't explosives. Or refills for the weapons his uncle carried. Or explosive refills, which was, Tayno sighed to himself, entirely likely, but all would be fine so long as—

Tarerea Vyna stumbled.

—he didn't have to stop quickly.

Disaster, as usual, happened in precise order. Tarerea grabbed for a wire to save herself, the wire snapped producing sparks. Tayno, meanwhile, busy getting his feet to stop without tripping and falling on the Vyna, flinched from the sparks, his claws fly-ing up.

The box sailed through the air to smash on Huido's back. White lumps careened from walls, shell, and floor, most shatter-ing to dust on impact.

Without blowing holes in the station. Relieved on that score, Tayno focused on his own predicament, having punched his lower left clawtip into a pipe while wrapping the upper right into wire. Maybe if he moved the left first—but then what might spray out?

Something struck him in the top head plate like a hammer.

It had been a hammer, Tayno realized, now flat on his back. The position afforded an excellent view of the cluttered ceiling and the spray of foul-smelling liquid arching overhead. There were, thankfully, no more sparks.

"Tayno!" Small hands patted him. "Are you all right? Why did you hit him?" Fiercely. "I should get rid of you—"

"No! Please. My esteemed uncle helped me," Tayno explained hurriedly. There being no graceful way back to his feet, he banged and clattered against both walls, Tarerea wisely giving him space. "See? I'm fine."

"A matter of— What are you doing, Fem Vyna?"

She tried to kneel, Tayno saw, for Tarerea a difficult and awk-ward procedure. He put a claw in reach and she used it, but didn't look up or thank him; her attention was for the floor. When she reached it, she plunged her hands into the growing puddle of nasty muck, searching with desperate haste.

"Tarerea?"

"Help me, Tayno. The Glorious Dead. What I need. There's one here!"

Huido gave a deep bell-like tone. Tayno looked at him, startled. Grief, that sound. "Uncle?"

"It's too late," Huido said heavily. "Come."

No. It couldn't be. "We can help, Uncle." Tayno crouched and began to collect whatever bits of the crystal he could see.

"Not those," she told him. "I must find the whole one."

Huido crouched, filling the corridor behind her. His once-shiny carapace was streaked with white powder, what wasn't slimy with whatever continued to rain from the pipe, but he moved with care, using a handling claw to touch Tarerea's shoulder. "You misunderstand me," with terrible kindness. "It's time for you go home, Tarerea Vyna. To listen to the voices calling you. You don't belong here."

She stared up, her lips parting. "You know—" More breath than words.

What Tayno knew? This was his fault. Everything was. As usual. He searched frantically, freezing when something he touched rolled away. He stretched. There.

He picked it up more carefully than he'd ever picked up anything in his life. "I found it."

Tarerea snatched it from him, her hands no cleaner than the lump of rock. "You can't stop me," she said, low and hungry.

"No need." Huido tucked his claws against his body. "You know it's true. I sense it in your grist."

His friend's grist was fine, Tayno thought. The finest. "Uncle—"

"She doesn't belong here, Nephew. None of them can stay."

He rose, raised his claws. Mean didn't begin to describe this feeling. This was *rage*—

"It's all right, Tayno." Tarerea's voice had changed, softened. He stared down at her, shocked to see a weary smile. She held out the crystal. "Take it. Crush it."

He crouched, uncaring how any many eyestalks retreated. "I don't understand." They couldn't make him. "You said you'd die without one. You mustn't die." It was very simple. "You need this."

"I've been this," a nod to the crystal, "and reborn, too many times not to be tired of it." Her smile grew tender. "All I want is to see my people free of the Dark. To join them. You are my friend, Tayno Boormataa'kk. Heart-kin. Do this for me."

He took the cold and priceless thing she didn't want and closed his claw with all the power of his grief.

The dust sparkled as it fell.

✳ ✳ ✳

"Can this starship take us to the Vyna?"

Tayno, his fate to wallow in misery for the remainder of his life, tried not to hear Tarerea Vyna's questions or Huido's answers. To be sure they knew he wasn't listening or interested, he walked as far behind the pair as possible without risking being left behind and lost.

He didn't notice his preoccupation made him less clumsy, rather than more, nor the number of eyestalks his uncle bent his way.

"My blood brother will know." With confidence. "Ah. We're almost there."

The "ah" signaled their arrival where three corridors met with a frenzied interchange of overhead plumbing. While he no longer cared for the future, personal safety, or, Tayno thought in a moment of wild rebellion, the budget, he quickened his pace to be sure they stayed together.

"My, my. There's two of you."

Having already quickened his pace to a near gallop, Tayno couldn't easily slow despite his shock when the Brill spoke. He surged forward, knocking over someone the size of Tarerea, who wasn't, thankfully, her at all.

But was— "Mathis Dewley?" He was too surprised to notice he'd remembered the name and used it for the correct Human-esque being.

The Assembler, having squeaked, climbed back to his feet. "Why are you two?"

"Hush."

Tayno went rigid, sending an eye to look over his shoulder.

The giant female Brill from the *Infant Emporium* stood there, with the *Galactic Mysterioso.*

While Huido faced the other Brill. Smaller, yes, no bulkier than a large Human, but the totally illegal weapon aimed his way did, in this instance, count for more than size.

Tarerea reached her hand back, for him. Her other slipped toward Huido. Suddenly, she stopped moving.

"That's right. No touching," the female said, pushing Tayno aside. "Your Clan tricks won't work. Gryba will make sure of that, my pretty thing."

The Omacron's grist was a fetid horror; the weird little *hum* it made hurt his elbows, and Tayno shouted over it, "Leave her alone!"

"Quite the protector, aren't you? You're the one who brought us here," the Brill informed him, and pointed to his claw. "You let me put a tracker on you, fool."

The claw she'd pressed—Tayno's eyestalks tangled trying to see what she'd done.

"Stop!" Huido looked meaner than Tayno had dreamed—in his worst nightmares—a Carasian male could look. Meaner, if regrettably not so large as two Brill. "Don't you—"

"She comes with us, and you can't do a thing about it," the Brill said in a bored tone. "Can we be done here?"

"But this is such a special moment." The female stroked the bulge at Tarerea's abdomen, the helpless Vyna unable to do more than look down. "I've always wanted one of their get. So close to Human but not. Too well protected—until now."

Meaning him. The tracker. This was his fault, too. "The baby's dead," Tayno blurted. "That's why we're leaving the station. To—for the funeral. To—" what had happened to Lones great-grandfather? "—bury it in home soil. Go away!"

The female Brill frowned. "You're lying."

"Why would we?" Huido's rumble was menace itself. "Leave while you still can."

"You're no threat, Carasian. You're already dead," the male announced, his tone bored. "Both of you. Your wives. You just haven't noticed yet."

"About them."

All eyes, except those Huido left on the Brill, shot to the Assembler.

"They didn't go to the pool," Dewley pointed out. "The wives."

"They'll still die," the big female said with horrifying confidence. "Gryba's concoction will have spread."

Huido *grew*, but Tayno wasn't sure if he felt mean or scared. Could you feel both?

"About that." The Assembler's foot turned sideways as though planning to escape. "Plexis put up forcefields. Biohazard forcefields. Means no spreading."

The Omacron spoke, over that *hum*. "A move I predicted. Concentration will enhance the second stage. The Humans will all die."

With a roar, Huido launched himself at the male, heedless of the weapon—

Tayno didn't wait to see what would happen. He threw himself past the female Brill, claws out and snapping, going for the true evil here.

The Omacron's skin flared as red as its cloak as it spun away, nipping into the side corridor and, impossibly, running up the wall to disappear in the plumbing. Thwarted, Tayno rocked himself around.

The Brill were gone, as was the Assembler. Huido lay unmoving against the walk, looking like a heap of discarded servo parts. Tarerea, again able to move, went to him, then looked up, her eyes going unusually large. "Tayno!"

A flood of red-eyed vermin poured down the corridor.

"I can take us away! Where, Tayno?"

For once, Tayno found an important decision easy to make. With no idea how to find Morgan or his ship, they'd one choice offering protection—and a vital duty to perform. "The security office!"

Deputy Inspector Jynet should consider information on the Brill and their threat against Humans as good as an appointment— so long as their arrival didn't break furniture or shock her into shooting at them. Oh, dear.

As for his grist? At least he wouldn't be the only male afflicted—
With Tarerea's touch, the corridor vanished . . .

* ✳ *

Plexis

Apart, the bits of Mathis Dewley could move faster than the whole, something the right foot kept trying to prove, causing the rest to lurch and complain, subvocally, of course.

The rest agreed the foot was stupid. Being apart wasn't an option. Plexis was empty, this concourse the most exposed place Dewley'd ever been forced to occupy, whole or apart. He was disturbed those with him appeared unconcerned. Casual, though they walked with firm, long strides. Hard to keep up with strides, one-minds being larger and inconsiderate as well as, he was beginning to fear, less than reliable group members. The term "stuck with" possessed significant additional meaning to Assemblers, including "mutually assured destruction."

That nonsense with the Carasians, wasting time for Choiola's "hobby" when Plexis could be onto everything and, dire thought, everyone?

It could, Dewley decided, be time to expand his options. His parts enthusiastically expanded theirs, making the whole stagger.

A Brill hand gripped a shoulder, hard. "I wouldn't," Choiola advised sweetly and the parts, terrified in equal measure, firmed their connection. "We're on record." She swept an arm in salute to a pole topped with a vid banner directing customers to the nearest *Clear-Coat Shower* installation, a pair of strangely immaculate Festors singing *Sweat Got You Bored? Let's fill those pores!*

Being seen was bad, Dewley knew, hunching as they passed the pole. Why did the Brill seem eager for it? There was something he was missing.

"Cheer up, Split." The one named Manouya beat his chest with a fist, surely painful. "It'll be over soon. You'll be famous."

Famous?

The Assembler fragmented. Bits scampered for the nearest

pots of greenery, diving inside. Those of narrow shape burrowed with their cilia till they hit bottom.

The head shoved itself between sharp nasty branches as the best it could do. It heard the Brill laugh, but "famous" wasn't good. Being in the pot was better.

Rustle.

Unless the pot was already occupied.

Chapter 31

LEVEL 5 WAS ANOTHER shopping level, and something more: home for the majority of beings who worked on Plexis. The signs weren't subtle. Unlike the deliberate slow-the-shopper maze of pots and growing things sprinkled throughout the other levels of Plexis, Level 5 featured—if you knew where to look— low-walled gardens complete with tidy plots of vegetables. The ceiling was the usual height, but fruit hung down the walls, where there weren't rental units or balconies, and had the occupants not been locked inside, and customers not been trapped in stores, the entire concourse would have bustled with the sounds of families.

And escort services, the appeal of species-appropriate nesting behavior not lost on professionals.

This odd distinction from other levels arose from the then-shocking realization staff needed homes. Plexis, needing staff and plenty of them, grudgingly allocated space. Rental space, of course, taxed and costly, with suites reserved for paying custom-ers, encouraging a boom in hotels and inspiring business owners to offer rooms to entice employees, rooms ranging from closets to shelf space, but, as the saying went, "thespaceyoushareon Plexis" at least got you paid.

Such a concentration of staff, a proportion of whom in desperate

need of sleep at any and all hours of the station's rotation, led to
Level 5 being the only concourse free of night-zones and associated entertainments. Making it less appealing to the usual spacer
and trader riffraff.

And, in Morgan's opinion, the least likely place to host a gathering such as theirs, yet here they were.

To the right of the ramps, twenty-three Carasian females
formed a wall of brooding, glistening black; they'd spread out on
the way down and hadn't, for reasons making sense to them, re-
formed their aggressive phalanx. Plexis security stood a rather
sheepish guard over the left side, half in biohazard suits and that
many again in their gray uniforms under battle armor. The pair
towing grav carts loaded with autograpples and string-steel nets
had taken one look at the female version of a Carasian and
pushed those tactfully out of sight.

Deceptively solitary, Trade Pact Sector Chief Lydis Bowman
stood at the opening of the ramp from Level 6. Terk and Finelle
flanked her at a distance that kept them close enough to intervene, their hands loose and near weapons. The *Conciliator* was
attached to Plexis, with over a thousand armored and trained
enforcers ready and waiting.

While Bowman rarely used force, there was no denying she
liked others to know it was there.

Morgan and Sira stood between the Carasians and Terk; he
preferred having the down ramp a step away, especially as Plexis
had to release those forcefields, and the crowds within, sooner
than later.

"Sight lines," Sira said suddenly. "That's why we're here." Her
boot stamped.

Terk grunted as though surprised.

She was right, Morgan realized, grinning at her. She'd learned
the notion as part of her training to be a trader; the importance
of having a clear view of all interested parties in a room—as well
as any exits.

Viewed that way, Level 5 became that rarity on Plexis: wide
open space. You could see to the distance where the floor began

its slow curve to meet the ceiling. With no foot- or servo traffic in the way, it was easy to see something else, too. "The accesses." Morgan nodded ahead.

You forgot that, about Plexis: how it was more than ramps and concourses, glittering stores and those come to shop. Remove the people, and you saw the circulatory systems: grates over airducts, flaps over drains, doors disguised as walls or ornamentation meant for servos and those who repaired them. A second station, larger, busier, as close to autonomous as economics and prudence allowed.

Beyond that, connected more intimately to that station than the living part of Plexis, the ranks of starships that docked, latched in, hooked on, and depended on the station's services.

Available at discount for shoppers.

Making here, where Sira's small boot stamped, as close to the center of it all as you could get and still see around you.

Why?

"GREETINGS!" The roar from the Carasians startled Morgan. By the haphazard whine and clicks behind him, it had done the same to Plexis security.

Sounds that ceased when Bowman lifted her hand, then gave a short bow.

With the rest, Morgan and Sira turned to face the ramp.

Two figures, both humanoid, both tall. A Trant and— "Board Member Sta'gli," Sira whispered to Morgan.

The Papiekian who'd stood with Bowman and the late Human Board Member to officially bring the Clan into the Trade Pact. Whatever had happened since, Sta'gli had done all she could to help Sira's people. To help him, Morgan thought, bowing with the rest.

Bowman spent a moment, heads close, with the pair, before leading them to the focal point of their arc of living beings. With suspiciously precise timing, messengers arrived, the little servos high overhead, but completing the circle.

"It's a show," Morgan declared quietly, but with disgust. "Politics, when we've—" a murderous Omacron to catch, a helpless

Chooser to rescue, a missing friend, and the universe to save, "—we've no time for this." He took Sira's hand. *We're leaving.*

She resisted. *Wait.*

"I introduce myself. Sta'gli." Board Member Sta'gli bowed to the Carasians, to security, and to Morgan and Sira. Vids in the messengers would broadcast those bows as directed to the audience.

She spoke in a soft, singsong voice, the fine scaling of her cheeks pearlescent in the light. "We are here to-o reveal ourselves, in this place, Plexis, that brings us to-ogether. I present Board Member fo-or the Trant, Trilip *nes* Fartho-o."

The Papiekian could pass, at a distance, for Human. A Trant never could. So thin were the creatures they looked more like stick drawings than living things and, while sturdy in their way, they swayed as if to breezes no one else felt. Their faces were narrow, heads flattened so their large eyes bulged from the sides. A Human-similar mouth and lips were shadowed beneath a hook-shaped nose. Like Sta'gli, the Trant was well, if conservatively dressed, its long four-toed feet in tidy knit socks.

Like Sta'gli, Trilip bowed to those attending. "We are of the Trade Pact," its voice a dry rustle. "We represent our home systems and species. We represent history as well, for our species were of the First, here before many others."

"To us, the Trade Pact is a-iy wonder," Sta'gli said next. "Busy. Inno-ovative. Full of movement and opportunity, yet species co-operate. There is order." A bow to Bowman. "We owe much to the new. To Humans."

The Trant made a wheezing noise: amusement, that was. "So many Humans," Trilip continued. "You are everywhere. Into everything. Like the glue that holds my home in one piece. Irreplaceable. Essential—"

"I disagree."

Change! At the taste more than the words, Morgan drew Sira to the side, closer to the Carasians.

Who gave a single thunderous heave, then settled.

Two Brill stepped from the ramp, a female the size of a Carasian and a male, the latter dainty for his kind and all too familiar.

The bartender from the *Raunchy Retian*.

Morgan tensed. He didn't need to look to know Terk would be ready. He loosened the knife in the wrist sheath, but didn't move.

Bowman's play now, chit.

With them caught in it.

Interlude

Plexis

DEPUTY INSPECTOR JYNET wasn't as surprised to have two Carasians—one collapsed—and a gold tag customer "appear" in front of her desk as Tayno'd expected.

Unfortunately, her lack of shock had more to do with what had recently done the same.

The Rugheran, for its part, seemed content to fill the back of the Eima's office, draped languidly over her desk, two arms flowing along the carpet. It might have been asleep.

Did they sleep?

"This is most irregular." For some reason, despite learning which Carasian paid taxes, Jynet kept directing her attention at Tayno who, for his part, maintained a several-eyes watch on what was irregular, indeed. "What am I to do with it?"

He was to know? "I don't think it means any harm," Tayno ventured hesitantly. Beyond cracking the furniture. The desk would never be the same. "Its grist is—" Charming, was the word he wanted, utterly so, but it didn't feel like a word to use at the moment. "I think it's the same one who visited the kitchen. It—" Oh, he shouldn't mention that.

"It brought me to the station," Tarerea stated for him. She'd found an unbroken chair and sat, beads of sweat on her fore-head. The business of 'porting, however easy for participants, took its toll. He should find her some water—a cushion. "I'd thought it wanted to be rid of me," softly, "but I've found help here. Friends."

Tayno felt much bigger. Until he sent an eye rolling to check on Huido, who'd yet to stir. The culprit was the dent on the back of his top head plate, a dent the size and shape of the female Brill's fist, the pair having combined against him. No permanent damage, from something so minor, but he'd be grumpy when he awoke.

At him, Tayno knew, feeling smaller again. Hadn't he chased the wrong villain—to no avail—thus missing the battle they were to fight together? Huido would be right to separate his head disks from his shoulders and use them for trays. They'd make, he sighed to himself, very nice trays. Or tureens for soup.

"Fem Vyna, do you know how to talk to it?"

"They don't listen to my kind." Tarerea had yet to look directly at the Rugheran. "I knew of one who could. Sira. She's the Chosen of the one Huido spoke of: the Human named Jason Morgan."

Sira of the wondrous grist, lost forever. Tayno sighed, tipping his head from side to side, but he did have better news. "Morgan's here, Deputy Inspector."

"We're aware. Outside my jurisdiction, I've been told. Repeatedly. Need to know and all that. But I think our guest changes the game, don't you?" Having made no sense, Jynet nodded cheerfully, her cheeks flaps a relieved yellow. "Let's go find Captain Morgan."

"Wait!" Tayno heard himself protest as the Eima strode to the com panel on the door—the one on her desk unavailable. The Rugheran was a surprise, granted, but for a Plexis official, Jynet's priorities seemed—were, he told himself, certain of it—wrong. "We told you the Brills' plan to kill Humans. What about that?"

"Outside my jurisdiction," this time grimly. "I trust you can appreciate how I feel about having my station and my staff preemptively put under Sector Chief Bowman's control. 'Situation well in hand,' I'm to believe."

She should believe it. Bowman? Tayno's eyes whirled. This was the best news he'd had in too long. Bowman was a friend—not of his exactly, though she'd complimented his serving skills on two occasions—but on their side, definitely. A personage, moreover, who could make good things happen and, most importantly, bad things go away.

"Coming?" Jynet asked.

"Of course. Could we have a grav sled for my uncle, please?" Tayno asked.

Go to Morgan and leave Huido behind?

Not even Bowman would risk that.

* ✳ *

Snosbor IV

Not long now, witch.

Wys slammed down her shields and threw a vase across the room in Erad's general direction. Six dead. Half of her followers. Her Chosen knew as well as she did they couldn't afford to lose so many—not and survive.

Was it down to that? She buried her face in her hands. Survival?

"I can come back at a better time, Gracious Queen."

Wys jerked her hands down, barely able to resist throwing the remaining vase at the obsequious Retian in the doorway. At least it wasn't one of her people. She mustn't show weakness or doubt, not now. "What is it?"

Talobar removed his mask. "I've good news."

Moving deliberately, the Clanswoman took her time going to her seat behind the table, paused, then waved the other to plop itself in the facing chair. The creature's energy was offensive. She'd become easily tired of late—

No. It wasn't her age, it was the incompetence surrounding her.

Talobar balanced on the seat; chairs ill-suited his anatomy, but he knew better than to ask for anything else. "Very good news."

"You'd be the first." They'd all felt the deaths of those on Plexis—of Tren, here. Their Omacron servitors had been affected as well, how being a mystery, but they'd all abandoned their tasks. Fled into the surrounding city or hills. Fell into ponds. Wherever they'd gone, their absence was a nuisance about to be a problem, if they couldn't be replaced, quickly.

She wasn't about to exert herself to wipe fresh ones.

Wys steepled her gnarled fingers, glowering at the Retian over their tips. For once, the creature didn't cower. Could it have made a breakthrough? "Tell me."

"The *Ikkraud* has the key components on board. All three. They've left Plexis and are coming here with all speed." A cautious pause.

"And?" she prompted without emotion.

A bulbous eye blinked. Then the other. "The captain wants to alter our arrangement."

"Let me guess. They lure my people into a deadly ambush and then raise the price on what belongs to me."

"You think they did that?" Shock did unpleasant things to a Retian's skin texture.

It's what she'd have done, Wys thought. Not that the Scats would escape her vengeance, but clearly they continued to be of use. More than use. The Retian was right; this was very good news. "You're ready for the delivery?"

"Yes. I can start at once."

To make the next generation, to sow the seeds of a future even she'd begun to doubt. Wys shared her *pleasure* with her Chosen, enjoying Erad's answering *dismay.* "Go," she told the waiting creature.

Her son was coming home.

Aside: The Sakissishee

IT WOULD COME on silent feet.

There would be no betraying scent, no warmth to detect, no *thing* to be seen.

There could be no protection, no safety alone or in number, no weapon or defense.

All knew this.

Mindcrawlers were its hands. To tear open—create weakness—to prepare the way.

The Sakissishee knew this, above all. Had they not been first to tell the Consortium? The Clan did not belong here.

For behind them would come the Dark.

Interlude

BOWMAN'S PLAY, indeed, I thought with some admiration, that admiration vanishing as I looked at the Brill. Rich silks. Swagger. Each twice or more the mass of the Human in front of them, confidence oozing from every pore.

Yet Bowman's calm dignity held the eye.

Despite my trust in her, I shared Morgan's tension. He'd *tasted* change. If it had arrived with this pair, things weren't as they seemed.

They weren't. The so-secretive Manouya, the Facilitator, out in the open? As for the female—

"Board Member Choiola," Sta'gli identified. "You were expected."

The female Brill's smile split her face. "We'd hoped to flush you out. You and this one." A hand that could snap the Trant like the twig it resembled reached out and closed into a fist. "Traitors." She spat, missing Bowman. Had she not, I thought, glancing at Terk, this confrontation would be over. "The First rejects you."

"You claim to speak for the First, then," Trilip said calmly. "Note."

Sta'gli nodded. "Noted."

"I claim nothing!" Choiola's fist struck her chest with a boom that echoed. "I state. Humans are a disease. They and you are no longer part of the future. The First shall arise!"

"FOOLISH."

Even a Brill should be shaken by that floor-shaking condemnation by the gathered Carasians. Instead, Choiola chuckled. "Oh, I think not." She pranced, I'd no other word for the disturbing way she moved, to stand before that wall of eyes and claws. "Dead. Dead Dead. You're all dead. Your Consortium is finished."

"NO!" A massive black form burst through the line of security.

Not how I'd expected to find Huido, though when had his claw been replaced with a shiny hammer?

A second massive form didn't so much burst as dodge cautiously—claws held high—through the confusion of beings sensibly getting out of the way.

Both Carasians thundered toward the Brill. Bowman was shouting, Terk shaking his head, and Finelle urging the Board Members back—

—when my head snapped around, drawn by *attention.*

There, at the edge of the ramp.

Someone watched.

⁕ ✳ ⁕

As distractions went, you couldn't beat a battle between huge angry aliens. They made more noise than crashing a servo freight into a stack of pipes—a sound with which I was regrettably familiar. Not to mention the morbid fascination of claw versus nail, fist versus—hammer.

Suffice it to say, even my Human was too engrossed in the proceedings to notice I'd left his side.

I narrowed my awareness, slipping around a grav sled loaded with metal nets that might have been of some use in ending the fight had anyone thought of them sooner, intent on my quarry. There, just ahead. A head lifted, as though whomever this was had to see what was happening.

In hindsight, I might have been more inspired by the physical struggle than was wise, for I leaped, arms out, intending to grab the Omacron—

Instead, I knocked over the very last person I'd expected to see again.

"Tarerea Vyna?"

She was decidedly pregnant, hunched as though in pain. Well aware of her Power, I moved to keep distance between us, tightening my shields. Morgan had wanted answers. I'd one, at least. Here was the Chooser Yihtor had sensed.

Along with a host of new questions, starting with what was a Vyna doing on Plexis?

A louder bellow raised her head. "Tayno! No—" She struggled to her feet again, ignoring me until I tried to help. She jerked aside, eyes wild. "He can't fight those monsters. We have to stop this!"

"Trust me, nothing can." Other than armaments normally employed against ground assault vehicles and then, Morgan had assured me, an enraged Carasian would only notice a direct hit. "What are you doing here?"

"We came with the deputy inspector to find Captain Morgan," as matter-of-factly as though the gold tag on her cheek was real and I hadn't last seen her on a dying planet beyond the Trade Pact.

"Why do you want Mor—" In the sudden hush, I realized I was shouting and closed my mouth.

The fight was over.

The Vyna started to move at the same time I did, then both of us stopped in horror.

The floor was *moving!*

Not the floor—

Things!

Chapter 32

THERE WASN'T A THING that could stop a fight like this, short of killing the participants before they could do it to one another.

Not with Carasians involved or, it turned out, Brill. Morgan had assumed anything capable of thought and independent movement would retreat as quickly as possible away from a charging Carasian.

The Brill had ripped off their clothing, boomed with joyful rage, and charged right back. The species' fighting styles were remarkably similar: smash into one another, grab hold, wrestle till breaking apart again. Smash and repeat. Eyes squeezed shut or closed inside plates, of course.

Claws scraped but didn't penetrate thick blubbery skin; fists dented but didn't crack shell. Yet.

"Where'd he get the hammer?" Terk shouted in Morgan's ear.

He gave a noncommittal shrug, though it wasn't hard to figure out. Huido had traveled to Plexis on the *Heerala*. Present the adoring, inventive Drapsk a problem to solve? They should all be grateful it was a hammer and not a missile launcher.

Morgan was more interested in where Sira had gone, but she'd contact him if she needed him. And his friend just might.

"I see security's being useful." Security presently making themselves scarce, other than a tight group of five going the long way 'round toward them, or rather Bowman, the Sector Chief standing beside Terk.

"Jellies," Terk grunted, as if that said it all.

Bowman turned to Morgan, a rare look of frustration on her face. "How long's this going to take?"

Morgan studied the combatants, none of whom seemed to be flagging, then looked toward the Carasian females. By the intensity of their many-eyed regard, they were enjoying the spectacle. "Your guess is—"

"Sector Chief Bowman!" The group of security personnel had arrived. Three constables, a comtech, and, by the bars on her uniform, the Eima who dropped Bowman's name like a gauntlet was the acting head of Plexis security.

"Deputy Inspector." Bowman had no problem being heard without shouting. "Why aren't you in your office?"

Morgan, with Terk, began to ease out of the line of verbal fire.

"Stay." The deputy inspector pointed at Morgan. "You, I need. I'm here because there's a threat!"

"Jynet, I've told you. This is outside—"

"Don't you cite jurisdiction at me when my customers are at risk!" The Eima's cheek flaps were swollen black with restrained fury. "I'm placing those two—" Her finger aimed at the seething mass of combatants, "—under arrest!"

Her constables looked ready to faint.

"I am," Bowman snapped.

Morgan, eyes on the fight, started to smile. "Watch this."

The four had moved apart, as they had several times already, but he'd spotted the difference. Tayno had shifted to challenge Choiola, but this time, Huido took a few steps back, carapace rocking side-to-side as though working off a blow.

Manouya moved first, rushing Huido—

Tayno crouched to the floor, claws in—

Then Huido showed the difference between Carasian and Brill biology. The latter had heavy gravity, true.

But Carasians were adapted to a rocky coastline, where the higher you could reach, the safer your offspring.

Huido's thick legs *contracted*, then thrust up, driving his huge bulk into the air. He landed on Tayno's back as Tayno lunged upward, leaping again. Both Carasians hit their target, Tayno plastered against Choiola's chest, her arms in his claws—

Huido, like a bolt of lightning, coming down, hammer-first, on her thick skull.

The Brill dropped, only her fingers twitching.

Morgan quickly looked for Manouya—

The male Brill stood where he'd been, without a twitch at all, Bowman's needler nestled deep in his ear.

Silence fell again as the two Carasian males squared off, each at his full height, ready for battle. Before Morgan had to go over and name Huido to settle things, that worthy roared with laughter and smacked Tayno cheerfully with his hammer.

Suddenly, Sira and—Morgan wanted to rub his eyes, because with her was a Vyna and not any Vyna but one he'd met, clothed as a wealthy Human customer—this person came running from the side of the ramp.

Followed by a seething blanket of red-eyed vermin!

Interlude

Plexis

THINGS RAN AROUND and under him. One clawed up
sept's leg. Cursing, Gryba kicked it away. The thing chittered
back before scampering to join the rest.

Pest control must be at work in the accesses. The things continued to pour from this one, from all the others in view, a mass
of moving filth. A distraction, the Omacron thought, as useful as
the one provided by his thick-headed allies.

Former allies. The Brill were never in charge, never important.
A means to the end sept and all sept's kind desired, that was all.
To take the blame for the deaths to come, this needful test of
delivery and toxicity. If the authorities accused sept, Omacron III
remained untainted by suspicion, free to continue the great
work. Destabilize the Trade Pact from within. Kill and terrorize
the Human pestilence, so they fled as this vermin did.

Sept adjusted the cloak. Why then, slip back into influence.
Slowly, with care. Never be noticed—never discovered—always in
control.

The Consortium thought they understood secrecy.

Amateurs.

The Brill were in custody. The Assembler gone and good riddance. Gryba's attention was on the results of sept's tests. That and a reward. The Clan on Snosbor IV were for others to relish. The females here? He'd no way to *enjoy* them.

Fingers locked around a pipe, sept crept to where light spilled into the access, vermin running below. Yellow bloomed, anticipation. Sept could see the one waiting, the one who'd give the pleasure sept deserved.

Jason Morgan.

＊ ✳ ＊

Plexis

Huido's hammer blow was tender. "Well done. And look, they're sizing you up, Nephew."

Tayno peered between almost closed head disks at the glorious array of females; it was peer or risk being blinded, for he'd never seen anything so beautiful since his last sunset over Mother Ocean—no, he decided, never.

"Timid won't catch their eyes. Don't worry, there're enough for both of us!"

He didn't have a pool. Didn't, Tayno thought wistfully, have a budget for a pool and might not have a job once Huido's good mood met the debts he'd incurred. Still, he gave a stalwart rattle and straightened, for he had, had he not? Done battle!

And hadn't died, that was key. Everything hurt and his right handling claw had lost a tip, but—he dared another couple of eyes.

Finding eyes looking back, his whirled in confusion.

"My brother!" Huido bellowed in greeting, heading away. "Great fight. Did anyone get a vid?"

Tarerea. Thoughts of females and missing tips vanished as Tayno looked anxiously for her. They'd left her out of sight, but close. To wait in safety while—he felt a bit of *mean* returning—they dealt with those despicable Brill. And dealt they had, an experience that while exhilarating now was likely to give him nightmares in future.

Where was she?

And why, Tayno thought with growing alarm, were there vermin out in the open?

Chapter 33

MORGAN RAN TO MEET SIRA, vermin parting to let him through as though he ran through a field of flowers, if flowers had red eyes, wicked bared teeth, and wiry black hair where there weren't scales. They weren't rabid.

He hoped.

"Jason!" By the look on her face, Sira was wondering the same thing. "Where did they all come from?"

"The accesses." Every one was open, each releasing its horde. "Could be from the entire station." He turned to the Vyna and gave a short bow. "Tarerea Vyna."

She inclined her head. "Morgan, Chosen of Sira."

Her resemblance to the Hoveny he'd known, Lemuel Dis, Pauvan Di and his family, was striking. It had to be, the Human knew. The Vyna had been Cersi's control population, the Primes who weren't to change, while the remaining subjects were given urgent reason to evolve. How much worse for them it had been, he thought with pity.

Questions of how and why could wait. Already pale and thin, Tarerea looked close to collapse, not something he'd advise, given the vermin. "Let's find you a place to rest—"

"No. I must be sure Tayno is all right."

"My brother!" Huido rushed toward them faster than vermin

could evade, several being crushed beneath his foot pads. "Great fight. Did anyone get a vid?"

"Tarerea!" Tayno, right behind.

Sira got out of the way as Morgan took a quick couple of steps away from the Vyna in time for Huido to sweep him up in his claw. "Your grist is better!"

"Put me down, you big oaf." He rapped knuckles on a shell rumpled and scratched, but thankfully whole.

Fortunately for the Vyna, Tayno's idea of a greeting was to crouch before her, tenderly offering a handling claw for her touch. "We vanquished your enemy," he said in a small voice. "I don't think I like vanquishing."

"That makes you braver," she told him.

There's a story here, Sira sent.

Tarerea turned her head, for the sending hadn't been private. "This is you? Ah. A rebirth."

"In a way," Sira said. "We'll trade tales later."

Huido set Morgan on his feet, offering a handling claw to Sira. "Welcome home. Tales, yes. Over beer. Much beer. But first, it is time."

Tayno's eyes whirled. "Time, Uncle? Haven't we saved everyone? Aren't we done?"

"We may have. Or not." A claw snapped, producing a somber bell tone. "We may be. Or not. But first," he repeated, "it is time." With that, Huido turned to face the expanse of the concourse.

Morgan and Sira moved to stand beside him, Tarerea using Tayno's arm for support.

Past time, the Human thought grimly. The messengers hovered overhead. On this level, they were surrounded by homes and stores filled with those waiting to be released; on every level, the same situation as well as on starships. Every being would be growing understandably anxious.

Soon, if not already, they'd be more than anxious and Plexis would have to consider the use of broad-species tranquilizers—not a safe option, by any means.

Bowman stepped into the space where titans had battled moments ago. She kicked aside a scrap of silk.

Vermin seized it, rolled over, played. The things were every-where.

Morgan's eyes narrowed. Including on the Carasian females, placidly allowing the filthy things to perch on their heads and shoulders. "I'm missing something," he whispered to Sira.

"We all are," she agreed.

Sta'gli and Trilip joined Bowman. Then one of the female Car-asians lumbered forward as well.

"Glorious," Tayno said, heartfelt and a little too loud.

The female's eyes converged on him. To his credit—or be-cause of Tarerea—he didn't cower, though from this vantage point, Morgan could see the claw he held behind him tremble.

After a long moment, her eyes spread to consider them all. When the Carasian spoke, it was in one sure voice, loud enough to carry, deep enough to be felt inside bone.

"We are the Consortium."

Sta'gli and Trilip spoke, one after the other, "I call the Trade Pact Board to order." "I second."

Images appeared over the messengers, projected upward. The interior of meeting rooms, atmospheres suited to those within, each room filled to capacity. Impossible, without time to count, to tell if every species' representative was present, but he'd bet on it.

Bowman, Morgan noticed, didn't look surprised. Then again, when did she?

"WELCOME!"

"We reveal ourselves to all beings," the single Carasian ex-plained, "because the time has come to put aside petty matters—"

"You're dead!" Choiola shouted. The two Brill were in metal nets, surrounded by Plexis security and guarded by Terk and Fi-nelle, but she struggled and pulled forward. "All of you! The First has triumphed!"

"You failed before you began. We—" the Carasian swept out a claw with ponderous grace, "—are the Consortium."

Vermin leaped upon one another, *sorted* themselves with a meaty snick of part to part, until tall, treelike beings—still scaled and covered in wiry black hair—towered above them.

"Assemblers," Sira whispered.

These weren't remotely Human-like. If anything, they resembled plants—or some deep-sea life able to move on land—little leaflike claws arranged in graceful lines, a glitter of red within deep vertical furrows, as though the eyes remained as they'd been and watched.

Not all had unified. More solitary vermin appeared, heading for the center. These carried objects in their claws, moving with care.

"No!" from Manouya. Choiola's mouth worked without sound, no longer straining against the net.

"These would be your traps," Bowman said calmly, though Morgan noticed she remained very still as the vermin—he'd need a better name now—deposited object after object near her feet. Heaps rose; there had to be hundreds. "Each contains a Human-specific toxin to be released into every shop and home of Plexis. The one left at the *Claws & Jaws?*" Her hand rose and tipped, palm down. "Dealt with at once."

"INTENDED FOR OUR KIND!"

The treelike Assemblers swayed with the angry shout.

When the echoes faded away, Bowman raised her voice. "Plexis-com, you're authorized to drop forcefields. The station is secure."

It hadn't been. The plot could have worked, Morgan thought, and there'd be changes in future, starting with the accesses, to prevent another try. Pest control could suffer some pangs—then again, why? The Vermin Assemblers thrived despite them—or was it because?

What else was there? wondered Morgan. Overlooked, yet anything but ordinary?

"We have this," the Carasian continued, "willing to testify." Vermin ran up, less carefully, dropping hands and feet, other parts.

Parts that crept with visible reluctance to one another, the head last, until the more familiar sort of Assembler stood, trying to make himself as inconspicuous as possible.

"That's Mathis Dewley," Tayno said quietly. "He's a bad person."

"It's all about the group," Sira observed, and Morgan would have loved to ask her more, but more was happening.

The remaining females stepped forward, carapace to carapace.

The first spoke for all. "We, the Consortium, do not intervene in the affairs of others. The species of the Trade Pact agreed to be governed by mutual respect, with any lapses the rightful business of authorities they have set in place." Mighty heads dipped in acknowledgment to Bowman, who actually looked shy. "We, the Consortium, think. We identify patterns. We watch."

This last with an ominous undertone.

"Those who possess grist are troubled. We, the Consortium, know why. We see the danger facing all life."

Jason. We aren't alone! NothingReal—the Trade Pact—acts, too.

Every eye converged on Sira. The tree-form Assemblers leaned forward as though pulled. Standing beside her, despite an impression of great good will, Morgan couldn't help but be intimidated. He held his ground. The Vyna hid behind Tayno, whose eyes disappeared within his head disks.

"Oh, my," his Witchling said faintly.

Their regard changed again. A crowd was gathering—at a distance—as those released from lockdown came forth. "WEL-COME."

That distance increased sharply.

As is the way of crowds, when nothing else happened, curiosity took over, those who couldn't see from the back pushing the front ranks forward until a cross-section of Plexis, from gold tags to none, spacers to staff, formed a ring around them.

When the movement settled to an uneasy shifting of appendages, the Carasian resumed. "We, the Consortium, reveal ourselves at this time of mutual peril. To succeed, we must work as one. Before we proceed, it is for the Trade Pact to deal with a threat from within."

More vermin, many more, this time dragging between them what looked like a corpse on a red cloak.

But still lived.

A threat! Beware! The Vyna's sending thrilled with *fear. It possesses power over us.*

Interlude

THE OMACRON DIDN'T LOOK like a threat, but here appearance lied. Sept used weakness as camouflage and, seeing sept like this, prone and disheveled, a shiver of dread ran through me.

Then anger. Then—understanding. This evil being wasn't mine to combat.

Sept was theirs.

"I bear witness," I said, walking toward the Omacron.

"SIRA!"

The identification, with the subtlety I'd expect from Carasians, came with approval. I had to smile.

You aren't alone, Witchling. Morgan walked with me, as it should be.

The *Galactic Mysterioso* rose to face us, sept's sinuous body coiling this way and that as though torn between targets, skin a putrid yellow-green. "Sira, is it? Whatever you think you know, Fem, whatever you do, he dies." Sept stared at Morgan with a terrible *hunger.*

"I wouldn't say that to her," my Human responded, tone amused, shields tight.

"Oh?" I heard the oddest sound. It came from the creature. A *hum.*

A *hum* that reached into the M'hir as well as here, that filled my senses until I could barely breathe, couldn't move. I heard shouts. Bellows!

They were nothing to the *hum*. I felt it press and slither, like something alive, seeking an opening into my mind—no, expecting one. In how many had the Omacron left their doors?

One too many. So even as I *felt* Morgan *scream*—

—cold, sure, I *carved* my own.

The *hum* faltered and fled. The Omacron's skin flared red, blue, grew transparent as though my intrusion drained sept's color.

I chased the *hum* to its source, destroying that part of the Omacron's mind with a flick of Power. Considered what worse I could do, sept's every thought and memory spread before me, the creature helpless in my coils—ready—I'd only to *enjoy*—

Witchling. Morgan, like a dose of clean fresh air.

I see it. Another sort of weapon, those waves of shared foul *pleasure,* and I pulled myself free, feeling in desperate need of a bath.

The Omacron stood, twisted at both waists, and smiled, as though sept had won.

I ignored it, my attention for those waiting and likely wondering what, if anything, had happened. "The Omacron cannot be trusted," I said, hearing my voice amplified. "They've used their abilities to create flaws in the minds of other species, flaws they exploit at will."

"We are misunderstood!" The *Galactic Mysterioso* bowed. "Telepaths come to us for aid. We do what we can—"

"You are the Poison Makers!" The Assembler named Dewley edged around the Omacron to get to me, words tumbling out. "Liars! Wanted Clan gone. Fine, who likes them. Carasians? Bad idea. Bad." At their rumble of agreement, he ducked behind me, peering around. "Humans, maybe bad, maybe—" Morgan raised an eyebrow "—bad. Very Bad idea. Who'd be next? What the end? Bad one-minds. All want everything but them dead."

"Testimony is complete," Board Member Sta'gli said.

A species' doom in her voice.

* ✳ *

The defeated were taken away; the Brill, wrapped in nets and on grav carts. The Trade Pact Board continued their deliberations over our heads, mercifully muted. Some beings on the concourse were using goggles to watch. Lip-reading or to find their own member.

The Clan had no representation up there, for the very sound reason we were soon to be extinct. To leave, I reminded myself.

Leaving had fresh appeal, given I stood not surrounded by the Trade Pact, but in the midst of the Consortium, a group none of us—with the exception of Bowman—had known existed until moments ago. The shadows cast by the Carasians formed a dark ring, like a warning against trespass. I'd no desire to go closer, thank you, and stayed in the only spot of light. If I'd ever imagined warmth in Huido's shiny black eyes, I couldn't now. Calculating, these many eyes. Assessing. I'd have been daunted by that regard—let alone the size of the claws, politely tip down, around me—if not for what was worse.

The tree-form Assemblers leaned into the circle. To keep their balance, more vermin had attached themselves to make braces. Braces attached to the shoulders of the Carasians.

It was disturbingly like being inside a mouth, granted a final look through teeth before the swallowing started.

Before that image went any further, I said, "Hello." Morgan would be proud. Was proud, I sensed, as well as worried. "You wanted to talk to me."

"SYNERGYREQUIRED"

I covered my ears and glared. "Stop that!" Which wasn't terribly diplomatic, but at this distance their bellow drove the air from my lungs and I'd trouble enough standing here.

"Our apologies," a single Carasian said in a decently quiet voice. She gave a delicate *ching* with her upper claw. "We'd hoped to commune within the Expanse. What you call the M'hir."

I blinked. "Between."

A low rumble. "A useful description." Another *ching*. "We agree to use speech."

"Wait, please." Cautiously, I opened my *inner* sense. Watchers. I felt their presence, but distant. Felt the Singers, holding tight, my anchor to AllThereIs. I avoided the glow that was Tarerea Vyna, the warmth of Morgan, and looked for anything remotely like the *twist* of Carasians.

But the rest was the Dark, a storm building within as I paid too much attention. Before I fled, I cried out, *Where are you?*

The Dark flowed, pushed aside by what couldn't be here.

A ship.

Sira? Morgan, feeling my *shock.*

It's—all right, I sent, staring with what weren't eyes at a shape I'd seen before.

The starship *Wayfarer* had almost rammed on Plexis approach. Massive, though size was a slippery concept here, with those strange lines, and somehow it hung in place, stationary despite the wild churning of Between.

Colors without name danced across its hull—skin?—then it became a mirror, awash in burning light. Mine, I realized. What must be *me* here. The mirror became night; the ship *flexed* and dove away.

I pulled free, staring up at the Consortium, reassured to be dealing with what I could see and touch. With what breathed and lived in this universe.

Yet did more. "That—that's yours?"

"We are the Consortium."

Not an answer, unless—I was thinking too small. "It's M'hir-life. Alive." One of them. "And your ship."

"We each contribute as we can. The—" that soft *ching* again, "—hosts synergy. Within him, and his kin, we share our deepest, most meaningful communion. And, yes," the Carasian sounded amused, "he's willing to carry those of us who lack mobility. We try not to impose."

Manners, with M'hir life. The Carasians simplified concepts for me, for which I was grateful, but they'd a reason for being here, for talking to me, and I didn't flatter myself it was my grist.

I sat, cross-legged, on the floor. Step one with aliens, according to my Human?

Establish mutual understandings.

"So," I began. "I'm a noncorporeal entity from another universe, temporarily in a Hoveny body to do what I can to prevent possibly catastrophic damage to existence. You?"

* ✳ *

Flesh and shell, Carasians were wholly of this space. That said, grist was, so they told me, more than a sense. When their females molted into their mature and glorious reproductive form, their ability to detect grist became a means of direct communication between them, allowing synergy through the Expanse.

Coming from a species with the Power-of-Choice and Commencement, I took this in stride.

It was the part where they could communicate—commune— with what lived in the Expanse I found startling. To their amusement. Had not the Drapsk shown me the variety of life there?

Some of that life, like the *ching,* existed across universes. At my stunned look, they'd begun talking over one another, earnestly describing life that could spontaneously duplicate. Be in several folds of space at the same time. Create folds in space. Or—

I threw up my hands. "Enough!"

In the pause that followed, whirling eyes converged on me. "We are corrected," the Carasian said, sounding almost abashed. "It is our common purpose that matters now."

For the Consortium had revealed themselves not only because the Clan had weakened what kept our universes safely apart—a more than sufficient problem, in my opinion—but to stop those who would tear it open.

The Rugherans.

Morgan would not, I decided, be pleased.

Chapter 34

BY SPECIES, waiting could put you in a pleasing semi-dormant state, such as the group of Oduyae snoring in front of the pet dealer, or have you literally climbing walls. There were, Morgan squinted, several Skenkrans presently climbing, despite the attempts of homeowners with balconies to shoo them away. The beings would glide down if anything interesting happened.

Several Human adults looked at both species wistfully, as if they'd love to have their offspring either nap or be someone else's problem. Meanwhile, because this was Plexis, a flurry of carts selling refreshments and newly minted commemorative coins had appeared, doing a brisk business in the crowd.

Morgan leaned a hip on the security grav sled, content to watch Sira. Not that he could see her, surrounded as she was at the moment by the Consortium—Carasians closest, then the still-disturbing tree-form Assemblers in an outer attentively-bent ring.

"Gonna take weeks," Terk grumbled.

Two-Lily Finelle laughed. "Partner Russ-Ell, there has yet to be a Trade Pact decision that took so long to reach." If cart owners were happy at the business they were getting, the Lemmick was ecstatic. She'd been handing out cards for her relative's now-publicly tested balloon-skin to any and all. By the level of interest, she could retire tomorrow.

Be a shame, the Human thought. The pair were shaping into an excellent team.

Terk scowled. "Could be the first time."

He stirred himself to answer. "The Consortium isn't here about the First or the Omacron." After that initial *shock*, Sira had locked herself away. Whatever she was learning could well explain why the *taste* of change hadn't left him. Why he felt on the verge of *something*—

"Yeah, that." Terk's eyes were hard. "I don't like waiting for the other boot. It's always bigger."

Finelle laughed. "How can that—Sector Chief!" She came to attention, her partner startled into doing the same.

Morgan raised an eyebrow as Bowman came to stand in front of him, dismissing her constables with a sideways tip of her head.

"Quite the show," he commented.

The meeting rooms were still being projected. By the vehement appendage waving and plumes of expressive gas, a decision remained elusive; several food vendors were taking bets on the side.

She didn't bother to look. "Not my problem. This?" A lift of fingers toward the Consortium. "Out of our league. It's what comes after. Your future—"

Instinct made him thrust out a hand to stop whatever she'd say. Terk came to alert, settling when Bowman merely nodded. "Not a topic you want. I get that." She leaned on the sled beside him. "I don't trust many beings."

"You trust anyone?" Morgan countered.

Gods, a chuckle. "There's that. Let's say there are individuals— very few—I find set a compatible course. I might disagree with the direction, and I don't enjoy surprises," grim, that, "but the result's worth my wait."

It was the most convoluted compliment he'd ever received, from the most dangerous person he knew. Morgan gazed down at her impassive face, torn between curiosity and suspicion. "Is this a job offer?"

"If it was, you'd say no." Her eyes were serious. "It's a reminder you aren't alone, Jason."

As if summoned, a slender figure in spacer coveralls came in their direction, dwarfed by the giant shapes behind her, yet, to him, greater than any. Sira.

"I'm not alone," Morgan said softly, eyes drinking in the sight. Shaking her head, Bowman left it at that.

* ✳ *

Sira pulled him from the others with a glance. Where they met became a small eddy of peace, those nearby taking one look at Morgan—and wisely moving on.

He didn't notice, too busy trying to grasp what she told him. "They plan to protect the universe with a supermarket?"

Almost a dimple. "When you put it that way—" Sira brushed hair from her face and sighed. "The Consortium has identified the point in this space corresponding to where the M'hir is weakest. That's where the Rugherans intend to break through to All-Theres. Why, they don't know and the Rugherans aren't saying, but they've been scratching at the door as long as the Consortium has existed."

"Now they've a chance to succeed."

She nodded. "I showed you the damage we did—" The corners of her mouth turned down, though it wasn't her fault, none of it. "Combine that with what the Great Ones caused when they retrieved the Hoveny artifacts, and we're running out of time." Her eyes lifted to survey the concourse. "There's a power here," slowly. "Not like ours. The species who sense grist, who naturally touch both here and there—their very existence is like glue. The Consortium has calculated how many would be needed to create what they call a countering inertia. They're convinced that would heal the weakness, thus stopping the Rugherans. They've sent out invitations."

There were no words. Morgan sent an incredulous look toward the Consortium. Lines of calm, shiny eyes gazed back.

A Rugheran had haunted him. Followed Sira. Crawled on the outside of Plexis—still did, for all they knew. They'd need to run scans—if the creatures could be scanned.

"Who's coming?" he finally said.

A dimple appeared. "Everyone."

* ✳ *

Before saving the universe—with a supermarket—the Consortium insisted the Trade Pact deal with the Omacron and their anti-social behavior. It came down, in the end, to what could be done. The Trade Pact Board Members were, after all, a conglomeration of species with wildly differing systems of justice and government, with even the concept of antisocial behavior, for that matter, a stretch for many. In the end, and to avoid unfortunate precedent, the Board decided to leave the Omacron alone.

"Alone" being defined as banned from Trade Pact space, while encouraged to remain within those star systems the Omacron could legitimately claim as theirs. Any non-Omacron in those systems would be informed, in full, of the reasons for the ban and offered relocation should they choose to run, and quickly.

As the decision was read aloud, nav-systems were being updated. "Here Be Monsters" Morgan thought, would be an adequate label for what would become blanks on the maps. Perhaps isolation would open minds so far willfully deaf to diplomacy and cooperation.

He wouldn't bet on it. At best, they'd bought time; to learn how to guard against the Omacrons' propensity for toxics, to find ways to repair the flaws they'd placed in so many minds.

He'd paid to let them into his—had thought himself improved. Morgan shuddered.

I should have killed the foul thing, Sira sent, her mindvoice like ice.

"Chalk it up to another life lesson, chit," he told her, unable to trust his own.

"Huh." Unconvinced, that was. She'd been around Terk too long.

No time was long, not now. Morgan handed her a cup of sombay, obtained from a cart dispensing the beverage—with just the right sweetness. "While you were communing, Tayno found an easi-rest for his friend," he told her. The Consortium having insisted Tarerea Vyna remain, to the young Carasian's visible distress, he'd done what he could for her comfort.

Sira took a sip, then passed it back for him. "What the wives—what they all do—they called it synergy." Her brows met. "Some takes place within the M'hir—the Expanse. They've a place, or members, there." Her frown deepened, then relaxed. "They politely gave up trying to explain. How Carasians communicate is beyond me."

"Because they are brilliant as well as beautiful!" Huido swaggered—deservedly so—though he bore his latest scars and dents, and hammer, with such pride, Morgan fully expected his friend to be depressed post-molt. "Are my wives and the others not magnificent?" A pause, eyes going to Sira. "As are you, dear friend."

Sira smiled. "Is it polite to ask how many are, ah, your shell-mates?"

Eyes whirled. The Carasian tipped toward them, his big voice as close to conspiratorial as possible, given the size of his chest. "Eighteen of these lovelies already grace my pool. Another four may join them. I was impressive, you know. There's a vid."

"You were," Morgan agreed, quickly doing the math. One female left, of the group here. Did that mean?

From the sparkle in Sira's eyes as she looked toward Tayno, busy with the Vyna, he thought it might.

"After the announcement," Huido continued, "there must be a feast. I will arrange everything."

Is the restaurant open? Sira sent.

Morgan shook his head. If his friend was involved, there'd be a feast—

"ATTEND."

Skenkrans who hadn't plunged for the Trade Pact announcement whooshed down now, causing those below to duck. Carts stopped where they were, anti-theft covers whipped into place, and the crowd closed in once more.

Fingers laced with his.

A single female Carasian had moved into the open, standing

where she—or another—had stood before. To identify individuals, he'd have to memorize the pattern of nicks and marks in their carapace and head disks; three had stubs in place of claws, but they kept their claws tucked tightly to their bodies. Once they molted, those clues would vanish.

"We are ready to receive the message."

A pinprick of night blossomed before their eyes into a star-filled oval with outflung fibrous arms.

Having burst into view, the Rugheran unceremoniously plopped onto the deck, defeated by station gravity and looking anything but a threat to reality.

/identity/~triumph~!~/identity/
/identity/~SIRA~/identity/

Interlude

/*IDENTITY/~SIRA~/IDENTITY/*
The tip of an arm gave me a limp but decidedly jolly wave. That, with my name, made this the same Rugheran who'd found me on the *Wayfarer*. Now here. Had it been outside the hull, waiting?

A message, the Consortium called it. Was it that, or an ultimatum?

"Let me through," a voice insisted. Deputy Inspector Jynet came forward, shaking off the tentacle of one of her own staff. "This fine being arrived in my office. Plexis claims it as a customer, under our protection."

/*query/~?~/query/*

While I admired her courage, the nature of this species outside the norm even for this hub of the Trade Pact, the Eima was—

"It came to our kitchen first!" Huido—goodness, that bellow came from Tayno? Who promptly crouched and hurried back, having surprised himself, too.

Meanwhile, the Carasians were—crooning. The one elected to speak went so far as to lean over the Rugheran, eyes whirling with pleasure.

Not the reaction I'd expected. "What's happening?"

"Remarkable grist," Huido said happily. "Simply—"

Morgan grabbed my hand, tight. "Sira . . ."

We were engulfed in purple feathers.

No, antennae. Antennae, I thought, holding my mouth closed despite having to smile, and tentacles. The Drapsk, dear little beings, patted every part of me they could reach, which tickled, and I patted round rumps and chubby arms. All the while they exclaimed their joy: "It's true!" "You're here, Mystic One!" "We've found you!" "Would you care for a beverage?" "Not now, she's busy!" "You're here!"

A smug—

/identity/~SIRA~/identity/

—only added to the frenzy.

"Sira. CHIT."

Morgan's captain voice reached me through the happy bedlam. The instant I tried to extricate myself from the mounds of squirming Drapsk, the Heerii fell over themselves to free me, each giving me a tiny pat first. I found myself standing alone, remarkably disheveled and grinning widely.

In front of the Trade Pact Board, the Consortium, and a large segment of Plexis.

I did the only thing I could do. I waved.

The Rugheran did, too.

And the Drapsk.

Suddenly, with the exception of the leadership of the Consortium, every being was waving, and laughing, and smiling—however was species-appropriate—for no reason but that friends had found one another and amid all else—from alarms to threats to bureaucracy—

That mattered, too.

* ✳ *

"You done?"

There was a smile in my Human's voice, if none on his face. Set to negotiate, his expression told me, assuming the Rugheran was here for anything so reasonable. The outpouring of Drapsk from the *Heerala*, docked to Plexis had to be a good sign. They'd been

invited, after all. Timing their arrival to the Rugheran's implied
a connection.

It didn't guarantee congruence.

Predictably, having granted me space, the dear little beings
were ensconced on the Carasian females, resembling feather
boas draped over grim-eyed rocks, though a few had scampered
to fondle Huido.

And Tayno, who, unlike the other Carasians, seemed paralyzed
by their attention. He really shouldn't let the captain sit on his
head plate, but it wasn't my place.

The Vyna reached up and gave the Drapsk a firm push. It
bounced down without complaint, leaning fondly against Tayno's
leg. Seeing all this could make you wonder why anyone took
Drapsk seriously.

Unless you knew the Drapsk.

"We are the Consortium." The Carasian lifted a claw to which
three Drapsk clung, giving it a little shake as though to make the
point.

"Of course," Morgan breathed. "The Scented Way. Drapskii."

"We will hear the message."

/attentionurgent/~SIRA~/identity/

I felt Morgan ready himself. "You're up, Witchling."

"Sira." Another claw invited me closer to the mass of "urgent"
goo.

It wasn't as though others couldn't hear the creature.

For some reason, it had fixated on me. Time to find out why,
if I could. I felt Morgan's presence, offering *confidence* and *belief*.
His *strength* should I need it. We weren't Joined, I thought, looking into those remarkable blue eyes, but in what mattered, we
were one still. I nodded, to say what I didn't know, but his eyes
brightened.

/identity/~help!~/urgency/

What it had said on the *Wayfarer*. Was it the Rugheran equivalent of a Board Member, able to speak for its kind?

Or more like me? I thought all at once. Alone, venturing where
it didn't belong, doing what it could to try and prevent disaster.

/ terror/~STOPGO!~/urgency/

Knowing Morgan would hate this, knowing I already did, I squatted near the Rugheran and offered my hand.

An arm flailed high above, slamming down like Huido's hammer—where I'd been, Morgan having pulled me aside. "Careful," was all he said, but his jaw worked.

Care we couldn't afford. This time, instead of offering my hand, I quickly grabbed hold of the arm.

Wet, rather than slimy. Cool. I opened my sense to the M'hir. There, the Rugheran glistened, its thought patterns like music.

Confusing music, with no rhythm I could detect. It wanted something, desperately. My understanding.

/agreement/~joy!~/urgency/

"You should talk to the Carasians." I formed an image of the female.

/confusion/~?~/help!/

That'd be no.

I felt a strong grip on my shoulder. *It needs an interpreter, Witchling.*

So did I, I thought, but kept it to myself. Start simple. "Were you outside?" I sent an image of the Rugheran crawling over Plexis' hull.

/anxiety/~BADSTOP!~/DREAD/~STOPTAKE!~/urgency/

"Jason!" My shoulder was cold where his hand had been. I heard running, urgent voices.

I stayed where I was, my senses alert to the now-roiling M'hir and this being who belonged there more than here.

"Take where? Take what?"

/Terror/~TAKEALLUS~/Terror/~TAKEALLUS~/Terror/

The arm moved, flinging me backward. The Rugheran *WAILED*, and I covered my head, shaking.

Silence. I looked up to find it gone.

Everyone else was motion. The tree-form Assemblers were fragmenting. The rain of vermin sent the crowd running for cover, vermin running with them. The Carasians snapped and stamped in agitation, fueling the panic.

I helped myself to my feet, rather annoyed by all the fuss.

Until I saw what was being projected from the hovering messengers.

The exterior of Plexis. There wasn't one Rugheran crawling over her hull. There were hordes, crawling toward one another to lock arms and stretch, as though creating a net with their bodies.

They covered the surface of their planet. Why this station?

"Plexis-com. Shut that off!" I heard Bowman order, then the Eima's sharp: "Do it now!"

The image disappeared.

The aftermath was hardly reassuring. The concourse was empty of all but overturned carts and discarded purchases. The last of the crowds who'd endured forcefields and announcements could be seen crammed on the ramps leading up and down, anywhere but here.

If ships could leave, they'd be able to charge what they wanted, but with the Rugherans out there, none would try. I looked for Morgan. Waited, like the rest, for a com broadcast or other explanation.

But no com broadcast could have the sheer heart-stopping potency of the Consortium's "ATTEND!"

Aside: The Drapsk

WALKWAYS CURVED AROUND and up, moving steadily, each filled with long, low bowlcars, each of those filled with Drapsk. There were Heerii and Makii. Doakii, Niakii, and Pardii. Tookii and in fact, every tribe—every Drapsk—and here and there, like punctuation, the bright yellow of Skeptics.

Antennae fluttered in the breeze of their own passing, sharing what was needful. "Together." "It is time." "Did you leave the kettle on?"

As well as some that was not, but no one minded.

Each bowlcar paused on the vast slope of the amphitheater to allow its passengers to hop out. Once coated in Drapsk, the slope itself moved upward. A wind came down in greeting, creating billows and waves among the antennae.

A wind of warning, of determination, but also of hope.

The city fell away, mountains shrank along the horizon, and still the slope moved up. Up. Up. Until it crested the lip of the amphitheater and over, Drapsk drifting gently downward like a rain of plump white seeds, their colorful antennae slicked back.

As each landed, they sought not their assigned seats, but the floor, gathering tighter and tighter together. When the floor was covered, those next to arrive stood on shoulders, held by hands below, for this gathering required—density. More arrived, and more, until the amphitheater itself began to fill with carefully balanced Drapsk.

And once every living Drapsk on the planet was together, tribe among tribe?

They gave forth the scent of the world.

DRAPSKII

Chapter 35

IF THE CONSORTIUM'S PLAN depended on secrecy, they were, Morgan judged, as good as dead and should therefore enjoy Huido's feast while they could.

If not—they were still in trouble. The problem being, what?

The Rugheran who'd come to warn them, for that much seemed clear, had terrified the station with its wail of "TAKEUS ALL."

He'd a bad feeling where—

"Morgan!" Terk beckoned him to the console. At the Consortium's request, they'd relocated, quickly, to the command deck of the *Conciliator*. "They" included Deputy Inspector Jynet, it being her station wrapped in aliens, as well as the two-plus Consortium members: a Carasian female, a Drapsk laden with com equipment, and the plus: a cluster of red-eyed vermin.

Captain Lucic and crew were too well-trained to react to a reputedly bloodthirsty and mindless Carasian female; the vermin received at least one second look.

Tarerea Vyna, accompanied by Carasian bookends—Tayno and therefore Huido not to be parted—waited in a nearby room, a medtech summoned to assess her condition.

"Dying" encompassed the options, Sira'd told him. The Vyna stayed because her people remained in the grip of the Rugherans.

And for Tayno, who'd become as quietly grim as Huido at his darkest.

Sira stood to one side, her eyes on him, quiet also, inside and out, but hers? Waited.

"Rolling external," the comtech at the console announced. "On main."

The Rugherans had multiplied, or more arrived. Both, maybe. Having girdled the station's forward end, strands of them reached aft, heedless if they coated Plexis or the unfortunate starships parked against her.

The *Wayfarer* was one of those ships. Morgan had contacted Captain Erin and told her what he could—ending that she and Noska were safer inside. She'd responded with a quip about using her leisure to fine-tune the engines.

Then offered him the captain's chair—if they survived the current crisis—having proven himself a capable pilot.

Another unlooked-for compliment, another friend concerned for a future he didn't plan to have. It warmed the heart.

And changed nothing.

Bowman sat a chair beside the captain, slouched, chin in a palm. "Can Plexis get out of here?"

"No. It's as though they knew where to start," Jynet said grimly. She'd a live link to station-control, its distraught staff bolstered by off-shift officers. "The field generators are coated in the things."

"Weapons."

"Atyourcommand," Captain Lucic replied, its voice calm. The Ordnex either had ice in its veins or something had happened recently to put swarming Rugherans well down its list of concerns.

Bowman would know, Morgan judged.

A claw snapped, gaining more than a few looks. "The Rugherans aren't fully in this universe," the Carasian said. "Only the station would be damaged."

"Stand them down, Captain." Bowman was another who might have been ordering sombay, not staring into a growing abyss. "Any idea what they're doing out there?"

"We know their purpose. To hold us here, keeping us from our destination until they succeed. After that, it will be too late."

For everything, Sira sent.

Not done yet, chit, he replied.

"Chief! The *Heerala* has launched."

Interlude

TAYNO DIDN'T LIKE THIS ROOM, with its pleasant array of chairs and tables, its dimmed lights. It made him feel meaner, which helped make him less afraid, but wasn't in any way helpful when surrounded by friends and their expensive furniture. When he peeked at Huido, he couldn't tell if the other struggled with instinct or not. Aspiring to such self-control was a worthy goal.

Aspiring to survive was another.

"Tayno?"

He crouched by Tarerea's side, eyes whirling. A medtech, of some species he didn't know by name, had given her something to drink and a shot. If a stim, it hadn't helped. Her skin's normal pallor had gained a yellow tinge and he worried, which didn't help his fear at all. "Do you need a blanket?" he asked. "Are you too hot?"

"Take me to Sira," she ordered, her voice terribly faint. "Quickly."

No, he wasn't to move her. Wasn't to take her where she might— "You have to stay here. They told us—"

"Don't argue." Huido took one end of her cot in his handling claws. "Come along," in a tone so unusually gentle—

It made his fear worse.

* ✳ *

No one argued. Not the crew who moved out of their way, nor the one who opened the luckily wide doors into what looked to be the breeding ground of breakable devices and important things, a space moreover filled with beings who turned to stare at the sight of two Carasians carrying a Vyna on a cot.

Including a cluster of vermin who were now, Tayno reminded himself sharply, to be thought of as colleagues. When not in the kitchen.

Such thoughts kept him from dwelling on how Tarerea's breaths were shallow now, and rapid, as if she exerted herself by lying still. They'd done this, Tayno decided, daring to glower at the Carasian female.

Who gave the tiniest tilt of her head in acknowledgment.

Confounded, he almost dropped the cot.

"We've got her." Two Human-ish beings took over.

"I must—Sira." The Vyna's six-fingered hand lifted.

Between

Singers strained but didn't let go. Wouldn't, despite the gathering of those with *teeth*, those that *pushed* and *fought* one another. Sira was the Song they'd chosen; they refused to abandon it.

A Watcher did, drawn by something *other*. A Stolen had entered Between, not calmly, but as prey *harried* by these unusual hunters. Frantic, confused—powerful.

She threw herself forward—

Too late.

The Stolen was trapped. Fought to be free. Used POWER.

And more pieces of Between *cracked* . . .

Chapter 36

CARING FLOWED BETWEEN THEM, carried through the brush of Sira's fingers over his wrist. The one with the bracelet. Morgan didn't look at her as she continued to the cot. Like him, she sensed time running out. For the Vyna.

For them.

Possibly for everything and everyone, but keeping a useful focus on what was present and urgent with that thought rattling around would be impossible, so Morgan dismissed it. Instead, he watched the *Heerala* ease away from Plexis.

Leaving her newly minted cargo supervisor, and former captain—not to mention former Skeptic—Heevertup. The lone Heerii stood beside him, sucking a tentacle, rocking back and forth. A member of the Consortium, yes, but first and foremost, of his tribe. Drapsk didn't leave their own behind. He hadn't thought them physiologically capable.

Until now.

Bowman turned her head. "Anything you care to tell us, Heevertup?"

"Only that our captain seizes opportunity, Sector Chief," the Drapsk said, another tentacle joining the first. "We must reach the gathering point. The *Heerala* goes to White."

The Rugheran planet? Morgan shook his head. He should

have known. The species' physical link to this universe. The system was a subspace hop from here, making Plexis' schedule the Consortium's all along.

The Carasian female made a *ching* sound. "All must try, or all will fail."

"Huh." Bowman scowled. "I prefer the version where we get these things off the station."

"As do we."

"They're leaving!" someone said, snapping eyes back to the screen.

Morgan looked with the rest. Rugherans were peeling themselves from the station in droves. Were they leaving, or simply hard to discern against a backdrop of stars—

Suddenly, a black web of bodies began to coat the white of the Drapsk ship. So many attached themselves at once, the *Heerala* appeared to drown—

Then, vanish.

"Report," Bowman, calm and quiet.

The tech's voice trembled. "Gone from scans. Just gone."

"Confirmed. No response to hails."

A ball of Drapsk thudded very gently against Morgan's leg.

The Rugherans reappeared, whirling through space like a flock of Darkness against a forever night, to resume coating Plexis and all those within.

They knew what "Takeusall" meant now, Morgan thought bitterly. How many other starships had they taken? How many so-called unexplained accidents had seen hapless crews and families swallowed whole—

Sira—

Interlude

"SIRA."

The Vyna's voice was barely stronger than Morgan's sorrowful sending. Both filled me with dread I'd no time to face. If the Rugherans could drop a giant starship into the M'hir, if that's what they'd done? They'd be able to do the same to Plexis. The Consortium's hope to save us—if it was a hope—would be lost.

Not yet.

"Are you ready to go home, Tarerea?" I asked, kneeling beside her. Tayno rumbled a protest. I didn't bother to look up, unable to fear him, of all things.

"You—must save them, too." Despite the catch in her breath, there was fire in her eyes. "My heart-kin. I feel their fear. Their hopelessness. Sira, they are hunted—" Her hand, with its paired thumbs, reached for mine.

Sira. The Consortium says we must get to White.

Where the Vyna must be, because that's where the Rugherans were strongest.

Where Between was ready to crumple, because of what they'd done. Had I—had we—started it? With our meddling in the sex life of worlds?

"White," I said aloud, as if we were talking about menu choices.

"That's where Tarerea needs to go." Tayno gave himself a triumphant little shake, then continued, much too loudly, "Jason Morgan can get her to White. He knows the way."

Chapter 37

"**Y**OU'VE BEEN TO THIS 'WHITE'?" Bowman looked across the command center at Tayno, then to Morgan. "Explain."

"An off-books stop," he said, keeping it simple and safe. There were—should be—no records the *Silver Fox* had been to White. No records, for that matter, of White, except—no doubt—those of the Drapsk and so the Consortium.

And from them to all the species invited to this gathering of grist.

"Happens we're stuck." Hands on the arms of her chair, Bowman thrust herself to her feet and turned to the one person she knew had another means of travel. "Well?"

Sira stood, her face stern. "I know what you're asking. No Clan could 'port an object this size. I wouldn't dare if I could. It would cause the very harm we're trying to prevent."

Something tugged his pant leg. Expecting the Drapsk, Morgan froze when he saw his feet ringed with red-eyed vermin.

A claw snapped. Another made a *ching*.

They didn't—

"We, the Consortium, concur," the Carasian announced. "Sira is correct to fear further damage. It's how we all knew the Clan did not belong here. Humans do. They cannot affect the Expanse. Jason Morgan. You know the way."

"But—" from Sira, who subsided at his signal. He sensed her
concern.

Shared it.

"Morgan," Bowman echoed, returning to him, that brow up.

The screen showed Plexis, three-quarters smothered in writhing black. It wouldn't be long before the reaching arms connected across the rest. The *Wayfarer* was already covered—

—and he'd do anything to save these beings, the ones in the
station, the ones on worlds he'd yet to see. Morgan met Sira's
steady gaze, asked a question with his. What good was a secret, if
no one survived?

Gods, the trust in her smile.

All in, then.

"There's a thing I can do," Morgan told them, feeling oddly
light-headed. "I don't know if—" How could he? *Pushing* a
starship through the M'hir should have been impossible. A space
station? "I'll need—" to drain the inner strength of every telepath
on Plexis, including Sira's? "—help."

Another, urgent, tap on his leg. Resisting the impulse to kick
what he shouldn't, the Human looked down.

The Drapsk's mouth tentacles were spread in exultation. "She
knows! She's coming!"

Morgan's mouth dried.

"Who now?" Bowman snapped.

"Drapskii!"

Interlude

DRAPSKII ANNOUNCED HERSELF to me as she had before, as a *brilliance* in the M'hir, an attraction like gravity. Her gravity I had felt, for she was a world, orbiting a star of pleasing warmth. I'd stood on her ground and tasted her rain—

As a world, she remained in her orbit, home to the dear little Drapsk.

As this *presence*, I felt her be *HERE*. Felt her *grief* at the loss of the Heerii, her *determination*.

"She's arrived," I confirmed rather breathlessly, looking at Morgan. "You've your help."

I watched his throat move, a swallow, nothing more. Outwardly, my Human appeared almost relaxed, a camouflage earning him a suspicious eye from Terk.

"Then let's do this."

"Do what, exactly?" Bowman asked.

Morgan's smile was a beautiful thing. "Move."

* ✳ *

I'd missed watching Morgan *move* the *Fox*, being preoccupied with staying alive. He'd shared some of the wonder and all of its cost, but little of the how. It was a Human Talent, and part of

me looked forward to seeing him use it. The only part not terrified.

"I'll need a seat," Morgan said.

Bowman stepped aside and waved him, not without irony, into
hers. "What will we see?"

"I've no idea." He closed his eyes and—

Sira. Show me.

My task, to guide him through the M'hir to Drapskii, but she
was already waiting. After all, they'd met. As the three of us remembered in detail, I felt myself blush.

Then felt a deep and painful *sorrow* and understood what
should have been plain from the start.

I'd been right, to believe the Great Ones of AllThereIs had
their equivalents, here, in NothingReal, but they weren't the
same. Drapskii. White? They were worlds, yes, but semi-sentient,
aware, partly Between. Instead of Singers, they'd inhabitants: beings of flesh who also existed here and there. In a way, theirs was
a more settled, peaceful universe.

But that assumption disregarded Between.

The Expanse.

The Scented Way.

The Dark.

Whatever the name, it also held life, life every bit as strange as
a Watcher—capable of violence.

And *hunger.*

Drapskii's *sorrow* wasn't only for her Drapsk, but for her coun-
terpart, White, caught in the schemes of those who craved a new
and larger hunting ground. The Rugherans—enough, perhaps
all but one—sought to move their world fully *inside* Between and,
from there, reach more.

I'd have liked to introduce them to the *Galactic Mysterioso.*

READY, WITCHLING? SHOULD BE QUITE THE RIDE.

My love's mindvoice, now the size of a world's.

Chapter 38

HIS VOICE was the size of a world.

The rest of him minuscule. The rest focused on what he *knew* of Plexis. He'd a Talent for discrimination, to identify objects.

If nothing so large as this.

But he *knew* the station, the parking spots with better equipment, the corridors that missed checkpoints or the ones that led to safety. *Knew* the cargo warehouses and the posting boards, the ramps and glittering shops, the *Claws & Jaws* and the Whirtle who sold sheets and shoes. Holding all that in his mind, refusing to doubt it was enough, he summoned his memory of White, formed the locate, and *pushed* . . .

The M'hir was in trouble. That was his first thought, and though the Consortium believed a Human Talent unable to cause harm, who were they to know? His beach was gone. Sira, out of sight. His grasp of Plexis, of where he had to go, were the only realities in a universe gone mad.

That, and a refusal to fail. Another joined him, *strange* and too small.

Too *BIG!*

Power surged through him, lifted him, *pushed* ahead what he gripped with what remained of consciousness . . .

He opened his eyes to find himself sitting in the captain's seat of a battle cruiser—enough to make him doubt his senses, but *she* was here.

Not a world. Nothing strange.

The other half of his heart. *Sira.*

Interlude

White

THEY'D COME FROM SYSTEMS so distant from one another this journey had taken weeks translight. Goth ships. Thremm. Papiekians and Scat. Drapsk, Carasian, and more.

Met over a planet none of them dared touch, sensing the grist of those swarming over its surface as poison. Space *rippled* as other ships, what weren't just ships, flowed in and out of reality around them, chasing back the hunters. *ching.*

Waited.

Despaired as some were swarmed—

And disappeared.

* ✳ *

When a space station pops out of nothing, especially one with a garish sign proclaiming "Plexis Supermarket: If You Want It, It's Here," prudence dictates a shift in orbit, preferably higher. Ships made their adjustments even as coms flared with messages. As hearts—or the appropriate organ—throbbed with hope, the answer came.

"We are the Consortium."

Between

The Watchers gathered, being what Watchers do when noticing something *new*. Wary of threat, always. Ready to act.

One hesitated, holding place.

Others did the same.

New, they whispered among themselves.

While the Singers held on, circled by *teeth*.

In this place where size meant nothing more than *will*, a single, *strange* and small being swam and laughed to itself, growing larger with the *pull* of so many who belonged *there* and not here . . .

. . . reached with *arms* to find them. Connected. *Pulling* in turn.

Growing larger and larger.

The Dark swam and *pulled*, too, but those within it were growing smaller and smaller, their influence waning.

Until the being circled back where it belonged, growing—
LARGE.

And *sorrow* became *recognition* became *joy* as the solitary Rugheran who had been White and so very small and alone . . .

Became, once more, a world around a star.

Beloved.

While the hungry went without, except for those they'd already *caught*.

* * *

Snosbor IV

Wys di Caraat stood on her balcony, staring out at Caraaton—her city—through sheets of rain. Fire continued to rage on the horizon, north of the park. The Retian had proved braver or more obsessed than she'd expected. The Scats had, of course, lied. They'd no special cargo. Hadn't landed. Extorted payment, that was all, while Talobar burned in his laboratory, with the future of the Clan.

The Omacron scum had stolen the present, one Chosen pair at a time.

Leaving her till last. A compliment of sorts.

"Mother."

Wys closed her eyes, savoring that deep voice. If the Omacron sent illusion first, let it be this one: her son alive.

"Witch."

Her eyes shot open, and she turned with a gasp.

Erad di Caraat stood in her quarters, freed. Beside him stood—

"Yihtor!" Without thinking, she loosed her Power in reacquaintance, eager to sense him again, feel him again.

To bounce painfully from shields every bit as strong as she'd once gloried in and Wys smiled, giving the gesture of recognition between equals. "My son." She frowned. "What's happened to your hair?"

"I'm here to send you home, Mother. Take my hand."

The words from nightmares, where the dead swarmed behind her eyes and called, over and over. *Home . . . home . . .*

"No!" Wys backed until rain of this world blinded her, until she felt the rail behind. She put out her hands. She'd have her empire. "Never!"

Her Chosen looked to her son. Her Yihtor!

"I told you," Erad said, then *pushed* her over the rail.

Stepping around the still-warm husk of his father, Yihtor di Caraat walked into the rain and tilted back his head, reveling in the sensation.

This, he'd remember.

Sira, it's time to go home.

He *pushed* himself Between, to lead the way.

AllThereIs

Night's Fire glowed overhead, a glory among dark dripping branches, luring hapless flying creatures to land on what was as much mouth as flower.

By that untrustworthy light, Wys di Caraat stepped with agonizing care. The narrow path—it would be a road, a wide road, one day—sent vines to snare her feet, vines with thorns to scratch her legs, scratches that not only itched but bled, attracting *things*.

They'd be gone, too, one day. A jungle was no proper place for a civilized being—let alone the progenitor of the new Clan. She'd have Acranam's burned to the ground. Replaced with her empire—

Wys stumbled and went to her knees. Her outthrust hands sank into a filth of rotting vegetation and mud; beneath her fingers, *things* crawled.

Paved, her road would be. None of this. One day.

She'd only to endure. Find the way for the others. They'd come—

Snap.

Some *things* weren't small nuisances. Rising to her feet, Wys staggered forward, reeling from tree to tree. They'd all be here, one day. She'd made a plan—it would be perfect—

SNAP.

AllThereIs

The Singers who remembered being father and Chosen and hated, son and never complete and used, burst free of their buds of Between, voices raised to greet their kind. Home, again.

Behind, they left one that shriveled.

The light within?

Gone out.

Chapter 39

"IT'S TIME—" Morgan folded over his knees, wondering where the words came from, wondering how he could fit inside a body this small.

And, urgently, if he was about to vomit on Bowman's feet.

The universe having turned itself inside out with his stomach, for some reason he wasn't shocked when Bowman herself took hold of him, firmly, and sat him back up, then kept her hand on his arm as if unsure if he'd stay there.

While around him came applause.

Applause?

Then he wondered the most important thing of all— "Where's Sira?"

SIRA?

Interlude

*S*IRA!

Oh, good, I thought. Morgan was conscious. Mostly. What little I let through my shields appeared whole, if confused.

Channeling the life force of an entity the size of a planet could, I thought, almost amused, do that.

Here, I replied, adding a soothing *calm* that was more how I wanted to feel at the moment than did.

"We're here," Tarerea Vyna breathed. She looked up at Tayno. "Thank you."

His eyes converged on her, every one unhappy. Then parted, to let those needle-sharp fangs protrude, and such was the trust between them that she smiled when those fangs gently touched her cheeks.

I looked away. When a subdued little rattle told me they were done, I turned and wrapped my fingers through hers. *It's time to go home.*

We'd healed Between. I sensed the difference as soon as I opened my *inner* awareness. No cracks, no rot, only the usual mad turmoil of the Dark, trying to tear me from myself.

How odd, to find that a comfort.

Keeper! This way. Hurry!

We both moved in answer, having both been Keepers, though I held Tarerea close. She'd used the last of her strength to reach this far. Would gladly have let go and spun away with the nearest Watcher, but her sense of duty was a match to mine.

And she would not leave alone.

Hunters prowled. I hadn't thought of the Rugherans as predators until I'd seen them as rumn, sliding through the depths of Vyna's lake. Muscular, powerful, *hungry.* It was their nature, here, where they belonged.

Had the Stolen lured them too far? Had it been the Hoveny? The Om'ray? We'd unbalanced more than Cersi, without intention or plan, and I was fiercely glad, all at once, to be here, searching the Dark for the last of our strays.

There.

To my sight, the Vyna were a cluster of fading lights within a violent circle of *appetite.* A circle growing smaller.

Tarerea was daunted. *Sira, how do we save them?*

And I laughed, letting free the Power I'd held in and feared, snapping it out like a whip of joy—

Scattering the hunters.

Watchers came instead, howling the names of those waiting. I felt Tarerea leave me.

Felt *attention.*

<<*Sira, it's time to go home.*>>

From one voice, from every voice, warm and welcoming and glad.

Soon, I promised.

And found myself back in the Trade Pact.

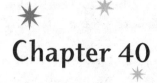

Chapter 40

THE *CLAWS & JAWS: COMPLETE INTERSPECIES CUISINE* was famous throughout the Trade Pact. Or a good part of it. At least this quadrant, which was more than enough business for one restaurant, on one space station.

Though not yet open for business—a shame, given the number of potential new customers orbiting with Plexis—a dinner party was underway in the private lounge. The elegant decor was literally overshadowed by giant rib bones propped in each corner, vertebrae keeping them from slipping while offering alternative seating. The food, on the best porcelain, was takeout from the Skenkran next door; she'd have gloated for the next station year had not her favored eldest offspring known the guests of honor personally, having welcomed them to the highest level of Plexis.

Menu and bones—or gloating Skenkrans—aside Huido was in fine form. The saving of multiple universes, including the Trade Pact and the station, was reason to celebrate, as if he needed more. After all, his pool was full of impatient wives who'd done, as the Carasian put it with a fond glisten to his whirling eyes, a great deal of thinking lately. He'd supplied them with vids of his epic battle, from several angles including above, to keep them aroused while he visited with guests.

Huido insisted on waiting on them all, leaving his staff free to entertain themselves, and the *Wayfarer*'s crew, by inventing names for the Skenkran takeout. "Glider Goobles" made Noska laugh so hard, Erin had to catch the Whirtle before it fell off its stool.

The Oduyae chefs were resting with their families, not being part of this one yet.

Two-Lily Finelle was, and present. Noska, now a firm believer, insisted she sit with him. The constable came bearing apologies from her partner and the sector chief. They'd business that couldn't wait.

With the Facilitator sitting in the *Conciliator*'s brig, Morgan wouldn't be surprised if Bowman was throwing her own party.

Morgan let the joy and anticipation of others wash by, having none of his own. He found a smile when it mattered, aware Sira did the same. Whether the feast took hours or ended soon, nothing changed. They'd run out of time.

As if Huido had reached the same conclusion—or was struggling with arousal of his own—he rose to deliver his infamous post-feast toast before most plates were empty.

"Friends and family. This will be a day to remember. We learned even vermin have their purpose! To the Vermin!" A noisy slurp invited all to join him, though two of the sous-chefs turned green and the Ordnex dishwasher disappeared under the table.

"Today, my nephew and I showed the Trade Pact the might of our claws! To our battle!"

Tayno's claw shook on its way to his mouth, but he stood straight. "Uncle! A toast to Tarerea Vyna, who carried us to that battle and who was very brave."

Eyes whirled uncertainly, it being an awkward point with Huido to have traveled the M'hir so close to his wives' return, but then he dipped his head. "And was a friend." Huido paused after that toast, then gave the bell tone of grief. He poured beer into his handling claw and raised it. "To our other friends no longer with us, the brave Drapsk of the *Heerala*." Instead of slurping the liquid, he trickled it over the metal hammer. The rest drank in silence, more than a few aware the ship's fate had come close to being their own.

If any good came from the loss, Morgan thought, it was having a possible explanation for the mysterious disappearance of other starships over the years. The Rugherans and their actions had been recorded by every device the *Conciliator* carried, data already being analyzed. It wouldn't be long before nav updates included notes on the risk of predation, as well as piracy.

Spacers might think it a joke; they'd still pay attention.

As for 'porting Plexis? The others who'd been there knew it had taken a partner who spent most of her time as a planet, and if that leaked out? Well, as Terk said, it'd make a fun vistape adventure.

"Finally," Huido boomed, "To my blood brother and sister, Jason and Sira! May your love be an example to us all. Go find yourselves a pool!"

Those who didn't know the truth laughed and applauded, along with the few still confused about why Huido kept calling Rael di Sarc by her sister's name.

Those who did know avoided their eyes.

Sira rose to her feet, glass in hand. "To our host and brother," she said simply, then added with a twinkle in her eyes, "you go first!"

Causing an uproar that caught even Huido by surprise, not that he was capable of blushing, for they all stood, Morgan starting the chant, "To the pool! To the pool!"

The massive Carasian hesitated, eyes torn between him and Sira, but this was the right exit, the carefree and happy one she asked for with a graceful sweep of her hand to the door, that tremulous smile.

Huido understood, as he always had. "Eat, drink, and don't break the porcelain," he ordered them all, eyes lingering on Morgan before clanging hammer to claw. "To my wives!"

* ✳ *

Morgan noticed Tayno remained subdued. "You'll have a pool of your own soon," he said quietly. "You made quite the impression."

Every eye winked out of sight between head disks.

"Oops," Sira mouthed.

One at a time, the black orbs reappeared. "Hom Morgan," sadly, "I cannot. There are absolute necessities. Success. Stability. Employment."

Ah. The inhabitants of Plexis had seen two Carasian males. "Trust me, Tayno, most beings can't tell the two of you apart," Morgan said soothingly. "You can still impersonate Huido."

"It's not that." Tayno attempted to whisper, but his voice grew louder with his woe. "I've critically overspent the restaurant's budget. When he finds out, my esteemed uncle will have no choice but to fire me. He may have to fire all the staff, including poor Lones."

Who, catching his name from the other end of the table, grinned and raised a glass.

"Overspent it how?" Sira looked puzzled. "I thought Plexis was covering the repairs."

"That's true." The massive head tipped from shoulder to shoulder. "I shouldn't like to say. You've saved us all." Tayno straightened. "The *Claws & Jaws* honors your debt as our own." Followed by a sad little, "And on top of everything, the new chefs might want to leave. Huido doesn't know that yet, and we can't afford their fare home either." A rattle of pure despair.

Morgan frowned. "What 'debt'?" He'd left none behind, well aware Plexis welcomed any opportunity to sneak in a charge, with interest, and worse, would consider what you owed as much a tradable commodity as anything in a store. Not to mention he'd been in another section of the galaxy—

"The rent was never paid on your apartment." Tayno produced a crumpled plas sheet from a crevice in one arm, passing it to Morgan. "I received this from the deputy inspector."

Definitely something wrong here. He'd always stayed with Huido; Sira, too. Nice address, though, Morgan noted, nothing fancy, but Level 5, spinward—

That rate? Jynet had done them a favor, bringing the bill to them instead of a collection agency, the sort that took body parts in lieu of payment. This would be outrageous for a grandie suite with full staff.

He passed the plas to Sira, whose eyebrows shot up. *Something's wrong,* she agreed.

"Hom, Fem. Friends," Tayno said. His claw reached for the plas. "Please do not think I'd ask you for the amount. Besides," with touching frankness, "you don't have a ship or a job."

Sira gave a nod of understanding. "Barac and Ruti."

"The landlord saw Bowman's voucher and felt—inspired." Morgan took the plas from Sira and went to put it in his pocket. "I'll deal with it."

Tayno attempted to snatch it back. "Hom—"

Not quick enough. Morgan closed the fastener. "Now, tell us why you think the chefs want to leave."

* ✳ *

With Tayno's equilibrium restored, though not even a relieved Carasian should eat that many "Glider Goobles," Morgan and Sira rose together to take their leave.

"Tell Bowman and Terk they missed a great party," he told Finelle.

The Lemmick regarded her still-full plate doubtfully. "If you say so, Captain Morgan."

"I say Terk is lucky to have you as a partner," Sira said firmly, offering her hand. "Please tell him—tell the sector chief—tell them—" she faltered and sent Morgan a pleading look.

"Tell them," he said, quiet and sure, "it has been a privilege."

"I will." The dip and wag of her pororus meant respect.

It could also, Morgan remembered, mean "the final farewell."

Sira was right, Terk had an excellent new partner.

And quite possibly the Lemmick could help someone else. "Finelle, if your fourth-over-sixth uncle needs help with his new business venture, talk to Tayno. He could be looking for an extra source of income soon—and he has a fondness for fonts."

"For—?" She thought better of asking. "I will, Captain Morgan."

Nicely done, Sira sent, as they walked away. *Tayno's ready to make his own way.*

There was that. *I did it just as much for Huido,* Morgan admitted. *By the size of those feet, Tayno's next molt could make him bigger.*

Best not leave a threat to his blood brother's pool too close.

Erin met them at the door, eyes bright with curiosity. "Morgan," a nod. "Not Rael, I'm told. How's that work?"

Sira didn't quite smile. "It's complicated."

"I bet. Well, my offer to *Captain* Morgan is open to you, too. Sira." A grin. "The *Wayfarer*'s ready to seek new adventures. You're welcome aboard. And to tell me all about 'complicated.'"

"Thank you, but it's time I went home."

How could she say the words so calmly?

"Fair Skies," Erin said, her gaze shifting to Morgan. "Undock tomorrow, midday. Either we see you or we won't."

"Fair Skies," he replied.

Knowing the answer.

Interlude

<<*TIME TO COME HOME . . .*>>

Soon, I answered without rancor, aware why they were eager when I was not. Once I let go, the Singers could, too, pulling us through Between to AllThereIs . . .

And nothing.

Until then, I'd now and this. An echo of our first time on Plexis, walking through a night zone, when I'd thought to leave Morgan, afraid of the strange bond between us and how it might harm him. I'd fallen in love with my Human so long ago, with no need for my instinct and Power-of-Choice to test him as a Candidate. I'd known then.

Our footsteps matched. They did, that was all. Walking together was as natural as breathing and we moved through the giddy post-almost-apocalypse crowds like one being, neither leading nor following.

Together.

It was this, I thought sadly, my kind didn't grasp about us. Morgan and I were two halves of a whole, a whole greater than our sum.

We worked through a throng of Turrned Missionaries who immediately turned their limpid, soul-searching gaze on us. "Stay. We will pray with you," they promised, singly and in pairs, and I'd have been willing, would do anything that could change the future.

But Morgan didn't look down or slow, so I didn't either.

We were on the rampway before he spoke. "What happens now?"

I didn't pretend to misunderstand. "I'll 'port Rael's body Between. The Watchers will guide me the rest of the way."

Morgan caught himself. No one else would have noticed. To me, used to his sure-footed grace, he might have staggered.

I searched his face, saw the flash of—was that relief?—and understood with a sickening lurch beneath my heart. My poor Human. My love. He'd believed I'd come with him so he could end Rael's life. Presumably in this apartment we were going to see.

Then what, be charged with my murder? Confess and accept punishment?

He'd brushed aside Erin's offer as if he hadn't heard it. Spoke to those we'd left behind as if he, not I, was the one about to disappear forever.

There'd been a time I'd been afraid to stay with Jason Morgan.

Should I be afraid to leave?

Chapter 41

S HE COULD LEAVE ON HER OWN. Would leave. Must.
When? The question he dare not ask, in case "now" became
the answer, now being a fragile, fleeting thing you didn't notice,
didn't stare at, because if you did, now would be gone and after
take its place.

Now, Morgan thought wistfully, was nice. Walking together
through Plexis, steering around maudlin groups of celebrants
while trying not to step on what appeared to be equally cheerful
vermin, was more than he'd had, the last time—

"Can this be the place?"

They'd reached the twelfth in a row of unornamented doors;
the entry pad was moisture-proofed for those obliged to key in
the code with a tongue or other damp part. Morgan checked the
plas sheet. "This is it. I'll read out the code."

Sira made a face as she entered the digits, the pad having been
slimed recently; a would-be burglar or housekeeping.

Housekeeping, Morgan judged, once they'd stepped inside
and closed the door, portlights activating to the left and right.
The floor sparkled and there wasn't a speck of dust to be seen.
Not that anyone had lived here. The furniture was new, a delivery
label on the back of the nearest of two easi-rests. Nothing hung
on the walls. Instead of a kitchen, there was a counter with a

replicator, still sealed and waiting for use. A step down a short hall found a fresher and bedroom.

"You were right. This isn't worth the rent." Sira put her hands on her hips, eyes hot with indignation. "What do we do about it?"

Morgan pulled out his voucher. "Trick with these," he explained, "is they work both ways."

Her indignation was replaced with puzzlement. "What do you—oh," with a slow grin.

His matched it. "Exactly. I didn't want to tell Tayno, but if Barac had applied the voucher, not just shown it, the landlord could only bill what the accountants deem fair value for service. Since the apartment was never used for its intended purpose, that would be zero." He held up his voucher. "Watch."

Morgan went to the com panel, accessed the credit slot, and shoved in the voucher. The panel lit up to display a truly incredible amount owed—that swiftly began to count itself down. He pulled it free at four days owing, the number going green as that bill was paid in full. "For the cleaning," he said casually.

That was, he thought, only fair.

* ✳ *

The second easi-rest in the apartment was covered in gifts, intended for the baby Barac and Ruti hadn't had, but who was with them in AllThereIs. Hard as that was for a being of flesh and blood to grasp, seeing the collapsed balloons, Morgan found himself smiling.

Sira moved forward as if in a dream and bent to examine the gifts, hair slipping over her shoulder. She pulled up an untidy mass of string. Spoons dangled from it, chinking together. "Tayno's creation."

There was the cradle from Enora and Agem, Barac's parents. In it a card for a prototype stroller, from Rael. A stack of practical bedding and wardrobe essentials from Huido—selected by Hom M'Tisri, who'd that knack for knowing what someone truly needed, though Bowman's gift of the voucher had been needed, too.

They'd thought.

"Jason, look."

Sira held up a painting—his painting. A flower from Acranam's jungle. Ruti'd told him the name. "Night's Fire."

"I have this one, too," she said softly. He must have shown his confusion, for she smiled and touched fingertip to forehead. "I remembered it so well, it's part of—I've all your paintings."

Paintings. All he'd had of her. All she'd have of him.

Something inside Morgan broke—

In one quick stride, he reached her. Had her in his arms. Pressed his face into her hair and couldn't stop himself. "Stay."

I can't.

Sira eased herself free, taking the warmth from the universe; put her lips to his cheek, stealing its hope.

As you love me, Jason Morgan, have a future.

He watched her walk out the door and close it.

"Sorry, Witchling."

Morgan flexed his wrist, dropping the force blade into his hand, and headed for the fresher.

"I can't stay either."

Interlude

STAY. STAY. STAY. I tried to outrun the word, the passion and *need* in it, my own just as strong, just as impossible, going faster and faster, blinded by tears and heedless of where I went, so long as it was away from *stay,* careening off soft and hard obstacles—until I stepped on some being's tail—or whatever. The yowled curse was enough to make me jump out of the way before the backhanded slap could connect.

I staggered, still running, now with one hand on a wall. Around a garden, not that gardens mattered or walls. Only paintings did, and starships, and—

Morgan.

I stopped before realizing it, staring down at hands pressed against stone, startled to realize they weren't mine. Rael's hands.

Mine.

Hers. Did it matter? These hands had touched him. These fingers had brushed over his skin, so warm and alive, and why did I stay—

Here?

Holding stone?

I'd only to concentrate to leave. Why—

My fingers clenched, skin tearing on stone. Was it because I *knew*—this time—

—he wouldn't stay without me?

I concentrated with furious haste . . .

* ✳ *

. . . finding myself back in the apartment, running again.

He'd be gone. Of course, he'd be gone—I'd left him again. Why would he stay here?

Lies, I told myself, flying down the hall. He wasn't in the bedroom.

A shadow slumped in the fresher stall, dark against the white tile, then eyes sparked blue, caught in the tiny glow of an activated force blade.

I lunged forward with no plan but to stop him. Stepped on some part and heard a pained curse every bit as vehement as the one yowled at me moments before and would have laughed—

If I hadn't been sobbing and beyond desperate. "I'll stay. I'll stay." I couldn't, but the words were all I had to offer, to keep him from this, to buy time.

To find hope.

* ✳ *

Fingers trailed over my stomach, tracing the line where I'd had a scar, then gently found the outline of the medplas over what boded to be a new one. We'd had several such conversations over the hours past, my body new to us both.

Morgan returned to a topic of particular interest. "The artist knew orchids," he mused. "Though this petal? Hmm."

"Critic," I began then gasped, arching with pleasure as he illustrated his point most thoroughly.

* ✳ *

My hair *stirred.*

Wrapped in love, heavy with content, I thought nothing of it and slept.

A Watcher stirred.

Something had changed. It wasn't Between, for that Dark was strong again, its deadly storm a song in its own right.

Song. That was it. There shouldn't be Song here. The Singers had been quiet, saving their strength to hold the traveler.

Sira. She had a name. Insisted on it, when others left theirs in dreams.

<< . . stay? . . .>>

Impossible. More Watchers paid *attention.* They were done, ready to go home.

<<. . . stay? . . .>>

One Singer, then two. More and more sang the soft question— as if what couldn't be, could, as if they'd seen a possibility.

<<. . . stay? . . .>>

<<. . . Stay . . .>> emphatic, that voice, and familiar.

But Watchers had no fondness for the different, the trouble-maker, the innovator. They respected *will,* if only their own, and understood a truth.

Shared it, with *FORCE*:

<< *All things begin.*

And all have an end.>>

Then, this

<<. . . *is it yet?* . . .>>

* * *

I startled awake, eyes open on a dark that was real and here, wondering what I'd dreamed. If I'd dreamed.

My hair *stirred.* I froze, feeling it growing. Lusher and richer, flowing down over my bare skin in search of his, *warm.*

Morgan growled happily in his sleep, then went perfectly still, awake in that abrupt, alert way he had. His hand stroked up my thigh, higher, met— "Lights!"

I wasn't sure if I laughed because of the stunned look on his face, or because you did, that's all, when you'd no idea what any-thing meant or the future held, but any change—this change—had to be good.

Auburn, this hair, a red so dark as to hide black within it, the ends with a curl I didn't remember.

The look in Morgan's eyes when a curl slipped around his neck?

That I did.

Chapter 42

WHATEVER THEY DID, however long this moment lasted, he'd take it, Morgan thought. He held up his hand, watching with delight as a lock of hair—such hair—wrapped around his wrist, covering the bracelet, then flowed over his sleeve to nestle along his neck.

To flick like a scold against his ear and drop, the hair displeased with his being dressed. Morgan rubbed his ear ruefully. "I remember that."

Sira laughed. "Then you should have known better."

He took hold of her chin and planted a firm kiss on those soft, very-well-kissed-already lips, rewarded by another, warmer laugh. "Gods," he said, staying close to share her breath, her taste, "I don't believe any of this." *I want to—*

Then do, with such *love* he felt dizzy. "The Singers are there— Rael is—but the Watchers are too quiet. I've a feeling they're—" her brows met, "—arguing."

"How long?"

"Can they argue?" Sira stepped back, doing up the fastener of her coveralls. They'd used the fresher and were now ridiculously hungry, which said a great deal about how the night had been. "If I had my way, it would be forever." Her lips lost their happy curve.

"But Singers don't belong Between, Jason, and they're all that holds me here. When they leave, I do."

"Then we'll hope this argument of theirs keeps up long enough for breakfast," he said lightly. *We live each moment they grant us, Witchling.*

Every one, Sira agreed, her stomach picking that moment to express itself. "Starting with breakfast."

Interlude

An Undisclosed Location

CARE, IN THIS ROOM, came as a servo nurse.

But care hadn't come, nor any food or drink, nor anything else, and the two waiting knew they'd been forgotten.

They held each other as they weakened, and if they understood anything more than their discomfort and fear it was that there were worse futures than this one, where they would end together. Just fall asleep—

The door with only one key didn't open.

Until the moment it melted.

The two blinked wearily at this new and unexpected development. One couldn't make a sound and the other knew better, but both shivered when a huge figure appeared, making loud noises.

"You're scaring them, idiot." Sector Chief Lydis Bowman stepped over the puddled remnants of what had been a door the makers intended to be impregnable, into a room whose owner—confined to one she'd personally ensure offered the greatest discomfort possible—thought impossible to find.

On second thought, maybe Choiola should be sent back to the Brill. Her species had an internal justice system that would prove far worse.

Or given to Lucic.

Terk opened his visor and crouched beside the two toddlers. "It's okay. We're the good guys." His craggy face folded into a warm, reassuring smile; at least, that was the expression Bowman assumed he attempted.

The girl stared up, her eyes wide in her emaciated little face.

Others streamed in, medtechs who saw their patients and blanched, but moved with urgency. Neither child protested, beyond clinging to one another. They were so small, the medtechs kept them together in a carrier.

Once they were gone, Terk gave a final string of curses, kicking sand for good measure, then glared at Bowman. "Cut it too tight," he accused.

They'd made it here with all the speed she'd could order, but she nodded. "I know." They'd saved two; but not the others, Bowman judged, surveying Choiola's room with a critical eye. This wasn't new. "I want the techs on those blankets in the Brill's closet. I want victim idents. I want—find out if any were Ordnex." Her voice threatened to fail; she gritted her teeth, refusing to allow it. "Get me the suppliers."

With a stark look, Terk wheeled and went out the door.

Bowman heard him call for the comtech. "I don't care what you're doing—get Plexis. I want my partner out here, now!"

Saving the Trade Pact—and who knew what else—from some Dark no one seemed able to properly explain was for others. The Consortium, for starters.

This kind of dark?

With a settling shrug, Bowman pulled out her noteplas and stylus, and got to work.

Chapter 43

THE SEAT FELT—RIGHT, Morgan thought, wiggling a bit deeper, then looked around sheepishly.

Erin grinned. "Looks good on you."

"Not committing myself yet," he warned, but had to return her smile. His fingers gripped the arms. "It feels good." It all did, crazy as it was when you knew you lived a moment at a time.

When each could be the last, but he refused to believe it.

Denial of the facts doesn't change them. With *amusement*, Sira no more sane than he. She sat at the com station, letting Noska show her controls she knew full well how to operate. Living the moment.

Dreaming. That she would stay. They'd talked about her name, her new face and hair; what to tell the handful who'd take it for anything but cosmetics, that being the Human habit, to change yourself at whim—

Dreaming this could be home, this ship—

"Jason." Sira rose to her feet, turned to him, her face stricken and hand outstretched.

Cold replaced the blood in his veins, slowed his heart. "Not now—" he whispered, the words like ice cutting his mouth.

But it was.

Interlude

BUT WAS IT?

I felt Morgan's horror—had ample of my own, feeling the *tug* on who I was, what I was—but fought to remain calm. After all, I still had feet.

Still stood on the deck of this grand ship, with Morgan nearby. Yet was *here* as well. Between.

Surrounded by Song. They didn't Sing here, I thought, confused. Not that anything about Singers was less than confusing. *Rael, what's happening?*

<<*We Sing!*>>

Well, yes, but—*It's Between.*

<<*We know where we are, Great-granddaughter.*>>

Aryl? With that, names flooded me, even as hands held me, and voices *Sang!*

Then another voice, with a Watcher's dry, harsh tone. Taisal. <<*They can stay as long as they Sing.*>>

<<*We will Sing as long as you stay!*>> came a joyful chorus.

I could have sworn I *felt* Taisal's answering scowl, but it wasn't quite as dour as usual.

But what does that mean?

Rael came close. <<*Stay, heart-kin. So long as we Sing together, the Great Ones care not where, be it here, or AllThereIs. They don't touch that which has purpose and place. Stay with Morgan, live the life that gives us all such joy. Love.>>*

There had to be a catch, I thought with all the suspicion of that master trader. *What about you?*

<<A lifetime in NothingReal is barely a spin of the Dance.>> Aryl. *<<Now go.>>* Firmly. *<<You've saved us all. Let us be grateful. Go to your Human and fly the stars. Bring us wonderful songs when you return.>>*

Because I would, that being the way of our kind. To live our lives, then die and Sing. To remember, always.

Deal!

I probably should have thanked my noncorporeal kin—

But I found myself in a hurry.

Chapter 44

MORGAN HURRIED to where Sira stood, but dared not touch her. The expression on her face flickered through emotions faster than he could pick them out, this being a face he didn't know as well—

"Captain Morgan? Plexis-com says we have to go now—"

—then her eyes opened, green and fiercely bright. "Hello."

Oddly formal, that "Hello."

"If we don't, we'll lose the window. There'll be a fine."

"Hello." He felt as though he'd one foot over a precipice, the other on the trembling edge and dared not move.

"Can't you see he's busy, Noska? I'll take her out."

But Sira took a step forward, so he could.

"Do you know how? Not that I'm worried, but you've never done this—"

Her hands flattened on his chest, as if seeking the now-wild beat of his heart, and she looked up.

"Hush!"

Then his love smiled her glorious smile, and said the words that made everything right.

"I'm home."

Beings of a Permanent or Temporarily Corporeal Nature Named in This Book

Alla'do Go: Papiekian

Ambridge Gayle: Human, former Syndicate Head, Deneb Grays

Ansel: Human, former assistant to Huido

Argyle Touley: Assembler

Baltir: Retian scientist who worked with Clan Council

Barac: Sira's cousin, Barac di Bowart, nee sud Sarc, Chosen of Ruti

Chert the Masher Nyquist: Neneman, Trade Pact Enforcer

Choiola: Brill, Trade Pact Board Member

Erad di Caraat: Clan, Chosen of Wys, father of Yihtor

Heevertup: Heerii Drapsk, Captain of the *Heerala;* was Skeptic Levertup

Henerop: Heerii Drapsk, cargo supervisor on the *Heerala*

Hom M'Tisri: Vilix, host of *Claws & Jaws*

Huido Maarmatoo'kk: Carasian, owner of the *Claws & Jaws*

Jason Morgan: Human from Karolus, former Chosen of Sira, Trader, former Captain of the *Silver Fox*

Jesper: Plexis Security, Jynet's assistant

Kero di Licor: Clan/Destarian, Chosen of Taze

Lones: Human, personal assistant, *Claws & Jaws*

Lydis Bowman: Human, Sector Chief Trade Pact Enforcers

Lyta di Kessa'at: Clan/Destarian, Chosen of Odar

Manouya: Brill, smuggler known as the Facilitator

Mathis Dewley: Assembler

Merin di Lorimar: Clan/Destarian, Chosen of Tren

Noska: Whirtle, Hindmost on the *Wayfarer*

Numnee: Festor, Parts Maker on Auord

Odar di Kessa'at: Clan/Destarian, Chosen of Lyta

P'tr wit 'Whix: Tolian, Constable, Trade Pact Enforcer

Jynet: Eima, Deputy Inspector Plexis Security

Pysyk Oes: Skenkran employed as a greeter/airtagger on Plexis

Rael di Sarc: Clan, Chosen of Janac, sister of Sira

Renn Symon: Human, telepath, former acquaintance of Morgan

Russell Terk: Human, Constable, Trade Pact Enforcer

Ruti di Bowart: Clan, Chosen of Barac

Sira di Sarc: Clan, former Chosen of Morgan, sister of Rael

Sta'gli: Papiekian, Trade Pact Board Member

Talobar: Retian scientist working with Destarians

Tayno Boormataa'kk: Carasian, works in *Claws & Jaws* as Huido's impersonator

Taze di Licor: Clan/Destarian, Chosen of Kero

The Righteous SeaSea: Master Chef

Thel Masim: Human, Auord Shipcity Manager

Theo Schrivens Cartnell: Human, Trade Pact Board Member

Tren di Lorimar: Clan/Destarian, Chosen of Merin

Trilip *nes* Fartho: Trant, Trade Pact Board Member

Two-Lily Finelle: Lemmick, Trade Pact Enforcer constable

Usuki Erin: Human from Stitts VII, Captain of the *Wayfarer*

Wys di Caraat: Clan/Destarian, Chosen of Erad, mother of Yihtor, leader of the Destarians

Yihtor di Caraat: Clan/Destarian, unChosen, son of Wys and Erad

Yo'lof: Auordian, Captain of the *Paradigm*

Zetter Byi: vid producer who built and raced the *Wayfarer*

Zibanejad Cluster: Oduyae Master Chefs

Acknowledgments

Nine books. Wow. The Clan Chronicles began as "Story X" in a faded file folder. I'd wrinkle each page after typing to make the folder look nice and fat. No need for that now. Today, there's well over a million published words of story, plus nine works of stunning, insightful original art: six by Luis Royo and three by Matthew Stawicki. The books have come out in mass market, hardcover, and SFBC editions, as well as audiobooks and ebooks (as those technologies came around—yup, been that long). There are even two in Russian. Who knew?

Sheila E. Gilbert of DAW Books. My Hugo-winning editor-dear (who is up for her second award, so appendages crossed). I remember Sheila correcting me, after I apologized in a little speech for doing everything "you weren't to do" in my first book: first person, an amnesiac heroine who, yes, views her reflection, telepathy . . .

Sheila? Said, quite firmly, those things are fine when done well, and I really should trust her.

I do. I've never forgotten that day, nor her belief in these characters and their story. Thank you, Sheila.

Thank you to the whole wonderful family that is DAW Books. (Welcome, Leah!) Twenty plus years feels like a blink of an eye, till I add up the words. Suffice it to say you're my family, too. (Yes, it's New York and a big-time publishing house, but I'm not the only mushy one in this, trust me.)

On to more specific name-calling. Despite our moving twice this past year (during *Gate* and during *Guard*), I was able to write in peace and make my deadlines because Roger did everything. I am not kidding. Best hero-partner a person could have. Did I mention his blue eyes?

Thank you, Matt Stawicki, for this stunning cover!

My thanks to Luis Royo for the Lemmicks, the aliens he created for the cover of *To Trade the Stars*. I'd simply said "put aliens in view" and he did the rest. So much fun to bring them to life!

There are new Tuckerizations in *Guard*. My thanks to Jeanette Glass, who inspired Deputy Inspector Jynet, and has been *very* patient with me. Lance Lones? You're here at last. And to our dear Erin Czerneda, who I've no doubt could command a starship in her sleep. Meet Captain Usuki Erin, of Stitts VII. Happy Birthday!

I had to cut back appearances—my clothes and toad stamp were packed—but between moves, there were these spectacular events: Keycon, in Winnipeg, Manitoba (Hi, Auntie Joyce); When Words Collide/Canvention, in Calgary, Alberta; Acadia Dark Sky Festival, Bar Harbor, Maine; CanCon in Ottawa; and Halcon in Halifax NS. Oh, my goodness. Go to any and all of these! I'd like to thank our gracious hosts, especially: John Mansfield, Sherry Peters, Katrina Thiesson-Beasse, Edward Willet, and Gerald Brandt (and offspring) of Keycon; Clifford Samuels, Randy McCharles, and Stacey (the birds!) Kondla of WWC/Canvention; Derek Kunsken, Brandon Crilly, Nicole Lavigne, and Marie Bilodeau of CanCon; Melinda Rice, Ruth Eveland, and Kayla Chagnon of Jesup Memorial Library, and Kristen Britain for getting me into it all, (Dark Sky), as well as Davonnne Pappas, teachers, and students of MDI High School for their warm welcome. Last but not least, my deep gratitude to Lisa MacIver, Adam Sigrist, and Patrick Charron of Halcon, where we'd the pleasure of meeting so many wonderful new people, including Peter Foote and Missie Brown, I can't name them here.

I must also thank the hosts of my "blog tour sans internet" for *Gate*. Your enthusiasm and support—and patience—was fabulous and most certainly needed! Special hugs to Andrea Johnson (Fantasy Book Café) and Jorie-loves-a-story. Made me cry, you did, in a good way.

Some tears, this year, weren't that sort.

Ruth, I told you a secret, how *Guard* would end, to hear your warm and happy chuckle. Told you about my secret new project, to hear the excitement in your voice. Hung up the phone, still feeling your smile, still smiling my own. Nothing new there, right? You've heard all my secrets. You've been there, to chuckle, get excited, and smile, from the start.

No longer. As endings go, heart-kin, maybe we did okay. I know I hear you, even now.

As for beginnings?

Jennifer and Jeff, Scott and Erin, John, Johanne, and Jamie. All our family and all our friends, who gave me distance while shouting encouragement as steam poured out the various windows and we crisscrossed the province in our little red Ranger.

Book's done, we're unpacked, the deck's open for company.

We're home.

31901060874700